MEMENTO MORI

A ***Digital Horror Fiction***
Anthology of Short Stories

DigitalFictionPub.com

 Print 1st Edition
ISBN-13 (paperback): 978-1-927598-56-6
ISBN-13 (e-book): 978-1-927598-55-9

Contents

Foreword

Bruce Lockhart

When I pitched the idea for Memento Mori to Digital Horror Fiction, the publisher produced, without hesitation, a 'killer' cover to coordinate with the theme. Toss up a picture of a grinning skull and watch the horror writers crawl out of the woodwork! The broad topic of death inspired the imaginations of some of the top authors of the genre, so the outpouring of submissions was no surprise.

A few of these writers have even stared death in the face and lived to tell about it…

The title, Memento Mori, is Latin and literally means: "Remember you too must die." An ominous-sounding phrase, the saying derived from Puritan settlers who would often display tokens of death as a reminder to the living of the fragility of life…not to mention the eternal punishment awaiting those who wallowed in wickedness.

Death has always been a fascination to the living, meaning different things to different groups of people. Edgar Allan Poe nailed it when he said: "The boundaries which divide Life from Death are at best shadowy and vague. Who shall say where the one ends, and where the other begins?"

There is a wealth of truly incredible talent within these pages, each storyteller attempting to explore that very question, and I must say that reading each and every one of these stories was truly a pleasure. I love the remark our publisher made concerning the 30 stories selected… "A healthy book full of decidedly unhealthy stories." With Death being the key element in each one of those stories, you might be expecting a morbid ride, but rest assured, there are quite a few pieces of comedic gold lined inside this skeleton's spine, along with the many that will send a chill down your own.

I want to extend my gratitude to all the spectacular authors who contributed to this great assemblage of literature; you brought your own great style to the table. I also want the thank Michael Wills for appointing me as Managing Editor and making all this possible, as well as the editorial team that worked so hard piecing this anthology together. A story of my own, "Death's Final Request" appears in this anthology—it was one of my very first Horror pieces.

If you're looking for an array of Horror stories to sink your teeth into, look no further than Memento Mori…pay the Ferryman, and prepare to take the ride of your life.

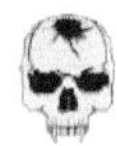

My Wasteland

T. Fox Dunham

The stainless-steel bed chilled my naked body, and I shivered. The white face of the linear accelerator hung over my bare chest. The wax tongue—made to fit the contours of my jaw and the shape of my mouth—penetrated my mouth, gagging me. Not a technician stirred, nor did the heavy arm turn or fire its lethal medicine—the invisible x-rays that churned and mutilated cells, healthy and cancer alike.

I searched the chamber for staff, and looked through the glass shield that protected technicians in the control room. They'd abandoned me, and I waited for them to return until my thoughts screamed against my skull. I had to get up, get out.

Pain ached down my spine, and my legs twisted. Finally, I broke the tape securing my arms and neck, grabbed the metal arm that secured the wax tongue and wrenched it, twisting the screws. It came free, and I tossed it away, hitting the base of the linear accelerator. My legs nearly collapsed, and I steadied myself to put on a wispy hospital gown.

I'd dreamed of Allison while I slept on the table, waiting for them to burn me again. The treatment depleted me, and often I drifted off to sleep throughout the day while waiting in the waiting room or on the train to my apartment. Her golden hair haunted me. Would we ever meet, or was she just a ghost in the dream?

We'd met in a bookstore, two months after the end of my

treatment. She served cappuccino. Through some miracle, I had survived the lymphoma and recovered. Dandelions blossomed in her hair, and her eyes burned stars whenever she saw me.

Time flowed in intended currents. I sensed the river, felt its path as I aligned with death; yet its course was not guaranteed. Chaos insisted, disturbed and interrupted the optimistic nexus set in place by a loving deity. She was to be my mate, but the cancer devoured me, pulling me further apart.

The cancer would ever distort our lives, but such was the nature of chaos inherent in the system. My reveries comforted but disturbed, and the visions of my future burrowed into my skin.

The hall stretched beyond sight. Doors multiplied doors. Stretchers filled the hall, and I supported myself along the beds. A shrill note plucked through the still ward, and I traced the sound to a small gurney—a bed meant for a child. I knew the song of a heart monitor, the music of the pulse-ox machine. Red eyes blinked furious. I knew the swansong. A child died.

I couldn't look, so I pushed myself away from the bed and kept looking. . . so tired. I'd dropped down to fifty pounds during my chemo and radiation. My neck and chest were inflamed as if from sunburn, and I could no longer swallow against the swelling in my throat.

I climbed into an empty bed and put down my head. Cut flowers littered the sheets, violet crocuses—the first flowers of spring, a gateway to the growing season. I fell unconscious.

"Such a beautiful day for a funeral," Allison said. She turned her Nissan into the Serenity Street, pulling into Saint *Somebody's* Cemetery. I couldn't make out the sign. "You awake? I know my company must be boring you by now, but you could pretend to be interested. You're going to have to fake it for a lifetime."

"It would have rained at my funeral," I said. The vision of the radiation ward faded, but the energy lingered in me like I'd swallowed nails.

"Not today, honey." We parked in the lot, joining the queue of cars lined up behind the limo and hearse.

"You didn't really know your great aunt," I said. "We're here to make your mother happy."

"Ruby," Allison said and tied back the length of her golden flow. She wore a simple black dress to the event, and black stockings. "Weird to have a funeral on a Tuesday."

"Why?" I asked.

"Marriages on Sundays. Births on Monday. Funerals on Friday."

"Saturdays?"

"Engagements." We hadn't told her family that she'd proposed to me.

We got out of the Nissan, and wet grass soaked through my shoes. Allison led us to a throng of family and friends assembled by the pit. The funeral stone had yet to be erected—problems with the estate. "Well, goodbye Ruby Tuesday," I said.

"Behave," she said.

Her mother wore a similar black dress. A pearl necklace hung over her top. The rest wore the standard funeral uniforms, dressing with veneration and defense. We celebrated the death of Aunt Ruby in grand style.

"No one threw me a party like this when I survived cancer," I said.

"How about a huge wedding then with a beautiful woman waiting for you?" she asked.

"I hope . . ."

At 10 a.m., the Catholic goalie would commence the ceremony with a prayer. Then, he'd end the ritual with a prayer. They'd end the event by dropping the ol' girl in the pit, knock dirt over the coffin and grant her a few token memories, a few moments of precious sentience in pity and memorial. I ran my fingers through the grooves carved into a pillar, marking remarkably in death the life of an unremarkable man. We carved the dates and names deep into stone to carry the burden of remembering, so we didn't have to.

Finally, the funeral began, and by the first prayer, my thoughts wandered. In the distance, beyond the white and gray monuments that neither tarried nor grew, a child danced in front of a mausoleum.

"Whose little girl is that?" I asked.

"My nieces and nephews."

"Up there. She's all alone." It had to be one of Allison's relatives. The river course of their faces ran coeval, and daffodils blossomed down their necks. She twirled below a plum tree and danced with bare feet, digging her toes into the rotten fruit. Bees buzzed around the pale child, and she spun sans regard of being stung.

"I don't see anyone." She scanned the horizon. "You sure you're okay? You've been . . . funny." A priest prayed, and the crowd hung their head.

"She's over there dancing on the grave," I muttered. Allison's mother hushed me.

"How much morphine did you take today?"

I rolled my eyes. "I've seen her before, at a family function, maybe. She has to be someone's little girl." They lowered the coffin into the pit, and the priest made the sign of the cross. I broke from the group as they departed and climbed up the incline to the mausoleum. "What's your name, baby-girl?" The child ceased her dancing, looked up and mouthed a word. She never spoke. Instead, the child vomited down her white dress, and her hair fell away like cobwebs. Allison grabbed my shoulder.

"What is going on with you?"

I flinched, turning back to see her. "She's sick." When I looked back, she had gone.

"I didn't see anyone," she said. "Come on. We're going to brunch with my parents."

"I don't feel much like it," I said.

"We should tell them about the engagement."

"Right after a funeral?" I asked. "Let's not."

"Why?"

"I'm not ready," I said. "Just go without me."

Her cheeks reddened. "And what are you going to do?"

"Stay here," I said. "I need to think."

"Fine."

The next morning, Allison sensed me awake, and she stirred. Her black dress from the funeral hung on the closet door from the day before. My fiancée entwined her slender leg around mine and kissed up my chest, avoiding the red sunburn that cut over my shoulders.

"Good morning, Luvie." Light shined through the spaces between the slats. The photons reflected off the snow, danced on the face of brilliant crystals and shined fulgent into the bedroom. She curled up to me and plucked my ribs, like playing her guitar.

Pain surged through my back, never easing. My doctors had mutilated my spine and nervous system with the treatment. The pain would never stop. "We should get up, Boo," she said, calling me one of her many names. "We're going to be late for your appointment."

"What they did to me." Allison flinched at my words. My attitude upset my fiancée. I didn't mean to stab her, but I lived my past every moment, obsessed with the lymphoma and treatment. It refused to release me. "It snowed last night," I say.

"In summer?" she defied. "You dreamed it."

"I'm freezing. Ice is growing on the window."

Allison showed me the calendar on her phone: June. The weather betrayed, or her phone lied. Winter smothered me, and I longed to see the white silky blossoms of the magnolia trees that spilled milk down the chocolate branches. We lived for spring, fell in love under the sun. Allison was the sun. Clouds occluded my eyes. Snow fell again. I heard the sleet pricking against the glass.

"I got lost somewhere in winter. I can't find my way to you in spring. I miss my sun."

"Get up," she said.

"It's too cold."

"You can't miss this appointment," she said, getting out of bed, and put on my robe.

"Why?" I asked. "Will he tell me it's summer?"

"It's your first appointment with this new guy," she argued. The doctor who had treated my lymphoma had returned to Scotland and cast me into new hands. I didn't trust doctors. Doctors did this to me.

"I never had cancer."

"Go take a shower."

I dressed, then tied my winter cloak around my neck. The dreams of the night haunted me, hanging on my skin like smoke. Gravity yanked me. "I hate being cold."

"This isn't funny," she said.

"No. It's not." We exited our apartment, heading to the car.

After a short car ride and a stop at Starbucks, we sat in the waiting room. Other patients—pale and emaciated like scarecrows—hung their bodies on chairs. A fish tank bubbled and teemed with swimming creatures. Allison sat silent and played with her phone, not looking up at me. The sun rose in her eyes; I shivered in the dark.

"What's the problem?" I asked.

"I'm afraid you're self-destructing in front of me," Allison said. "I'm losing you."

"I don't think I ever came back," I said. I hadn't realized that I'd felt this way until we got engaged. I never expected our relationship to last. I couldn't let go.

The nurse called me back to see the doctor. Canine ears perked from her head. Her nose extended into a snout, and fangs hung from her jowls. She pawed a folder and growled as I followed her into a squat office.

"Are you wearing a mask for Mardi Gras?" I asked. She said nothing. Saliva dripped from her mouth.

The nurse showed me to an examination room. My feet dug into crunchy sand. She slammed the door behind me. It hit me in the ass, and I looked up on a swollen pale moon.

The door stood in the middle of a desert. No stars shone above. Wind-sculpted pillars cut from sandstone reminded me of a collapsed temple. Memorial stones decorated the hilly sand, some buried and others clear to their base, revealing the roof of a mausoleum.

Shadows wore a man. Long hair fell in clumps around his kidney bean head. He folded his legs, wearing boots, and his breath reeked of rotting deer.

"You've come to exorcise demons?" he asked. I couldn't make out his face in the shadows.

"I'm a slave to my doctors," I said. "Just healing and dealing."

"I wouldn't be here if you were dealing," the shadow said. "I'm Doctor Sullivan."

"Is that your real name?" I asked. "I've met you before." The familiar sensation pervaded me, digging into my chest. I knew his feel, smelled the acrid smoke coating him, but I couldn't match him to memory. Wind whipped sand onto my lips, and I tasted the metallic earth—metallic like the ozone the linear accelerator used to pour over me when they radiated me.

"I'm going to cure you of your disease," the doctor said. "I'm the Good Doctor."

"I thought I was in remission. I wouldn't be getting married if I wasn't free of the shit."

"Getting married? When?"

"In a few months. Then we honeymoon in Ocean City, New Jersey."

"Remission is not a cure," he replied. "It is the cancer sleeping. But the cancer is not your disease. You are stuck."

I sat down on a tombstone at his foot, then traced the carved lettering out with my finger. I couldn't read the writing in the dim light of the swollen satellite, but I could feel the name. I wouldn't remember it. What would be the point?

He lit up a cigarette. The red coal hanging off the stick pierced the dark. I choked on the vapors, tasting the dirty smoke.

"Doctors aren't supposed to smoke," I said.

"And people are supposed to live. How long have you been frozen in winter?"

"It's a wasteland," I say. "My wasteland."

"A soul sometimes can get stuck between life and death, the past and present—the in-between places."

"You're a priest too?"

"I wear many hats," he said.

"So how do we proceed?"

"You must move on from your nightmares, either to this world or the next."

I sighed. Crows fluttered overhead. "I don't think it's my choice."

"And we'll do some scans just to make sure. That's your life now." The Good Doctor drew notes on a chart of flat sand. "See the nurse on the way out to set up a time to get a CT scan."

I left the examination plane and walked out the lone door. Allison looked at her phone in the waiting room, and we walked to the car.

"What made you love me?" I asked.

"You're a remarkable human being. You're so different."

"What makes me remarkable is what makes me so broken. You should run. I should run before you do."

"You kill me when you say things like that," Allison said.

"Did you think you could change me?" I asked. "True love cures all?"

"You can be so selfish," she snapped, and started the car.

We drove to a small park outside the hospital. I used to watch the stream flow from my room on the third floor. Daffodils sprouted yellow along the bank. She kissed me and moved her hand under my shirt, sliding it down under my jeans. I moaned into her mouth, and she climbed over the seat then straddled my thighs with her legs. The winter melted to summer, and a lightning flashed over the sky. We moved into each other, through each other's bodies. She felt so real. Then, I fell asleep in her embrace.

I woke up moving through the darkened wards of the radiation oncology wing of Penn, searching for a way out. The park had vanished. My sun fell. Ozone hovered around my mouth, and my tongue tasted metallic air that the linear accelerator exhaled after it irradiated my head and neck. I finally came to double doors. A silver button on the side of the wall activated the opening mechanism.

Skin grew over the hospital doors. Veins pulsed with violet blood through the skin, and the flesh blossomed several mouths. When the mouths opened to speak, black feathers fluttered from the orifices, as if the door had swallowed a raven and spit up the indigestible bits. Black bile vomited from my desiccated stomach. I hadn't eaten in months, sans a few cappuccinos and some milk—the only thing I could tolerate. The silver plate used to operate the opening mechanism swelled pink and saturated with fluid. I refused to touch the giant boil. Pus dripped from its tip, and I vomited again.

I would have demanded passage, but the door had no ears. I would have pleaded for pity, but the hospital bore no heart.

"I don't believe in ghosts," the mouths sung in choir. Each lip unified and synchronized to deny my existence.

"I'm not dead yet," I argued.

"Dead is only a matter of flesh," the mouths replied. "Dead you will be, so dead you are now."

"I don't want to die," I whispered. My eyes moistened. I'd never actually thought it before, never entertained the possibility. My lymphoma hadn't been real—just a lump in my face for a day. Doctors burned me with caustic chemicals and invisible rays. I vomited and burned. Still, I dreamed this trial, suffering nightmares. I wouldn't die. No one died. I would just live on into oblivion and never stop feeling. No one could truly understand the cessation of their own sentience. Now, the guardian teeth confronted me as the hospital animated; or I dissociated.

I didn't demand my survival. My fists didn't pump. My lungs drew little air to speak. I spoke beneath my own breath and declared my intention. "I could die," I said.

"What do you wish?" the mouths asked. More ebony wings fluttered from the lips, and I recognized the voice of the Good Doctor Sullivan. The oncologist served as doctor and door at Saint Mary's Hospital.

My head spun a merry-go-round. I punched at the door, but the teeth bit my knuckle, drawing blood.

"To see tomorrow and the 'morrow after," I defended.

"How terribly selfish," the mouths accused. "What right do you think you have to time? Children die every day, and babies born still." The little girl sleeping on the stretcher flashed into my mind; she wasn't sleeping. The hospital lights flickered, glimmered, then died. I waited in darkness.

"Just let me leave," I said.

"But you don't want to leave, not really. This is all a dream you've cast, a story you've spun and sung. I am a rhyme on the door, warped wood, glass made of loose sand. You've woven me onto the door to keep your hand from hitting the button."

"You lie," I said.

"You are not afraid of the door. Just walking through it." He smirked. "Time for another distraction."

I heard organ music droning and rolling, playing from down a side corridor. I followed the notes, and the music always dashed ahead.

I found my suit hanging up off an abandoned IV pole. I donned a black frock coat and silver waistcoat. Allison waited for me at the end of the aisle in a vibrant dress made of white lily leaves. Verdant ivy wove through her golden curls, and she stood as tall as I in Miami blue heels, capturing the sky spirit.

I hesitated at the start of the path. I couldn't break my gaze from her vision.

The jug band played Pachelbel's "Canon" with the plucking of a banjo and the scratch of a gritty washboard. I cried from the song, then stepped against the wind.

Her family filled the audience, all wearing their funeral garb. She waited for me and held out her hands. Her palms fell from the magnolia tree that blossomed outside the grand window of the Unitarian church. Ivory blossoms glowed in the afternoon light. The band increased tempo, then slowed, drawing out each note. The tones stabbed my ears until they degraded into buzzing noises.

The hall morphed. Pews melted away into corridors. Flowery perfume changed to the rank odor of stale coffee mixing with old vomit, the spoiled meat smell of the old and decaying. My Victorian suit sloughed off, and I wore my old jogging pants and hospital gown. I tried to run, but the strength drained from my body, emptying out with the vital energies of my spirit. I reached for her, trying to find her, and a plastic tube pinched my arm, tugging on my skin. It joined me to an IV pump that pumped saline into my body. I staggered forward, trying to find an elevator to reach the ground flood. I could find a cab on South Street and just get away. I had no pockets to carry money, but who would charge me? The skin of my emaciated face clung to my skull and ribs. My starved body had devoured my muscles.

"Call me the ace of spades," I said to a passing nurse.

"You're next, Timothy," the nurse said and guided me into linear accelerator room one. I stripped like I had and lay naked on the cold steel table.

"You'll burn me to dust," I said and twisted against the bonds of my own weakness. My body resisted my efforts to resist. Gravity weighed me heavier than others, and fatigue wormed through my body, devouring my muscles and bones, filling me with rubber. I couldn't think through the mud filling my head.

"We're all become dust," the Good Doctor Sullivan said. He positioned the blank square face of the linear accelerator, aligning crimson lasers to the tattoos dotting my face, then my shoulders and arms, matching the pattern to the pattern. The radiation poisoned me, killing healthy and malignant flesh alike in holistic method; thus was my hope.

"You're supposed to heal me," I said.

"I can only heal your body," the Good Doctor Sullivan corrected. "Your soul is not my bailiwick." I shivered on the chilled steel. The doc stepped into the side room and activated the accelerator. Particles spun. Electrons whipped.

When I first began treatment, I couldn't feel the invisible radiation. They said I wouldn't feel a thing, but over time, it tingled, then burned, and finally raked steel wool down the site. I tasted the metallic ozone, and my stomach churned from the electrical flavor.

"First dose is done," he said.

"I've already been through this." I had lived through this, endured the treatment and survived. "This isn't my future. It's my past."

"Are you so sure?" the Good Doctor asked.

"Allison is my world." I longed to live out our lives together, to grow old, to see her honeyed hair harvested by bees then dried to silver wheat, growing wild in the fields of our time. I would die at a ripened and wrinkled age, then spread my ashes in those fields of time and sun. She would set there, and our shared lives would rise over the nameless tomb in testament and command. "What's keeping me here, so I can kill it?"

He released me from my bonds and handed me a robe. I donned it and followed him out in the ward, dodging gurneys as I walked—patients waiting. I recognized the child's cot ahead. Its monitors rang fast, singing death like funeral bells. Finally, I looked upon the face of a little girl. Her plump face blossomed out of the blankets like a plump gray strawberry.

"How old is she?" I asked.

"Not more than three," the Good Doctor Sullivan said. "Not less than a hundred."

I touched her fevered cheek. "She's just a baby," I said, recognizing her face, trying to place it. I knew it, and then I remembered. I imagined her with Allison's hair, dancing below a plum tree in a graveyard.

"She's your baby," he said and adjusted his crow mask. His nose stank of burning herbs. My eyes watered from the perfume. "She will be born two years after your marriage."

"This is the past," I said. "She can't be. I've never had a daughter."

"Time never mattered to the ward," Doctor Sullivan said. "You just never left this place—always trapped. Your soul will never want to leave."

"She's Allison's?" I asked, looking over the countenance of my child with my fiancée. I assumed we'd marry; at least, that was the potential if I ever left the radiation ward.

"Looks familiar, doesn't she?"

"My cancer is killing her," I said.

"She's undergoing a regimen of image therapy, but there hasn't been any significant shrinkage in the tumors. We're going to try an experimental therapy. Such a therapy put you in remission."

"It destroyed me," I said.

"For you, that was the same thing."

My child breathed shallow. She lay still, nearly frozen in time. She'd never age, always remain young. Her death would destroy my wife.

"I did this to her. I brought her into the world, made her from my broken body."

"You don't have to," the crow said. "You never need leave. Just let go."

"She'll never live," I whispered. "If I don't live." He didn't know the little girl, though I fell into the gravity well of her soul. She was more than my offspring. I could see her mother's aspect—her spirit, intelligence and beauty, all the forces that had created such love in me. "How can I do that to her? I would be bringing her into the world just to murder her."

"And never giving her the chance to live."

"It's not fair," I said. I reached to touch her hair like I would her mother, and I rubbed the skin of her tiny head. She sighed in her sleep. Monitors beeped. Pumps dripped. A respirator forced oxygen into her lungs.

"You're a selfish being," the doctor said.

"I'm a prisoner here."

"You are hiding—comfortable and safe."

I looked at my child, seeing Allison's face in waiting to emerge. I saw my mother's face hiding in the creases, her ears listening. Allison had never known my mother. She had died of human failing, and now she had been reborn to me, to us.

"Her light is the only one that should shine now."

"A new star born from the plasma of the old."

I wept and lost time. My past, present and future shattered, and the shards mixed, then sliced down my skin. I'd been so lost in myself. "Forgive me," I said and bundled the little girl in my arms. Her legs dangled over my forearm—legs that fell, not dancing. I tore off her sensors and wires, then pulled out the tubes from the pump. The machines shrilled, complaining of their disconnection. I carried her down the endless ward, walking through coeval corridors, looking for the fleshy door. My fortitude depleted, and I struggled to carry her. When I could no longer walk, I stumbled. When I couldn't stagger, I crawled, pushing her still body on the floor tiles. Finally, I found the fleshy door. A heart pumped and pulsed at the heart of the portal. I threw my body against the door, felt my arm snap and collapsed onto the floor, shielding my baby girl.

She whimpered in her slumber, and I kissed her forehead. Her skin soaked with my tears, and I hit the portal with my other shoulder, striking its heart. The door shuddered. Veins snapped. Blood poured down the rips and wounds in the hospital's skin, pooling on the floor. I beat against the beating heart, and the rubbery organ resisted my weak blows. Bruises blackened the rotting red apple, but it would not burst. My child whimpered again, then shook, and I pressed my ears to her white lips.

A light breeze blew on my cheek, then paused several moments before blowing again. I refused to let her die in this pit, in my lost world, my prison. I chomped at the heart and tore off a hunk of red flesh, then spit it out. Salty blood flooded my mouth and poured down my chest, soaking me in crimson juice. I vomited from the spoiled flavor, but kept biting.

The doors bled out, etiolating until their flesh grayed. My own chest ached, and the pain from my broken arm surged through my shoulder. I nearly collapsed.

I hit the silver button, and the hospital doors parted, allowing me direct exit to green fields. Lush grasses grew right to the edge of the phantom building. I stepped off the floor tiles, and my toes tickled tulips. The sun burned white, blinding me, but I kept going, pushing into the open space.

I ran as far as I could, then my body gave out. Golden daffodils swayed in the wind, and the breeze breathed for us as our lungs stopped. I laid her little body out in the sun, then lay next to her.

The blood dried on my body, and it started to rain, cleansing us of the hospital sediment, washing us in holy waters, preparing us for death. The rain filled my mouth like a cistern, draining down my nose, and I allowed it to fill my lungs.

Allison locked her arms around my shoulders and lifted me above the ocean crests. I choked on seawater. Kelp tangled around my legs. We swam naked, exposed only by the moonlight. Lights of the boardwalk sparkled along the shoreline and down the Atlantic pier. Seagulls claimed the midnight skies. I coughed up the water.

"The ocean nearly took you from me," she said, holding my mouth to air. "The bitch."

"When seagulls fly at night, they're carrying souls lost at sea."

She clamped her hands to my back and pushed my chest against her body. Her pert breasts floated on the surface and bounced with each wave. My mouth hungered, and I kissed the curve of her breast. She exhaled hard and shuddered. We floated in the waves, and the inclinations of our bodies joined. I released my burden, let go the battle, and I moved my damaged body into hers. The treatment had killed the cancer, but Allison cured me.

I stopped. I couldn't do this. "My dreams," I said. "This is the moment. I can sense her. Our daughter. We create her in the ocean, in the constant waves, and she'll always dance."

"I feel her too, baby," Allison said. "She wants to be born."

"She got sick too. I made her sick."

"Just a dream, baby," Allison said.

"But if you knew you were bringing a child into the world, and she'd only live for a few years . . ."

"If you're right, and she dies, I'll probably hate myself for thinking this. But right now… she deserves that time, if it's even a few years. We'll love her, Timothy. She'll be ours, always our daughter. And nothing is forever. It could all change. Now make love to your wife."

My memories renewed. We'd been married in a civil ceremony in New Jersey. Her parents witnessed. We went out to dinner, then drove to Ocean City. We didn't need a party. We only needed each other. I pushed deeper into my wife.

"Is this real?" I asked. "Am I still on that table waiting to be burned?"

"Does it feel real?" she asked. "Does it hurt? Do you love?" She moaned as I pushed into her, ready to fill her with my seed, my essence. I looked ahead and watched more seagulls silhouetted over the ripe moon. They flew low, mayhap burdened by souls they carried to the shore.

T. Fox Dunham lives in Philadelphia with his wife, Allison. He's a lymphoma survivor, cancer patient, modern bard and historian. His first book, The Street Martyr, was published by Gutter Books. A major motion picture based on the book is being produced by Throughline Films. Destroying the Tangible Illusion of Reality or Searching for Andy Kaufman, a book about what it's like to be dying of cancer, was recently released from Perpetual Motion Machine Publishing and Fox has a story in the Stargate Anthology Points of Origin from MGM and Fandemonium Books. Fox is an active member of the Horror Writers Association, and he's had published hundreds of short stories and articles. He's host and creator of What Are You Afraid Of? Horror & Paranormal podcast. His motto is wrecking civilization one story at a time.

His blog is at: tfoxdunham.blogspot.com.

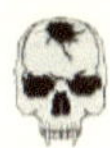

Death, Dying, & 3 Credits

Ken Goldman

From the Swatmoore County Community College Fall 2006 Course Catalog:

> **Death & Dying: (3 cr) Instructor: Dr. S. Byron Hoffner**
>
> A study of historical attitudes, customs, and myths surrounding our culture's various perceptions of death and dying. Professor Hoffner has written extensively on both the psychology and physiology of the dying process in his book "Exploring The Fear Of Death." (Please note: this course is open to a limited number of senior students pending written staff approval.)

Swatmoore's lecture hall filled quickly, the auditorium's atmosphere unusually somber for college students fresh from summer vacation. One might think some powerful figure lay in state near the podium onstage. The cloak of mystery surrounding Dr. S. Byron Hoffner's unorthodox teaching methodology and his unconventional field of research demanded that kind of respect—and that kind of fear.

Melanie Cerra selected her seat alongside an attractive blonde coed, the two girls exchanging polite smiles while each set up her laptop.

Unlike Melanie's other morning classes, during which social interaction seemed practically a course requirement, this morning's unwritten code of silence felt especially awkward. If Melanie were going to remain awake during the next ninety minutes, she would have to change that. She turned to her seatmate.

"I'm Melanie. Does this place feel like a funeral, or what?"

The blonde smiled but kept her voice low. "Bobbie. I need the three credits to graduate and this was the only class I could fit into my schedule. I haven't seen this course listed before, so I don't know much about it or the instructor. It *does* seem kind of creepy in here, doesn't it? But what would you expect from a course about death?"

"Do you believe we had to sign a release form just to get in? I hear the instructor won't allow anyone under twenty-one to register for this class. What's that about? Does he plan on having Happy Hour here after this wake?"

Bobbie's interest was piqued. "Maybe the college doesn't want any lawsuits. This guy Hoffner is new here, but I hear he's quirky. His questionnaire sure was. He wanted an essay about how I felt watching my mother die last year, and I wrote the paper, all right. But I added how I didn't feel it was an appropriate question to ask. I guess that was okay with him because here I am."

Melanie busied herself with her laptop's cursor, opening a new file for her class notes.

"My father died last winter, three days before Christmas. Pancreatic cancer. It was awful, and I'd never experienced grief—not like that, like I was being choked. So that's what I wrote. Maybe Dr. Hoffner prefers his class filled with orphans."

Some bookish-looking guy wearing thick coke-bottle glasses turned in his seat. Melanie felt certain he would ask them to shut their mouths, but he wanted to talk too. "With me it was about my Labrador, Skank, so I wrote how I felt really upset when I had to put him down last summer. I don't live in the safest neighborhood, and you need either a dog or a gun. But Skank was old and kept shitting everywhere in my apartment, so I couldn't keep him. Hoffner just wrote 'Good enough' on my answer sheet then signed my class slip. I never even met the guy."

"I don't think anyone has," Melanie said. "He keeps a low profile. His book jacket mentions his methods are a little unorthodox. His course is like some big campus secret."

Bobbie turned theatrical. 'More like this is some clandestine secret society, and we three are among the select few to be granted membership. Knights of The Living Dead. *Hoo Hah!*"

Melanie studied the faces of other students. She didn't doubt that everyone in the lecture hall had a nodding acquaintance with death. It seemed a course requirement. Bobbie nudged her to turn around when Dr. S. Byron Hoffner took the platform. She hummed the Addams Family theme until Melanie poked her in the ribs.

Melanie had expected some rumpled old academic type with uncombed hair and a cheap tweed sports jacket with elbow patches. But this guy was young, and wore a fashionable olive-green corduroy sports jacket covering a chest more thick than his facial features suggested. Hoffner seemed the youthful professorial type right out of central casting, cute in an Opie-from-Mayberry sort of way. He paused at his podium, studying the crowd, allowing his students time to check him out too. Mutual scrutinizing completed, Hoffner began his lecture, offering no wooden introduction of himself, or even a "good morning". With his first words, the man went for the gut.

"Let's clarify two things at the get-go. I have no intentions of being politically correct today, and no one leaves to pee. Them's my rules. Capiche? Comprende?"

Waiting for a response, he smiled when he didn't receive one.

"This course is about death and dying, just like your catalogue says, and I'll start with my basic premise: No person has ever passed away nor gone to his eternal reward. No hospital patient has ever expired, nor have any of your loved ones played the harp in heaven. Those expressions are lies, tacky euphemisms intended to make death palatable, because throughout history dying has scared the living bejeesus out of everyone. But the truth is, when you die you're fucking dead, not deceased nor resting in peace. I won't sugarcoat death for you in this class. I won't even embalm it. Death is ugly, and it smells bad. Someday you'll be rotting inside your coffin and you will stink. My purpose is to teach you to accept death with all its hideousness and grossness intact, just as nature intended."

A few students laughed although the man did not seem to be joking. Melanie typed Hoffner's objective into her computer: *Lesson Goal: To accept death for what it is. (Real)*

"All right, then. So, how many of you in this room are dying? Hands?"

Dumbfounded students turned to one another, then stared back at their instructor. The room fell silent. No one ventured a raised hand.

Hoffner grinned and leaned forward on his elbow. He seemed about to reveal the answer to an elaborate riddle.

"Well, gang, here's your wake-up call. All of you—and me too—are dying. Being born is your death sentence, and you're ten minutes closer to that expiration date than when you walked into this lecture hall. Even as I speak, your brain cells are shorting out, your internal clock is ticking. Death is real, and it's out there waiting. Your date of death is as real as your birthday, and it's coming, you can be absofuckinglutely certain of it. Does that thought frighten you? Does it make death any more real? Probably not, so I'll demonstrate my point."

In three minutes Opie had transformed into Vincent Price. Melanie tapped her keyboard: *From the moment we're born we begin to die.* Back at the podium, Hoffner held a small fish bowl. Inside swam a tiny gilled creature with long and golden fins.

"Anyone here from the P.E.T.A. or the A.S.P.C.A? I'm hoping not. Class, this is Ariel, like Disney's Little Mermaid. Beautiful, isn't she? I found her in a mountain stream last spring, fed and cared for her all summer. She's pretty plump now, and seems happy just lolling inside her little bowl all day long. Ariel, she doesn't ask for much, just a few daily specks of food and some clean water. I've grown rather fond of her."

Melanie distrusted the professor's sincerity, but this class could take it. Seniors could comprehend life's sudden horrors better than their younger cohorts. Back in high school she'd had to chloroform a hapless frog before dissecting the poor creature's innards, all in the name of education. Now she found herself mouthing the words, *It's just a stupid goldfish.* Expecting her instructor's worst brand of histrionics, mindlessly she typed the same lip synched words onto her laptop's screen.

"Do I detect a reaction from the crowd, an uneasy stirring in your seats?" Hoffner asked, the smile never leaving his face. "Come on, don't be afraid to think it. You're expecting me to kill this helpless little fish to prove my point, to bring to the forefront your absolute aversion to death, am I right? It's not a bad idea, for the purpose of demonstration, wouldn't you agree? Just like Reality Television, eh?" He spilled some water from the fishbowl to the floor.

Some murmuring arose. Even Bobbie gasped, quickly covering her mouth.

"I heard that!" Hoffner continued. His dark eyes drew a bead on the coed. He continued to stare at her. "This young woman expressed her revulsion, even though two hours from now she'll be inside the cafeteria ordering the tuna salad without thinking twice." He looked right at Bobbie and the girl turned crimson. "Am I getting through? Have I made a splash?" He spilled more water.

"I think I want to leave," she whispered to Melanie.

"No pee breaks, remember?"

The goldfish named Ariel struggled to remain below the diminishing supply of liquid, desperately puffing air bubbles close to the surface. As the bowl emptied the little fish began to flop inside.

Melanie's finger thumped upon one key of her laptop.

?????????????????????????????????????

"I'd say our finned friend is having some difficulty breathing," the instructor continued. "It would be a simple matter to refill her bowl if I chose to do so. But that would be giving in to my fear of death, demonstrating how the thought of it repulses and terrifies me, wouldn't it? And I have a point to prove. So I'll ask you to indulge me while I do this…"

Hoffner reached into the bowl. He held the wriggling fish upside down by its tail.

"I'll refill her bowl if someone requests it right now, perhaps some naturalist who is willing to receive an 'F' for this course by asking me to spare little Ariel's life. Any takers?"

The instructor waited. No fish saviors sat in this classroom.

"All right, I think we can begin." Hoffner dropped the fish to the floor, allowing it to thump about for a moment. He chased it around the platform, stomping at the fish like a man performing a river dance until a thick golden paste clung to his shoe. "Can you believe I did that? Did it anger you, depress you? That little goldfish, so alive and content a moment ago, is now jelly. Death is one fast bastard, eh? Ariel was here, and now she's not. Can you accept that simple fact? Is it real to you now?"

Melanie stared at her keyboard. She had no idea what to write.

Bobbie whispered, "That man is nuttier than a Snickers Bar."

"Three credits," Melanie whispered back.

Hoffner stepped from behind his podium, sat on the edge of the platform and removed a handkerchief, wiping the sticky fish goo from his loafer. Without missing a beat he continued as if he were discussing whether it might rain.

"Elizabeth Kubler-Ross. Does the name ring any bells? She was a woman who made a lifetime study of death, if you'll excuse the seeming contradiction. Old Liz has since bought the farm herself, but while she was with us she believed the process of dying occurred in five significant stages, something to remember when The Grim Reaper crosses your path or a loved one's." He walked to the chalkboard, wrote '**DENIAL**' in uppercase letters.

Melanie tapped the word into her computer, while Bobbie snapped her laptop shut. For her this lesson was long over.

"There's this old joke. Mr. Smith's doctor tells him, 'I have some good news and some bad news. The bad news is you're going to die in six months.' 'Six months?' cries Mr. Smith. 'What could possibly be the good news?' The doc answers, 'See that luscious receptionist out front? I'm fucking her!' But that's not the punch line. See, Mr. Smith goes home and assures himself, 'I'm not going to die, nope and nuh huh, not me! Dying is what happens to the next guy.' Smith goes for a second opinion, maybe a third. Then one day six months later Mr. Smith keels over into his mashed potatoes. Is that funny, or what?"

No one in the lecture hall seemed to think it was.

"Okay, let's bring it closer to home. If I informed you that someone in this room was going to die before this morning's class is over, you would tell yourself *'That's total bullshit!'* You would deny it. Deny, deny, and then deny some more."

"That *is* total bullshit," the guy with the thick glasses mumbled to the two coeds. "What's with this sadistic fuck?"

"Of course, little Ariel probably awoke this morning believing all she had to worry about was when her breakfast was coming. Who could know that before noon she would be scraped off the good professor's loafer like a wad of Juicy Fruit? Death? Hell, that only happens to other fish!"

If the man were batshit crazy or some Marquis de Sade wannabe, it still wouldn't hurt to score some points with him. Melanie raised her hand and identified herself.

"Suppose a person is terminally ill and his doctor tells him he's got six weeks? He starts feeling sick, sees in his mirror some skeletal imitation of himself, becomes weak and tired. He can't keep denying his death is inevitable."

Bobbie whispered, "Brown Nosing 101, that's down the hall." But Hoffner seemed impressed with the girl's question. He scribbled a second word on the chalkboard.

BARGAINING

"Miss Cerra, your terminal patient is about to go through a process. 'Please, Mother Mary-Jesus-Allah-Bozo,' he begs. 'I'll do anything. *Just don't let me die!'* It's another form of denial, of course. Your bony patient, maybe he suddenly finds religion, tells himself 'I'll be good so God won't let me croak.' So he begs, pleads, prays…

"Think of it like this. If I tell you there's a bomb under one of your seats right now, something I disguised that looks like a dropped pen—and if I get you to genuinely believe it—wouldn't you beg me not to set the fucker off? If you'd like to play God for a while, put someone's life in your hands, then watch them plead with you not to let them die, hallelujah and amen! I promise it'll be good for a few laughs."

Melanie turned to Bobbie. "See any pens under my seat?"

"He's just fucking with us, making us paranoid," Bobbie said, but she took a quick peek under Melanie's chair just to be certain. "Does a pencil count?"

Melanie checked for herself. Nothing was there. "Bitch!" she said.

Bobbie leaned close to her seat mate.

"Paranoia… the game the whole family can play!"

Hoffner's death rant continued going strong.

"Death makes no bargains. When it comes to your mortality you're betting against the house, and the house always wins. You lose, and losing pisses you off. So…"

He wrote **ANGER** on the board, and Melanie dutifully wrote the word down. She felt pretty angry herself that Hoffner was getting his rocks off playing with her head, first stomping some poor goldfish, then planting crazy suspicions about bombs beneath her seat. Still, she had to admit Hoffner knew how to make his point.

"Of course, anger burns itself out pretty fast. You can only rant at a storm for so long before you realize it's not doing a whole lot of good. So you're left with a whole mess o' the blues, emotionally busted. Good for creativity maybe, not so good for your mental health." He added another word to his board, separating it from the others.

DEPRESSION

"I'd like to share a little secret with you people, okay? Anyone mind if I smoke?" Without waiting for a response Hoffner lit up. He was soaked in sweat, and the cigarette shifted inside his mouth while he spoke. "I know, I know. These things will kill you. Well, let's say I'm past that denial stage and I no longer give a rat's turd. Smoke free environment, my ass. Smoke 'em if you got 'em, gang!" No one took him up on his offer, but Hoffner didn't appear to mind or even notice. "Up your ass with a Marlboro, Mr. Death!" he shouted, inhaling a mouthful of smoke like some defiant pimpled adolescent, but now the instructor's bravado seemed forced and unconvincing. Something odd was going on here, some lunatic shift in tone that exceeded brazen eccentricity. "Oh hell, I almost forgot. About that secret I wanted to share…"

Hoffner's smile twitched, then disappeared. For the first time he seemed unable to find the correct words while he sat on the edge of the platform smoking. He stubbed one cigarette out, lit another. Sixty students waited for whatever demonstration of insanity he planned next.

"I have lung cancer. Stage four, I'm told, advanced enough to eventually kill me very dead and very soon." He took another long drag pretending to savor the smoke filling his lungs, but he wasn't that good an actor. Seated on the small stage he didn't say another word.

The room fell silent. Someone dropped a book and several students flinched at the sudden crack of noise. Given the tenor of Hoffner's lecture, Melanie half expected the man to jump up shouting "Gotcha!" while chortling like a maniac. But that didn't happen.

Finally he got to his feet and said "There's more." His voice had the tone of a man at confession. "See, I wasn't kidding about someone in here dying before this class is over. There's no death denial going on in my classroom, kids." He walked to the chalkboard and scribbled the fifth word.

ACCEPTANCE!!!

Melanie didn't bother typing. Her eyes fixed on Hoffner.

"Christ, the man is having some sort of nervous breakdown."

Bobbie nodded. "And I think he's planning on sharing it with us."

Hoffner was losing it, but he didn't appear about to slow down. "I know I'm going to die, so I'm giving the Reaper his due today. A man can't get more accepting of death than that, can he? The house always wins, but I still get to choose the game."

Sopping with sweat, the instructor removed his corduroy jacket. Beneath it he wore a thick black vest, and Melanie's brain didn't immediately register what she saw. Some sort of wired tubes, maybe a dozen of them, adhered to the vest and were lined up like little soldiers. Focusing hard, suddenly she gulped for air.

"That's right, sports fans. It's a bomb, home made and ready to bring the house down on each and every one in here, enough explosives to spatter the four walls with the dripping remains of your arteries and intestines. All I have to do is pull this little cord here and today's class will be summarily dismissed. See, I've worked out a way to make today's lesson a genuine exercise in show and tell. Want to see…?"

A boy in the front row left his seat. Hoffner raised a hand, then quickly returned it to the thick cord dangling from his side. *"Nuh uh! No piss breaks! Sorry!"* Another beefy student pulled the kid back into his chair.

"Oh, I'm not going to blow the place up just yet, don't you worry. That is, unless anyone here is thinking of using their cell phone, of course." His eyes scanned the lecture hall. "That's good, kids. Real good. Now let's shut those laptops too, shall we? Wireless access at Swatmoore is state of the art, but we wouldn't want any IM's upsetting the outside world." He waited while two dozen laptops snapped shut.

From the back row a girl started crying. Another student shouted curses.

"You're faking!"

"You crazy prick!"

Hoffner ignored all of them. He reached into his pocket, withdrew a small revolver.

Several young women were whimpering. Hoffner ignored them also. Instead he beelined to Melanie's seat and held the gun out to her.

"Go on, Miss Cerra. Take it. It's only a .22, not much more than a cap pistol, really, and you seem reliable enough to use it."

She stared at the weapon in his hand as if the instructor were offering her a steaming turd.

"I don't know what you want me to—"

"Take the fucking gun!" some guy shouted.

"He's crazy!" from another. *"Can't you see that???"*

Melanie rose from her seat and took the .22, gazing at her hand as if the revolver might suddenly on its own blow her head off.

"What do you want me to do with it?"

Hoffner smiled. "I want you to point it at me and shoot me, of course. I want you to stand right here, take careful aim, and put a bullet right between my eyes. See how well I accept death? Hell, the Grim Reaper and me, we're old pals."

"I can't do that! Shit! I can't…!"

"That's denial, Miss Cerra. You *can* and you *will,* or I bring the house down right now, *Boom, Boom, Ka-boom!"*

"Please, don't…"

"Yes! And there it is, bargaining!! You're going through the stages well, so, let's cut to the chase, okay? Unless you're angry enough to throw that .22 right in my face. Of course, that would defeat your purpose entirely, wouldn't it?"

"Shoot him!" from the back.

Melanie's hand shook, but she pointed the revolver at him.

"He's bluffing!" the guy wearing coke bottle glasses shouted at her. "The gun isn't loaded! There's no bomb! It's a set up, all of it! He's fucking with you!!"

The tears came quickly. Melanie swiped one hand at them, trying to hold the gun steady with the other.

"I can't do this… don't make me do this…"

"Good, Miss Cerra. We've hit depression now. Let's take it home..."

"I... I..."

"Shoot him!"

"Do it!"

"The clock is ticking, Miss Cerra. Ten... nine..."

"Please. Oh, God... please!"

"...six... five... four..."

"Kill him!!!!"

Melanie's hand was shaking badly. She aimed the pistol at Hoffner's head. Her finger twitched on the trigger.

"...two...one..."

A single shot rang out, one quick unimpressive pop in the expansive lecture hall. But it did the job. A sudden small red hole appeared dead center above the man's eyebrows, and Dr. S. Byron Hoffner crumpled like a sack. For a moment on the floor his legs kicked, and the image of that damned goldfish replayed inside Melanie's brain. The professor didn't kick for very long. Melanie looked at the gun she still held.

"I didn't... *I didn't shoot him!"* she said. She turned to Bobbie. *"I swear, I didn't—"*

"*I* did," the guy with the coke-bottle glasses said. He held his own gun up for all to see, some toy-like thing that could have passed for a cigarette lighter. He approached Melanie, touched her shoulder. "I hoped he was bluffing, but I couldn't take the chance." He turned to the startled students surrounding them. "Hey, I'm licensed for it. I swear!"

Murmurs all around.

"He's dead, isn't he?"

"He isn't moving! Someone call 911!"

"There's a bullet in his brain, asshole. 911 can't do shit!"

"Does this mean the course will be canceled?"

Melanie turned to the guy with the goggle eyes.

"You may have saved our lives. I don't even know your name."

"It's Henry. And I guess I'm the new marshal in town."

Bobbie was pointing at the professor's body. One of the tubes attached to his vest had broken with his fall. She climbed from her chair, pulled the tube from the vest.

"It's empty. There's nothing inside… no powder." She tore away another tube, shook it, then broke it open. It was empty too. Bobbie looked at Melanie. "It's fake. Just a hollow plastic tube. There's no bomb here."

A girl who had been hysterical managed to ask, "Do you think that cancer story was just…?"

"…Bullshit?" Melanie asked, and now she too was drying her eyes. "How could that man be so intent on making his point? Would he do something so completely insane just to create this whole scenario?"

She stopped herself, remembering the notes she had written into her computer earlier.

Lesson Goal : To accept death for what it is. (Real)

[I won't sugarcoat death for you in this class.]

Bobbie managed some composure. "There's only one way to find out what's bullshit here and what's not." She reached for the gun and Melanie handed it to her. Running fingers through her blonde curls, she raised the hand holding the revolver. "I never fired a gun before. We're in this together, everyone in here, right?" She turned back to Melanie.

"Three credits," Melanie said.

Bobbie managed only a half smile.

Henry came to her side. "Go ahead. The first shot is free."

That almost earned a grin. Bobbie tightened her grip on the weapon's handle.

"Okay, here goes…"

She aimed the .22 at the professor's body that lay crumpled on the floor. Struggling with uncertainty for a moment, she pulled the trigger.

A little red flag popped from the gun's barrel.

It read "BANG!"

Ken Goldman, former teacher of English and Film Studies and a member of the Horror Writers Association, lives on the Main Line in Pennsylvania and the Jersey shore. His stories have appeared in over 825 independent press publications. Ken's tales have received seven honorable mentions in *The Year's Best Fantasy & Horror*. He has written five books. His novel *Of a Feather* (Horrific Tales Publishing) was released in 2014; Sinkhole, his next novel, is coming in 2017. Find some of Ken's stories at amazon.com/Kenneth-C.-Goldman/e/B004QVWTTE.

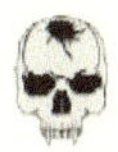

Eve

John McIlveen

Guy read the text message. It was one simple word—not actually a word, but what had become the standard expression of boredom between him and his friends.

Whazzupp!!

He had just toggled the send button, responding with the same nonsensical expression, when he felt an impact that tore the steering wheel from his left hand and sent his iPhone hurtling to the rear of the vehicle. Before he could make sense of what was occurring, the Escalade hit the guardrail with enough force to catapult over it and land on its roof on the opposite side. The SUV slid another fifty feet, toppled over the embankment, and rolled seven times before coming to rest on the leafy forest floor, sixty feet below the highway. Guy lay on the hillside, halfway between the roadway and his Escalade, launched through the shattered windshield to collide against a large spruce with jarring force.

Guy opened his eyes, but didn't move… not before assessing his condition. He felt no pain, which he found peculiar, because he remembered the forcefulness with which his body had hit the tree, and he could see the mangled scrap that moments earlier had been a late model Cadillac Escalade, only months off the showroom floor. He licked his lips and inhaled; no blood or difficulty breathing, only the earthy musk of fallen leaves in the early stages of autumnal decay, mingled with the smell of steam and antifreeze from the vehicle's fractured engine, which clicked and pinged as it cooled.

Guy wiggled his extremities, flexed his arms and legs, and rotated his head on his neck. All seemed well, so he gingerly pushed himself into a sitting position, stood up, and bounced on the balls of his feet. He felt a momentary elation that quickly dissolved into dread with the realization of just how deep the pile of shit he had just gotten himself into was. He had made only three payments on the seventy-thousand dollar vehicle. Insurance would most likely contest it once they found out he was texting… and they would find out. They routinely checked phone records nowadays, since texting accidents had become an epidemic. He considered reporting the truck stolen, but just as quickly dismissed it. He'd be caught in that, as well. *At least I'm sober,* he thought, but it was a small victory… he was screwed any way he looked at it. May as well call 911, tell the truth, and face the music.

The tumble down the embankment had jammed all the doors of the SUV except for the rear hatchback, which had folded onto the roof. Searching through the smashed windows, he looked for his phone, but couldn't find it, and reaching beneath the seats only turned up remnants of shattered glass and other strewn items. He'd have to backtrack up the embankment, and look for the phone there. If he couldn't find it, he could flag someone down from the roadway.

… *If he could only find the embankment.*

Around him lay only forest, flat and dense with trees—endless oaks, birches, locusts and maples in every direction, rising skyward on thick trunks… and one smashed-up Escalade.

Guy knew this wasn't possible, but denial dampened his reaction. Hills don't simply disappear. There had to be a logical explanation, like shock, or maybe delusions from hitting his head. That had to be it, because he thought he could also see what looked to be a young girl moving among the trees, about a hundred yards deeper into the woods. He refocused, and sure enough, there she was, long strawberry-blond hair falling halfway down her back and dressed in light blue overall shorts. She appeared to be writing or scraping something onto the trunk of the tree, but it was difficult to be sure from such a distance. Guy took a few hesitant steps toward the child and stopped.

"Hey, little girl!" Guy called. "Hey!"

She looked up at him indifferently and dutifully returned her attention to whatever she was doing. Guy started walking towards her, and when he had cut the distance in half, the girl moved to a tall elm about a dozen trees away from him. She deftly climbed the tree and propped herself at the crux of a branch nearly sixty feet overhead. There was nothing natural in it, the way she had ascended with the dexterity and ease of a squirrel; Guy had never seen anything quite like it from a human. He watched her for a few moments, wondering if she were avoiding him, but she just as deftly climbed back down and headed in another direction.

"Wait a minute!" Guy said.

The little girl stopped and watched him expectantly. She looked about nine years old, thin-limbed and fawn-like with vibrant blue eyes. Under closer observation, guy realized her hair was dark brown, not strawberry-blond as he had first thought, and attributed it to the play of sun through the trees.

"I got in an accident," Guy told her. "I can't find my way out of the woods."

"I know," the girl responded, her tone neutral. She resumed walking.

Guy followed, dually concerned for himself, and as to why a child her age would be alone in the deep woods. "Are *you* lost?" he asked.

"You're lost," she said in the same impartial manner. She looked at him, her alert brown eyes reflecting him and the surroundings, and walked over to another tree.

Brown eyes?

Guy felt prickles of unease run through him. There was no question that her eyes had been a striking blue before she climbed the tree. He looked back at his Escalade, trying to get his bearings so he could get the hell out of there, but the SUV was no longer in sight. He ran a few steps in the direction he thought he had come from, but stopped, feeling anxious by the idea of letting the girl out of sight. Everything else he had looked away from had disappeared.

He returned to where the little girl stood. She now had rich ebony skin, but the same light blue overall shorts, which Guy found more disconcerting.

Isn't it the clothes that are changed, not the child inside them?

She seemed unconcerned, giving him the impression that *she* wasn't lost, which meant she was faring better than he was. She again scribed something onto the tree.

Guy moved beside her, feeling as if he'd fallen into the rabbit hole. "Something's going on here that I don't understand," he said to her.

"Something's always going on," she replied, matter-of-factly.

Guy couldn't tell if she was being disparaging, or just answering him the way most children her age would, but she was making him feel quite dense. Frustrated, he asked, "Can't you give me a direct answer?"

"I can," she said, pinning him with glimmering green eyes. She skittered up the tree, spent five minutes high above, moving from branch to branch, and climbed down.

Guy followed her thirty yards to a huge, majestic oak. "What are you doing?" he asked.

The girl, now with straight, shiny, coal-black hair to her waist, started writing on the tree with what looked like a simple wooden stick, but as she moved it, the name Joey Wilkerson appeared as if engraved. "Writing," she said.

"Writing what?"

"Names."

"Who is Joey Wilkerson?" Guy asked, understanding that his questions would have to be precise if he wanted precise answers.

"A broken heart," she said, but offered no explanation.

She again climbed the tree and moved from branch to branch. Guy meanwhile walked to a number of trees and saw that most of them had names engraved onto them—Dedrick Aaldenberg, Luis Rosios, Peter Craig, Hirohito Ishushima, Glenn Levesque—and hundreds, maybe thousands more. She descended, now wearing a mane of tight auburn ringlets.

"Are all of these broken hearts?"

"Yup," she said, the simplistic word making her, for the first time, sound her age.

"Why are they all men?" Guy asked as he followed her to another tree.

"Boys, too… mostly boys," she said. "There aren't enough trees for girls and women, their names are on the leaves."

Guy thought about this for a while and asked, "Why so many females?"

She looked at him and smiled sadly. "Thirty-one years," she said.

"How do you know how old I am?" he asked a little defensively, and even more confused.

"That's how long your eyes have been closed."

"I don't know what you mean."

"You will when you have to," she said, rubbing an almond-shaped eye with the back of her hand.

"Who are you, Confucius?" Guy blurted with frustration. "What little girl talks in circles like this?"

"Me." she answered. "You are angry at the wrong person." She engraved the name Abubakar Kwabena.

"You've already written his name," Guy said, noticing the name was already on the trunk once, and again. "Twice."

"His heart has broken three times." She looked around them and held out a pale arm. "Girls, women, they grow another leaf. Some trees have many names; some names have *her* own branch."

Guy followed her gesture and looked back at the pale-skinned girl with Afro hair and Asian eyes. "Speaking of names, what is yours?"

"I was never named," she said. "What would you have named me?"

Her look and question were so sincere that he seriously considered it.

"Eve," he said.

"For you, I am Eve."

"Okay, Eve, why are you writing the names of all the broken hearts?"

"Broken hearts deserve recognition."

Guy chuckled and said, "I should have a dozen or two here somewhere."

"You have one," said Eve.

"One! How do I have only one? I've been trashed by more women than…" Guy quieted when he noticed the way Eve looked at him. Her smile was much too knowing for the Samoan child's face that wore it.

"A wounded pride is not a broken heart," Eve said.

Guy's indignation was defused when Eve took his hand. She led him a long way into the woods, during which her features changed numerous times.

"Why do you keep changing?"

"Is there a specific way a girl is supposed to be?" she asked.

Guy felt the question was layers and ages thick, and any answer he gave would be insulting to her and condemning to him. He didn't answer. Eve smiled.

They stopped alongside a heavy oak. Eve pointed to Guy's name on the trunk and met his eyes. "This is your heartbreak," she said.

"Which one was that?" he asked, feeling diminished, like a child trying to defend himself.

"Your mother died."

"I was four!"

"Four-year-old hearts break."

"I know! I mean…" Guy sputtered. "That was the last time my heart broke?"

"That was the last time anyone could reach it," Eve said. "You locked it away."

Guy wondered if he was unconscious, or hallucinating from the accident, and if that were so, would it be this coherent, or even have these thoughts? "How do you know about my mother?" he asked.

Eve gestured to the surrounding trees with her sun-weathered Cherokee arms. "It's what I do," she said.

"But how would you know? You're, what… nine years old?"

"I'm what you need me to be," Eve said.

"There you go again with your befuddling comments, confusing me even more," Guy complained. "Why are there no evergreens here… where are we?"

"Here is also what you need it to be," she said. "To understand."

Guy blew out an exasperated breath and looked at Eve. "Understand what?"

"Your accountability. You have broken hearts."

"Okay, so whose heart did I break?"

"Many."

"Many? How? I don't remember being such a bad guy."

"*Bad* is an assessment, as is inconsiderate, neglectful, and unconscious." Eve said. She pushed a strand of her platinum blonde hair behind her ear. "Some hearts you broke intentionally, some out of spite. Some were unintentional, yet still broken."

"Who?"

Eve climbed to the lowest branch of the oak and quickly returned with a leaf. She handed the leaf to Guy who read the name inscribed on it.

"Carla Rinaldi? I didn't break her heart!"

"Really?" asked Eve.

"Okay, I was sort of a dick, but she was whacked. We dated in college for about a year, but we agreed we were better off going our separate ways," Guy said. "And then she started stalking me."

"Odd behavior for someone who agreed to separate," Eve said.

"Well, okay… she didn't exactly agree, but we were better off apart," Guy said.

"Absolutely," Eve agreed. "You can't make someone love you,

although she loved you immensely, as you knew."

"All right, if you're trying to make me feel guilty, you succeeded," Guy said. "She had serious problems. I heard she killed herself."

"She did."

"I wasn't with her then. At least *that* wasn't my doing."

Eve held his gaze, but didn't answer.

"Now wait a minute! You're saying that I broke her heart and caused her to commit suicide?"

"I didn't say anything… you did," Eve said. She started for another tree. "You broke her heart, but you weren't the direct cause of her suicide—you weren't that influential. A far more painful heartbreak caused her to take her own life, although you did play a part in it."

"How was I responsible for that?" Guy asked, flustered.

"The baby died," Eve said. Her skin darkened to a warm Brazilian bronze as quickly as if someone had dimmed a light inside of her. It was the first time Guy had actually witnessed her face change.

"She had a baby?"

"Stillborn. She was in her ninth month," Eve explained.

"It was mine?" Guy cried.

"It's simple math," Eve said. "Carla was already alone and depressed; the death left her utterly heartbroken."

"I had no idea," Guy said, shifting to a new level of surreal. He felt sick to his stomach.

"You threw her letters away unread, ignored all the calls, and deleted the texts. Carla didn't want you back; as a mate, you're no prize." She crinkled her nose in effect. "She *was* hoping her child's father would acknowledge his own child so she wouldn't go through life feeling her father had abandoned her."

"It was a girl?"

"Yeah," Eve said, engraving the name Kenneth Mossiman on a tree trunk. "She would have been nine if she had lived. Her name would have been Eve."

Guy stared at her, unable to speak for a long time. "Are you…?"

"As I said, I'm what you need me to be for your situation," Eve said.

"What do you mean by my *situation?*" he asked, but Eve simply smiled. "I didn't want this to happen," he said.

"Is that a comfort to you? What kind of monster would you be if you did?" Eve asked. "Most consequences of most heartbreaks are not fully intentional, and many are unknown by those who cause them," Eve explained and pointed at the name she had just engraved on the tree. "Like him," she said.

"Kenneth Mossiman?" Guy read aloud. "Well, I know I didn't break his heart."

Eve held his gaze, but said nothing.

"Oh, come on!"

"As I said, most broken hearts are not intentional. Those who cause them, directly or indirectly, are unconscious of the pain suffered," Eve said, her hair altering to a fiery copper as if to stress her words. "Bethany, Kenneth's wife, was the driver of the car you hit while you were texting. Her pain was intense, but it didn't last long. She had just dropped her three-year-old son off at daycare."

Guy reeled and had to use the tree for support.

"Kenneth's heartbreak will last another forty-seven years. It will fade gradually with time, but it will never leave him," Eve said.

"Are there more?" Guy asked. Feeling disoriented and very old, he rubbed a hand over his face.

"Many," said Eve. "But for heartbreaks, these are the worst."

How can this be? Guy wondered. He was having a conversation with a child who ethnically fluctuates and could be the nine-year-old spirit of a stillborn child he might or might not have conceived with an erratic ex. It was nonsense, and regardless as to why he was having this episode—be it a head knock, nightmare, or daydream—it was just a matter of time before he came to. He opened his eyes and looked at a Korean Eve, still with fiery copper hair. She offered him a sweet, understanding smile, but said nothing.

"All right, I'll play along," Guy said. "We've already established that I'm inconsiderate, unconscious, and despicable beyond the norm."

Eve laughed and said, "Don't give yourself too much credit. On the grand scale of things, you're pretty common. Everyone plays a part in heartbreaks somewhere along their lifeline, deliberate or not, and some thrive on purposely causing it. On the bad-guy-good-guy scale, you're as usual as salt… but you have a decision to make."

"And what would that be?" Guy asked.

"Your situation," Eve said. "Haven't you figured out why you're here?"

"I'm either dreaming or hallucinating."

"You're dead, Guy," Eve said. Guy gave a harsh, derisive laugh, but Eve silenced him with serious hazel eyes. "Bethany Mossiman wasn't the only fatality in your accident. Right now, your body—your shell—is lying forty feet from your vehicle. You are suspended in the between. I am your guide."

Guy felt a sudden inrush of pain. He fell to the ground, writhing as scorching blades of agony stabbed and twisted throughout his body, in both of his legs, his right arm, the right side of his chest, and his head—dear God, his head! Lying on his back on the forest floor, the pain became so complete he couldn't move. Eve knelt down beside him and took hold of his left hand. The pain on the right side of his chest intensified and Guy cried out. He tried to focus on Eve through the hurt, but his vision kept shifting from light to dark and back. Shadows moved around him, swelling and ebbing with a stir of voices.

Blunt trauma head… tree. Compound fracture… leg… arm… need backboard.

"Can you hear me?" asked a man's voice. "Stay with us, buddy. Talk to me."

Guy focused on the face of a man… friendly looking, wearing some kind of uniform. The man gradually diminished as Eve returned.

"It's time for you to choose, Guy. You have to choose between returning to your present life, and moving on to your next," Eve said to him, but her voice was deeper and satiny—soothing and alluring—a woman's voice.

She still held his hand, and gently moved it onto his chest, over his heart. He could see the flesh of her arm was now black like onyx, as was her face and her hair… everything. She was no longer a child, but a woman, draped in robes made of the darkest shadows. She had become the night—terrifying, yet beautiful… so beautiful.

"In a few minutes, the window will close," Eve said. "You will default into death and move to your next life, unless you choose to remain in this life."

An intense stab brought the paramedic back into view as he maneuvered Guy's shattered arm. "Can you tell me your name?" the paramedic asked.

"But, before you decide," Eve was saying, fading back, "there needs to be balance in whichever choice you make."

"Balance…" Guy muttered.

"That's good! That's good! Talk to us…" said a hopeful EMT with large, compassionate eyes. She opened a large package of gauze and handed it to an unseen person near Guy's head.

"If you return to your present life, you must resolve your past," Eve continued, tugging him back to the in-between. "You will live with a new resolve." Something moved behind her—something large, dark, with feathers. *Eve has wings,* Guy realized through his gauzy consciousness. Her hand gently touched his cheek and she coaxed him to meet her eyes, which were black opals, hypnotic pools of oil with fire flashing within.

"You will live to rectify your old way of life by avoiding the thoughtlessness and neglectfulness that dictated that way of life. You will live with the knowledge that each person you encounter is like a well. If you only look inside, what you see is only the surface. Below the surface, there may be treasures, danger, horrors, or beauty such as you've never witnessed before, but you will never truly know that person, or what is below their surface, until you make the effort to explore. In your present life, there will be times of happiness. Though much loneliness."

Guy's body exploded with pain as the paramedic and EMT carefully maneuvered him onto the backboard.

"If you choose to move into your next life, there must still be balance," Eve said, her voice somehow weaving through the agony. "While you will create little heartbreak, you will experience much, though there will also be much love. You cannot experience heartbreak without love." The black angel leaned forward as if to kiss him. "Now," she whispered. "Decide."

Guy's whole existence became agony, and with his last coherent thought, before the blackness swallowed him… he chose.

He opened his eyes to a chaos of motion and light…

John M. McIlveen is the author of the paranormal suspense novel, *HannahWhere* (Winner of the 2015 Drunken Druid Award (Ireland) for high literary merit and Nominee for the 2015 Bram Stoker Award (HWA) in the First Novel category.

He has more than fifty short stories in print, two story collections, *Inflictions* and *Jerks and Other Tales from a Perfect Man*, and the well-received novelette *Got Your Back*. A father of five daughters, he works at MIT's Lincoln Laboratory and lives in Haverhill, MA with his wife, Roberta Colasanti. You can learn more about John at johnmcilveen.com.

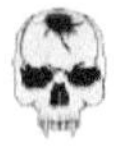

Tomorrow We Be Free

Jean Graham

Folks were saying that Washington City might fall by sunup.

If General Jubal Early and his Reb raiders got their way, there'd be no more capital, and no more Union left to fight over.

But not if we could help it.

When the 151st arrived by the rail cars, Nick and me marched the regiment right through the town out to the camp at Fort Stevens. Quite a proud show we made of it, too, even if it was after midnight and hardly a soul around to see us. I'll bet we woke 'em up, though! We led the defenders straight down the city streets, all tramping in time to our music–to Syl Foster's fife and Nicodemus' drum. Didn't matter none that, being so young, we lacked a good foot in height on any other man in the regiment. They had to follow us, 'cause we two were the drill corps, and for at least that one hour, we felt like kings for sure.

I think we were both surprised to reach camp at last and to see the "fort" we'd been sent to. It was poorly lit by torches and weak moonlight, but any fool could see it wasn't a proper fort at all–just three broad cannon ramparts built up against the wide ditch. That ditch had been dug out, almost overnight, all around the capital for miles. But I guess I'd expected to see a fort like the ones in those pictures in my school books back home; something like those wood spiked affairs they built out on the frontier, or better yet, the big stone castles with moats in the fairytale stories. A ditch and three cannons was a trifle disappointing, for a fort.

Nary a man of us could sleep, even if it was the middle of the night. We were all sure that Jubal Early could be just brazen enough to try storming the defenses in the dark, and we were going to be ready. So soon as all the bedding assignments were done with, I went down to the colored soldiers' tent to find Nick. I figured we could maybe work out what songs to line up for tomorrow, just in case we had drill as usual, instead of a battle.

If we got a chance to drill with the drum and bugle corps that was already here with the 3rd Massachusetts, maybe we could learn some new songs, or maybe teach them a few. I'd ask 'em if they knew *Lorena* yet. Didn't matter none to us that it started out a Reb song. We Yanks liked it, too, and so we took it for our own.

I found Nick out behind the Negro bivouac, sitting by a campfire and whittling himself a new drumstick.

"Broke one on the way in," he said when I came up and sat down on the other side of his fire. "Nobody's sleepin' nohow, so I thought I might as well do sumpthin' useful."

"Makes good sense," I answered, and found I had to scoot back a ways from the fire. It was July, and so sticky-hot in these parts, you didn't really need a fire except if you wanted the light. "You think maybe we should use *Old 1812* and *Minstrel Boy* for drill tomorrow?"

Nick's whittling knife stopped in mid-stroke and his large black eyes blinked at me, little flames dancing in 'em. "*If* there's drill, you mean?"

"Yeah. If."

"Them's fine. And maybe *Hell on the Wabash*, too. I got the beat on that'n *real* good."

I nodded, and Nick went back to whittling. His knife made soft *skritch skritch* noises as he worked. The fire popped and snapped when his wood shavings flew into it.

"You think Jubal will do it?" I asked at length. I had to admit, part of me hoped the Rebs would see the capital wasn't defenseless after all, and would turn tail and run before morning. "You think he'll attack?"

Nicodemus didn't answer for a long while. He rubbed the finished drumstick on the sleeve of his too-large uniform, then, apparently satisfied, slipped both stick and whittling knife into a pocket. Only then did he push back his kepi and look across the fire at me, as though I'd only just posed him the question.

"Scared?" he asked.

I pretended to a sudden need for rolling up the cuffs some more on my own ill-fitting trousers, and didn't answer his question any more than he'd answered mine.

"We just gon' hafta stop him, is all." Nick said it as though the declaration alone made it a sure thing. Then he looked me over good and smiled sorta grim-like. "What's givin' you the heebie-jeebies, Syl? Ain't you never seen no battles before?"

I supposed I might as well admit it, so I shook my head "no" and stared back into the fire some more. At fourteen, Nicodemus had only a year on me, but he was already a veteran. He'd grown up a slave, but had been drumming for the 151st Ohio ever since the start of the war, when the Yanks had taken Nashville and told him he was free. Me, I'd only signed up two months back, after trying three times and getting sent back home, till I could finally get my pap's consent.

"Since I joined up," I said, "I haven't seen anything but a whole lot of drilling and marching, marching and drilling. I've never even got within spitting distance of a Reb. Don't know what I'd do if I ever got a real shot at one, or him at me."

"Don' worry none." Nick weaved his long slim fingers in between each other. "You'll see fightin' soon enough. And you'll get used to it."

"Yeah," I said, hating myself for the coward I must sound like. "I guess so."

Camp rumor said Abe Lincoln himself might be coming out to watch Early's attack. I thought that was odd, 'cause I couldn't think of anything would make the Rebs any happier than having Old Abe to shoot at. I wondered where he planned to watch from.

"Tell you what..." Nicodemus had got up and come around to my side of the campfire. From somewhere under his coat, he pulled out a round, palm-sized thing the color of blood, and pressed it into my hand. "You keep this in your pocket tomorrow. An' if we gets a battle out of ol' Jubal, you reach in and squeeze this jus' as hard as you kin squeeze."

I tilted the thing into the light and saw it glow a more fiery red. "It's beautiful," I told him, but then I had to add the next part, 'cause I didn't have any idea. "Uh... What is it?"

"Wish stone," Nick said. "Come from Africa. Used to belong to a king, so they say."

"Who said?" The pretty rock's smooth edges were starting to warm to my hand.

"My Gramma Huru. She give me that on the day she died, two weeks before Nashville done got itself lib'rated. She told me whoever holds this stone and squeeze it *real* hard, he'll get a wish. Jus' one wish, though."

I had to smile at that, and almost handed the trinket back to him. But on a whim, I put it into my tunic pocket instead and asked him, "Did it grant you *your* wish?"

He looked a shade disappointed. "Not yet. Will, though."

"Well, what'd you wish for? Or does telling spoil it?"

"Nope." He sat down beside me and stared into the fire, too. "I jus' done like Moses, that's all. Wished my people free. Wished all the Negroes free, everywhere. Made that wish out loud, the very same minute Gramma Huru gived me the stone. An' you know what she say?" I shook my head. "She say, 'It'll be, Nicodemus, it'll be. Maybe not right now, not today, but tomorrow. *Tomorrow* we be free.' Well, we didn' all get free on the next day. So I figured she musta meant some other tomorrow." He grinned at me. "You see Old Abe in the mornin', you tell him for us that we's still waitin'."

I didn't know what to say to that, so I just smiled back and nodded again, and we both sat and watched the fire till it burned itself all the way out.

As a rule, I didn't put no stock in magic charms. Back home in Lima, there were plenty of old wives who swore by the "magic" in those little asafetida bags they hung round your neck when you got the croup. Only thing they ever gave me was more croup and a powerful stink besides.

Nick's wish stone, though, I took back to the tent with me. I fished it out of my tunic before I hung that up and then got onto my bedroll and held the stone up to the moonlight coming in the tent flap. I looked into its dark depths and wished there *was* such a thing as magic. And I thought to myself, if there was such a thing, Sylvanus Foster, and you only had one wish, what would you wish for?

I had to think some on that.

While the sentries outside scuffed the dirt path back and forth from the flagpole and the few other men in the tent snored and muttered in their sleep, I stared at Nick's "magic" bauble and decided that just wishing to live through a battle was maybe a pretty big waste of its powers. I wondered why it hadn't granted Nick his wish yet, and if it ever really would. I'd never met any colored people till I joined the OVI, but I knew I didn't hold with slavery nor with all the bad things some folks said about Nicodemus' people being cursed of God, and such nonsense. I liked Nick well enough. So why shouldn't he get his wish that the Negroes all be free?

That set me wondering how much longer the war could go on for, and after it *was* finally over, then what? General Grant was supposed to have Lee on the run down in Richmond: he'd pulled so many troops out to help him, he'd nearly left Washington City defenseless. Which was why we were here. But even if Lee did surrender and the war come to be over, I wondered how much would be left to start over with. And how on God's earth did you put Rebs and Yanks back together again and expect 'em to just shake hands like all was forgiven, after so many years of shootin' at each other?

I couldn't see any way to do that. But then, I guessed it would all be Abe Lincoln's row to hoe when it was over.

Just like freeing the slaves would be.

I didn't see how exactly he could accomplish that, either, but I'd sure give a lot to come back in a hundred years or so and see how it'd all come out.

Then I thought, *All right, Nicodemus. Here's a wish for your magic rock after all.* And I squeezed the pebble hard. *If it can really grant a wish, then I'll ask it to show me your children's children and my children's children and how they fare with each other a hundred years from now. That's what I'd wish.*

Nothing happened, of course. The charm didn't grant my wish any more than it had granted Nick's two years ago in Nashville. Maybe it planned on waiting, like he said, for some other tomorrow. Shrugging, I slipped the bauble into my trouser pocket for safekeeping, and turned over to get some shut-eye.

Shots and a bugle call woke me. It was barely after dawn and all hell was breaking loose in camp, with men scrambling for shoes, tunics and guns all at once and the officers outside bellowing orders over the sound of more gunfire. My rifle was taller than me by eight inches and I tripped over it twice just getting out of the tent. Didn't need it after all, though, as I wound up ordered to join the relay lines passing shells from the bunkers up to the cannon ramps. They were eight-inch bore 69-pounders, those cannons, big enough to shake the ground and dull your ears when they went off. The shells were mighty heavy, too, especially after you'd hefted the first five or six of 'em.

Smoke, cannons, shouts and gunfire were all I knew then for what seemed to be hours. I never did see a Reb, but I heard 'em shootin' clear enough, and every now and then there'd come a cry from one of the sharpshooters who got hit up on the breastworks.

The smoke got so thick I could hardly see or breathe, but there was nothing for it but to cough and wipe my eyes and keep on passing shells. I also kept one foot up against my rifle on the ground beside me, even though I prayed all along not to need it.

After a while, I caught a glimpse of Nicodemus up the relay line a ways, standing with the other colored soldiers close to the leftmost cannon ramp. Every time a guidon fell and signaled one of the cannoneers to fire, Nick would put his hands over his ears, even if someone was trying to pass him a shell at the same time. I wished I'd thought of that, but right now in all the thunderous noise, I couldn't tell if my ears might be ringing or not.

I almost didn't hear the order to cease passing and come to attention: I only made sense of it when everyone around me did that. So I stood at attention and wondered what was going on. The gunfire from the battlements hadn't stopped, so the fight couldn't possibly be over.

Someone shouted something. The men on either side of me stiffened up even more. I looked where they seemed to be looking, and through the haze, saw Generals Wright and McCook and two officers walking with a tall man in a black coat and a high hat. I didn't realize it was Abe Lincoln with 'em till they'd walked right past us and continued up the center ramp all the way to the parapet. I wondered why he hadn't taken that hat off, such a handy target as it would make, but then the order to resume passing came, and we got back to business.

Fort Stevens had been dug out around a big oak tree that rose front and center of the ramparts, and it was next to that President Lincoln chose to stand and observe the battle. Cannon smoke almost obscured him from our view, but it wasn't long before Jubal's troops must've spotted him, 'cause a Reb shell landed smack on that oak and split it, with more shots flying close behind. One of the officers with Lincoln pushed him down just as another soldier who'd been moving to protect the president got hit, cried out and fell. The Yank sharpshooters up on the wall opened up, and in another moment they'd whooped and hollered that they got the sniper.

I started to turn and look for Nick again, only a loud whistling noise made me look up instead. The man next to me dropped the shell he'd been about to pass and hit the dirt. Before I could do the same, the loudest noise I'd ever heard and something that felt like a ton of cinder blocks knocked me clean off my feet.

I think I flew a ways. Don't remember hitting the ground, though. The cannons and gunfire all faded into stone deaf silence, and smoke blinded my whole world gray.

Strangest thing is, the next sound I could hear was a bird singing. No explosions, no battle cries, no guns–just one little mocking bird cheerily practicing his repertoire.

I couldn't smell smoke anymore, and the ground under me didn't shake. The fight must be over, I figured. So I opened my eyes.

And saw green grass.

I was sure there hadn't been any grass in the camp last night, but maybe I'd just missed it in the dark.

I found I could move, so I pushed up and got to my feet. My rifle was missing. But when I looked further, I realized that so was the camp. Our bivouac, all the trees and most of the ramparts were gone, replaced by a soiled brick-sided building and a tiny whitewashed church. I stood in the middle of a half-acre greensward that vaguely resembled Fort Stevens only because it retained a piece of the embankment (that, too, was grass-covered), three cannon ramps (only one had a cannon on it, and that was a rusting hulk), a flagpole and the ruins of an ammunition bunker. The bunker's wooden doors had been replaced with huge slabs of white sheetrock, but even that was cracked and crumbling, as though some titan with a giant hammer had taken his spite out on it.

I didn't see a soul around.

Only thing I could figure was I had to be either dead or dreaming. After some thought, I ruled out dead just because this didn't look like any Heaven I'd ever read of in the Good Book. So, if there was nothing for it but to wait till I woke up, I supposed I might as well have more of a look around.

Something made flapping noises over my head, and I gazed up at a flag up there on the pole, whipping full out in the wind. It was Old Glory, sure enough, but it wasn't quite right. There were too many stars on it.

Another block of that white sheetrock stood not far away, and it had a bronze plaque bolted to its top that mapped out what the camp should have looked like–*had* looked like, more or less, just this morning. The bronze was dark, like it'd been there awhile, and in the bottom left corner it bore the inscription DEDICATED SEPTEMBER 1956 BY THE DAUGHTERS OF UNION VETERANS OF THE CIVIL WAR, 1861-1865.

Two pieces of that inscription sort of stared right back at me: the year 1956 and the word DAUGHTERS. My hand went straight into my pocket to pull out Nicodemus' wish stone. Hadn't I just told it before I fell asleep last night that I wanted to see how Nick's children's children and mine would fare in about a hundred years? Could this shiny little rock really grant wishes after all? It lay in my hand, deeper red in the sunlight, and didn't part with a single one of its secrets.

The roar of some terrible engine sounded from beyond the embankment. My first thought was to get down and hit the dirt again, but if this was a vision, hadn't I ought to be safe enough? The sound faded off. Emboldened, I climbed a cannon ramp up to the parapet, where another bronze plaque pictured Lincoln under fire, and gazed over the top at what I knew had been open ground north of Washington City: the ground Jubal Early had attacked us from this morning.

It was all gone.

No fields, no farmhouses, no trees. Just dirty brick buildings as far as the eye could see, all cramped and crowded together, surrounding my greensward on all four sides. A wide stretch of tarred road and a smaller one of white sheetrock lay between, and on the road's edge, unattended, sat a row of gleaming glass and metal carriages. Leastways, they *looked* like carriages, as they each had strange, fat black wheels on 'em. But there wasn't a horse in sight anywhere.

The crack-whine of a gunshot made me duck fast behind the embankment. Someone shouted something, and three more shots went off in rapid succession. I hunkered down behind the Lincoln marker till the shooting stopped, then carefully peeked around its edge till I could see the road.

Two colored boys, neither of 'em much older than Nick, had run into the street, and right behind them had come five white soldiers in peculiar dark blue uniforms I'd never seen the like of before. They carried guns and clubs, those soldiers, and they caught up to both boys right there on the sheetrock in front of the dugout, where they commenced to beating them senseless. Black folks started pouring out of the buildings then, some with bricks or rocks or bottles in hand, and they set upon the soldiers with shrieks louder than any Rebel yell. They smashed the shiny glass carriages into splintered ruins, set 'em afire and ran like hell when more white soldiers showed up and started shooting.

That terrible roar I'd heard before came again, along with a fearsome wailing, and right quick at least a dozen horseless wagons, all black and white with blazing red lanterns, came barreling into the fray. Dozens more soldiers spilled out of 'em, guns blasting.

Quaking like a damn coward, I clutched the edge of Old Abe's bronze likeness, stayed hidden, and watched the bloodshed. My first look at a real battle, and I couldn't do nothing *but* watch, 'cause my feet rooted and just plain refused to budge.

I saw Negroes shot down in cold blood and soldiers beaten into pulp by blacks who'd managed to gang up on them. The two boys the first soldiers had set upon were shackled and dragged, screaming, off to a wagon while a colored woman followed and cried that they hadn't "done nuthin' wrong." Her pleas for mercy fell on deaf ears.

Bigger wagons arrived, and now the soldiers had clearly won the skirmish, for they quickly herded or carried every last Negro into those transports. Then they picked up the dead ones and took them as well. Their own dead and wounded they hauled away in a different sort of wagon, but in the end, they took everyone, and roared away with their red lanterns blazing.

The burned carriages stank and smoldered. Glass exploded out of one of them and scattered itself with an almost musical sound across the oiled road. Behind me, a stiff breeze snapped and fluttered the flag with too many stars.

I don't know how long it took me to convince my feet to hold me up again. I climbed up onto the parapet for a better look at the battlefield, but somehow all I could look at was a bright pool of blood on the white sheetrock where the soldiers had beaten the two Negro boys.

When I did tear my gaze away, it was because a glint of sunlight caught my eye. I looked up and away, past the burning wagons and the squalid brick houses, over the rooftops to a thing familiar from the Washington City I knew. There, not more than a ten-minute march away, stood the white Capitol dome. It should have been a comfort, seeing something I recognized in this grim, war-torn place, but it wasn't. Would our children's children's world really come to this? Could the law of our great land truly have allowed this horror to go on for so long?

I made a fist, and shook it at the gleaming white dome.

"What did our boys fight and die for?" I shouted. "Nick's people are still in chains! It was all for nothing!"

I raged at it for several minutes more, but the dome only glittered at me in the bright sun, and staunchly refused to care.

"He'll be fine," I heard a gruff voice say. "Shell concussion knocked him flat, that's all."

I had to think on it a spell before it seemed I remembered how to open my eyes. When I did, I saw two hazy forms standing at a tent flap. From his black bag I figured one for a sawbones. The other one was Nicodemus.

"You can go in now, boy," the doc said, and he hustled off, the leather bag making *skiff-skuff* noises as it rubbed against his long black coat.

Nick came in, and seeing my eyes were open, he knelt down next to my bedroll and grinned at me. "'Bout time you waked up," he said.

"Sawbones says you'll live, but I could tell he was powerful disappointed not to be cuttin' no arms or legs off you."

"Powerful sorry to disappoint him," I replied, borrowing his words. I realized then that I couldn't hear any cannons or gunfire. "Battle over?" I asked.

Nicodemus nodded. "Hours ago, right after you got knocked out. Gen'ral Jubal, he got in his shot at Old Abe, then seein' as he missed an' our boys got his sniper, he lobbed that last shell up over the 'bankment and took off runnin'. We been celebratin' ever since."

"They missed Old Abe," I repeated, and smiled 'cause I remembered seeing the officer push the president down just before the shell had gone off.

"Shore did," said Nick. "Lieutenant Holmes, he grabbed Lincoln and yelled 'Get down, you fool!' jus' like he was talkin' to some green recruit. Landed square on top of 'im, too! You'd a thought Old Abe'd be hoppin' mad, only he jus' picks 'isself back up when it's all over, dusts off his stovepipe and says to Holmes, 'Son, it sure is a good thing you know how to talk to civilians!' Had the whole lot of us fallin' down laughin' till we couldn' laugh no more!"

I laughed too, though it made my head hurt. I remembered the wish stone then, and had to squirm some to fish it out of my pocket and hold it out to Nick. "Reckon I can give this back to you now," I said.

He frowned a bit, although he took it. "What'd it show you?" he asked, just as if he already knew about my vision.

I didn't rightly know what to say. I just couldn't tell him that a hundred years from now, there'd still be a war on, and his people would still be slaves, and the only thing white folks would've learned is how to build shiny wagons without needing no horses to pull 'em. I couldn't tell him none of that, so I just said, "It showed me that your Grandma Huru was right."

He looked puzzled at that. "About us gettin' free, you mean?"

I nodded. "Tomorrow," I said, and closed my eyes again because

my head still ached and I felt suddenly very tired. "Tomorrow."
And before I fell asleep, I prayed that somewhere, in some future tomorrow, Nick's wish really would come true.

Jean Graham's stories have appeared in Misunderstood, Dying to Live, Arcane 2, Daw Books' Time of the Vampires, and in several other anthologies and magazines. "Tomorrow We Be Free" is based upon her great-grandfather's experiences, at age 13, in the US Civil War. She lives in San Diego, CA with husband Chuck, 5000 books, and six cats. For more of her fiction, see jeangraham.20m.com.

Fire and Stone

Jonathan Shipley

I strode into the cavernous mess hall, and stood stiffly behind my assigned seat. I stared at the banners on the far wall—the center one blood-red with a swastika, the ones on either side dead-black with two silver lightning bolts. I tried to appear inspired by the emblems of the SS academy. Appearance was the only thing keeping me alive.

The gypsy blood in my veins damned me, but I was blond enough to pass. Blond enough to be accepted as an SS officer-cadet with only a cursory background check—and a bit of nudging from the small Romany magicks that came with the blood. Gypsies weren't the soul-stealers of folklore, but not all Romany traditions were myths.

"Walk among them," my father had said. "Survive. Do it for all of us who can't."

There had been no more discussion. Among my people, a father's word is still law. Blending into the Reich's New Order became my life. But I grieved for my old life. I should not be hiding while the Clan suffered. This charade, this pretending to be one of them, stuck in my craw.

Lohsen, the cadet beside me, nudged my arm. "I think those were your best rifle scores to date. Another week of improvement like this one and—"

He fell silent as the Commandant and senior officers entered and took their places at the head table. The room remained deadly quiet for a few seconds, then at the signal we all drew out our chairs and sat down. The meal proceeded wordlessly, the only noise the clatter of forks against the plates and the tread of the duty officer as he walked among the tables, checking the cadets for proper table manners.

"Cutlery is held with the fingers and not with the whole hand," he said to someone at the next table. His voice boomed as if through a megaphone. The cadet in question turned red, quickly readjusting his hold on the fork. For the sons of farmers and butchers aspiring to join the National Socialist elite, the SS academy was finishing school as much as training ground.

Then I felt the chill. Like a door suddenly opening and closing, a breath of the Otherworld wafted over me. An omen? I tried to continue eating, but my stomach felt tied in knots. Finally I gave up and waited. Lunch ended and the Commandant rose to make general announcements.

"Cadets will appear in the lecture hall in full dress this afternoon," he said. "*Hauptsturmführer* Eckhardt from the *Reichsführung-SS*, Berlin will speak. No passes will be issued this evening. Be prepared for special orders later this afternoon. That is all. Heil Hitler!"

We all rose to our feet and snapped our right arms upward in salute while the Commandant and officers filed from the hall. After a momentary silence, a rush of words came from all quarters as cadets relaxed and resumed interrupted conversations on their way to the door.

"Well, *komerad*, this will be something new for you," said Lohsen. "Or did you practice the rites in Vienna?"

A distinct prickling started at the back of my neck. "The Commandant said nothing about rites."

Lohsen gave me a knowing smile. "What else would it be on this night of the year? Something to look forward to, eh?" He turned and left me standing by the table.

Even when I was the last one left in the hall, I didn't move.

Lohsen's words had my imagination running riot. Tonight was the Summer Solstice, a time when the boundaries between worlds thinned.

"The essence of the German soul is Blood and Soil. From the good earth arose the German *Volk*, whose destiny it is to pull mankind back from the brink of extinction that is the byproduct of modern civilization..."

I scrupulously scribbled down every idea that *Hauptsturmführer* Eckhardt poured forth from the podium. I had heard it all before, but more than ever I needed to cling to appearances. I needed to make it through this night.

Eckhardt turned suddenly to the blackboard behind him and slashed the SS symbol across it. "From the past we find the inspiration for the present. The twin lightning bolts represent the sun's life-giving power and carry a heritage and energy far beyond any mere acronym. Just as with the old stone altars of our ancestors, the runes are a long-overlooked energy source, waiting to be tapped. The runes in themselves are power."

I gave a start. What did the Reich know about runes and stone altars? Runes *were* power, of course. The Clans had known that for centuries, but we kept the knowledge to ourselves.

I stole a few furtive glances around the room to see how the other cadets were taking this information. Nothing showed on their faces except the usual blank acceptance that accompanied all lectures.

At length the lecture ended, and we were dismissed to our rooms for the rest of the afternoon to contemplate what we had heard.

Was the average cadet supposed to understand any of this? I wondered. Why would we be force-fed mysticism as part of our training? I kept wondering if the whole afternoon was an elaborate trap of some kind.

A knock on my door startled me. "*Herein*," I said, getting to my feet and noticing for the first time that the afternoon sun had given way to twilight.

Lohsen pushed open the door. "It's sundown, *komerad*," he said. "It's time."

We marched from the barracks to the central courtyard. The cobblestones resounded with the tread of boots as we took our regular drill positions.

When every cadet stood in his assigned phalanx, Eckhardt mounted the platform in the center and began speaking. The words echoed off the stone walls, and I had to strain to follow what he said. Most of the speech seemed to be familiar slogans like "*Ein Volk, ein Reich, ein Führer.*" Old garbage. I relaxed a little.

The sense of dread that had been building up inside me all afternoon faded. Now that the "rites," as Lohsen called them, were upon me, everything seemed too commonplace to be threatening. The courtyard was still the courtyard, the cadets were still cadets. If anything, an extra solidness seemed to surround me. I felt rooted in the good German soil like an ancient oak.

The thought was odd. I turned my attention back to the speaker's platform in time to catch something about the shrine of the oak tree. Eckhardt continued with the symbolism of the birch and beech and linden tree. His words seemed to wander in the forest, drawing on the ancient energy of the land. Like fire, they spread from tree to tree, person to person, igniting the individual will and uniting them all into the Will of the *Volk*.

I blinked and drew a ragged breath. My thoughts were not my own. Eckhardt's phrases kept slipping inside my head.

I tried to fight it, tried to feel the strength of the Land flow through me like a great river—

Again I wrenched my thoughts out of Eckhardt's current. It wasn't the words, I realized, it was how he spoke. His voice had a mesmerizing effect. Even though it sounded dull and flat, he could somehow make me see and feel certain images.

I must have lost another few minutes for the next thing I knew, the cadet next to me was handing me a wooden shaft. I stared at it.

"Pass them to the end of the row," he muttered, handing me another.

Torches. I wondered why it had taken me so long to spot the obvious. Of course they were torches, one end dipped in tallow.

My hackles rose. Something was very wrong. Eckhardt had done—or was doing—something to me that I didn't understand. *Trap*, a little voice in my mind kept whispering.

I conjured up the best defense I could—an image of a thick, solid wall. I tried to build the image the way an artist painted in oils, overlaying detail upon detail. Bricks and mortar to block out *Reich* and *Volk*.

Orange flames rose up in front of my eyes. I blinked. A lit torch passed in front of me. Eckhardt began speaking about the power of the fire, but I refused to listen. I lit my torch from the comrade on my right and touched it to the one on my left. The heat seemed extraordinary, the flames compelling.

Suddenly I was cold, freezing cold, despite the flames all around me. Except there wasn't any fire around me. I was alone in a gray landscape.

I knew this place from the old tales, the place that sundered mind from body. The Otherworld. It didn't mean I had died. It was a place to gather yourself, to draw strength from Beyond—but not a place to visit alone. Never send your soul Beyond, it was said, without a brother to guard your body. I had to return.

I focused on the academy, on being back among the stones and torches of the courtyard. The gray landscape shimmered.

Suddenly I plunged back into the physical world where I stood staring at the torch in my hand. My fingers were numb and I couldn't feel my legs at all.

If I break rank, I thought as my knees started to buckle, they'll know. They'll know their ritual has found me out. Have to maintain appearances.

I tried to straighten but the cobblestones rushed toward my face.

"Cadet?"

Someone hovered over me, calling me. I wanted to tell him to leave me alone, but my mouth wouldn't work right.

"*Komm, Mann! Wach' auf.*"

The voice above me grew more insistent. I managed to open my eyes. A man in uniform stood over me with a worried expression.

I opened my mouth, heard a few muddled syllables come out, and gave up for the moment. My head cleared a little. I stared up, trying to place the face above.

"Finally, you return to us," the man said. "You've been out for hours."

"What happened?" I mumbled. "I had a torch—" The ritual. The trap.

"And passed out cold," he nodded. "Fortunately your comrades on either side were able to grab you on the way down, or you would have had quite a concussion."

I attempted to sit up, but my arms were like rubber.

"None of that," he ordered. "Just lie quietly."

Suddenly, I realized who he was—Eckhardt! The one who had done this to me.

"You had quite a reaction to our torchlight ceremony," he said, leaning over me with a smile.

My mouth went dry. I could think of nothing to say.

"We planned this ceremony precisely to find people like you." He smiled again.

Cold panic seized me—I couldn't move, only stare at the smug face above me.

Eckhardt leaned even closer, his eyes running over my face in minute inspection. "According to your records, you're from a very old family—Austrian, isn't it?"

My stomach knotted. "Yessir," I forced myself to answer. If he had my family history, he knew all.

"Sometimes old families possess—" he paused, watching me closely "—old powers. The power of the Stones and the Sacred Sites."

"*Hexen*," I murmured. The word was out before I realized I'd said it aloud. But I recognized the old phrase from tales handed down among my own people.

Eckhardt's smile grew. It was the word he'd been waiting for. "Yes," he said. "Witches."

"But I'm not—" Not a witch, I started to protest. Then what was I, he would ask. I closed my mouth and stared at the ceiling. The trap was sprung.

"I am seconding you to the Ahnenerbe," he continued. "Berlin has already been notified."

I looked up, startled. "Ahnenerbe?"

"Yes, the SS Occult Bureau. We actively recruit those with the old powers. The Reich has enemies who traffic in the occult—Freemasons, gypsies, half-breeds. We have learned to fight fire with fire. We have work for you—important work. Our first assignment is in Westphalia."

The pieces finally clicked together. This was the reason my father and the Clan had sent me to the Nazis—to sabotage their fire.

I smiled at Eckhardt, to all appearances a cadet bewildered by a sudden promotion. I would join this Occult Bureau. And see what havoc my small Romany magicks could spawn among these SS witches.

The stone outcropping rose out of the Westphalian forest as we bounced along the dirt road in a military transport vehicle. There were twelve of us in back. Eckhardt rode in the cab with the driver. The twelve of us were new to the Occult Bureau, all recruits personally culled from SS academies and barracks. I discovered that I, the newest member, completed his special circle. Counting himself, he now had a full complement of thirteen to work his magic. Thirteen had always been a number beloved by witches, I remembered—their coven number. And I was part of the coven.

The rock formation ahead was our destination. The Ancestral Research Bureau of the SS had recently discovered this place of pagan worship and was painstakingly excavating the caves. The Occult Bureau had a less archeological interest. Raising power in the ancient worship site was the first assignment for Eckhardt and his newly completed coven.

The Rom knew many of the old sacred places scattered among the forests and hills of Central Europe. Although they were not our sacred places, we held them in healthy respect. The Christian priests had not destroyed the old stone gods, merely driven them underground.

Eckhardt was playing with fire. I could only hope that this site had been just a minor center of worship whose power had faded over the centuries.

The trees finally opened to a clearing where several wooden cabins had been erected to house the research personnel. As we climbed out of the truck, my gaze slid past the buildings to the rocks beyond.

"There are many of these sites throughout the Fatherland," Eckhardt told me in a hushed whisper as he came up beside me. "Many are lost to us, but this, the greatest of all the power sites, we have reclaimed. From this center, the power shall again flow to bind *Volk* and *Land* into one unstoppable force."

The uneasiness that had plagued me since I had been briefed on the assignment climbed several notches higher. Whatever power these SS witches possessed could well be amplified by the old power sites. And I suspected that people like Eckhardt had already unearthed the old rituals from the commentaries of long-dead scholars. They would use blood, of course. That was the dark path, the gift that the ancient stones craved. My people usually gave the old power sites wide berth. The Rom remembered the appetites of the stones.

I took another look at the jagged silhouette of the massive rocks against the setting sun. There was almost no indication of shaping or tooling. The formation stood as it had been thrust up from the bowels of the earth, a product of nature, not man. That was rare among the power sites. It conjured blurred memories. Did I know this place?

"Does it have a name, this place?" I asked Eckhardt.

He smiled. "The Externsteine. We have found the Externsteine."

I felt a sudden chill. The Star Stones. Yes, I knew this place from the old tales. Once, it had been among the most powerful of the stone worship places. The Wild Magic ran deep from the core of the earth to this outcropping. For a thousand years or more it had slept, forgotten, but now these SS witches would have the power flow again.

They say that the Rom have no conscience, hold nothing sacred, and much of the time that is true. Our life is the Clan. Beyond that, the world holds only enemies and fools. But the stones truly have no conscience. They will give of their power to whoever feeds them. Good and evil do not exist in the bowels of the earth. If I could not stop whatever the SS had in mind, no one else would.

The "research" would start tomorrow. I had already seen the prisoners they had shipped in from the detention camp at nearby Wewelsburg. When the transport truck stopped and the brace of SS Death's Head guard began unloading their human cargo, I was gripped by the fear that I would see some of my own Clan among the prisoners. But the shaven-headed dozen that appeared were all pale, thin creatures with no hint of Romany in their appearance. I watched until they had been marched into the windowless bunker at the heart of the camp.

I would have to act tonight. Tomorrow—whether Eckhardt knew what he was doing or not—the blood of these victims would awaken the stones. But what could I do? I still carried the moonstone of my birthing disguised as a fob for my pocket watch, but it served only as a personal charm. Small magicks I could wright with it—glamours, illusions, even love potions on demand. But to bend the ancient power of the Externsteine to my will—this was beyond anything in my experience. Perhaps the Clan Elders assembled together could accomplish such a thing, but I was only one person, and not very old.

As the camp settled into silence, I gathered my meager arsenal—the moonstone and a few sprigs of monkshood that I had been able to harvest undetected near the academy. Only one guard had been posted near the prisoners' bunker as a formality.

I had walked the site that afternoon and knew exactly where to go—the crypt stone facing the lake. The emanations were stronger here than any other accessible location. The caves were too filled with debris, and the chapel chamber high atop the tallest of the stones could only be reached by a rope ladder precarious even by daylight.

As I rounded the formation and placed the wall of stone between me and the camp, I turned more of my attention to the mystic problem. Perhaps with the aid of the moonstone I could slip into trance and contact the wild magic lying dormant around me. But what could I offer it? A cupful of my own blood?

I knelt beside the crypt stone, placing my moonstone on the ledge in front of me. Then crushing the monkshood between my palms, I wiped the pungent oil across my forehead and laid my hands flat against the coffin-like hollow.

A cold, leaden feeling coursed up through my hands to settle in the pit of my stomach as the landscape faded to a silvery gray.

The Otherworld. Again I was drawn here, alone and unprepared, but perhaps this was the door I needed. Then a sudden movement across the lake caught my attention. There should have been no movement, because I was standing outside of normal time. But it happened again—a ghostly horse wheeling in the shadows of the far trees.

My skin prickled. I had forgotten the dangers. Only a fool would enter the Otherworld here at a site of Old Power, where reality was already stretched by the very nature of the place. Whatever hovered in the shadows around such places would bear no love toward humankind.

I glanced back at the ghost-horse and forgot everything else. The horse was solid enough now, and had picked up a rider, a huge figure with horned helmet and spear. Behind him, several more riders were beginning to materialize. Riders masked in antlered skulls. The waters of the lake swirled red around their horses' feet.

Murky memories stirred. This was the Wild Magic at its wildest, the Wild Hunt that fed off the souls of the unwary. Nothing in my gypsy blood would protect me if they came for me.

I saw one of the riders wheel his horse and start across the smooth lake surface as though it were solid under hoof. The skull mask turned toward me. I could feel his gaze from behind the empty eye sockets, could feel the pull on my soul. Dimly, I realized he was lowering his spear and charging...

I lurched back into my body and fell shivering beside the crypt stone. I could hear the wind in the trees again. When I opened my eyes, I was back in real time, in full color.

So the Otherworld was closed to me in this place. I would have to find another way to speak to the stones, though I had no other way. With a ragged sigh, I struggled to my feet.

"What are you doing?" a harsh voice demanded behind me.

I whirled and found myself face to face with a leering Death's Head guard. He swaggered closer, one hand resting on his holstered Luger.

"What are you doing?" he repeated.

"I heard noises—across the lake. Horses." I shouldn't have been so terrified. As one of Eckhardt's coven, I should have been beyond interrogation by a mere prison guard. But I couldn't stop shaking. I could almost feel the Wild Hunt creeping closer. They had caught my scent and would have my soul, one way or another. They would use this loutish guard without his ever being aware.

The guard half turned toward the shore. "There's nothing over—"

I didn't plan it. It just happened. Suddenly I was tackling the man, my fingers working his SS dagger free of its sheath.

He fought back, going for a choke hold.

Time seemed to flow backward, taking me back to the academy and the endless combat training. My body reacted with a will of its own, blocking his hold and plunging the dagger into his chest. It went in part way and hit bone.

He grunted. His hand groped for his service pistol.

I pulled the dagger out and plunged it in again, slicing upward through the ribcage this time to reach the heart.

The wind rose suddenly to a howling gale.

He gurgled and went limp. I let him fall into the hollowed sarcophagus of the crypt stone. The rock walls drank in the spurting blood like a sponge.

"Take him," I cried to the wind. "Take his blood and taste its arrogance. Take his kind as your prey, not your priests."

The wind abruptly faded. I sensed that my invocation had been heard, though with what result I could not guess. I only wanted to get away. It was no longer clear who was using whom. Such was the way of the old stones, I remembered.

Staggering back to the compound, I checked my hands and clothing. I didn't see any blood from the struggle. The stones had taken it all, leaving nothing to connect me to the guard's death.

The next morning, the camp erupted into chaos. The guard had been found in the crypt stone, completely mummified. And the other Death's Head guard who discovered the body fell within moments of sounding the alarm and broke his neck.

With such circumstances, Eckhardt must have suspected the Old Powers' involvement, but it was not a thing he could tell the investigating officer sent out from Wewelsburg.

For my part, I no longer cared what he suspected or what he attempted. I had awakened the stones and given them a taste for SS blood. The Occult Bureau would find little joy in this place, for the stones—and perhaps only the stones—were crueler than the Nazis.

Jonathan Shipley is a Fort Worth writer of fantasy, science fiction, and horror. Although he self-identifies as a novelist, it is short fiction where he is currently enjoying success and he has sold over seventy stories. Jonathan is a contributing author to the *After Death* anthology that won the 2014 Bram Stoker award, as well as a finalist for the 2014 Washington Science Fiction Association's Small Press Award. He maintains a web presence at www.shipleyscifi.com where you can find a full list of his publications.

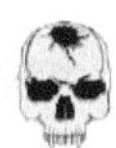

Wanda Hargett's Last Date

Cathy Moeschet

...And now here she was, with the cutesy, absurd question cards in her hand, thinking that this was the weirdest dream she'd ever had. Except that if it really was a dream, then she'd dreamt everything that had happened in the last few days, and *there* was a thought that was too good to be true. Wanda Hargett was the kind of woman to whom strange things frequently happened, but this took the cake.

She was shocked to find that the game show host was the same guy who'd given her his business card in the bar two nights ago. He'd cut his hair since then, and had somehow managed to grow a mustache, but here he was, all right. He couldn't disguise the booming cheer in his voice that had made her want to tighten his gaudy Hawaiian tie until his eyes popped. Who did this loser think he was fooling?

She could see the shadows of three figures lounging casually in chairs behind some sort of screen. The would-be host wiggled his nose. Wanda was relieved to see the ridiculous mustache shift a little. Good. It *was* fake.

"And now, Wanda, welcome to 'Your Last Date!'"

Last date?

"Excuse me," Wanda said, pulling on the host's sleeve. "You said this was –"

"It'll be the experience of a lifetime, Wanda, we guarantee it!" he interrupted heartily, but shot her a stern look. "Before we begin, let me tell you about our three Mystery Men, and explain the rules of the game. Mystery Man Number One is one cool guy, Wanda. He likes getting falling-down drunk and playing Chicken with cops in unmarked cars. Sounds like a bang-up time to me!"

This was greeted with wild applause from the darkness around her, but Wanda could see no audience. The silhouette of Mystery Man Number One waved unsteadily.

"Mystery Man Number Two comes to us from Washington, D.C. He collects assault weapons and says he enjoys hunting small animals, children and vagrants. Just be sure to wear those colors, big guy. We wouldn't want any nasty accidents, now would we?"

More applause. Mystery Man Number Two waved his gun, accidentally discharging a spray of bullets. A collective gasp escaped the audience, followed by a scatter of nervous giggles.

"And finally, Mystery Man Number Three. This wild man is in sales, Wanda. His specialty is hard-to-find recreational substances. His hobbies include pyromania and risky sexual encounters. Welcome to our show, you old stud, you!" There was pandemonium from the invisible audience. Mystery Man Number Three sniffled loudly.

What WAS this?

Wanda was damned if she knew, but one thing was for sure. It was going to stop right *now.*

She'd been sitting in the lounge of the Regal Inn, having a consolation martini and thinking of novel ways to kill her boss. Hands Malloy had always been a lecherous old fart, but sometime during the last two days that they'd been thrown together on this trip, Hands had decided that Wanda was crazy about him and trying not to let on. Wanda had spent the early evening playing chase around tacky, generic motel furniture. Now, finally, the dirty geezer was tucked safely away in his room, sleeping off his nightly quota of Jack Daniels. She wished there were somewhere else to go, somewhere far, far from Hands, and work, and… well, *life*.

She wished she were dead.

As if on cue, the guy plopped down on the stool next to hers. He reeked of perfumed soap and breath spray, and he grinned idiotically. It took her all of two seconds to peg him as a tourist or a salesman, the kind of guy who wore suits ten years out of style and read things like *HOW TO BE YOUR OWN BEST FRIEND* in the john.

Some days, things just got better and better.

"Hi there!" he boomed, falsely large and chipper. "Sonny's the name, and image is my game! And you look like your subscription to sunshine just expired. Maybe I can help you." Sonny stared at her expectantly, no doubt prepared in the event that she should fall at his feet.

"Drop dead," Wanda mumbled, staring into her drink.

He laughed heartily. So heartily, in fact, that he fell into a coughing fit. Wanda made no move to pat him on the back. Heads, he recovered on his own; tails, the barkeep called the EMS squad.

It was heads. When he had himself under some kind of control again, Sonny reached into his shirt pocket and brought out… *Horrors!* A business card. Wanda groaned inwardly.

"I like you!" he enthused. "I'm promoting a new game show, and we're always looking for players with the right attitude. Call this number, if you'd like. It's legit. And it's guaranteed to solve all of your problems." He pushed the card across the bar at her and left in a cloud of Binaca and Irish Spring.

Wanda looked at the card. It read:

"Tired of losing? Life getting you down? Giving up on finding that special someone? Put an end to the rat race! Play the game and find eternal happiness! Call 555-3323 today!"

Wanda sat for a long moment, debating… Oh, what the hell. She dug down into her purse and unearthed her cell phone. Taking a deep breath, she dialed.

Sonny-the-host had by this time launched into the rules of the game and was firmly ignoring Wanda's mystified attempts to get his attention.

"Now wait just a—"

"Remember, Wanda," he said to her, avoiding her gaze, "the object here is to get to *know* our Mystery Men. You'll ask them the questions on the cards you're holding, in any order you like. Based on their answers, you'll select one lucky guy, and together you'll stroll off into the sunset!"

"Hold it!" protested Wanda. "What's going on here? Are you all *crazy*?"

"Sounds too good to be true, eh, Wanda? Well, I don't blame you. First question, please!"

Wanda gaped at him. Still, she felt her mouth move, heard her voice asking the first nonsense question.

"Mystery Man Number One, what food best describes you?"

"Hamburger."

"Wha—? Would you care to elaborate on that?"

"No, that about covers it."

Wanda had the sinking feeling that she was losing some sort of battle. She motioned to Sonny, who had ducked into a shadow and was doing his best to be invisible.

"Keep going!" he hissed. "You're doing fine!"

She looked at the next card.

"Mystery Man Number Three, what kind of gift would you give a lady to mark a special occasion?"

"The kind that keeps on giving." He chuckled darkly.

"Oh, like a book."

"I had something a little more personal in mind."

Wanda looked pleadingly at Sonny, but he was having none of it. He gestured wildly at her to continue. She sighed and moved on to the next question.

"If you could be any famous person you wanted to be, Mystery Man Number Two, who would you be?"

"Adolf Hitler," he said, without hesitation. "Now *there* was a dude with a plan!"

"That's IT!" Wanda screamed. She rose and stalked to the corner where Sonny stood, watching the proceedings with maniacal glee.

"What are you doing?" he yelped, as she took his arm and yanked him into the circle of light in which she had been sitting.

"You're going to tell me just what the hell is going on here, or else!"

"I don't have to tell you anything!" he said, but she had taken off one spike-heeled shoe, and he made the mistake of imagining the various kinds of damage it could do him. He fidgeted, weighing his chances of bare-facing Wanda, but the look in her eye and the shoe in her hand put a stop to that. This one wasn't going to swallow any bullshit. He sighed, resigned. This was the third one in a row. The Boss was going to have his ass.

"Okay, okay. Here's the deal. I work for… Well, I work for Death, Wanda. See, he feels that he's gotten kind of a bad rap over the years. Always the bad guy, lurking on the fringes, robbing good, deserving people. Bad for business, right? Everyone's morale was in the toilet. Even the harbingers were leaving faster than he could replace them. And what else are *they* gonna do, for crying out loud, work at McDonald's? Can you imagine '"You want fries with that?" quoth the Raven'? Poe would be sick! So the Boss, he decided to put together sort of a PR package. To put Death in a new light, so to speak. Make himself more appealing to the masses."

He reached into the shadows and came up with a water pitcher, which he drained in four swallows. Wanda was mildly amused to see that he was sweating furiously.

"It's a good idea, really," he went on. Was it her that he was trying to convince, or himself? Wanda wasn't sure. "And the game is part of the package. We're pretty careful about who plays. Usually they *want* to. But lately… I don't know. The old radar's been a little off. But I was sure about you. You wished you were dead! I *know* you did! You're the third one in a row to back out on me. If this doesn't work, I'm history here. The Boss'll just… Oh, I can't even *think* about it!" Sonny threw his face into his hands and sobbed.

Wanda found herself reaching out in an impulsive gesture of comfort, then stopped herself. This guy wanted to…wanted to kill her. There it was. He wanted her *dead*. So why did she suddenly feel sorry for him?

"I don't suppose there's any way around this?" she asked, half-knowing his answer.

"Nada. Zilch. Zippo."

The unseen spectators, who had gone solemnly silent when the festivities ground to a halt, were finding new ways to amuse themselves. The air now rang with curses and insults, and various grisly and exotic items rained down on Wanda and Sonny.

"What are your rules about all of this? Is there some sort of guideline that you follow concerning… contestants?" Wanda had the germ of an idea; now she just had to get Sonny to cooperate.

"Not really," Sonny replied morosely. "Just that the player has to be the one to call us, and he or she has to be willing to play the game all the way through."

"But it doesn't have to be me?"

"Well…" Sonny paused. This had never occurred to him. "Not as such. I don't *think* so. But the actual numbers have to match up. We all have a quota, you know."

Interesting. Wanda looked at Sonny speculatively. He looked desperate enough to go for a deal.

"I can get you someone."

"Someone who won't back out?" Hope dawned in Sonny's beady

little eyes.

"Absolutely." Wanda said, in her best professional, reassuring voice. Sonny blinked at her.

"Sold."

Wanda enjoyed her relief the way she normally enjoyed a cigarette after a really good meal. A quiet voice in the back of her head told her she shouldn't do this. It was the same voice that nagged at her when she forgot to water the plants or didn't call her mother. But it was nothing she couldn't live with. She was doing what she had to do to survive... and she would also be doing a good deed, of sorts.

Sonny collected himself and turned to the screen, behind which the Mystery Men were exchanging social outrages with the audience.

"That's it, guys. We're done for tonight. I want to thank you for participating. Please be ready in case we call you back. Next time, I promise we'll finish it."

"Sure," said Number One. "Just like last time, right?" The Mystery Men filed lazily out from behind the screen.

Wanda froze, terror thick in her throat.

Mystery Man Number One was a mass of blood. His clothing hung in shreds, and Wanda could see jagged slivers of glass protruding from his wounds in some places. He carried his head under his arm. With his free hand, he waved to his two companions.

"Adios, fellas. I'm running a little late."

Before Wanda could even wonder how he could still speak, Mystery Men Numbers Two and Three emerged. Number Two sported at least four bullet holes from which blood still trickled; a few others looked less recent. He didn't seem overly concerned, however, and raised a polite hand to her in greeting as he passed.

Mystery Man Number Three was cooked to a turn, black and shriveled, with wisps of smoke escaping from his shirt collar and his open zipper. Wanda saw that his nose was completely gone. He sniffled and nodded at her. He stopped when he reached Sonny.

"You promised me a woman, Sonny-boy. I'm getting tired of

waiting. Get on the stick, will you?" he growled, poking at Sonny's chest with the charred stump of a finger. Air whistled merrily through the gaping hole that used to be his nose.

"Next time, big guy. Scout's honor."

Two and Three slouched away together, mumbling. Something hit the floor with a soft plop.

"Bummer, man," Two consoled. He knelt and retrieved the blackened penis, handing it gingerly to Three, who regarded it with little interest and stuffed it into the pocket of his sport jacket. "Don't you hate it when that happens?"

"Yeah." Three shrugged mildly. "You get used to it."

Eldon Malloy, known in wider and more realistic circles as Hands, rolled over and yawned. There was no one in the other half of the bed. It was still almost perfectly made. Damn. He hated waking up alone. But no matter. One of these days, Wanda would see the light. Wanda, or someone else. He guessed it didn't really matter in the final analysis, but he'd been having some *spectacular* dreams about Wanda just lately.

He got up and walked unsteadily to the closet. He recognized the light-headed feeling that told him to expect the juicier parts of his hangover to drop in around the middle of the afternoon. He looked at the clock. He was supposed to attend a lecture at 10:00 a.m. Wanda should have called to wake him. He frowned. It was half-past eleven. *Damn!* To hell with it all, he thought. It was a series. He'd make the next one at…what time? Jesus, his head was really swimming. He hated that feeling almost as much as he hated to wake up alone. Almost. But he could fix both problems. It was lunchtime. Wanda would be in the restaurant.

It was all Wanda could do not to laugh as she watched Malloy stumble over to the bar for an eye-opener. This was going to be so easy. All she had to do was get him to admit that his life wasn't worth living. But she had to do it now, before he drank enough to feel normal again.

Quickly, she headed for the bar.

"Good morning, Mr. Malloy," she gushed, reaching for the double shot that the bartender was about to hand over. "Don't you think we should eat something first?" Malloy, fumbling shakily with crumpled dollar bills, looked up in surprise.

"We? You mean, you want to have lunch with me? Usually, you disappear."

"Of course. We work together, don't we? We should talk, especially since I couldn't seem to wake you up for your seminar this morning." Wanda was all but purring. Was she overdoing it? If so, Hands didn't seem to notice. A spark of lecherous hope crept into his bloodshot eyes.

"Here, let me help you with that," Wanda said, smoothly. She took the bills from her boss, handed them to the bartender, and picked up the drink. As she steered the bleary old wreck of a man ahead of her to her table, she downed the drink herself.

Malloy sat, relieved to have something solid under him, and eyed the empty glass on the table. "Didn't mean to down it all in one go," he mumbled. "Maybe you're right. I really should eat something." He picked up the menu and opened it, studying it intently for a moment before turning it right side up. "Oh."

Wow, he was still hammered from last night, Wanda mused. Would this make her job easier or harder? "Do you know what you want to eat, Mr. Malloy?"

"Can't read this damn thing. Where are my glasses?"

"You don't need them in here," Wanda assured him. "I can read you the menu, and you can pick something."

"Why are you being so nice to me all of a sudden?" Malloy peered at her suspiciously.

"Honestly, you look like you feel terrible. I'm just trying to help." Wanda picked up her own menu and began to read off items, embellishing them with impossibly disgusting ingredients and condiment combinations. She was gratified to see old Hands begin to go a little green around the gills. She kept it up until he stood up and wobbled as fast as he could go in the direction of the restrooms. The laughter she'd been biting back finally found its way out. This was the most fun she'd had in days. She would thank Sonny, except that she never intended to see him again. But she wasn't finished yet. She had to make him wish he were dead. It would be even better if he said it out loud, just to be safe. Those were the rules, and she was going to follow them to the letter. She didn't want Hands popping back up on a technicality.

The queasy Malloy emerged from the corridor that led to the restrooms, doing his best to escape a diminutive, screeching old lady, who was whacking him stridently in the head with her handbag.

"Pervert!" She chased him most of the way back to Wanda's table. "Keep your sugar daddy out of the ladies' room!" she advised Wanda, giving Malloy a final whack and Wanda the finger.

"It was an honest mistake," he said. He rubbed his head ruefully as he slumped back into his chair. "I didn't even look at the sign. I was just looking for a toilet. She didn't have to be so *rude*."

"I kind of admire her freedom of expression," Wanda said, carefully innocent. She decided to give Hands a break. He really was pitiful. When the waiter came, she ordered soup and a sandwich for him, exactly as it really stood on the menu, and a salad for herself. Go easy on his stomach for awhile, she told herself. Making him miserable was one thing. Ending up wearing his lunch was another.

As she ate and Malloy poked warily around in his soup with his spoon, Wanda filled him in on the seminar, which Hands had been required to attend by his own boss. Fitz MacGregor, the CEO, was Malloy's immediate superior, and a real hard case. While Hands was merely a grabby drunk, who was happy when Wanda covered his tracks well enough to keep him out of trouble at work, MacGregor was all business, and actually expected his orders to be followed and his people to be productive. He'd be surprised, Wanda knew, if he had any real idea of how much of Malloy's production was actually her own; she'd been doing his job for years, only without the title and commensurate pay. Some days, she really did think it might be easier to be dead.

The seminar he'd missed had been a real snoozer, full of statistics, graphs and projections. The second part was slated to begin in an hour and a half. She'd have to work quickly. She read from the notes she'd taken in a deliberate monotone, making sure to inflate all of the negative information he'd be required to present to the Board of Directors when they returned home.

He sagged, elbows propped on the table, his stubbly chin in his hands, regarding her with a stare not unlike that of a panicked animal in a trap. "Shit, I hate this job," he moaned. "Do we really have to go back? I don't want to have to tell them we're swirling the bowl. They'll fire my ass."

"Oh, I'm sure something will happen before you get to that point," Wanda consoled him, earnestly. That was, if she had her way… "Have I ever let you down?"

"No," he said, mournfully, the hangover really beginning to kick into high gear. "You've been great. And I've been awful to you. I've been such an asshole." He choked back a sob. "It's just that you're so pretty, and I'm old and fat and—"

"—Drunk," she finished for him.

"Right! I probably wouldn't even still *have* a shitty job to complain about, if it weren't for you," he admitted.

Isn't that the truth, Wanda thought. Aloud, she said, "Try to eat something. We have part two of the seminar coming up."

Malloy stared morosely into his soup. "Not going," he said. "What's the point? I'm useless. You won't even eat with me most of the time, let alone go out with me."

"Well, dating the boss isn't very professional, is it?" Wanda cooed, back in pacifier mode. "You need to find someone outside of work, who has your same interests and will appreciate you for who you are."

"She doesn't exist!" He was bawling in earnest, now, rivers running down his fat, flushed cheeks. "Nobody wants me! I'd be better off dead!"

As if by magic, Sonny appeared in the bar and made a beeline for their table. He winked at Wanda as he went into his corny, high-pressure salesman shtick.

"Hi there!" he boomed, falsely large and chipper. "Sonny's the name, and image is my game! And you look like your subscription to sunshine just expired. Maybe I can help you." Uninvited, he pulled up a chair and handed Malloy a business card. Malloy squinted at it, barely able to make out the print. It read:

"Tired of losing? Life getting you down? Giving up on finding that special someone? Put an end to the rat race! Play the game and find eternal happiness! Call 555-3323 today!"

Smiling, Wanda slipped away from Sonny and poor, distracted old Hands. She would just make her seminar.

And with a little luck, soon there might be an opening in management.

Cathy Moeschet has been writing since childhood. She has had short stories published previously in the now-defunct *Jackhammer II*, *Planet Relish*, and *Storied Hours* e-zines. When she's not working as an editor, formatter and script analyst or writing, she enjoys darts, reading, cooking, movies and hanging out with her spoiled rotten lab/border collie mix, Maddie.

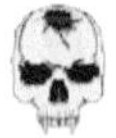

Dead Men Tell No Tales

Elaine Cunningham

The ship closing hard on our port side was a brigantine. Two masts, twenty cannons, maybe a hundred men aboard. Pirates hereabouts favor the brig, so Cap'n Mayes sang out the make-ready long afore the black flag started climbing.

She come in fast and mean and sure, like a man raising a fist to an old Quaker knowing he'll only hold up his hands and say, "Whist now, Friend, there's no cause for brawling!"

If I was manning the brig, I'd be thinking much the same. The *Donkeybow* is a Dutch flute, broad as a barrel and built to haul cargo, not win a sea battle. Her real name is *Donkerblauw*, which Natty says means "clear blue skies." A fine, good-omen name for a ship, if you can twist your tongue to it. Natty, now, he can speak six different kinds of foreign, navigate by dead reckoning or with a sextant, make a wood flute sing like a meadow bird, and a half hundred other things I could no more hope to do than fly. Me, I can work and I can fight, and I don't mind telling you I was itching to get to it.

The captain gave over the wheel to Mister Nichols and quick-footed his way to the rail. "Make ready the pinnace, Little John, then get you below decks." He reached up to clap me on the back. "One look at you, and they'll not believe we mean to give in without a fight!"

Why he calls me Little John, I couldn't say. I'm a head taller than any man aboard, broad and strong as any plow horse. And my name is Thomas. I asked Natty once, and he said the captain is powerful fond of old tales. That was no answer at all, so far as I could see, but most men find answers in what looks to me like a pile of more questions. So generally I just haul in the slack of my jaw and do as I'm bid.

"Aye, Cap'n Mayes."

"*Mister* Mayes," he corrected me, and I'm ashamed to admit that it wasn't for the first time. When pirates are about to come aboard, he's "Mister." I forget that betimes. Being a gentleman, he don't often chide me for my lacks.

I hauled the pinnace into place and set the winches so it could be lowered quick and easy. Natty stood ready, three lads with him to help with the oars. The pirates would be expecting the captain to come aboard the brigantine to talk surrender. Instead, they'd be getting Cook, looking the very picture of a merchant captain in a fine light-blue coat and a fancy white wig. The cook's got a rich man's belly and a Dutchman's whey-colored face, and he does look the part, but I don't mind telling you he's as dumb as a stump. That don't much matter. He pretends he can only speak foreign, and he mumbles something in Natty's ear for show; it's Natty who figures out what to tell the pirates that'll tempt them to empty the brigantine of men, the better to carry loot off the *Donkeybow*. They're a mismatched pair, them two, what with Cook so big and round and pale, and Natty black as molasses and scrawny besides. But it takes the pair of them to make a captain, and that's a fact.

Mister Surrey, the boatswain, bellowed out the call to strike colors. We harbor in Newport, and Rhode Island is an English colony, but the captain was flying the Dutch flag—a strip of orange atop, then white, then blue. As it come down, the men pulled out neck scarves in the same colors and tied them on. Some of them gave me hard looks and I passed by on my way below decks. I been known to cut down *Donkeybow* crew along with the pirates once I get to fighting. Even shot a shipmate once—shot him deader than salt cod. The crew's always changing, you see; I've no head for names and faces, and that's a fact. It helps considerable when they wear the colors, and I'm proud to say I never once killed a man wearing orange and blue.

The men in the hold—and most of the *Donkeybow's* men was in the hold—made ready for battle. A pair of nimble-fingered lads was loading flintlock pistols. I took two pistols and tucked them into my belt.

"Don't you be firing those in the hold again," warned Mister Sawyer. Being a ship's carpenter, he has to think on these things. He was tugging at his fox-colored beard, which is what he does when he's riled up, so I promised him I would fight topside.

I checked the edge of my cutlass. The tang looked a mite rusted; I'd meant to have that mended.

Just then we heard the crash of grappling hooks and the screech of iron scraping across wood. Boarding planks slapped down, quicker than I could count them. Natty must have spun them some grand story about our cargo. Slaves, is what he mostly told pirates, and him being black as the devil himself and the slave trade at Newport's Brick Market being what it is, pirates generally lapped up this lie like cats on new cream.

The men blew out all the whale-oil lamps but a small, dim one and crawled into the wooden shelves meant to hold slaves left over from the Barbados. Before Cap'n Mayes took over *Donkeybow*, slaves was mostly what we carried, and I don't mind telling you it wasn't work I relished. The able-bodied slave men stayed behind to work the sugar, and beddable women we sold along the way. It was children we brought to Newport.

I ducked behind some barrels of hardtack, for there was no hope of me fitting into one of the slave-shelves. We hadn't long to wait until the pirates come down the ladders like a swarm of bilge rats. They roared into the hold quick and happy, yelling insults at the one man in plain view.

He meekly held up a fistful of keys, which he spilled out over the broad plank that served us as a table. "Take any one of them, lads," he said in a quivery voice as he backed away. "The locks on them chains is all the same. Unhitch the chain from the bolt just outside the shelf, then you can use the chain to haul the slaves out."

They set to. We waited until Mister Harris—a fine sailor and fighter, he is, next on the list to captain his own ship—sang out the attack. Cutlasses flashed out of the slave-shelves as the men slashed open whatever part of a pirate was closest to hand.

Some of them fell dead at once, big gaping grins on their throats to match their greedy smiles. Others stumbled away screaming, clutching at their opened bellies and tripping over more screaming men who'd been hamstrung.

While the crew rolled out of the shelves and finished the task, I hurried up to the deck to join in that bit. There was plenty of pirates topside, and I pulled my pistols and picked two of them to kill.

Small cannons, that's what pistols are, and the flash of powder and the back-blowing smoke always blinded me for a heartbeat or two. That's all the time it takes to die, so I threw aside the pistols straight away and pulled my cutlass from my sash, slashing at the smoke as I charged.

My aim was good today and my luck better. One of the pirates I'd shot was flat on his back and twitching, the other slumped against the mast, holding himself up by the ropes and screaming as he stared at the blood pouring from what used to be his knee. I cut his throat quick and clean, then looked around for Cap'n Mayes.

He's not like most gentlemen, in that he does his own killing, and he's a good hand at it. It's a sight to see, him being a London man and gentry besides, brawling like a cornered badger. Once the fighting starts, he's another man altogether.

There he stood, over by the wheel, fighting two men and holding them off handily. I started to push my way toward him through the noise and confusion of battle.

A big man come at me, cutlass held high and ready for a down-coming slash. I caught his blade just below the hilt of mine and swept his arm out wide as I drove my other fist into his face. Bone crunched like boots on gravel.

The pirate dropped his cutlass and set up a howl to beat the damned in hell. He was a sight, with his flattened nose and the blood pouring into his beard, and the noise he made set me back on my heels. When I raised my cutlass to meet his I saw that my blade had snapped clean off, leaving me holding a rusted hilt.

But I know how to fight the way birds know to fly, and afore my head could think of what to do, my hands grabbed Mister Bloody-beard and spun him toward another pirate. The second man's cutlass drove deep into Bloody-beard's gut. Before he could pull it free I gave the dead man's head a hard shove, slamming it into the face of the man who'd killed him. They fell together.

Bloody-beard's cutlass was a mite small for my hand, but it would serve for a single battle. I stepped over his body and grabbed ahold of a small man wearing the orange and blue neck rag. A quick shove sent him sprawling and put me face to face with the man he'd been fighting.

The pirate looked surprised, and then he looked dead.

I spun around and cut the throat of another man who was about to kick my fallen shipmate. I shouldered the pirate's body over the rail—the deck was getting as littered as a tavern alley—and then kicked the small man myself for not getting up quick enough. Some men, they'll take any way out of a fight they can find.

Not Natty, though. He come thundering over one of the boarding planks, hollering in some heathen tongue.

The captain looked over, startled-like, as a pair of pirates come over the side, daggers held between their teeth and blood in their eyes. Him being busy with the men in front of him, he hadn't much hope of dealing with two more. I'm surprising fast for a big man, but I stood too far away to get to him while the getting still mattered.

But Natty, he kept on running and he threw himself off the boarding plank, arms spread wide like he hoped to take wing. He slammed into both the new-come pirates and down they all went.

I killed three more men on my way to the captain's side, and by then he'd taken down his two. The fighting was mostly over by then, and the second part of the killing well underway. This part, I didn't much care for, when the clang of steel gave way to moans and pleas for mercy. But that noise was almost over with, too, for aboard the *Donkeybow*, the louder a man begged, the quicker he died. Cap'n Mayes is a fair man, but he got no use for a coward.

The captain finished off Natty's two afore they had a chance to plead. He was crouched in a pool of their blood, his face grim as he gave study to Natty's small, dark form.

I don't mind telling you I was mighty happy to see Natty's eyes open. His loss would be felt, and that's a fact. I done well enough for a man of my birth, but Natty was a pure marvel. Slave children brought to Newport was apprenticed to learn a trade. They work in all the town's crafts: distilling rum, building fine furniture, casting silver, making tallow candles. Some of the Jews down on Touro Street bought Natty, and from them he learned to scribe and cipher so well they made a good profit selling him to a sea captain to learn map-making. The sea captain turned pirate and was caught and hanged and buried on Goat Island, but not afore he taught Natty all there was to know about seamanship. Cap'n Mayes often said Natty was the best of us all. He would have had his own ship years ago, except that most men wouldn't take orders from a freed slave no matter what his skills.

The captain looked up and saw me standing there. "Pick him up, carefully, and carry him to my cabin."

Something in his voice raised fear in me, and when I bent over Natty I saw what troubled the captain. In the close fighting, one of the pirates had got a knife between Natty's ribs. The wound was small, but the rough, wet sound of Natty's breathing told the tale. His lungs was filling up; he was drowning in his own blood. A slow and ugly death, that was. I wouldn't wish it on a poxed and thieving whore.

I lifted Natty up, gentle as I could, and followed the captain to his cabin. Cap'n Mayes didn't seem to mind Natty's blood on his quilt, though he'd paid good coin to an old Quaker dame to fashion him one in bright pieces of orange and blue. Money well spent, he'd said with a laugh, if it kept Little John from accidentally killing him while he slept.

The captain pulled the cabin's only chair up to the bed. He sat down and took Natty's thin, black hand in both of his. I don't think he noticed I was still in the room, or that he would have cared if he did.

I had no better place to be. Mister Harris would be busy claiming his new ship, choosing men to start his crew. He wouldn't choose me. No one ever did. Cap'n Mayes, gentleman that he was, told the men he kept me on because I was a fighter worth any three of them, but I suspect he wouldn't have me either, except that I come to him along with the ship.

What was happening topside was a tale often told. As far as the Court of Vice Admiralty knew, Cap'n Mayes was one of theirs, an English gentleman following England law. And on the English king's say-so, pirates was no longer welcome in Newport. Not long ago, Newport loved pirates. When Cap'n Tew come ashore some years back, most of the town turned out to greet him. But after a time, too many pirates in the waters is like too many goats in the yard. Here's the long and short of it: the merchants complained, the king commanded, and Cap'n Mayes went pirate hunting.

Some of the ships we took he turned over to the court and Crown. As far as his friends in Newport knew, the rest of those ships went down in battle. Now, that just wasn't so. Over the years, Cap'n Mayes built up his own fleet of pirate ships, crewing them with his own men and sending them to Madagascar and the Caribbean and suchlike. Not every man had it in him to become a captain, but every man who sailed with Cap'n Mayes had a chance to grow wealthy. Every man could expect to be treated fairly, for the captain was known as an honorable man, in his own fashion.

What he was saying now to Natty proved the truth in that tale. "You saved my life, lad. That's not a debt easily repaid."

"No need, Cap'n," Natty managed. He was no fool; he knew he

was dying.

"This *is* need," he said. "There's a great need for men of your caliber. So I want you to listen to a tale, and listen well. Do you mark me, lad?"

When Natty nodded, the captain started in. "Some years before I acquired the *Donkerblauw*, an ambitious young man came to Newport. He had been appointed as a judge in the Court of Vice Admiralty, and it was his intention to build a fine house for his bride, a young woman of good family who would join him the following spring. Do you know of whom I speak?"

Natty nodded.

"Have you heard this story?"

"Aye," he gasped out. "Or better said, part of it."

"Better said indeed," the captain agreed. "Well, spring came and summer followed, but no word of the judge's bride. He sent letters to England, and the last ship of autumn carried back an angry reply from her father. His daughter had set sail as scheduled, in good weather and calm seas. If she did not make port, he said, no doubt there were pirates at work, and the judge had no one but himself to blame for not doing his duty.

"At that, the judge went a little mad with grief and guilt, and in his fervor he hanged every pirate brought before him, even a privateer or two who carried letters of marque. After the fact, he learned that one of the pirates he hanged had worn a ring on a chain around his neck, a gold ring with a single ruby. This ring had belonged to the judge's young wife.

"The man became obsessed with learning her fate, but none could tell him. Had she been slain when her ship was boarded? Was she living unwilling in a New York brothel, or sold in some distant port where her golden hair would be a curiosity? If she'd come to disgrace, did she yet live? Since all the pirates who might answer these questions were dead, the judge went to certain wise men among the slaves and learned from them how to seek the spirits of the dead."

Now, I must have made a sound, because the captain looked over at me. "Does this tale trouble you, Little John?"

"I'm not afeared of any man alive," I told him honestly enough, "but I don't like talk of spirits and haints and suchlike."

"Do you believe in such things?"

He asked this like my answer mattered to him, and I told him truly that I did believe. Many a man I'd sailed with over the years come from heathen lands. From what they told me, it seemed like their dead stayed close to hand, having no Christian heaven or hell to repair to. As for that, there was ghosts aplenty in the ruins near the village where I was born, and people in that part of Ireland are Christian, or close enough.

The captain turned back to Natty and went on with his tale. "At first the judge sought the spirit of the pirate who'd had the ruby ring, and when that failed, the spirits of the men who'd sailed with him. All efforts came to naught. Finally, in desperation, the judge purchased the home of a former sea captain and sometimes pirate, a man he'd previously hanged, who was said to haunt the premises. A man you knew well," he said, looking fiercely into Natty's eyes. "A man you know still. Do you mark me, my lad?"

A strange look come over Natty's face. "Aye, captain," he said in wondering tones.

"Then you might well guess what followed. On the night of a full moon, the judge entered the house alone. Come morning he left in time to catch the tides. He became a sea captain himself, and spoke no more of his lost love. Most men believed he had put aside his grief and found a new way to do his duty. Only one man—now two men—knew the truth:

"In that house a battle had been fought, a battle without swords or pistols. At the end of it, the living vessel set sail under new command. The house, they say, is haunted still. To this day, when the moon is full and high overhead, people who enter the house sometimes see the glint of a ruby and the ghostly shadow of a man, holding out a ring and pleading, 'What became of my bride? Tell me, have you seen her?'"

Natty's eyes drifted closed, and a smile curved his lips. "The better man won; the better man left that house."

The words came faint and thick, and bloody foam gathered at the corners of Natty's mouth. The captain wiped it away with his own lace-edged handkerchief.

"Aye, lad, that he did, and so he will again." He leaned in closer, and what he said next made little sense to me. "But before you do*, be sure to give Judge Mayes my regards.*"

We made port two days later, and Cap'n Mayes made report to the Vice Admiralty court of the pirate ship we'd lured to our bait and burned to the waterline. Many of his men was killed in the fighting, he told them, and he added, all sad-like, that Mister Harris would never again be seen in this port. As I said afore, the captain is powerful fond of stories, and he has the knack of making a whale-sized lie out of two small truths. The men of the court believed him, as men generally do.

And they was all in a fine mood, being that the meeting was held in the White Horse Tavern and since the Crown was paying for their dinner and their ale.

I didn't sit with the captain, of course, but I had a good meal at the common table and afterwards a tumble with a big whore I favor. Her hair is red when it is clean, and she looks a little like the girls I remember from my village. The captain had been uncommon generous when he counted out my share of the brigantine's booty, so all in all it was a fine afternoon.

The sun was still high when I met the captain at the ship and carried Natty's mortal remains onto a small, quick sloop. He was to be buried on Goat Island. Didn't seem right, seeing that Goat Island was where pirates were planted, but no doubt Cap'n Mayes had his reasons.

He sailed the sloop himself, with only me along to carry Natty's body and dig the grave. The captain spent a long time saying heathen words over the grave. A strange, cold wind come up while he spoke, and I don't mind telling you I was glad to leave.

Seems like that wind stayed with us all the way to Newport, and by the time we tied the sloop to Long Wharf, I felt chilled to the marrow of my soul. By then the sky and sea had faded to that tarnished-silver color that comes just short of full dark, and I was ready for a mug and a meal.

But the captain said he had one thing yet for me to do. We walked through the Brick Market, past the Quakers' meeting house and the fine houses merchants had built along Thames Street and Marlborough. After a time we turned down a narrow side street.

I did not like being here, though I could not say why. The air felt even colder, and this place seemed uncommon dark, even though the moon was full and high overhead, and the street better lit than most taverns.

A half-starved dog slunk out of the shadows and crawled forward on his belly, tail wagging, like he hoped for a kind word and maybe even a bone. He stopped all of a sudden, and his lip curled as if he meant to snarl. For some reason he thought better of it and lit out, tail between his legs.

The captain led me to a tall house with a fine iron fence. Now, I'm not the cleverest man you're likely to meet, but somehow I knew where he'd brought me.

"This house belonged to a man I once knew," he told me. "He was a sea captain of considerable skill, and yes, a pirate. Still, in his own fashion, an honorable man. He rewarded men who deserved his favor and those who did not, each according to what he had earned."

Good words, those, but I didn't take any comfort from them. "Why have we come, Cap'n?"

He didn't answer me straight away. We stood there a while, the captain thinking his own thoughts and me trying not to tuck tail and run.

"You could have your own command, Thomas Hale," he said suddenly.

The sound of his voice startled me, and so did his use of my true name, so a few moments passed afore the meaning of his words hit me. And even then, they didn't make much sense.

"Me, a captain? You'd trust me to command a crew, to sail one of your ships?"

"You've more natural talent for fighting than any man I know, and your size and strength could lend you a powerful air of command. Of these things, I have no doubt." He shook his head then, like he was thinking of all the things I done wrong over the years, things no sea captain could do and hope to hold a ship. "*Thomas Hale* could command a ship, but first you must battle what you fear most. And so we have come here."

I remembered then what he'd asked me about spirits and ghosts and haints. He must have caught wind of my fear, and decided this was the way to test my mettle.

But I did not want to go into that house, not even for my own ship. Not even for Cap'n Mayes.

"We part ways, Little John, whatever you decide. If you face your fears and spend the night in that house, then Thomas Hale will take command of the next ship we acquire. If you do not, well then, that is your choice to make, and I wish you well in whatever you do next."

That, I understood straight away. I was not a man who feared many things, but the loss of the *Donkeybow*, home to me since my tenth summer, was foremost among them.

"I'll do it," I told him.

"Good man." He smiled at me then. "Did you listen well to the tale I told Natty?"

"Aye. There's said to be a spirit here, a man who holds a ruby ring and asks after his lost wife."

"In truth, I believe there are now *two* unquiet spirits hereabouts. If you see the judge's ghost, give it little heed, and instead seek out the other."

This was ill tidings, but I saw no better choice than to do as I was bid. As I started through the gate, though, I was struck by a powerful fear. "If I go in that house, Cap'n, I'm not never coming out."

The captain, he reached up and clapped me on the back. "Take heart, lad. I expect to see that face of yours come morning," he said heartily. "And I've no doubt that a better man will leave that house than went in!"

Elaine Cunningham is a *New York Times* bestselling author whose publications include 20 novels, over 4 dozen short stories, poetry, non-fiction, and a graphic novel. She is best known for her work in licensed settings such as the Forgotten Realms, Star Wars, and Pathfinder Tales. For more information, stop by her Facebook page or visit elainecunningham.com.

The Broken Silence of Fanghan

Jennifer Brozek

Jia gave the young man an appraising look as he stood before her. He didn't fidget, and that was good. All he did was bow and give his name. Kim Zhou. He looked prepared in his dark blue coveralls. His hair was too long for her liking… but the youth today. Finally, she nodded. "Wen Jia. Call me Jia. Not 'auntie' or any other title. We're both caretakers. Let's get to work." She was intentionally non-traditional with him, in hopes that he would understand from the start that this was a non-traditional job.

Zhou nodded, seeming to reserve judgment. He picked up the gardening tools and walked with her, examining her. She wore the same dark coveralls he did, only hers were stained, faded, and patched. She fought the urge to hide the old jagged scar on her left hand, but knew he would not ask about it. That would not be polite.

Still, his almost complete silence was unusual. Jia eyed him, wondering if he was only sullen, or something more dangerous… arrogant. She stopped at the driveway of the first mansion. "Do you see these twenty-nine homes?"

"Yes."

"As caretaker, you are in service to these houses and their lands. It is your duty to ensure they are properly kept."

Zhou turned dark eyes on the luxurious neighborhood. From

where they stood, only four of the twenty-nine mansions were visible. Each had the same basic layout: at least two levels, three car garage, an acre of manicured land, and a long driveway off the winding road that meandered through the community. "Why?"

Jia tilted her head. "Why what?"

"This is a beautiful neighborhood, but no-one lives here. Why do we take care of it? Why aren't we working closer to home?" Home being Changsha, the large city they contracted from.

"They will sell these homes someday. To do that, they must be beautiful and well maintained." Jia examined her words, making sure they sounded true. "You'll learn how to care for them as I have. There are some particulars you must follow. I have a list." She pulled a handmade, laminated booklet from her breast pocket. "Today, we tend to the lawns of these four homes: 1001, 1003, 1005, and 1007. Then, we do the walkthrough of 1001 through 1019."

Zhou looked at the notebook. There were daily chores, weekly chores, and monthly chores. He frowned. "Why not mow all of the lawns at once? Then do all the gardening? Isn't it less efficient to do it this way? Four houses at a time?"

The old woman shook her head. This is what she had feared. He was young and, of course, knew better than the woman who'd tended these homes for the last seven years. "No. This is the proper way to tend this neighborhood. This booklet was passed to me from my predecessor." She paused, debating, and then decided against telling him the bald truth. He would discover it in time. "This neighborhood needs special tending."

Zhou nodded, but said nothing.

Zhou forgot the need for efficiency as Jia showed him all that "must be done" to tend the lawns and grounds of the four houses assigned for the day. After finishing the mowing, edging, and weeding, Jia made him refresh the water in a small, ornate wooden bucket on the back porch of 1001 (the notebook stated this was to be done on a monthly basis). For 1003, he was required to put fresh flowers on the front porch (weekly). For 1005, during the walkthrough, Jia had him run out to the truck to retrieve a fresh container of apple juice (weekly). For 1007, she required him to dust the back window sills of the ground floor windows (weekly). But only the back window sills of 1007 and no other.

When he returned, Zhou found her washing out a stoneware pitcher. Jia didn't say anything as she wiped the outside of the pitcher dry, set it down on the counter, and held her hand out for the liter of juice. For a moment, he wasn't going to give it to her. He was going to demand an explanation. Then, seeing the tiredness in her eyes and the flush to her cheeks, Zhou handed her the juice without comment, and watched as she filled the pitcher and placed it back in the refrigerator.

The rest of the week was a repeat of the first one: gardening, lawn maintenance, and then incomprehensible little tasks: ensuring a back gate was propped open (1019, weekly), pounding a nail into a board (1027, daily), singing a lullaby (1031, daily), changing out a hunk of dried, cured beef (1043, monthly), and putting a letter—any letter—through the mail slot (1055, weekly). The list went on. More confusing was the fact that some of these things, like the fresh flowers and produce, were provided to them by the home office. They were packed in neat boxes with their names on them, along with their truck assignments. The rest, like the nails, they needed to get themselves from the garage supply.

Jia gave no explanation for these oddities, and Zhou did not ask.

As they packed up their equipment on the last day of training, she smiled at him. "I think you will do well. I think the neighborhood likes you."

Zhou gave her a small bow and returned the smile. "Thank you."

Jia pulled the small laminated notebook from her pocket and held it out to him. "This is for you." She paused, looking worried. "I know… I know you don't understand all that we do to care for this neighborhood of Fanghan, but it's important that you follow the checklist."

Reaching for the notebook, Zhou saw that Jia's hands were shaking. "I will follow your wisdom."

Jia tapped the notebook in his hands. "Follow *this* wisdom. It was hard-earned. You should probably make your own copy. Just in case." She paused, and then pulled another slip of paper from her coverall pocket. "If you need, call me. But only if you need."

Zhou frowned as he accepted the scrap of paper with her name and cell number on it. "What aren't you telling me?" Suddenly, he didn't feel so sure about this anymore. He needed this job, but why the strange tasks? Why did he feel so uneasy at the thought that Jia wasn't going to be there?

Jia wouldn't meet his eyes. "There are things your parents told you not to do, to protect you. You didn't understand then. You had to learn for yourself. You will learn about this neighborhood for yourself. If you follow the checklist, you will learn gently."

"If I don't?"

She rubbed her scarred hand before she glanced up at him. "Then I suspect you'll call me."

The first thing Zhou noticed as he began his second week of work, and his first week on his own, was the neighborhood's silence. He didn't like it. Any rare noise that bubbled to the edge of his hearing from time to time, like children laughing, seemed amplified and impossible. It was unnerving. Zhou was used to living in the city, where the noises of life included people talking, cars driving, generators humming, and music or TVs playing. There was always noise. Here, in Fanghan, there was almost nothing. Yes, electricity had been hooked up, so there was a soft hum of appliances in the mansions, but when you were outside, there was nothing except an occasional plane overhead or a caretaker's vehicle in the distance.

According to Jia's notebook, this week was all about dusting and sweeping the insides of the mansions. As empty houses went, a lot of dust accumulated throughout the month. It took longer than expected. One house, 1003, seemed to have actual tracks in the house. As if someone had walked through the garden and scuffed their feet on the floor as they went.

This last thought bothered him. He wondered if a *liulangzhe* had gotten into the house—not that it would do them any good. There was no furniture in any of the houses. Just some appliances. Still, Zhou couldn't remember if this was one of the houses that was supposed to be kept locked, unlocked, or a combination of one door locked and one not locked. He pulled the notebook from his breast pocket as he drove away from the neighborhood. Stopping at a stop sign, he saw that it *was* one of the locked houses… and that he was supposed to leave fresh flowers on the front porch.

"Pi shi." Zhou glanced into the back of the truck. And there they were. He'd forgotten them. As he idled, he debated going back and putting the flowers where they were supposed to go. No. The sun was setting and he was tired. It's not like there was anyone there to look at the front porch anyway. He'd clean up the old flowers tomorrow. "Besides, Song will love them. I haven't brought her flowers in ages."

The next day, as promised, Zhou made sure to clean up the wilted flowers from the porch. "I'm sorry I don't have flowers for you this week. My girlfriend loved them. She thinks I'm the best. I'll get more for you next week," he told the door with an impish smile.

Whistling as he took the dead flowers to the trash can, he stumbled and fell against the truck, smashing his hand against the bumper. Zhou swore as he pulled thorns from his hand and coveralls, throwing the flowers away. He hadn't realized there were thorns in the bunch. He sucked on his hand as he returned to his route. He had still had 1013 and 1015 to dust.

Checking his notebook, the notes next to the houses were "*incense*" and "*silence*", respectively. From the box in the back, he saw that there were three sticks of incense. He picked one of them up and gave it a cautious sniff. Amber and jasmine. Zhou nodded. He left the other two incense sticks in the box and grabbed the lighter.

Number 1013 smelled faintly of the incense as he opened the house to work. He found the incense burner sitting in the middle of the dining room floor, all of the ash neat caught in the tray, as it had been the first and second times he'd done a walkthrough of the house. He saw there were three burnt incense sticks and sighed. Of course. Eventually, he'd remember that the home office gave him exactly what he needed.

Again, he debated. Get the incense sticks now so he didn't forget, or wait until he was done dusting. He decided to dust and sweep first to make sure the incense dust wouldn't scatter as he worked. First, he wanted to wash his hands. The meaty part of his left thumb hurt like there was still a piece of thorn in it. He wouldn't be any good to anyone if it got infected.

Putting his equipment on the counter he turned the water handle and nothing came out. "What?" Zhou moved the handle this way and that, but nothing happened. It was the first time he'd seen something not work in this neighborhood. Scowling, he looked up, out the kitchen window and saw his scowl reflected in the face of a man standing right behind him. Zhou gasped and whirled around.

There was no one there.

Zhou looked over his shoulder at the kitchen window. Nothing was there. But, as he did so, a stink like fetid garbage wafted through the air. The miasma of rotting meat and spoiled yogurt choked him. It was so strong he could taste it.

He sprinted for the front door and made it to the trashcan before he vomited his lunch until he heaved nothing but bile. When he had control of himself, Zhou wiped his mouth and looked back at number 1013. He had the impression that someone had just walked by the front door. Someone who had been watching him.

Maybe he was watched. Maybe the stupid little incomprehensible tasks were one way home office made sure you did your job. Zhou grabbed the other two sticks of incense and returned to the house. The fetid smell was gone. He quickly cleaned out the incense tray, put the three sticks in their place, and lit them. As the fragrant smoke rose, Zhou put the tray back in the middle of the dining room floor.

The water in the kitchen turned on.

Zhou took a couple cautious steps into the kitchen, but didn't smell anything awful. He returned to the sink and washed his hands, pulling the last bit of the thorn from his thumb. "Thank you," he whispered to the kitchen window, but did not look, did not see the man there in the window again. This time not scowling, but still not smiling. Zhou refused to see the man's curt nod.

Instead, he pulled his cellphone from his pocket, found his favorite playlist, and turned it on. The music soothed his nerves and set him in motion. He made quick work of his dusting and sweeping, made sure that the incense was still burning, and then hurried on to number 1015.

The interior of 1015 was immaculate. No dust. No dirt. No cobwebs. Zhou looked around, surprised. He went over to the living room window and checked the sill. Nothing. It shouldn't be possible. Not with what he'd seen with the other three houses today.

But something was wrong. As he walked through the house, checking each room for dirt and dust, a heaviness in his chest grew and the wound in his thumb throbbed. Zhou looked around the empty hallway. "What? What's wrong?"

His answer was the chime of a text message cutting through the song playing on his phone. "Nǎo cán!" Zhou fumbled his phone out of his pocket and took two tries before he could unlock it. He turned the music off. "I'm sorry. I didn't mean…"

His phone binged again. Another text message. It popped up, showing its message. It was Song.

Headed to the hospital now.

He touched the message, the text thread opened, and his heart sank.

Allergic to the flowers you gave me. Covered in hives.

Zhou started to type back to her but his phone turned off. He hit the button to turn it back on and nothing happened. He tried again. Nothing. He held all of the buttons down for the requisite five seconds to reboot it. Nothing. His phone had gone from more than half charged to no charge at all. "No. No. No! Pìyǎn! No!" He needed to let Song know he'd gotten her message and that he hoped she was okay.

Movement caught his attention and he looked up.

A woman ran at him from down the hallway. Her mouth was open in a silent scream and her long black hair billowed out around her like a cape. Zhou screamed and ran. He didn't look back. He fled as fast as his legs would carry him. 1015's door slammed behind him, clipping him in the heel as he tumbled forward down the porch stairs and landed hard on the sidewalk.

He lay there stunned, bleeding from the eyes, nose, mouth, and scraped chin. Zhou didn't understand what was happening. He didn't want to know. He pulled himself to his feet and wiped at the blood covering his face. He grabbed a ragged, clean towel from the back of the truck and moved to the front, where he plugged his phone into the charger.

While the phone charged, he continued to clean his face with trembling hands, and wondered if he was going crazy from the neighborhood's quiet and isolation. He looked at his blood on the towel, and knew more was going on than he'd been told. This place was empty, and yet he'd seen two impossible people and heard children laughing. He thought about what he still needed to do that day… and what he had not done the day before.

The house walkthroughs. He was supposed to have done ten houses yesterday and ten more today. The thought of what he hadn't done made his stomach turn. What would he find? He gave number 1003's flowers to Song. Was it his fault that she was sick? Did he upset… the house? *Or whatever lived inside?* Zhou shied away from that last thought. He was too old to be thinking of such fables. Jia would know what was wrong and what to do.

His phone turned on. Leaving it plugged in, he pulled the small slip of paper with Wen Jia's phone number on it from his coverall pocket and dialed. The phone picked up on the second ring.

"Zhou?"

Her voice sounded tense to him. "Yes. It's me. What's wrong with this place? What's happening?"

"Did you follow the notebook?"

"Not exactly. I'm sorry. Help me, Jia-Qiánbèi, please."

"You young, stupid fool. I warned you! Are you still there? In the neighborhood?"

"Yes. In front of number 1015."

"Go back to the beginning of the week. Do the things you didn't do. Do them in order. Otherwise I can't help you. I'll be there as soon as I can."

"I'm bleeding…"

When there was no answer, Zhou realized that either she had hung up on him or that the phone had died again. Or both. The day was moving into late afternoon. He realized he might be here after sunset. His skin crawled as he felt the certain knowledge that this place would be very different after dark. But Jia was coming. She would help. He wiped at his face again. The blood was still flowing.

He left the cell phone charging in the truck. Pulling Jia's notebook from his pocket he read a list of what he hadn't done yet or done right. Flowers for 1003. Putting the juice in the pitcher for 1005, checking the gate for 1019, pounding a nail in the board for 1027—he wondered if he should pound two, since he didn't do it the day before, and it was one of the few daily chores; same with singing a lullaby in 1031, and putting a letter through the mail slot of 1055.

The impossibility of the situation struck him even as Zhou felt more blood trickle out of his ear. Denial kicked in. It was just a quirky neighborhood. Whatever he'd done wrong, he'd make it right. He had to. He couldn't lose this job, and he didn't want to be a failure… again. He'd start at the beginning and go house by house, fixing his mistakes and doing the walkthroughs for the others. House 1001 was quiet. He'd been there the day before. Technically, he hadn't made a mistake in 1001, but Zhou wasn't taking any chances.

For 1003, he carefully trimmed one blooming flower from each of the nearby yards until he had a respectable bouquet. This time, when he stopped on 1003's porch, he bowed low. "I'm sorry. I was forgetful and lazy. It won't happen again." He put the bouquet of flowers in their place and backed away.

Nothing happened and he breathed a sigh of relief. He turned and walked down the street to 1005. He had put the juice in the refrigerator. He just hadn't put it in the pitcher. He'd cleaned the pitcher out and left it on the counter. Zhou couldn't imagine how the house—he still refused to give voice to what he thought might actually be happening here—would punish him for this transgression.

He opened the back door with slow, careful movements, peeking in. The door opened into the kitchen. Nothing attacked him. There, right where he'd put it on the marble countertop, was the stoneware pitcher. Zhou stepped inside and approached it warily. It sat as still as the grave. Nodding to himself, he turned to the refrigerator, opened it, and retrieved the unopened quart of juice. The sound of stone on marble made him whirl about.

The stoneware pitcher rocked back and forth as a torrent of black spiders boiled out of it: tiny ones, large ones, medium sized ones. They tumbled out onto the countertop, and then to the floor, a ceaseless black wave of spiders flowing toward him. Zhou scrambled to stand on another countertop but it did no good. The spiders kept coming, crawling up and over every obstacle to get to him. Zhou screamed as they flooded over his legs and up his coveralls.

He felt each step of those thousands of legs as they swarmed up his body. "Please! Please! I'm trying to make it right! I swear! Please let me!" Zhou held the cold juice carton to his face as he screamed, feeling the spiders cover him from head to toe. He stopped screaming in fear of swallowing them. Silently, he prayed, shaking so hard he thought he'd fall. *I swear, I'll never do it wrong again. I didn't understand. Please. I'm new. I didn't know. Please!*

Then the sensation of the spiders was gone.

He stayed there, trembling and sweating, holding the juice next to his face, and waited until the count of ten to open an eye. No spiders in sight. Clambering down on shaking legs, Zhou wasted no time getting the juice into the pitcher and placing it in the refrigerator. He bowed to the appliance and the juice inside. He didn't know what else to say except, "I'm sorry."

The journey to 1019 was quick. All he wanted to do was survive the night. Fortunately, 1019's gate was still wedged open, as it had been the week before. Zhou tugged on the gate to make sure. He nodded to the house after he checked the gate and said, "All is well here." As he turned and walked away, he felt the presence of *something* walking from 1019 to the gate. Zhou refused to look back. He pretended that it was the wind.

Zhou got out of the truck and stood in front of number 1027. The sun was moving toward the horizon at an alarming pace. It was almost twilight. There were three things left to do: pound nails, sing a lullaby, and deliver mail. It was the first one that made him the most nervous. He'd missed the pounded nail thing yesterday. He didn't know if that meant he now needed to pound one nail, or two.

He took a breath and walked toward the back gate. It was such a silly thing to be required of him as a caretaker. Pound a nail in a board that's leaned up against the stairs each day of the week, and replace the board each month. It was busy work of the worst kind. What if he got sick? What if he got hurt? Would the… *houses*… get mad at him for missing work, or would they understand?

Zhou didn't know what he was expecting when he stepped through the gate. Whatever it was, it wasn't the violence that erupted as the gate slammed shut behind him.

He spun to look at the gate, and didn't see the first of the nails pull themselves free from the board and fly at him to puncture his shoulder, but he felt the pain. Zhou jerked around, grabbing at his shoulder and looking for what hit him. He pulled a small nail from his flesh. It came reluctantly with an audible sucking sound. He stared at it, and then threw the nail to the side.

The sound of the board shivering against the stairs brought his attention back to his sin. Zhou watched as another nail wiggled its way free. He flung himself to the side as the nail shot itself at him, point first. Then the air was full of nails aiming for his flesh. As Zhou sought cover behind a tree, some of them hit their mark.

He couldn't help but cry out as the nails punctured his legs, his arms, his chest. Every time he pulled one from his body, more of the metal struck. He curled up behind the tree, hiding his face, afraid one of the nails might take out an eye. Tears came as he silently begged for the torture to stop. But the sound continued: angry nails striking wood, stone, and glass.

Please. Please don't let me die here. Zhou knew this place would kill him, and he didn't understand why. Hopeless, he remained curled behind the tree with nails sticking out of his body, listening to the sound of his death as the deadly slivers of metal continued to seek their mark, but protecting his vital organs as best he could, fighting to keep from being hurt more.

The gentle hand on his shoulder made him cry out as he was sure that one of the ghosts—*No! Can't be!*—had come to take him away.

"Shhh. Shhh. Foolish one. You've done better than I thought."

Zhou looked up into Jia's face and was unsurprised to see she was wearing goggles. He looked at her hand. There was a nail stuck in it. He reached for it. "I'm sorry."

"No. Don't move it." Jia looked around and raised her voice. "He will do his duty." She pulled him from his hiding spot. "Don't remove any of the nails until I tell you."

Zhou obeyed, although each one was a small point of agony as they moved through the cloud of flying nails. He flinched as some of them came close, but Jia's hand was an iron grip on his arm. She led him to the board, now empty of nails, and pulled him to a kneeling position.

"Now. Take each nail from your body… and then mine… and nail them into the board. Then, take the fallen nails and nail them to the board until the appropriate amount is there. No more. No less." Jia looked around the yard.

Zhou followed her gaze and saw that tiny metal spikes covered the ground. "When… when do I clean up the rest of the nails?"

"Tomorrow. After you finish everything else," Jia said.

He nodded and did as he was told. He winced more than she did as he pulled nails from her hand and arm. His blood, and Jia's, stained the board for only a moment before something sucked it away. He sensed the moment when his job was nearly done. "I'm sorry," he murmured to the board as he pounded the last nail. "It won't happen again."

When nothing else happened, the two of them rose and left 1027's yard together.

They endured the screaming of invisible children in 1031, while they were pelted with unseen toys, until he had sung three lullabies. Nothing happened when they slid the letter into 1055's mail slot. Together, they walked back to the waiting truck. Parked next to it was Jia's tiny tan car.

Done, Zhou still felt heavy and sick. He had stopped bleeding from his wounds, but he wondered how much blood a man could lose before he died.

Jia gave him a head-to-toe look and shook her head. "We're not done, are we? What haven't you made amends for? We followed all of the tasks. You should be better now."

He shook his head.

"Look at the notebook and tell me."

Zhou pulled the notebook from his pocket, suddenly realizing why it was laminated as the blood on his fingers smeared across its surface. He hated this notebook. He hated it with all of his being as he opened it up and looked through the week's tasks.

Inside the truck, his phone chimed with a text message.

He looked from the truck to the notebook in his hand, stricken, and pointed to the word "*silence*" next to number 1015. "My cell phone. I had music."

Jia's confidence wavered. "This… will be difficult. She is very angry." Jia moved until she was in front of him, holding both of his arms, and looking up into his face. "You will need to be strong. Can you do that?"

Zhou ignored the fact that Jia's left hand was squeezing one of the nail wounds. He was too shocked that Jia was actually afraid. "Do I have a choice?"

Jia looked away and shook her head.

Zhou swallowed hard and took a breath. "What do I need to do?"

Jia smiled at him, her pride at his willingness to learn and to be strong clear in the wrinkles of her aged face.

The two of them entered 1015 as quietly as they could. They walked to the middle of the dining room. Zhou stood there, stripped to his t-shirt and shorts, next to Jia. The small woman raised her head, readied herself, and began to speak. Zhou closed his eyes and waited.

"Lady of Silence, we come to make amends. Kim Zhou is young and impetuous, but can learn. He is here to accept his punishment."

Claws ripped into his back without warning. Zhou clapped a hand over his mouth to keep from making a sound as he stumbled forward. Jia, ready for this, caught him and helped him to his knees as long bloody furrows carved themselves into his flesh.

"Forgive him his youth. Forgive him his ignorance." Jia's voice was very soft.

The bite of what could only be a cane switched across the back of Zhou's thighs. Hot waves of red flooded through him, warring with the pain in his back. He turned his face into Jia's shoulder, tears of pain soaking her coveralls. *I must not make a sound.* He almost broke this as the cane struck him once across the bottom of his bare feet.

"We beg you this, Lady of Silence."

This time, it wasn't Zhou who stiffened as an invisible assailant attacked. It was Jia. She rocked back on her heels but made no noise as she was struck in the face three times, the sound of flesh on flesh echoing loud. Zhou clutched her to him, keeping her from falling. *Silence. Silence.* The word was a mantra in his mind, even as blood dribbled down his back, his feet throbbed, and welts rose on his thighs. *Silence. Silence. Silence.*

"Please forgive the lack of training."

After an eternity, there was no more pain. Jia stood, pulled him to his feet and led Zhou from number 1015's property. It wasn't until they were at his truck and he was gingerly pulling on his coveralls again that he asked. "Is it over?"

"Making amends for the last two days' transgressions? Yes." Jia rubbed her face. "Your job? No. It will never be over."

He hissed as rough canvas fabric scraped over his wounded body, pulling clotted blood from his arms and scraping his back like sandpaper. "Why didn't you tell me?"

Jia scowled. "Would you have believed me if I told you your first week that our government, in its infinite wisdom, was building cities to keep the angry ghosts at bay? Would you have believed me if I told you that all this infrastructure wasn't poor planning, but a stopgap to keep the world of the dead from tormenting the world of the living?"

He looked at her, searching her face for the lie he wanted to find. All he could see was tired resignation stamped within the wrinkles on her face. "How many…? All?"

Jia shook her head. "Not all of the cities, but most. Most are specifically for them. Some are not. I don't know how many. Someone at the home office knows, but the rest of us?" She rubbed the scar on her hand again. "We don't."

Zhou was silent for a moment then shook his head. "Why are they angry?"

She shrugged. "The old ways are no longer followed, because we forgot why we followed them in the first place. In this modern age, we forget our traditions. We forget our ancestors. We forget ourselves. Of course they're angry. Not all of them, but many."

Zhou thought about that, frowning. "What if we didn't have these cities?"

"More of what you experienced, but on a far worse scale." She saw how deeply her words cut. "If you follow the notebook, this will be the easiest job you'll ever have. And you'll never get sick. They are sweet to those who show respect."

He winced as he struggled into his shoes. Then he looked around at the quiet neighborhood. It was beautiful in the twilight, and it felt more inhabited. Zhou wasn't sure if that was because he now knew the truth, or because Jia was with him. "We really are building ghost cities. Cities for ghosts."

"Yes." She shuddered and hugged herself. "Truth in advertising."

"What happens when we run out of room?"

"When that day comes, I pray I'm already dead." Jia paused, glancing at number 1015. "And that I'm not one of the angry ones."

Jennifer Brozek is a Hugo Award nominated editor and a Bram Stoker nominated author. She has worked in the publishing industry since 2004. With the number of different projects she juggles at one time, Jennifer is often considered a Renaissance woman, but prefers to be known as a wordslinger and optimist. Read more about her at her website: jenniferbrozek.com or follow her on Twitter at

@JenniferBrozek.

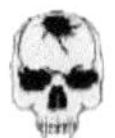

Father Figure

Tracie McBride

I met her during rush hour on a wintry Friday afternoon on the steps of Flinders Street Station. She stood slightly apart from her friends, an outcast amongst outcasts. Commuters migrating homeward bumped and jostled each other in the crush, yet the crowd instinctively parted to leave the little coven of Goths inviolate.

Untouchables. That's what they appeared to be. That's what I once was, before I grew up, got responsible, jumped on the corporate gravy train. Yet one look at Mia and all I wanted to do was touch her. Touch her in the most intimate and urgent ways, shake her, bruise her, drive her to her knees, wipe that sullen look off her face and replace it with one of flush-faced, open-mouthed, uncontrollable lust, run my hands through her long, black hair and pull real tight…

The impulse shook me; I considered myself a lover, not a fighter, and certainly not both at once. And right then I should have heeded my inner caution and walked on. But instead I stared at her, willing her to meet my gaze, and she did for a split second before turning away with a sneer. As well she should, for I was nearly twice her age and should have no business looking at her with the thoughts I was having. I was no stranger to sexual conquest, albeit with women closer to my own age and social milieu, but there was something… *different* about this girl. I dithered on the steps, pretending to fish around in my pockets for something, and trying like a lovelorn teenager to pluck up the courage for a direct approach. Surreptitiously, I studied her more closely.

She wore the traditional Goth costume: head to toe in black. Despite the cold, her shirt was sleeveless, made of a flimsy lace material that allowed tantalising glimpses of pale skin. I smiled – no doubt she rebelled against everything, even the weather. She turned to talk to a friend, thus affording a clearer view of the black-inked pseudo-Celtic tattoo adorning one bicep, and my smile widened – there was my opportunity. As I closed the gap between us, I bolstered my confidence with a mental image that I couldn't fully buy into; I was the Big Bad Wolf, and she my Little Black Riding Hood.

"I'm Andy," I said, extending a hand. She looked at it as if I had just offered her a plate full of dog shit. Only slightly deterred, I pushed on. "That's an interesting tattoo. Do you know what it means?"

"Of course I do," she spat, "but I'm not going to tell you."

"You don't need to," I said. "I know what it means. It means that we're destined to be together." A battle waged in my head - *Could you get any cheesier?* versus *But what if it's true?* The latter won out, and I leaned closer and lowered my voice.

"I have an identical tattoo."

"Bullshit," she said. Her gaze flickered from my face to my suit-clad arms and back again. For an instant her aloof exterior cracked, and I saw something akin to hope in her eyes. Hope that I might be The One, that I might succeed where others had failed (or perhaps not even attempted) to save her from whatever misery her life contained. No longer the Big Bad Wolf, I became the Knight in Shining Armour. Now *that* was a role I could sincerely play.

"C'mon," I said. "It's cold out here. Let's go somewhere to warm up and I can show you." This time, she accepted my outstretched hand.

And so, over a couple of glasses of absinthe in a dimly lit corner of an impossible-to-find-unless-you're-in-the-know back alley bar, I shrugged off my jacket and tie and slid my business shirt down over my shoulder to reveal her tattoo's twin. It wasn't really any great coincidence—no doubt she'd chosen the design the same way I had twenty years ago, by pointing at a picture on a tattoo parlour wall—but she was suitably impressed all the same. From the moment her fingertips caressed my inked skin, she was mine.

While a part of me still screamed *Wrong! Wrong! Wrong!* I slid quickly into love, in spite of—or perhaps, because of—her troubled background. Mia's drug-addicted mother had died from an overdose when she was a toddler, and nobody knew who her father was. She'd been raised by a series of indifferent foster parents—so beautifully damaged, a wild, rudderless child. When she told me seven months later that she was pregnant, I was jubilant, and proposed to her on the spot. Everybody counselled us against getting married. Everyone, that is, who cared, which was precious few.

Was I drawn to her youth? Yes. Her fragility? Yes. Did I want to protect her, to save her, from herself and the world at large? Yes. Was I tired, bored and lonely, and looking to stave off the oncoming ravages of old age a little longer with a vital young wife? Yes. Did we rush into our marriage, with little thought for the consequences? Yes. Yes, yes, a thousand times yes, yet all these tawdry truths did not come close to describing the profundity of our relationship. We were *connected* on some deep, indefinable level that transcended the clichés of our union.

The change in Mia became evident almost immediately after we got engaged. She put away the trappings of her misery—the thick black eyeliner, her exclusively black clothing, her extensive collection of drear, moody so-called music. The scars on her limbs from her self-harming episodes faded. Her eyes sparkled. She *smiled.* I was vindicated in my love and support. She carried and gave birth to our child with a joy and ease that other women envied. Bain, we named him, and he was perfection incarnate. Certain that nothing could spoil our happiness, we scheduled our wedding to coincide with Bain's first birthday.

On the eve of our wedding she came to me bearing a battered shoe box.

“Burn it,” she commanded, a glimpse of her former, defiant self flashing across her face as she thrust it into my hands.

“What is it?” I asked.

She shrugged. “Photos. Letters. Documents. Mostly old shit that belonged to my mother. None of it means anything to me anymore. You and Bain are my only family now.” She rested one hand on her belly, not yet swollen with our newly conceived second child.

I cradled the box in my lap as if it might contain a venomous snake. “Well, if you’re sure…”

“I’m sure.”

She did not say ‘don’t open it’, and even if she had, I would have disregarded her. When she left for the night to attend to whatever mysterious wedding rituals women observe, I removed the lid and examined the first item. It was Mia’s birth certificate; despite her instructions, I set it aside against some future need. There were a few blurry, poorly composed photos of a teenaged girl who I assumed was Mia’s mother Debbie. I studied them closely. The quality of the photos made it hard to learn anything from them; she looked familiar, and I was caught in an uncomfortable state of not-quite-recognition, unable to tell whether I knew her from a former time or was merely acknowledging the features she shared with her daughter.

I turned to the other items. Old concert ticket stubs, a lock of jet black hair barely held together with ancient, yellowing sticky tape, a cheap necklace bearing a small, blue stone pendant which I threw into the bin… they meant no more to me than they did to Mia.

At the bottom of the box sat a bundle of letters bound with a rubber band. I skimmed through the first few. They were almost laughable in their banality—badly written old love letters penned by adolescent admirers, and one angry missive from Debbie’s mother over some long forgotten grievance—and I was almost ready to toss the entire bundle back into the box, when something about the last letter caught my attention. It was from a young man, begging Debbie to abort, adopt out, pin the blame on someone else, say she was raped, do *anything* other than name him as the father of her unborn child. His life would be ruined otherwise, he claimed with staggering selfishness.

I knew the handwriting only too well, although I'd long since forgotten the circumstances that had prompted the letter, buried as they were beneath so many other careless close calls of my youth. I sat and stared at the pages for what seemed like hours. Big Bad Wolf indeed; I felt like I had been hollowed out and my stomach filled with stones that weighed me down until I could no longer move.

Then came the self-justifications. Perhaps it was a mistake. Perhaps this was just some horrible coincidence, this Debbie not the same one that I had once known, but some other callous youth's discard. Or perhaps it was my Debbie, but not my child. After all, she could have slept with any number of young men that summer, as free with her affections as I conveniently remembered her to be. Yes, that must be it; after all, wasn't Bain's robust good health and beauty living proof that Mia could not be my daughter?

I looked at the birth certificate again, at the "Father: Unknown." With one word, Debbie had both saved and condemned me. Still, a DNA test would settle the question, and it wasn't too late to postpone the wedding. And yet…

My favourite game as a child had been to 'hide' by covering my eyes with my hands; if I could not see my hunter, I reasoned, then he or she could not see me. It had always served me well as a problem-solving strategy and I saw no need to give it up now. I burned the box with its damning letter inside, and kept my mouth firmly shut about it. I was probably the only person alive who so much as suspected the truth of Mia's parentage, and I buried that suspicion deep down until it became as ephemeral a thought in my consciousness as the smoke that rose from the embers in the fireplace.

After Bain came Layla, then Charlize, Sebastian, and finally Poppy. Five beautiful, healthy children under the age of seven and all of them with the same black hair, pale skin and delicate features. Like a household full of Snow Whites, our neighbours used to say. After Poppy, I booked myself in for a vasectomy, citing a long list of sensible reasons, but in truth I did it because I feared that we were pushing our luck. Every pregnancy brought with it a deep anxiety on my part that the child would be born malformed in some way; it felt like we were playing Gestational Russian Roulette. Mia was happy enough with my decision, as you would expect for the mother of five. Our lives were cheerfully chaotic, and we immersed ourselves in love and a deep contentment. My family kept me feeling young, but they could not stop the physical signs of aging, not that I cared much about that anymore. I grew round of belly and grey of hair, and the only time it bothered me was when strangers mistook me for the children's grandfather. Too close to the bone by far, these innocent assumptions made me want to prove my vitality by throttling the life out of them.

The cracks began to appear when Bain turned fourteen. Literally overnight, he changed from a happy, if slightly highly strung, child to a surly and uncommunicative teenager. I was unconcerned; my own adolescence had been much the same, and I had come out the other side of it relatively unscathed (*not so for Debbie*, my subconscious whispered, and I squashed down the thought).

But for Mia, the change in her firstborn child sparked off her own, cataclysmic shift in outlook.

"There must be something wrong with him," she said, chewing on a thumb nail. She hadn't chewed her nails in fifteen years, and I resisted the urge to slap her hand away from her face. "Some hormonal imbalance or something."

I laughed. "Of course it's a hormonal imbalance! It's called puberty. He'll settle down eventually – just give him time."

"But still, it's not normal… is it?"

She ignored my reassurances, and became convinced that not only Bain, but our entire family was in the grip of some mysterious malady. Mia marched us all, one by one, to the family doctor, and when she pronounced us all in robust good health, Mia sought a second opinion.

And a third. She took our temperatures twice a day, and seemed almost disappointed at the invariably normal results. Every blemish, every cough, every little twinge became the subject of intense scrutiny. She visited dermatologists, chiropractors, dieticians and acupuncturists, dragging with her whichever child she could coerce at the time. A visit to the naturopath had her imposing on the family an organic diet free of meat, soy, dairy, gluten, wheat and sugar. A task as simple as mopping the floor set off a paroxysm of indecision, as she was unable to choose between scouring away potentially deadly bacteria and exposing her family to toxic chemicals.

The children had always been closer to their mother than to me, but Mia's obsession skewed the family dynamic in a different direction. I became their ally, their confidant and their accomplice as I snuck them out of the house on various pretexts to gorge ourselves on burgers and fries, slipped them extra cash to stock their school lunch boxes with more desirable items, invented alibis to get them out of medical appointments, or simply provided them with adult conversation that did not revolve around their health.

One day I caught Bain smoking behind the garden shed. A normal response would have been to punish the child, deliver a stern lecture and confiscate the cigarettes. But we were in no normal situation. Instead, I merely sighed and helped myself to a cigarette out of the packet. I leaned against the shed wall and lit up, inhaling smoke into lungs that had not been abused in such a fashion for the better part of fifteen years.

I smiled at Bain. "Don't tell Mum," I said.

"I won't," he said, smiling back. We finished our smokes in silence and luxuriated in our guilty camaraderie.

"I went to see a psychic today," Mia said one evening. It was the end of a particularly trying week; the children had gone from sly avoidance to open defiance whenever their mother tried to drag them off to some specialist or another, and Mia was angry at me for taking their side.

"And?" I pretended mild indifference, keeping my eyes on the TV screen as I channel surfed without taking any of it in. There was something in her tone that made my hackles rise, and I steeled myself for another confrontation.

"The spirits told her that my intuition has been right all along, and that we have some hereditary disease. Something genetic. It's rare, she says, and the symptoms haven't manifested yet, which is why it hasn't been diagnosed. Apparently, we're all ticking time bombs. She says I should go back to the doctors and request DNA testing."

DNA testing... panic made me explode. I leapt up from my seat, grabbing her by the shoulders and dragging her to her feet, and shook her until her teeth rattled.

"For fuck's sake, Mia, this has got to stop! We're all fine! We don't need DNA testing, or any other kind of testing! The only one sick around here is you—sick in the head."

I regretted my words the instant I uttered them. It was what we had all been thinking, or muttering behind Mia's back, but been afraid to voice for fear of making her worse. I expected her to react with tears or anger, or both, but instead a curious calm came over her. She took a deep breath and shook her head, even giggling a little as she spoke.

"A psychic told me... Yeah, I can see how you might think that sounds a little crazy. Maybe I'm just stressed, or overtired. I probably just need a little break. A couple of days away on my own to get a bit of perspective."

"Yeah, maybe..." I drew her into a hug and muttered an apology into her hair. "I'll book you into a hotel somewhere nice," I promised. "Somewhere in the country, with a day spa." She nodded her assent, but the rigidity of her body told me that this was only a temporary truce, and the battle was far from over.

For a few months after Mia's getaway, things in our household were almost normal. She let up on the dietary restrictions, and there were no more unnecessary visits to medical practitioners. The children began to relax a little, although they still held their mother at a slight distance, as if she were a not-quite-tamed animal that could turn on them at any moment.

Then one night I came home from work to a cold, dark and silent house. I thought at first that everyone had gone out, so I jumped, startled, when I switched on a light to find Mia sitting at the kitchen table.

"What's going on? Where are the kids?"

"I sent them all to their rooms," she said. Her voice was strained, as if her throat were in the grip of a giant, unseen hand. She stared down at an opened envelope and several sheets of folded A4 paper on the table in front of her, turning the pages over and over reflexively, her face obscured behind a curtain of glossy black hair. She lifted her head to look at me, her expression held unnaturally still.

"I had DNA testing done on all of us," she said. "I had to be sure."

I gripped the back of a chair to stop myself from falling. "How... how did you manage to do that without us knowing?"

She waved a hand in dismissal. "Oh, you'd be surprised where you can get DNA samples if you're trying to be secretive–toothbrushes, nail clippings, snot on a used tissue... saliva from cigarette butts..." she said, pointedly emphasising the latter. I had visions of her gathering her materials, not to conduct scientific tests, but to create voodoo dolls of us all.

She rose from her chair, suddenly incandescent.

"You knew, didn't you?" she yelled, punctuating each word by poking me in the chest with a sharp-nailed forefinger and sending me backpedalling into the kitchen bench. "I gave you that box of my mother's letters, and you must have read them, and you MUST have recognised yourself in that one letter, and you said NOTHING! You let me conceive all those babies, and you... you..." She stopped, speechless with rage and revulsion.

"I didn't know for sure," I protested. "I only suspected..." I glanced behind me, checking for any readily accessible weapons, not for myself but to keep them away from her; if she could reach a knife at that moment, she would surely plunge it into my heart.

The children, drawn out by the noise, emerged one by one from their various retreats about the house. They were all graceful and gorgeous, magnificent young creatures as they walked past their mother and came to stand at my side.

"'*Suspected*'? Just your suspicion alone should have been enough to end it. You should never have married me. I should have aborted Layla, drowned Bain in the bath and got as far the fuck away from you as possible." Spittle flew from her mouth and hit me in the face, but I did not wipe it away, my hands being too occupied trying futilely to shield my children's ears from her obscene rant.

At my shoulder, Bain stiffened. "What are you on about now, Mum?" he said scathingly. Mia looked at him as if seeing him for the first time. There was no rage left in her now, only a bone-deep despair.

"It's OK," I murmured to Bain. "I'll handle this." Poppy pressed closer to me and chewed on her thumbnail, just like her mother did in times of stress. Just like I had done at the same age.

"Look at them," I said to Mia, gesturing at our children. Except that with each passing moment they were becoming less *our* children and more *my* children. "How can you call them a mistake?"

And she did look, for long moments, assessing the physical and psychic distance between us. "They're just kids…" she muttered to herself, but whether the 'just' meant that they had yet to reach maturity or that, being only children, they had little value, I wasn't sure.

"OK, Andy," she finally said. "You want them so much? They're yours. For now. But they will grow up and come to understand what you have done, and then you'll lose them. Remember this: as soon as they turn eighteen, I will reclaim them." This last sentence she spoke with vehemence and ritualistic slowness, as if uttering a curse or casting a spell.

Then she turned and walked out of the house. It was the last time any of us saw her alive.

Mia had left the house empty-handed except for her car keys. She made no attempt to access bank accounts or contact friends, no witnesses came forward to say they'd seen her anywhere, and no body matching her description was ever found. The only trace of her was the car, which police found abandoned in a semi-industrial area some fifteen kilometres from our home. She had simply vanished off the face of the Earth. I took to visiting the site where they'd found the car in the vain hopes that I would find some hitherto undiscovered evidence there, or that she would reappear as magically as she had disappeared. The urine-soaked and graffiti-splattered alleyway yielded no clues, yet it became something of a weekly pilgrimage for me to go there; it was the closest thing I had to a grave. Sometimes I imagined I could hear her voice whispering at me from the darkest recesses of the alley, but it was only the wind stirring the leaves and the echoes from my memories.

As for the kids, I was at once relieved and disturbed at the ease with which they flowed to fill the space left by their mother. There should at least have been tears or misbehaviour, but instead they acted as if she never existed, as if they had sprung, godlike, directly from my loins. They never asked why she left, and I never volunteered the answer.

In fact, they thrived without her. Mia's absence seemed to have removed the shackles from their potential; all of them clever young things before she left, they grew tall and gifted, excelling at school and each possessing a particular prodigious talent. Bain was a sports star, Layla a mathematician, Charlize a musician, Sebastian a writer and Poppy an artist. The future for all of them was blindingly bright.

We'd all forgotten Mia's parting words when, three days after Bain's eighteenth birthday, a drunk driver steered her car into his, killing him instantly. If I'd had concerns about my children's lack of emotion when their mother left, I needn't have worried; the remaining four shed tears aplenty at their brother's graveside, and continued to grieve extravagantly in the months after his death.

We lost Layla to meningitis, which she contracted whilst on a camping trip with friends. I barely let the remaining three out of my sight after that, not that they wanted to stray far from home anyway in the wake of such tragedies. Charlize in particular became very withdrawn. She slept a lot, and during her waking hours she took to playing one mournful note over and over again on her cello. I put the changes down to depression and grief, but it turned out they were caused by the brain tumour that killed her the day after her eighteenth birthday.

I continued my visits to 'Mia's Alley', as I privately called it. Some days as I stared into the darkness, the darkness stared back, the shadows shifting and coalescing for moments into shapes almost human before dissolving back into meaninglessness. The day before Sebastian turned eighteen, I went to plead my case.

"Please stop, Mia," I whispered, feeling ridiculous but continuing regardless. "You have three now; leave me Sebastian and Poppy. Or one of them, at least. Surely you can see how much we've suffered already."

The wind moaned in response. *Bargain with your own children's lives, would you?* it seemed to mock. *Go home, old man. Go home to your grief.*

We celebrated Sebastian's birthday by closing the curtains and huddling inside, eating canned food and lighting candles for our fallen which I would blow out within minutes for fear of one toppling and setting fire to the house. Poppy and I took turns standing guard over Sebastian while he slept, and he complained about how creepy it was to have someone staring at him all the damned time.

Nine days later, he was still alive. For the first time since Bain died, I began to feel, if not happy, at least hopeful that Mia's curse had been broken, or perhaps never existed in the first place. We drew back the curtains and opened the windows to let in some fresh air—which is when a bee flew in the window and landed on Sebastian's neck. He couldn't have seen what it was, only felt it brush against his skin. I leapt to stop him but I was too late; he slapped at it, and yelped when it stung him.

He went into anaphylactic shock, and died before the ambulance could arrive. I racked my brain for memories of childhood injuries, but could not recall him, or any of the other children for that matter, ever being stung. This time at least I could be there to see my child take his last tortured breath, to usher him out of my arms and into his mother's, wherever she might be and whatever form she had taken.

Which left Poppy. My youngest child, my daughter who was so much like Mia in looks, mannerisms and personality that sometimes it hurt to be around her. Poor Poppy, who had endured more tragedy in her short life than anyone ought to suffer. And just like her mother, she simply walked out the door one day and never looked back. Unlike her mother, they found her body, splattered at the base of a multi-storey parking building from which she'd jumped; evidently she'd decided that if she had to die young, it would be on her terms. Bystanders who'd witnessed her plummet put her time of death at eighteen years after her birth, to the minute.

I went back to Mia's Alley at midnight—the Witching Hour—on the night of a new moon. The lighting was sporadic already in the area, but I took out the two closest street lights with a few carefully aimed rocks. The darkness was near absolute.

I felt rather than saw her at first, a tiny disturbance in the air currents and a sudden, sharp drop in temperature.

"Silly man," a barely audible whisper tickled my ear, "you didn't have to come here to find me." Substance formed around the sound, and there Mia stood. Her hair, her eyes, her spectral clothing that swirled and slid across her body like an unholy mist, were so black, they were somehow visible against the now insipid night.

"Where else would I find you?" I managed to croak.

"Anywhere there is death. Anywhere there is grief." Behind her, our children—*her* children now, I reminded myself—took shape, although not as distinctly as Mia; some kind of barrier separated us, insubstantial-looking yet impenetrable for one like me whose heart still beat. Their features were just as I remembered them, but their *expressions*... no human could bear such pain and knowledge and live. They now knew the truth of their parentage, I could see it in their eyes, and they condemned me for it. More than that, it looked like they'd been condemned to exhume the bones from every family's closets and make their beds on them.

Perhaps that's what death was—the sudden weight of the universe's most sordid secrets.

My every instinct told me to run, to get far, far away from these ghouls masquerading as my family. But hadn't I yearned for this moment of reunion, however twisted it might be, for years?

I laughed. The sound echoed dementedly off the concrete buildings around us. "Anywhere there is death and grief? If that were the case, you would have been with me all along."

Her smile flooded me with yearning and terror, and literally made me buckle at the knees. "I have been," she said, "you just didn't know how to see."

"So will I always see you now?"

"No, Andy," she replied. "But you'll see me again, when it's your turn to join us." Her children receded into the darkness, leaving her alone to gaze down on me, I thought perhaps in pity. But when her final words came, they were steeped in triumph:

"And that will not be for a long, long time."

Tracie McBride is a New Zealander who lives in Melbourne, Australia. Her work has appeared in over 80 publications, including the Stoker Award-nominated anthologies *Horror for Good* and *Horror Library Volume 5*. Her collection Ghosts Can Bleed contains much of the work that earned her a Sir Julius Vogel Award. Visit her blog at traciemcbridewriter.wordpress.com.

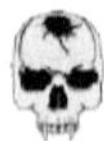

Wealth and Hellness

Gregory L. Norris

5 x 7. Silver. In the unforgiving white glare beyond her dimming vision, Ruth saw that the little picture frame was tarnished. The elegant, delicate scrolls were caked in a darkness they wouldn't likely be rid of again in her lifetime. And after she stole her final breath, what then? The picture torn out, tossed into the garbage pail at the side of her bed, presently containing a few candy wrappers and plastic from whatever pharmaceutical sponge or instrument of torture had been opened by a nurse or nurse's aide. Someone would claim the frame; it was sterling silver. But the picture…

Ruth Elizabeth Lester forced her gaze higher and greeted the eyes of the young man captured in that lost moment. He looked happy. Maybe he was, though she didn't think so. His smile owed to the photographer. College graduation? No, high school. He hadn't made it long past this snapshot frozen in time.

There were instances lately, too many of them, when Ruth couldn't remember who he was, only that he'd died in a car accident. Now, the truth sat heavy on her shoulders and fed whatever dark creatures lived in her gut and the regret that tumbled through her bloodstream.

"Jacob," Ruth whispered.

For a terrible second, she felt all the emotion drain as it got ironed off her face. Then the caustic sting of tears invaded her eyes and, for the thousandth or millionth time, she wept for her dead son.

"And how are we today, Ms. Ruth?" the chirpy, chipper young woman asked.

Ruth assumed the nurse in the plum paisley scrubs was Mimi, who worked the weekday shift at Hutton Hill, though it was difficult to tell one body or voice from another when everyone paid to care for your health and wellness in the last of your days among the living acted like your best friend and was so happy to see you. She'd never had so many cheerleaders. A whole cast of partygoers present to celebrate the end of eighty-three years, a jumble of months, and who knew anymore how many days.

How was she? Her entire body felt like one giant bruise. It was as though every cut, every scrape her skin had ever sustained, dating all the way back to childhood, had surfaced up from scars long healed and stitched together.

"Fine," she settled for instead.

Mimi—she wasn't sure who her new best friend was—wandered over to the wheelchair wedged into the small space between hospital bed and the outer wall of the bathroom. "Are you sure, Ruth?"

Ruth remembered the tears, her latest over Jacob. Proof lay in the wadded tissues clutched in her good hand. What was the point of lying? Still, she hadn't been the type to bemoan life's many sinkholes. Maybe-Mimi leaned down and checked the sling. Tenderly, of course—the adjustments were merely mimes, motions run through and something to do out of compassion, because that was what was expected of party guests waiting for you to blow out your candles at the last big hurrah.

The breaks in her arm—three, according to the unreliable information ping-ponging through her thoughts—were healing on their own, no cast or surgery required. Still, the miserable slowness, and so much agony.

She'd slipped out of the wheelchair, her second home after the hospital bed, which trapped her body at night but couldn't keep Ruth's mind from wandering back to people and places from the past. She'd fallen asleep in the chair, breaking a promise she made to herself never to do so, because in the chair, she was able to move about. It wasn't the same as walking; still, the closest thing to it at the end of her life.

What Ruth didn't tell them was why: because she was running, carried along by the wind. Running around the shiny exterior of Lester's Variety during the store's best and happiest years. Running toward the alley, which opened up on the patch of backyard behind the building. Inside the fence, somewhere between the pickets and the back door leading up to their homey apartment above the convenience store, she heard Jack and Jacob having one of their father-son talks. Her heart galloped in anticipation of joining them. Ruth's legs sped faster. And then the world erupted in red-hot agony, and the dream cracked apart. So did arm bones, Ruth later discovered.

She woke on the clean white linoleum floor of Room 209 at Hutton Hill, the nursing home for well-to-do old ladies. The pain was so intense that it drove out the fog, and Ruth remembered everything. The convenience store, long gone now. Her husband Jack, gone longer. And Jacob, whose body had been so mangled in the wreck that they'd held the funeral closed-casket. That pain knew no rival, not even breaking her arm in three places.

The Italian woman on the other side of the privacy curtain, Ruth's unwanted and loud roommate, screamed for help. It was the one time Ruth was grateful for the woman's big mouth.

Three weeks later, the pain roused Ruth awake. She unstuck her eyes and gazed to the foot of her bed, where Death stood dressed in maroon hospital scrubs. The air thrummed with its usual undercurrent of electricity, the pulse of machinery, and televisions playing in other rooms. The white glow from the hallway outside the room did little to illuminate the man's face, though she could tell by his silhouette that he was, indeed, a man.

Death held a penlight in one hand. He flicked it on and off, creating an effect Ruth equated with distant thunderclouds pulsing with furious energy. The storm stood frozen, watching her. A chill gossiped over her flesh, creating an unpleasant sensation in counterpoint to the burning from deep within her bones. He stared. Ruth's skin dimpled in goose bumps.

She conjured her voice. "Hello?"

The man answered with an exhale snorted through nostrils, nothing more. And then Death walked out of the room. Invisible ice encased Ruth's body. She waited, breathing no longer simple, or even an involuntary thing. She forgot to blink until her eyes started to burn, and sleep remained elusive until one of the nurses checking in saw that she was awake, and brought Ruth her next dose of pain medication.

Lester's Variety had been more than a place to buy cigarettes, beer, and cold cuts. One whole aisle was devoted to seasonal items—coolers and suntan lotion in the summer, and beautiful gift notions during the holidays. That's where the silver picture frame had originated, Ruth remembered during the too-short spell of clarity following her disturbed night.

The store was gone. So, too, were husband and son. She was stuck in a present whose reality was pain and infirmity of both body and mind. Limbo, land of lost souls.

One of the Mimis washed and dressed her and, with another Mimi's assistance, eased Ruth into her wheelchair for another day no different than the one before. The pain in her broken arm helped her to ignore the unforgivable invasion of hands touching her that Ruth always choked down and suffered through in silence. She welcomed the warmth of the long gray sweater, draped over the shoulder of her injured arm.

"Looks like we're gonna have snow today," one of the Mimis announced in a cheery voice before exiting the room.

Like that news mattered, or was reason for saccharin smiles. The last time Ruth had sampled the outside world she was being whisked away by ambulance to the hospital, her arm in pieces. And the cold on that journey untold days in the past had gotten deeper into her marrow through the breaks. Sometimes, she overheard the nurses complaining about the stifling heat inside Hutton Hill after they removed their birthday party hats and thought the guest of honor wasn't listening. Truth was, she always felt cold, even under the extra blanket in the prison that was her bed.

Right before Death moseyed back into Room 209, Ruth sat staring at the tiny, oblong patch of real estate her life's end occupied. In the apartment over the store, there'd been big rooms filled with plenty of furniture, books, and drapes she'd ordered from catalogues sent to Lester's Variety by vendors. There were rugs—a big oval one, dark green, though for a moment her mind colored it cobalt blue. A gallery of family photographs—snapshots of happier times—filled the hallway between the bedrooms and bathroom.

The photograph of Jacob on top of the nightstand near Ruth's bed was the last survivor to have escaped the hallway; the last relic of Ruth's life apart from the frail living corpse that still, somehow, held onto so many ghosts—the memory of the china they ate off of daily, with its butter-yellow stripe around the edges; the fancy plates for company and special occasions, Blue Willow; the night of the phone call, and how that deep *ringing* right before she lifted the receiver off the cradle had gotten into her and stayed, was still echoing in the dusty corners of her psyche, proclaiming the news of Jacob's death.

One photograph in a tarnished silver frame, set beside an impersonal altar of tissue box, plastic water pitcher, cup and straw, and a plastic vase with one silk flower, a gift from unknown hands. All sat beneath the stark white glow of the light from which the call button's tentacle snaked, along a length of drab beige wall.

Briefly, Ruth pined for the apartment. She'd kept the place immaculate, and had loved their small, guarded backyard. Jacob had wanted a dog, but there was Lester's Variety to run, a store that provided them an above-average life. She'd wanted to entertain—dinner parties, using the good Blue Willow china…

But always, there was the store.

A shadow cut across the top of the nightstand and engulfed Jacob's photograph. Ruth seized in place and returned to the present. A blur of crimson color materialized at the corner of her eye. She attempted to turn the wheelchair, using her feet. The pain in her broken arm reasserted its pull.

The earth moved beneath her. No, Ruth realized, it was only the wheels under the chair. Death's hands turned her around to face him directly.

"Hello, Ruth."

"Well, hello," she said in her usual voice, which always accentuated the positive, even as her insides clenched from the negative energy she felt radiating outward from the man in the crimson scrubs who towered over her, seemingly at a height of a hundred feet.

Their eyes connected, and the cold inside Ruth's bones worsened.

"*Go say hi to Ruth Lester*, they all said. *Ruth's the sweetest, kindest soul*," the man said, his voice deep, friendly.

Ruth instantly sensed it was a ruse. Decades had passed since some smiling customer had approached the register at Lester's Variety, intending to steal whatever was inside the cash drawer. The store had been robbed a total of seven times during its existence, and all of the criminals had spoken in that same slippery voice before revealing their true intentions.

"I told them," he continued, "you don't gotta tell me. I knew the Lesters a long time ago. Nice people. Especially that Ruth."

The man hunched down so that his face was close to Ruth's. Too close. She caught the thick stink of his cologne on her next sip of air and drank in the image of his face—long, mean despite the smile, especially in his eyes. His mean, dark eyes drilled into her.

"You don't remember me, Ruth? Sam Tillman? I was a pal of your son, Jacob. You know, before…"

He mouthed a sound meant to mimic screeching tires, followed by the *kaboom* of an explosion.

Ruth listened, too stunned to react. Her lips moved of their own will. "A friend of Jacob's? How nice."

The man's smile flattened. "Yeah, nice. How's the arm? Heard you landed pretty hard on it."

His hands moved to adjust her sling, only this time fresh stings rippled outward in concentric waves, engulfing her entire body, and Ruth knew the pain was inevitable because she saw it telegraphed first in his smile.

"How's that feel, Ruthie?" the man taunted more than asked.

She bit back a howl. The fear she remembered from the man's first visitation at night manifested in day—a snowy one, by all reports. The scream built in her stomach and clawed its way up her throat. Ruth ground what remained of her teeth and readied to release the shriek.

The man straightened. "You let Sam from the old neighborhood know if there's anything you need, dear Ruth."

He shuffled toward the door, and she got a better look—this former friend of the dead boy in the photograph wasn't the size of a skyscraper anymore. Tall enough. If he was the dead boy's friend—*Jacob*, proclaimed the voice in her thoughts—he'd be in his forties now. A tattoo snaked along one of his arms. The smirk on his mean face unleashed pins and needles over her skin. And deeper. Deeper than marrow. Soul?

"See you soon, Ruth," Death said. Then he winked at her before exiting the room.

Ruth sat paralyzed, fearing to blink, to breathe. The male nurse's name—*Sam Tillman*, that's what he said. Frozen in the wheelchair, she focused on his name, attempted to etch it into her grey matter through concentration. That was his name. Sam. Tillman. Tillman's Salvage and Scrap Yard.

The place jumped out of the background of muddy memories and she could almost see it clearly, a two-dimensional automobile graveyard on the bad side of town. Bad kids. Jacob was having problems with the Tillman brothers. Jacob wanted a car for graduation. Car accident. Dear God, the man in the crimson scrubs… he'd *mocked* Jacob's death. Who could be so cruel?

Ruth caught herself drifting past the rusting, sepia wrecks of Tillman's Salvage and Scrap Yard, and turned the shoulder of her injured arm, just enough, so that a bolt of exquisite red pain shattered the fog and left her head clear of distraction. Ruth imagined the jolt as a ballpoint pen, then as a threaded needle, and wrote his name out, in cursive.

Sam Tillman, he knew my son.

Ruth choked down a dry swallow and maneuvered her feet along the floor, closer to the nightstand. She reached for the cup. The water was warm, but she drank it down through the straw until she drained the cup.

Knew my son, she embroidered in her thoughts. *And he knew me.*

It could have been days later or only hours—in the jumble of concentrating on Sam Tillman's name to the exclusion of most else, Ruth lost track of time—when she overheard the birthday party revelers as they worked on the other side of the privacy curtain.

"So nice. And funny!" one of the Mimis said in a voice not meant for anyone else's ears. "He knew exactly what to do. Somehow, it was a loose battery cable."

"You're lucky," another Mimi said. "I feel so much safer knowing we've got Sam working here."

She heard them moving around, wrapping and taping. Presents for the party? The privacy curtain was closed fully around Ruth's little oblong patch of real estate. She imagined herself sitting inside a gift box, bolts of ribbon spilling down from a giant bow. Wheels moved across the white linoleum—the cart upon which the birthday cake sat, perhaps?

Movement stirred just beyond the curtain. Something snagged and dragged the curtain aside, enough for Ruth to see the stretcher as it slipped past, containing the shrouded corpse of the loudmouthed Italian woman from the bed next door. Sam Till…no, *Barbara…* had been in fine voice not long before. Clearly, the birthday celebration was for Big Mouth, not Ruth. Barbara had blown out her candles. The Mimis could focus on other shindigs, other funerals, now.

The curtain fell back into place, and a silence far worse that the loudest of her roommate's jabbering settled over Room 209.

He said he was coming back, warned the voice in Ruth's thoughts. *That boy who knew Jacob. The scrap yard kid. Tillsbury… no, Tillman. Sam Tillman!*

Food had long ago renounced its taste and pleasure. For a while, Ruth loved frozen yogurt, particularly the chocolate brownie variety served for dessert in Hutton Hill's dining hall, but even that had waned.

One of the nurses wheeled Ruth out of the room and down the corridor, toward the elevator.

"Barbara," Ruth said.

"I know. So sad, but it was her time."

Ruth pondered the partygoer's statement. "Do you know when I'll be getting another roommate?"

"Soon, hopefully," the nurse said. This Mimi's voice boasted a soupcon of Spanish accent. "Until then, be sure to enjoy the quiet. Rest, Ruth—get that arm back to where it was for the next tennis match."

Ruth laughed, even as the sense of dread thickened around her. "Is it still snowing?"

"No, dear, that was days ago. It's just cold and miserable."

"And Tillsbury?"

"You mean Sam? Sam Tillman?"

"Yes, him. That rotten punk from the junkyard. I don't want him playing with Jacob. He's too rough—and a bad influence. Every time Jacob comes home from that place, he's covered in scratches and bleeding!"

Mimi hesitated. Ruth wondered if she'd trapped her thoughts inside the tiny section of clarity where she attempted to sort out memories, names, and faces, or if she'd spoken them aloud.

"Ruth, you have the wrong guy," Spanish Mimi said. "Our Sam, the new nurse—he's a gentleman. So nice, so sweet and kind. We're all lucky to have him here. You'll see."

The elevator reached the ground floor, dinged, and its doors trundled open. Standing outside was Death, dressed in crimson hospital scrubs.

"Sam," Spanish Mimi said. "Ruth and I were just talking about you."

Ruth gazed up. The man's mean eyes captured hers, and their cruelty intensified in league with his slippery smile. "Were you? All lies, I hope."

Spanish Mimi snickered and wheeled Ruth past the lobby, a turn right, and then another into the lunchtime bustle of the first floor dining hall. She sensed his cold stare tracking her to the table beside the big window that looked out on the courtyard, presently draped in a coat of pristine white. A thick soup of meat and gravy smells and coffee sitting too long on burners, mixed with perfumes and sweat, hung over the place.

Spanish Mimi guided her wheelchair into one of two vacant spots. Colleen—the woman's last name eluded Ruth's memory—sipped either tea or some of that burned coffee, pinkie finger politely extended.

"Hello, Ruth," the Grand Dame of their dining table announced.

"Hello, dear."

Ruth nodded to the other lady at the table, all that now survived of Colleen's court. The two women were engaged in eating their dinners. Ruth's soon appeared—some kind of meat, pork or turkey, she assumed, cut into tiny bites; starchy mashed potatoes under a glaze of brown gravy; and bright orange cubes she guessed were carrots. One round bread roll and a single pat of butter. Tea with skim milk. She moved the food around on the plate with her fork more than she actually ate anything.

"Do you need help, Ruth?" one of the Kitchen Mimis asked.

Ruth lifted a glop of potatoes and gravy, showing them she didn't need spoon-feeding. She wanted the tea more than the rest. Anything to feel warm again.

"Terrible about Barbara," said Colleen.

Ruth roused from the fog and attempted to focus. "Barbara?"

Colleen rolled her eyes toward the vacant seat. "Your roommate. *Ex*-roommate."

News travels, thought Ruth. Especially bad news. "Have you seen that new man? Tall and mean. He was a friend of Jacob's."

Colleen tittered in that theatrical manner that drew attention from other tables, something the Grand Dame ate up as heartily as select castoffs from the rest of her court's unwanted lunches, like bread rolls and butter. "You mean that nice man, Sam? If I was thirty years younger…"

The statement went unfinished. More laughter. Saying nothing, Ruth lifted the plastic cup containing her tea and sipped.

The joy of food was gone. For lunch, which was also Ruth's breakfast following the daily morning humiliation of being washed and dressed, she forced herself to eat. Dinner was usually a small carton of skim milk, maybe something sweet, though even dessert had lost its appeal.

She sat in her wheelchair, her eyelids fighting the pull of gravity. It could have been a dream, but she was almost certain it was a memory. Jacob, sobbing. The Tillman boys, whose family owned the junkyard of rusting cars and car parts, had chased him home from the bus stop. Ripped his clothes. The skin beneath one of the tears bled.

"What happened?" the younger version of Ruth Lester asked. Before the boy could answer, she demanded, "Who did this to you, Jacob?"

"Sam."

"That Tillsbury boy?"

Ruth reached for the phone, that rotten crier of doom whose ring haunted both dreams and the background of her waking hours. The Ruth who dialed was an elderly shell with a broken arm in a sling.

"Yes, I want to talk to you about your boys. Especially Sam, and what he did to my son, Mister Tillman!"

Jacob tugged at Ruth's gray sweater. She turned to face him. He was older now, barely eighteen, and clearly scared, according to the look on his face. "Be careful, Mom—Sam's back."

Ruth's eyes snapped open. The confines of the apartment evaporated. Room 209 at Hutton Hill Nursing Home rose up from the fog and solidified in its place.

"Ruthie, wake up," Death cooed in a sweet voice. "I brought you something."

Sam Tillman's face leaned down, right into Ruth's. Her heart attempted to jump out of her chest and into her throat.

"You—!"

"Shhh, Ruthie, just a couple of friends from the old neighborhood hanging out here, catching up. How you doing today, sweets?"

He cupped her chin. She twisted away. Tillman pulled her face back toward him, hard enough to hurt. She thought about the call button, still within reach. She'd ring for help and, surely, help would arrive… unless he told them not to come. Then what? Try to convince whatever Mimi was on duty that she was being terrorized by the new favorite son of Hutton Hill? Hadn't she already tried that? Nobody believed her claims about Sam Tillman.

"Please," she attempted. "Whatever happened was a long time ago."

He dismissed Ruth's statement with a snort. "I got a long memory, lady."

Ruth persisted. "Whatever I did to make you angry… your mom, would she want you acting this way to me? I'm a mother, too."

Tillman released her chin, caressed her cheek, and, at first, the gesture seemed kind. Soon, his touch was overly familiar, unwanted.

"You sure are, Ruth. Go on, drink up."

Tillman reached for the small carton of skim milk on the nightstand and aimed the straw at her trembling lips.

"Drink up, mommy."

She caught his malevolent smile again. Every instinct told her no—*don't drink it, Ruth!*

"Do it," Tillman growled.

Ruth took a tentative sip. The second made her gag. She choked down the swallow as the sharp odor of urine struck her nostrils a fractured second before the taste ignited over Ruth's tongue. She pushed the carton away, sputtered.

"What? You don't like my little happy hour cocktail of piss and milk?"

He laughed and straightened. Turning, he entered the bathroom. Ruth heard the glug of evidence being dumped into the toilet, followed by the flush that washed his guilt away. She reached for the water cup—empty—and then the pitcher. Tillman intercepted her wrist and yanked the pitcher out of her hand.

"No, you rotting old snatch, you get to choke on the taste of my piss. Just like that fucking dick-smooch son of yours. You uppity, rich fucks, thinking you were so much better than us. Do you know what my mother did to me after you called to complain about me and my brother and your kid? We were only roughhousing with him. Know what she did to me? That was a day at the circus compared to what the old man did after you banned our family from your shitty store, and he had to go next town over for his beer and smokes. You want to see, huh?"

Ruth attempted to look away, but Tillman lifted his scrub shirt, and there were the scars—nearly perfect round burn marks drilled into flank and stomach. Scars from the ghosts of cigarettes past, she realized.

"Oh, no, Ruth-baby, I'm not done with you. Not even close, bitch."

Tillman smoothed out his scrub shirt, flashed his slippery smile, and shuffled toward the door.

"You have a great day, too, dear Ruth," he said, loud enough that she imagined other patients and nurses overhearing the exchange.

Bile rose up Ruth's throat on a sour burp and painted the back of her tongue. The contents of her stomach threatened to follow. Somehow, she willed the vomit into staying down.

Oh God, dear God…

Ruth began to pray. To God. To whatever saint, martyr, or deity would listen. To Jack. To Jacob. To the late Italian Big Mouth, who'd woken her up so many times with her endless babbling and snoring. She forgot the woman's name, but figured the least she owed Ruth was a good word with the Powers Above.

And then it struck her—a concept that would have seemed crazy if not for her predicament.

What if Sam Tillman had murdered the Big Mouth to get her alone, to further isolate her from prying eyes and loose lips?

Ruth sank into the darkness. She didn't want to sleep. Sleep gave Tillman yet another advantage over her. Age, exhaustion, and the pain medicine all conspired against her and, despite her promise not to, Ruth floated off, wondering about his accusation—*banned from the store.*

We reserve the right to refuse service—the words jumped out of the depths and played in the foreground of her dream. There'd been a sign posted on the glass door with the jingling bell that announced customers had entered Lester's Variety. After the funeral—Jack's—Jacob had gotten into another scrape with that Tillsbury punk. *No, Tillman,* her inner voice barked.

"Since you can't keep your son from acting like an animal and beating up on my boy, I have no choice but to ban you—all of you—from my store!"

The humorless, hulking brute that smelled like ashtrays and motor oil had gone off on her, using the kind of language that cemented Ruth's resolve. "The apple and the tree," she'd calmly stated while reaching for the phone. "Yes, Operator, give me the police…"

She'd been terrified then, more so than she ever thought possible, but no Tillman was going to bully this widow around, even if he was twice her size. And no Tillman brat was going to get away with beating up on her son.

"Fuck you, bitch," spat the long-dead memory of the Senior Tillman.

"You fucking bitch," the son whispered, shocking Ruth out of the dream.

She woke to the on-off click of the penlight, now aimed right at her eyes. Pain pulsed between the flashes.

"That's right, it's me again, you dried up cunt. Skeleton crew on tonight at the Hutton—the minimum staff required. Just you and me together, Ruthie."

A hand slid over her cheek as the penlight went out and stayed dark. Ruth gasped.

"Only the two of us…"

The hand slid lower, down Ruth's throat, over her nightgown and the shriveled lump of her left breast. She let out a yelp, which she imagined vanishing into the ether, smothered by all the other sounds of nightlife in Hutton Hill.

A hand clamped over her mouth, silencing any additional temptation to scream for help. The hand groping her breast pinched, savaged. Tears invaded Ruth's eyes.

"Go ahead, tell them," Tillman chuckled, his voice barely above a whisper. "Nobody will believe a senile old gitch like you. *Dementia*, Ruthie. You talk crazy shit all the time."

She attempted to bite. Ruth Lester had faced off against dragons before—seven thieves and Old Man Tillsbury, the chain-smoking, alcoholic mechanic, among them, even if standing up for her son against Death's father had sown the seeds that had germinated into this dark moment.

"Tomorrow, Ruthie," Tillman said, and released her. "You just wait for what I've got planned for you, bitch. Wait 'til you see what's coming next..."

He spit at her and stalked out of the room.

The clarity of her thoughts wouldn't last, she knew. Ruth imagined herself holding onto the details, each fact a bird with flapping wings attempting to escape her grasp.

"Mimi," she said to the woman who washed her body.

"Mimi?" the Spanish girl laughed. "Ruth, Mimi hasn't worked here in a jillion years. You know very well I'm Altagracia."

"You won't let him near me, promise me you won't."

"Him? Who do you mean?"

"That boy. The one who was so mean to my son. His family owns the scrap yard. Will you please call the police?"

"There's nobody like that here at Hutton Hill—you know everybody cares about you. You're just confused again, Ruth."

"That man—*Tillman*!"

"Sam?" Spanish Mimi giggled. "He's a big teddy bear. Every time one of us has car problems, there he is, saving the day. Man's a mechanical genius!"

"But..."

Spanish Mimi finished drying off Ruth and fixed her with a fresh adult diaper. Then, with another nurse's assistance, they dressed her, seated her upright in her wheelchair, and made sure she was as comfortable as possible.

"You won't let him hurt me," Ruth pleaded. "You'll check in on me, won't you?"

"I swear," said Spanish Mimi. "Cross my heart."

And then they left her alone.

At lunch, as was always the case, Colleen held court and Ruth pushed the food around on her plate. She eyed Colleen's butter knife.

Because they cut her meat, Ruth's own table setting consisted only of napkin and fork.

The fork, with its four tines, seemed a better weapon for defense anyway. During an interlude from Colleen's theatrics, Ruth wiped the fork on her napkin and slid it under cover inside her sling. The metal lay cool against her epidermis and helped her to keep a grasp on those many thought-birds scrambling to fly away.

She sensed his approach even before he entered the room. Ruth's heart beat a tattoo in concert with his footfalls across the linoleum or, perhaps, in response to sensing his dark intentions coming closer, closer.

"Hello, Ruthie," he said. "You're looking particularly lovely today."

He closed the door. The doors had no locks, but the Tillman punk didn't need them. He created a temporary lock by wedging what looked like a screwdriver or scalpel into the thin space between door and frame.

Death grabbed hold of his crotch. "Wouldn't want anybody interrupting our fun."

"Spanish Mimi promised to call the police on you," Ruth warned. "You stay away from me!"

"Altagracia? Her shift's over, and all the other nurses on this floor are busy. It's just you and me now, Ruth."

"*No*," Ruth said. "You're a rotten boy, Sam Tillman. I'm calling your mother. *Help!*"

Death hurried over and clamped a hand over Ruth's mouth. She struggled, ignored the pain in her shattered arm. The pain became her ally. She used it to locate the weapon, scrambled old but capable fingers into the sling, gripped metal that wasn't cold any longer but warmed by her body's heat, withdrew.

She took aim and lunged. Ruth swore she heard the pop as well as felt it, as the fork's tines punctured the soft meat beneath Death's chin.

Tillman howled and drew back. Drops of red rained down. Her aim for his throat had missed; still, the jab had proved effective. Tillman knocked the fork away and surged back toward her, and all else that followed was steeped in agony.

He pushed, driving Ruth's wheelchair backward, into the nightstand. Objects toppled off the altar. Then he pulled her forward, and Ruth spilled out of the chair, onto the floor. Onto her broken arm.

The wave of pain crashed over her, so intense that Ruth's voice shorted out and she lost the ability to scream. Fantastic colors leapt before her eyes, as beautiful as brutal. Continents collided. So, too, did galaxies. She witnessed the supernova of numerous stars and the spiraling plunge downward of the universe into black holes filled with exquisite agony. So this was the end of life, Ruth thought.

Jacob appeared beside her in the abyss. Her beloved son, taken too young from a world that needed his goodness, smiled at Ruth, seeming to beckon her forward. Only there was no accompanying tunnel filled with light and loved ones, and his smile, even at that horrifying instant, read as sad.

Darkness swept over Ruth.

"I have something to tell you, you rich cunt," Tillman said.

He straddled his body over her crumpled form. She smelled his breath, his cologne, his blood. Leaning his face down into hers, Death laughed.

"Always wanted you to know it was me. Yeah, that car accident, your faggot son—it was *me*. I was the one. Messed with his brake lines because of you messing with me."

A knock sounded. A woman's voice called out for whoever was in there to open the door.

"I did it, bitch," Tillman continued, unfazed. "*I killed your son.*"

5 x 7. Silver. Tarnished.

Ruth faced Jacob. She gripped the jagged shard of glass from the shattered picture frame containing her dead son's sad smile and, focusing the last of her strength into the upward cut, she drove its point into Tillman's throat.

Gregory L. Norris is a full-time professional writer, with work appearing in numerous short story anthologies, national magazines, novels, the occasional TV episode, and, so far, one produced feature film (*Brutal Colors*, which debuted on Amazon Prime January 2016). A former feature writer and columnist at Sci Fi, the official magazine of the Sci Fi Channel (before all those ridiculous Ys invaded), he once worked as a screenwriter on two episodes of Paramount's modern classic, Star Trek: Voyager. Two of his paranormal novels (written under his rom-de-plume, Jo Atkinson) were published by Home Shopping Network as part of their "Escape With Romance" line—the first time HSN has offered novels to their global customer base. Norris judged the 2012 Lambda Awards in the SF/F/H category. Three times now, his short stories have notched Honorable Mentions by Ellen Datlow. He won HM in the 2016 Roswell Awards in Short SF for his short story 'Mandered'. Norris lives and writes in the outer limits of New Hampshire. Follow his literary adventures on Facebook, or at www.gregorylnorris.blogspot.com.

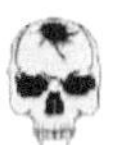

Cold Feet

Adrian Ludens

Even though I work with cadavers every day, *I'm* the one with cold feet!

I'll explain that in a moment, Doctor Mayes, but first I want to express how pleasantly surprised I am to see you. I realize I don't have an appointment, and the circumstances are unusual to say the least, but being able to talk to you one more time would mean so much to me right now. You've helped me through tough times before, and I sure could use your advice.

You see, about six months ago I asked Holly to marry me. She agreed, and I was ecstatic… for a while. The problem is, now that the wedding is only a few weeks away, I'm having serious second thoughts.

Not Holly, though. She's been running around as busy as a honeybee, making the final arrangements—

Oh my god. I can't believe I just said that: *Final arrangements*. You'd think I'm talking about a funeral. Let's see if I can choose my words with more care: Holly has been seeing to the last-minute details of our nuptials.

As for me, I've been spending more and more time alone, mulling things over.

I know what you're thinking: "What could possibly rattle Bill March, the senior mortician at Carlton Funeral Chapel?" Maybe I'm jumping to conclusions and subconsciously creating excuses so that I don't have to go through with the marriage. I'll let you be the judge.

A year and a half ago, when she first started her apprenticeship at Carlton, Holly and I hit it off immediately. Her first day on the job, she brought some compact discs in from her car. We embalmed our first cadaver together with a movie soundtrack composed by Angelo Badalamenti playing in the background.

As I've already told you, I felt an attraction to Holly from day one. I love her eyes. Picture a young Leeza Gibbons and you have a good idea of what my fiancée looks like. Holly's hair is blonde. I'd like it better if she'd grow it out and just tied it back when she's working, but she keeps it cut short instead. Maybe that's something I can get her to change once we're married.

Holly has an adorable button nose and oh-so-kissable lips; they're pouty, but not a collagen injection disaster. She gets her eyebrows waxed in a way that really accentuates her eyes. I think her eyes, eyelids and eyebrows are her best features. Did I mention that already? Sorry, I guess I'm fixated. As you have pointed out on more than one occasion, Doctor, I have a tendency to obsess.

See there? A bit of self-recognition. I have been paying attention during our sessions!

But back to my fiancée.

I don't mean to brag, but Holly has a great body too. *Now* she does, anyway. When she first started working for me here at Carlton, she had some extra pounds on her. Not morbidly obese; just chubby. Not anymore, though! Now I'd say she's smoking hot.

I remember one evening, as we cleaned up a high school kid who'd been ejected from his pickup during a rollover, Holly asked me what one characteristic about her I would change if I could. I guess lots of guys would have made the smart response by saying, 'Nothing.' I told her point blank that she could stand to lose about twenty or thirty pounds. She didn't get mad or fall to pieces over it; just went about her work without another word on the subject. Afterward, I felt bad about it, but she didn't bring it up again, so neither did I.

For a long time, my sense of professionalism kept me from making any moves on her. I've never been a guy who condones romantic entanglements at work. Not with the staff, not with the families, and definitely not with the clients. That's a joke, by the way. We had gone to dinner a few times, but I could never quite bring myself to proposition her, much less propose. A quiet, but insistent, voice in the back of my head kept finding things wrong with her looks or her personality. Don't get me wrong, I *wanted* to be attracted to her, but traits like her weight had a negative impact on me.

I realize I must sound shallow, but look at it this way: if you were five-foot-two and your prom date was six feet tall, would it make you feel uncomfortable? Of course it would. Now imagine spending the rest of your life in a situation like that. That's how it was with Holly and me. Now, I know what you're thinking: I'm fixating on one characteristic and obsessing over it. I'm trying to work on that, I swear. That's why I'm talking to you now.

Professionally speaking, Holly has progressed in her skill level as an apprentice to the point where she has less than six months to go before she earns her license. Then I'd like to make her a full partner. Here at the funeral home, I mean, but I suppose you could say that phrase applies in our personal life, too. Sometimes our professional and personal lives overlap. There was one time—and I do want to stress that it was one time *only*—where things spiraled out of control, and our personal life invaded the sanctity of this room.

It was a warm spring evening, just a few months after we had started dating. We'd completed embalming a stroke victim, and had transported the casket upstairs to the chapel for a late evening viewing. Since another funeral director would be overseeing the viewing, Holly and I returned to wash up before heading home. I guess we both had spring fever, because I found myself kissing her at the cleanup sink. She kissed me back and we both let ourselves get swept up in the moment. She said, "Come over here; I want to show you something." I followed her to one of the mortuary cots and she positioned herself on it so that her head hung down off the back of it. Then she directed me to unzip, and she...

Sorry, Doctor. There's a lot more I could tell, but I don't think it would be appropriate. Suffice it to say that my bride-to-be is not hindered by any gag reflex, if you catch my drift. That's a rare and cherished quality, in my opinion.

But enough of that subject.

You'd be appalled at the state of some of the cadavers that we see roll in here. Embalming requires a balance of art and science, and you have to possess a strong stomach for this kind of work, believe me. After a few bad car accidents or burn victims, you develop a stomach of steel. Holly was a natural from day one. She never had to leave the room, no matter what the state of the cadaver was.

The same can be said for me, although to a lesser extent. It depends on the situation. For instance, Holly's strong stomach extends to mealtime too. Me? I'm a burger and fries kind of guy. Or steak and potatoes, if we're dining fancy. But Holly goes for all kinds of nasty stuff I'd never touch. You know that sushi bar that opened a few months ago on Mason Lane? My fiancée loves it. Who in their right mind eats raw fish wrapped in seaweed? I find it disgusting. She watches that show on cable with the guy who travels all over the world eating bizarre food. I get so grossed out I have to leave the room.

Talking about that reminds me of the time we almost ran for the door here at work. It was the only time I can remember where we got rattled while processing a cadaver. Now that I think about it, that day marked a turning point in our relationship. Mostly for the good, but sometimes I wonder.

The deceased had died of natural causes. Her name was Minnie Markowitz, and she was one hundred and four years old when she died. But the reason I bring up her age is because Holly and I got to talking about it as we worked. Minnie's sixty-year-old grandson, who was writing the check for everything, nearly talked my ear off as we filled out paperwork and made the final arrangements. According to him, Minnie had been something of a sex symbol in her day. She'd started as a burlesque dancer, moved to acting in films when 'talkies' were new, and had gone on to star in several Broadway shows. He told me her stage name, and if I told you, you'd probably recognize her. Unfortunately, the details slip my mind.

Even after Minnie finally retired from acting, she didn't stay out of the limelight. Her slender figure was legendary, and as long as she kept it, Minnie still made plenty of television and public appearances. But she was more than just a celebrity. She got involved in charity work, took an interest in politics and championed a number of humanitarian causes.

I got all this from her grandson as he sat reminiscing in my office. It's something I always let the clients do. It helps with the grieving process. Anyway, he talked about how her mind was still sharp, but that she had slowed down noticeably near the end. He said she felt weaker and more exhausted with each passing day. He told me that Minnie admitted that she 'couldn't stay ahead of it anymore'. At the time, I thought that was her way of saying she couldn't keep up with the pace of life. I found out I was wrong.

I unzipped the black bag containing the late Minnie Markowitz and looked her over. Wrinkles had made a road map of her face, but otherwise she was still a beautiful and regal looking woman, even at one hundred and four. Her clothing and personal effects had already been removed and inventoried.

Holly smiled to herself as she lifted Minnie's eyelids to check her corneas for clouding. I placed a modesty cloth across our subject's lap and asked Holly what was so funny.

"Nothing," she said. "I'm just impressed that she lived to such a ripe old age and she doesn't look half bad."

"Chalk that up to the old 'Everything in moderation, including moderation' philosophy," I said. "According to her grandson, Minnie drank, smoked, and ate like a horse right up to the end."

"Good for you, honey." Holly told the cadaver as she started washing it with disinfectant solution.

The arterial embalming went smoothly and after that we started the cavity embalming procedure. Holly stepped away for a moment and changed the CD. She gave an impish grin as the soft piano of Ravel's *Pavane Pour Une Infante Defunte* filled the room. I rolled my eyes at the irony of her selection.

Holly defended her choice. "Hey, this one's for Minnie. Young at heart till the end."

I grinned and selected a scalpel from the tray. I made a small incision about two inches above Minnie's navel. Then I attached a trocar to the end of a suction hose, turned the water on and began the process of removing gas, fluids and semisolids from the body cavities.

I punctured Minnie's lungs and stomach and aspirated their contents without incident. None of Minnie's internal organs had been removed because no autopsy had been performed. The doctor on call at the hospital when Minnie died had stuck with a safe assumption of 'natural causes' on the hospital certificate. I had moved on to her intestines when the trocar struck something substantial and the hose jerked and bucked as it encountered resistance. Surprised, I set the instrument aside. I wanted to take a closer look at what could be causing the obstruction.

I used a pair of forceps to hold the incision open and leaned in for a closer view. Something slid away from my touch, deeper into the small intestine. I jerked my head back and hit the overhead lamp, sending it swinging. I palmed the back of my head and grimaced, more out of surprise than real pain. Holly stared at me with eyes widened and mouth hanging open and I felt my cheeks redden. Neither of us spoke. Something had slithered away from my forceps. It was dirty white, almost yellowish. And it was large. My mind formed a mental picture of an inflated condom, slick with mucus and unaccountably mobile. I saw what I thought were scales, though I later realized my error.

I grabbed the scalpel from the tray and made another incision further down in the cadaver's lower intestine. In my zeal, it was more like a gash than an incision. The lining of Minnie's intestine opened to reveal the undulating yellowish form. It moved rapidly with spasmodic jerks. I heard Holly gasp, but didn't look up.

Then it hit me: a *tapeworm*. It had to be, though I'd never seen—or even heard of—a specimen that large. Not in length, but in girth. I hope this isn't too upsetting, Doctor Mayes. We could move on to other topics. No? Then with your permission, I'll continue.

I used the forceps to grab the parasite and temporarily arrest its progress. It must have sensed danger and twitched forward. I clenched my fingers in an attempt at holding the creature stationary. The tapeworm tore itself free from my grip, and I was left with several feet of inert segmented tissue. If you're surprised, don't be. This was nothing but the tail end.

Tapeworms are amazing creatures. For instance, a beef tapeworm has the capacity to grow between twenty and thirty feet long, but they're extremely slender. Think of those long balloons used to twist into balloon animals. Tapeworms are even thinner and more delicate. The one that lived inside Minnie Markowitz was different. That one was, as I said earlier, much thicker. I used a condom as a reference, and I stand by that description. The parasite's appearance astonished me. I am quite certain that the tapeworm ended Minnie's life. The idea of that gargantuan vampire sucking the life out of her from within is appalling, to say the least. No wonder her grandson said she 'ate like a horse.' The poor woman was fighting to survive!

I decided to try to contain the tapeworm and then contact the biology department at one of the local universities. Surely this specimen would be of particular biological interest. "Help me flush it out," I instructed.

"What the hell is it?" Holly asked. She didn't move.

"It's a tapeworm, an abnormally large one," I explained. "If we can remove it intact, maybe we'll get our names in a medical journal or two."

"A tapeworm?" Holly didn't sound convinced.

"Damned thing sucked her dry," I said. "No wonder she was skin and bones."

Holly took a step closer, curiosity apparently getting the better of her. As I pondered my next move the tapeworm made my ruminations unnecessary. It had reached the end of the line and, having nowhere else to go in its flight from my forceps, started pushing its way out the cadaver's anus. I stared at the whitish knob-like head as it hung stationary for a moment and became aware of a shrill, girlish scream. I realized the sound emanated from me and shut my mouth. I felt my cheeks burning as Holly's eyes darted between my face and the tapeworm, which by then dangled close to the floor.

"Don't touch it, but don't let it get away either," I called over my shoulder as I sped across the room to the utility closet. I realized I was contradicting myself, but I'm not great at thinking under pressure. I threw open the door and grabbed the mop and bucket we use to disinfect the floors. I discarded the mop itself, which landed with a clatter and kicked the bucket toward the cot. Holly stopped the rolling bucket with her hands, tipped it sideways and lowered one edge under the tapeworm's head right before it touched the floor. The creature continued to un-spool from Minnie into the bucket while Holly and I watched in horrified fascination.

I realized we would need something to cover the top of the bucket so the specimen couldn't escape. I glanced around the room and, finding nothing that would suit my purposes, bolted for the stairs.

"Where are you going?" Holly called after me.

"To find something to cover it with!" I replied. Then I ran upstairs.

I raced around the building like a crazy person, but had no luck finding anything I thought would effectively hold such a lengthy creature. I finally rushed back downstairs, intending to flip the bucket over and cover it with something heavy as a last resort.

I re-entered the embalming room to find Holly kneeling on the floor, one hand covering her mouth in obvious dismay.

"What happened?" I asked.

Holly swallowed hard then squeaked, "It got away." She pointed down the drainage grate in the floor. "It was so aggressive, Bill! I tried to hold it in the bucket…"

I realized it had fled to a more hospitable location and shuddered as I imagined the tapeworm growing back to its original length—and perhaps longer—inside a new host.

I stepped forward and peered through the slits in the grate at the darkness. I felt disappointed that the tapeworm had escaped. And I know my emotion showed on my face, because Holly looked sick, like she was afraid I blamed her.

"This is bad," I said, shaking my head solemnly. "Someday someone patrolling the sewers will come across an anorexic alligator."

I gave Holly a broad grin then, to put her at ease. I hugged her, since she still seemed pretty upset, and assured her that everything was fine. I sent her home while I finished on Minnie myself.

Everything *was* fine, at least on the surface. But it was weird, too, because I felt emasculated. Does that sound strange to you, Doctor? I was called upon to be the hero and felt like I came up short. I ran out of the room. I wasn't running away, you understand, but I wasn't *there*. Did Holly think that I chickened out and used finding a cover as an excuse to run away? She said she never thought that, but how can I know for sure? Maybe she just wanted to spare my feelings.

That night became a turning point for me.

I felt like less than a man around Holly, so I no longer flirted with her. I kept our talk focused on work. When she asked me why I acted so cold toward her all of a sudden, I gave her a line about deciding it would be best if we kept our relationship professional.

Our lives continued for a while under a cloud of unhappiness. It was as if everything in the world had faded somehow. The sky seemed gray even on sunny days, but I maintained my stubborn facade of indifference.

It didn't last, as I'm sure you have already gathered. After a couple of months I noticed a change in Holly's appearance. She looked thinner, more fit. She started tanning. Not too much, but just enough. She got a cute new haircut and added a few eye-catching pieces to her wardrobe. She looked more gorgeous than ever, and she knew it.

And yet I still tried to deny my feelings. But then one day I entered the embalming room to find Holly wearing only a bra and panties and lying on one of the mortuary cots. The sight triggered a rush of memories and I just stood there flat-footed. My mind whirled. My former lover gave me a knowing smile and slid so that her head hung over the edge of the cot. It was the position she had used to achieve such memorable results in happier times.

"We were so good for each other," Holly purred. "I miss you so much and I love you more than ever. I'll do anything to make this work. Look at my body, Bill, aren't I what you want?

She arched her back. I threw in the towel.

That brings us to now. I'm engaged to the most gorgeous woman in the world. I agree with her when she says we're perfect for one another. I should be grinning from ear to ear and skipping around instead of moping over my predicament.

But here's where you can be of assistance. You are now in a unique position, Doctor Mayes. You'll be able to examine Holly at close quarters.

You see, there's something that's bothering me, something that's been keeping me awake at night. Sex? Forget it. I've been as limp as boiled spaghetti lately. Holly thinks its just nerves and that everything will be okay after the wedding. She's wrong. The problem I have—this mental stumbling block as you might refer to it—hinges on one question.

Knowing the situation as I've just explained it to you, and knowing what's at stake here, I'd like your professional opinion one last time. I can't help but wonder what lengths a woman with no gag reflex might go to in order to stay with the man she loves. I don't want to marry a crazy person.

But let's talk about you for a moment. Your family has my deepest sympathies, of course. You will be pleased to know that if I can overcome one key hurdle, I should be able to present you in an open casket for your memorial.

Was it the trailer of the big rig or the top of your convertible's windshield that beheaded you? It probably happened so fast that you aren't even sure. No matter. We can use your current state to our advantage; I'll position your head here at the top of the cot where you can observe the proceedings. We'll reattach it later in the embalming process.

Holly should be here soon to help me embalm you and prepare you for burial. She'll wash your body with disinfectant first so you'll have ample opportunity to look her over before we begin the arterial embalming.

Here, let me prop your eyes open. There we go. Before we part ways, I must have your professional opinion.

There should be enough time for you to make an assessment. Once you've seen her, Doctor Mayes, maybe you can help me decide once and for all:

Did Holly manage to swallow the tapeworm while I was gone?

Adrian Ludens is the author of the short story collections *When Bedbugs Bite*, and *Bedtime Stories for Carrion Beetles*, and is an Active member of the Horror Writers Association. Recent and upcoming publication appearances include: *D.O.A. III* (Blood Bound Books), *The Prison Compendium* (EMP Publishing), *Dark Horizons* (Elder Signs Press), and the weird western novelette *Bottled Spirits* (Grinning Skull Press). Adrian is a fan of hockey, music, reading, and exploring abandoned buildings. Visit him at adrianludens.com.

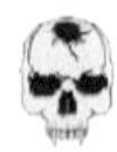

Road to Hell

Gary Power

"It's a gullorrrious Friday afternoon, and it seems everyone is taking to the roads for the big drive home. The M25 is busy but moving, a few holdups around junction 6, so why don't you let the radio take the strain and listen to the relaxing vibes on..."

Anthony Lerrom, disgraced MP, now media star, picked up his mobile phone while recklessly cutting across three motorway lanes and maneuvering his brand-new BMW Z4 3-litre sports car into the fast lane of the world's biggest ring road. With his attention away from the traffic, he selected the number of his agent and mentor, media publicist Rex Splifford.

"Yeah... yeah... breaking up a bit. Traffic's slow. Just going past Clacket Lane Services. Should be in Brighton about five-ish. Phone the station and say I left late from a kids' charity or something like that, something that makes me sound good. You know I'm worth it, Rexy. If you don't, just think of your ten percent," he added smugly, and tossed the phone onto the passenger seat without waiting for an answer.

"Now let's get this show on the road," he said to himself, while scanning the three lanes ahead. Rock music erupted from the speakers as he slipped in a CD, put on his pince-nez sunglasses and pushed his foot to the floor. Thirty grand's worth of finely tuned metal surged satisfyingly ahead. Drivers watched incredulously as he moved from lane to lane, cutting in tightly on other cars without indicating or giving space. He laughed at their reactions, at the same time making snide remarks about their sad lives and pathetic cars.

Anthony Lerrom was heading for yet another lucrative radio interview. No doubt there would be the usual questions about his various indiscretions—mainly his three-in-a-bed escapades so eloquently revealed for a hefty five-figure sum by kiss-and-tell bimbette Rebecca Fleece.

"Bitch," he snapped, as he used the slow lane to accelerate past a couple of lorries before swerving wildly back to the fast lane. Then he laughed at the irony of it all. It was the best thing that had ever happened to him, a blessing in disguise—and the sex had been mind-blowing. His political career had not brought the power and money that he had so desperately yearned for, and public awareness of over-inflated expenses had seriously curtailed his lifestyle. Most politicians were the same, with their mistresses and deviant practices; corruption, in all of its guises, was endemic. The difference was, he got caught out. There'd be a bit of mileage in bringing others down, though. He'd use that if the coffers began to dry up. And then there was always the book. He'd find a way of getting back at all those so-called colleagues who'd dropped him like a brick at the mere sniff of controversy.

"Bastards!" he growled. Then he smiled, and admired himself in the rear-view mirror while reflecting on life post-politics. He didn't see the balding, round-faced and slightly goofy man looking back; he saw more of a Keanu Reeves with maturity, a sort of people's Neo.

Now he appeared on quiz shows and media programs for extortionate fees. He'd even made the C-list as a guest on Parky—the one that comes on first as a prelude to bigger celebrities; that made him laugh out loud. Good old media publicist Rex Splifford had turned public perception of Lerrom from utter scumbag to likeable rogue. He turned up the music and rocked his head to and fro. A pounding heavy-metal beat blended perfectly with his manic driving. He changed gears and lanes like a rally driver. So people flashed and sounded their horns;

so what? By the time they'd cursed his superior driving ability, he'd left them for dust.

A subtle change in direction brought stark sunlight straight into his eyes. No problem. He flipped down his visor and turned his head away. Someone else sounded their horn as his car veered across the lane lines; the intrusive sound lasted for several seconds. He looked and saw an infuriated man in a sad little family car, surrounded by his wife and several overactive children. His wife was shouting at the children and turning her anger on her husband. Now the man was looking to vent his own frustration on Lerrom by hurling abuse at him. He'd pulled alongside and seemed to be gesticulating threats of extreme violence to certain parts of his anatomy; not the sort of behaviour to be displaying in front of his kids, thought Lerrom; have to teach him a lesson. He wagged his finger and swerved back into the middle lane, almost taking the front end of his car off. The man braked sharply and nearly lost control. Anthony watched with amusement as the boring family shrieked with terror.

"Losers," he mouthed, and then pressed metal to the floor. The family man and his pitiful car, that was no doubt bought on absurdly overpriced credit, soon became a mere speck in his rear view mirror.

He turned the CD up another notch. "Born toooo beeeee wild…" he howled, as he thumped the steering wheel in time to the booming bass line.

The day was glorious, and so was his life. The cloudless sky lifted his spirits. Doof, doof, doof went the music as he reminisced on how his life had changed so drastically. He'd been in a mind-numbing marriage with two spoilt and bleating kids. He'd been mortgaged up to his eyeballs, and was endlessly knocked down by his parliamentary peers as he tried to carve some kind of career in what had to be the most unscrupulous profession in the world. Now he had meaningless sex with airheaded beauties and made mountains of money catering to the public's inexhaustible demand for dirt. He was paid huge sums for talking about his colourful life and being a 'character'. Now he was on his way to a radio interview with Brighton's premier radio station. He had a nice little room lined up in the Hotel Pelirocco, a themed hotel on the seafront where he was meeting a couple of women from a previous evening's liaison in a dingy Soho bar.

Life just didn't get better than this.

But time was getting on, traffic was slowing and he was getting impatient. He still had a fair distance to go, and the interview was going to be a pain in the backside, but it would be paying for a night of drunken debauchery; he just couldn't be too late. Now was the time to up the ante. He scanned the road ahead and saw three lanes filled with traffic, but there was plenty of opportunity if he became a little more ruthless.

"Time to rock and roll," he said, and swerved wildly into the fast lane. He overtook three cars, switched back to the middle lane, made a bit more ground there, but found himself struggling to get back into the fast lane. They'd probably seen his tactics and closed ranks. No problem. Into the slow lane and make a bit more headway, then the master stroke. He accelerated onto the hard shoulder for at least a ten-car lead and then took a sharp, weaving turn across several cars and three lanes, manoeuvring himself back into the fast lane.

Nothing in front of him now.

He whooped with joy and turned the music up even more. The next few miles were driving bliss, a hundred and ten miles an hour of heavy-metal heaven.

Then came the next hurdle. Several lorries spread across the whole motorway loomed ahead.

"Shit," he growled. But he was on a roll; adrenaline was pumping, and his pulse was racing. Some flashy driving would soon put them behind him. He cut and swerved his way through the lumbering convoy, and in doing so received an even louder volley of abuse and headlight flashing. Getting through was harder than he'd expected. To add insult, the cars that he'd previously overtaken were making ground on him. He moved back onto the hard shoulder, a bit risky with all the motorway cameras around, but hey, that would just make another lucrative story. He'd launch a scathing attack on speed cameras and maybe criticize traffic wardens for good measure. "The bad boy just got badder," he growled as he throttled his way through the HGV jungle.

A fleeting glance of clearer lanes in the distance raised his hopes. He cut in between two lorries, leaving literally inches between them, then did the same in the next lane. A whole chorus of claxon horns blitzed his ears, but Lerrom was riding on an adrenaline high. He was moving from one slick manoeuvre to another, and could almost taste the freedom of open road. One more outing onto the hard shoulder should do it, but a juggernaut anticipated his actions and blocked his path, preventing him from overtaking. "Bastard," he snapped. "So you want to play games, eh?"

He slammed on his brakes, cut to the rear of the lorry, and saw his chance. A diagonal dash in front of a petrol tanker in the middle lane would see him clear. There was just enough room.

But he didn't see the motorbike.

He didn't see the damned motorbike.

There was a clash of metal and an enormous crash. The bike slewed sideways into the tanker, and the rider disappeared under its wheels. The juggernaut tried to move away, but a tyre blew and sent it careering into the path of the tanker. Anthony braked again and backed away from the two huge vehicles, but caught sight in his rear-view mirror of another lorry closing in at breakneck speed. It was obviously out of control, having tried to avoid the mangled body of the motorcyclist. Behind it, cars were ramming into each other. Everyone was trying to avoid crashing, but a massive pileup was inevitable, and Lerrom was in the thick of it.

To his horror, the petrol tanker suddenly rolled over. *They don't explode,* he thought as he watched it tumbling across the tarmac like a dinky toy. *They're made that way. They just crash, they don't explode*, he told himself.

But this one did. It exploded in the biggest ball of fire that he'd ever seen. For a moment there was a blistering blaze of colour and light and the most appalling cacophony of sound. That was it, he thought. His time had come. Flames surrounded him and raised the temperature to an unbearable degree. Bits of wreckage flew by the windows, but by some miracle he avoided collision. The car entered a boiling black cloud of burning oil, and suddenly Lerrom found himself plunged into complete darkness. For a few heart-stopping seconds he was driving blind, and then, with plumes of smoke curling away like massive curtains, he emerged from the conflagration onto three clear lanes of unfettered motorway.

He didn't stop. In fact he went faster; he just couldn't get away quick enough.

He looked in his rear view mirror and saw an image of complete and utter devastation. It was like driving away from an apocalyptic explosion. Nothing could survive that, he thought. Then again, there wouldn't be anyone to point the finger of blame at him.

Soon he'd be on the radio, though. People would be asking questions. He needed a story, and had to think quickly. He'd get to the radio station a hero for surviving such an awful catastrophe. Some mad bloke on a motorbike overtook him and cut straight into the path of the tanker, he'd say. He, of course, had been driving sensibly. Who wouldn't with a car like his? He even tried to flash the motorbike to slow down, he'd add. Maybe he'd get choked up and shed a few tears—show a human side. He'd say he had a premonition that it was going to happen and tried to warn people. Splifford would back him up on that one, especially if it meant more money. That would be a blinding story, one for the chat shows. That would probably get him on Richard and Judy; they loved heroic people with death-defying stories.

"Jesus!" he shouted—he was so damned lucky. Even God wanted him to stay alive. His heart was pounding and his body drenched in sweat. He took several deep breaths and shook his head. A guardian angel was definitely at his shoulder, and hey, there were two gorgeous fillies waiting for him in his own little fantasy room in Brighton. He'd become the man who dodged death, he mused. That would double his appearance fee, at least.

He glanced briefly in his rear-view mirror again and saw a hellish cloud of smoke spreading across the clear blue sky. "Poor bastards," he muttered, as he thought of the people that had perished in the pileup. He was inconsolable for almost a minute. He closed his eyes and shook his head, then he pulled a beer from the glove compartment and opened it on the dash mounted opener that he'd had fitted just under the fascia. Such was his compassion that he even raised the bottle to those now departed.

It wasn't long before a traffic bulletin announced the complete closure of the M25 at a location close to Clacket Lane Services. The crash was worse than he'd imagined. Estimated figures were of up to 50 dead, and countless injuries. There'd even been multiple collisions on the opposite lanes. After a prolonged hiss of static, the report continued: "Disgraced MP Anthony Lerrom has been killed in the M25 pileup," said a gritty voice. ""There have been unsubstantiated claims that his reckless driving was one of the main causes of what is being reported as the worst motorway pileup ever…" and then the report fizzled out. Anthony stabbed the presets of his radio but all he got was deafening static.

"I'm not bloody well dead!" he shrieked in disbelief. As he carried on with his journey, it occurred to him just how deserted the M25 was. There was no traffic in either direction. And that wasn't all. The light outside had taken on a surreal, pinkish hue; it was as though he'd driven into an episode of the Twilight Zone. He drove on a bit further at a more sedate pace while he tried to work things out. "Rex!" he said to himself. "He'll know what's going on." But all he got on his mobile was the same rasping hiss that had come from the radio. It was as though the outside world had ceased to exist.

He stopped and, leaving the engine running, got out.

There was nothing. No sound, no breeze. Just a perfect stillness and an eerie silence.

"What the *fuck* is going on?" he said.

He lit a cigarette and tried to work it out. The westbound lanes were empty, that made sense, but nothing in the opposite direction? That just couldn't be.

The UK's busiest ring road? Friday afternoon?

He flicked the barely smoked cigarette into the air and got back into his car. With a roar of his engine, he turned at speed and drove the wrong way up the motorway, back towards the pile up. The CD player still worked—that was some consolation—and he could see a boiling cauliflower cloud of smoke in the distance. For some reason that made him feel better. His heart sank as he got closer to the carnage, though. All he could see was a battleground of burnt-out cars and dead bodies. A few of the victims had actually made their way out of the inferno. Smouldering bodies littered the tarmac.

He stopped for a moment and, breathing deeply and slowly, tried to muster the courage to get even closer. He'd caused the carnage. In his heart he knew that he had, but in his head he was still in denial. He looked away and started to panic. His hands began to shake and he began to sweat profusely—he was having a panic attack, and his instincts were telling him to get as far away as he could get, as quickly as possible. Some tiny part of him (the last tiny vestige of civilized human part) told him to stay and help—to face up to the consequences of his actions.

The tiny part lost.

Without further thought he jumped back into his car, shoved it into gear and put his accelerator foot to the floor. The BMW lurched forwards and stalled. "Bastard car!" he snapped, and tried again. This time the engine didn't even turn over. The windscreen was sprayed with phlegm as he vehemently declared that his beloved car was in fact a "useless pile of shit". And when, after several attempts, he finally conceded that the engine was simply not going to start, he proceeded to get out and stomp on his mobile phone in a fit of vented fury.

For a while he just stood in seething silence and glared into space. When finally his frustration started to ebb, it dawned on him that, despite the devastation, there was a curious serenity about the situation. There were no emergency services present. No wail of sirens or people in fluorescent jackets running about like you see on TV. There weren't even any survivors crawling from the mangled wrecks. He looked closer and thought he saw a solitary figure sitting on a crash barrier. Shading his eyes, he took a closer look. A man was staring back at him. He could see him with surprising clarity despite the distance. The man was smiling at him; in fact, he was almost gloating. He was perched on the barrier and hunched over like a big black crow. His clothes looked seriously dated, like a 40s demob suit.

Things were getting just a little too weird now.

"Bugger this for a lark," said Lerrom, and he turned back to his car… except it wasn't there anymore.

"What the hell?" His words drifted into silence as he looked around. It was nowhere to be seen. His beloved babe magnet had disappeared into thin air. He felt a sinking feeling in the pit of his stomach as his mind tried desperately to find a rational explanation.

There wasn't one. Unless going mad was a rational explanation.

He could be dreaming. That was a possibility. But when he pinched his skin, when he rubbed his eyes and slapped his face, the sensation of pain was all too real. He took a deep breath and shouted at the man.

"What's going on?" he screamed. "What the fuck is happening around here?"

The man made a gesture. He was beckoning Lerrom over, and had that "I know something you don't" look on his face. Lerrom couldn't stand people being more smug than him—that really pissed him off.

"Tosser," he muttered. What else could he do but go and see what the freak had to say though? There was no other option. But as he got closer, he became aware of the gut-wrenching stench of barbecued people. He retched, and pushed a handkerchief to his face. Charred corpses were scattered all around. There were women and children barely recognisable as humans. Clothes were burnt from flesh and flesh from bone. Some were stuck in poses of panic and desperation, others were holding each other in final affirmation of love. One poor soul had managed to crawl onto the hard shoulder before curling up to die in a foetal position. His body was still smoking. A mobile phone was melted into his hand and pressed against the charcoaled remains of his ear. "Wouldn't want to have been on the receiving end of that call," thought Anthony.

Lerrom felt sick. He *was* sick. He leaned forwards, grabbed his knees and retched up whatever was in his stomach. When he finally stopped, he heard the man tutting. That made him even more angry. He looked up and glared through bloodshot eyes and hurled a volley of abuse towards his smug observer. The man merely chuckled. Lerrom clenched his fists and moved closer, but something in the man's eyes stopped him.

"Reckon you should be worried and not angry," said the man calmly; then he looked at the unrecognisable mess of burnt-out cars and lorries. "Ain't never seen anything like this in all my 65 years here."

"Who are you?" demanded Lerrom, and then, when the man didn't answer, he took a deep breath and asked more calmly, "What's happening here?" There was an almost pathetic tone in his voice now.

"You're half-dead," said the man, "and m'name's Shadrac Wilmsey. You might've read about me if you'd been around half a century ago." Lerrom just stared back at him; there was no answer to that. "The world's goin' on without you, but it ain't lettin' you go jus' yet."

Lerrom sat on the tarmac and put his head into his hands. He *was* going mad. Maybe it was the drugs he'd taken recently; some kind of hallucinatory after-effect.

"You killed a lot of people," said Shadrac, "an' believe me, they're really pissed at you."

Lerrom looked up. "So tell me something that'll cheer me up," he said. The man laughed loudly at that.

"Suffering and torment is all you got waitin' for ya. Those people that you killed; they'll be back for you in a few hours, when they're a little more settled in the afterlife. They have to finish things here before they can move on. They got scores to settle. Wouldn't want to be you, son."

Suddenly Lerrom was filled with panic. He saw the burned bodies and twisted metal, the black clouds and reddened sky, and he found himself gazing into a vision of Hell. He looked at the bizarre man, with his soul-searching eyes and chilling grin, and suddenly he couldn't take anymore. Something inside him snapped. He leapt to his feet and just stood there screaming until his lungs were raw. He tried to run away, but the further he got the more difficult it became to move. It was like trawling his body through a sea of thick syrup. Eventually it became impossible; something was stopping him from leaving. Exhausted, he returned to Shadrac and just glared at him.

"Oh, and there ain't no escape," cackled the old man.

"So why are you here?" he demanded.

"Pretty much for the same reasons as you. I caused an accident. Only killed a couple of people, though. I sorted it out with them when they came back for me. Wasn't really my fault. A burst tyre sent me careering into their car, and they left the road. Course it was just a small road here in fifty-four, not a motorway. I'll have to hang around here for a couple o' hundred years, probably, 'til I've paid my penance, that is."

"So what's going to happen to me?" asked Lerrom.

"You really want to know?"

"Just tell me, you stupid old fuck," he snapped back.

"Okay, seein's you asked so nicely. You'll be torn limb from limb. You'll have your eyes pushed into the back of your head and your tongue ripped from your mouth…wanna hear more?"

"Hah! That can't happen," said Lerrom, "not if I'm already dead." He was really losing it now. He laughed as though he'd caught Shadrac out, but his mirth was borderline hysteria, and there was a wild look in his eyes.

"*Half* dead," replied the man, "that's a whole lot different: you still feel pain—worse, really, 'cause you can't be killed again, so you suffer longer. Believe me, I've heard men tougher than you screamin' for their mothers for hours. I have to walk away sometimes. If people knew what was gonna happen to them, then I reckon they'd drive like saints for as long as they could drive." He shook his head and gently rubbed the stubble on his chin. "Reckon this must be one of the worst crashes ever."

Lerrom suddenly realised he'd heard the man before. He recognised the gritty tone of his voice. It had been on the radio.

"That was you," he said. "You were the one that said I'd been killed in the crash."

"So you heard it," he said, almost surprised. "Yeah, that was me, tryin' to make contact with the real world. Guess I can do it after all. Hah!" he uttered, and he rubbed his hands together like a gleeful child.

"How did you know my name?"

"How couldn't I? You were driving like a man possessed for ages. I'd been watching you and waiting for the inevitable. Us ghosts see an' know everything, y'know."

Lerrom shook his head and looked around. Light was fading; night was approaching fast.

Shadrac saw the fear in his eyes..

"That's when they come," he said. "At night."

"You're enjoying this, aren't you?"

"Not really; but it passes the time for me. Wish I could help, if truth be told. Nobody deserves what's gonna happen to you. Not even if they have caused the deaths of so many. Women and children, too. S'ppose you didn't want to do that. But you should have been a bit more considerate. Shouldn't take all your frustrations out in a fast car. Bit of thought would have changed the fate of a lot of good people."

Lerrom heard a strange sound. A sort of distant hum that was dark and ominous.

"That's them," said the man. "Quicker than usual. Reckon you must have killed more than I initially thought."

Night was falling quickly now. There was a blood-red swell on the horizon, and a cold drizzle in the air.

"Think I'll take my distance. Not sure I can watch this one."

"Don't you care?" pleaded Lerrom. "Can't you help me?"

Now there was desperation in his voice. He was sobbing as he spoke.

"Truth?" said the man. Lerrom looked back through begging, tear-filled eyes.

"Yeah. That's why I've got to get away. I'll say one thing, though. If you get a chance to be really sorry… 'cause sometimes us half-deads do… then think on it."

He climbed over the central reservation onto the opposite motorway, and ambled off into the distance, moving quickly despite his slow pace. Eventually his body became a silhouette that shimmered briefly and then disappeared completely.

For a while Anthony just sat on the tarmac and sobbed with his head bowed into his hands. He couldn't run or hide. All he could do was wait. Wait for whatever Shadrac had warned him of. But he felt so alone… and so utterly terrified.

The resonant drone of impending doom was growing louder in his ears. He looked up, but all he could see was a darkened battleground of wrecked vehicles.

Then he saw the eyes, like tiny red beacons of light burning in the darkness. They were just beyond the crash site, but they were getting closer. Lerrom scrabbled backwards. He got to his feet and put as much distance between himself and the approaching hordes as he could, but, as he'd found out before, trying to escape was futile. Exhausted by his attempts, he collapsed onto the ground. The drone grew louder. The glaring eyes became brighter. And then he saw their bodies clambering over the wreckage. At first he thought they were silhouetted against the sky, but as they got closer he saw just how terribly burned and disfigured they were. He saw their burnt faces and their angry, seething expressions. There were men and women. There were children and even babies crawling towards him.

"No," he said, and he shut his eyes tightly. "Please, God, no," he begged. He put his hands together and prayed for forgiveness. "When I open my eyes," he stuttered, "please… please let them be gone. I'll be nice to people. I'll… I'll drive sensibly. I'll give money to charity and… and go to church… occasionally."

The droning stopped.

He breathed slowly.

He breathed deeply.

"Please God please God please God…" he muttered again and again, "Please God, let them be gone."

And then he opened his eyes.

But they were still there.

Close enough for him to reach out and touch. Close enough for him to smell the fetid stench of death that he'd forced upon them. Close enough for him to see the livid flesh that had been stripped from their battered bodies. He saw hundreds of eyes glowing like candles. He saw stark white teeth glaring at him from behind charred and burnt lips. He saw impassioned expressions of rage and fury that struck fear into his heart.

Together they screamed in anger and reached out towards him. They lunged and lurched forwards until he was buried beneath a scrabbling mound of living corpses. He felt them scratching and tearing at his flesh, and he screamed the scream of a man who was going to suffer for eternity.

And then as the world became a black and terrible place, he heard a familiar voice.

"It's a gullorrrious Friday afternoon, and it seems that everyone's taking to the roads…" said the man on the radio. And it was a glorious day. Anthony Lerrom, disgraced MP, shook his head and looked at the cloudless sky, and remembered that he was heading towards Brighton for a radio interview and a night of debauchery with a couple of busty wannabes.

He'd been day-dreaming; but what a daydream. He was still shaking with fear. He'd popped some pills in a Soho nightclub the previous night. Must have been something weird in them, he thought. He had vague recollection of… of a huge crash… and a strange man… and horrendously burned bodies attacking him. The feeling of deja vu was so intense. He made a quick call to Rex Splifford on his mobile, much to the disdain of other drivers, then he tossed the phone onto the passenger seat and put his foot to the floor. Just fleetingly, he thought he saw a curiously-dressed man perched on the crash barrier that separated the opposing lanes of the motorway.

"If you get a chance to be really sorry… then act on it," said a voice in his head.

Where on earth did that come from? he wondered.

He even slowed his speed a little, and started behaving like a considerate driver. Then he laughed to himself. The day was great and so was he, and it was only going to get better.

Just a stupid dream, he thought. And the strange man with his portentous warning was nothing more than a mental apparition.

He put his foot down again. He weaved in and out of the traffic. He used the hard shoulder to overtake other vehicles. People flashed their headlights at him and sounded their horns. He dismissed them all as idiots. He saw lorries ahead, but they wouldn't stop him. He saw a chance to get through, and accelerated hard. He was going to make it. Just the petrol tanker now. His heart pounded with excitement as adrenalin flooded through his body.

Then he saw the motorbike.

Gary Power's short stories have been published in terrifying anthologies such as *When Graveyards Yawn*, *Spinetinglers*, BFS nominated *The Black Book of Horror* 7, 9 and 10 (Mortbury Press) and as October's featured writer in *The Horror Zine*. Manor House Audio are in the process of producing 'Flitching's Revenge' as a podcast play.

He is a member of the British Fantasy Society and the Clockhouse London Writers. At your peril visit garygpower.com.

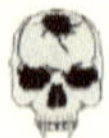

Keeping Score

Jay Wilburn

"I've never heard of this game," Dan said as he reclined on the bed.

He eyed the two dozen roses in the silver vase on the desk at the end of the bed behind her.

Evelyn smiled, "My sister and I made it up."

"Hills and Valleys," Dan repeated as he loosened his tie.

Evelyn nodded. The top of her dress hung down, giving a peek of her breasts, which Dan had only seen twice before their wedding night.

"Eve, playing cards is not what I had planned tonight, you understand."

She laughed, and accepted her new husband leaning up and kissing her hard on her lips and then down her neck. "Oh, I'm sure, but we have room service coming, and I won't be naked when they drop it off."

"We'll see."

He squeezed her immodestly and she laughed again. "There will be plenty of time for that tonight, and every night to come."

"That's what they all say."

She pulled back from his grasp. "That's what all of who says, Daniel Thomas Dorit? Do you have other wives lined up?"

"Stop, Eve. I just mean the other married guys say… nothing. Just pretend I didn't say anything."

"No, Mr. Dorit, pretend your night depends on you explaining."

"Oh, good. I'm in trouble already. I got that over with early. The other fellas say the sex drops off over time. That's all."

"You spend a lot of time talking about other people's sex lives. You talk about me like that?"

"It's not like that, Eve. It's 1928. Women have been voting for almost a decade, driving cars, and cutting their hair short. The rules have changed."

She crossed her arms hiding her chest again. "Disrespect is the new rule?"

Dan sighed and picked up the cards. "Eve, please, it's our wedding night. We are in a grand hotel on the lake on your father's dime. We have pricey room service coming. Let's not fight. Show me how to play Hills and Valleys."

"You're just trying to change the subject."

"Once we are done with room service, I'm going to change the subject on you all night. If you want to play cards, you better teach me to play now, Evelyn Conroy Dorit."

Eve covered her mouth and laughed. "Evelyn Mary Dorit … Conroy sounds like a boy's middle name."

"Your robber baron daddy is not going to like that, Eve."

"Don't call him that … and I don't care what he likes. Mary is his mother's name, that died when he was a boy. He'll want me to keep that."

Dan shuffled the cards once. "My guess is that he would want Evelyn Mary Conroy Dorit … or maybe me to change my name to Conroy. It is 1928."

Eve shook her head. "My father likes you fine. Don't be like that."

"He sent you two dozen roses to let you know he loves you best."

Eve shook her head. "The only way my father knew to show his disapproval of our marriage was to send flowers? Oh, yes, I see the rage now. I hope to see your disapproval regularly, Mr. Dorit."

"Ah, there is the trick, Eve. He wants to bankrupt me by giving you a taste for fine flowers."

"He is an evil genius, it seems."

"Hills and Valleys… this is a collapsing offer, as your father would say."

Eve crossed her arms again, but was smiling. Dan looked her up and down again as he shuffled against the soft spread on the bed.

"So, I'm expected to step up my wifely duties beyond what your other married tramp friends get, but we have to hurry to play one game of cards. I see how this will be."

Dan laughed. "I will play cards with you for years… we'll play the same game continuously."

"It only goes first one to five hundred. There are up to fifty-two points in a round, but they usually split between the players."

"We're playing to a thousand, then."

Eve fanned herself. "Oh, Mr. Dorit, please, you are giving me the vapors."

"Fine. We will play to one million."

Eve laughed. "You really won't be getting much wifely duties, if we do that."

"Oh, we'll take breaks for eating, sleeping, and such."

"And such?" Eve waved her finger at her husband.

"I'm serious," Dan said. "I'll play cards with you every night, and we won't stop keeping score until one million. We are not allowed to pass on to the great by and by until one player reaches the winning score of… one million points."

Eve stared at Dan. Her smile wavered, but only for a moment. Dan would see that waver on her lips in his dreams once he was in prison.

She suggested. "If we are in fact staving off death with this promise, then I say we set the bar at a billion."

"Oh, Dear Eve, I see your one billion and raise you to an even trillion."

He shuffled the cards one last time to punctuate his statement.

Eve shrugged. "Are you sure about that promise, Dear Dan? No one wants to live forever."

"Not forever," Dan set the deck on the bed between them. "Just to one trillion points… fifty-two at a time, I understand."

"Consider it our final vow of our wedding then."

Eve extended her hand. Dan shook it and then kissed her knuckles.

"Why did you invent your own game instead of just playing hearts, spades, or gin?"

Eve dealt out the cards. "My parents didn't think cards were appropriate for ladies. We weren't allowed to learn other games, so we snuck a deck and made up our own."

"Teach me the rules before you run me up on points and I never catch up."

Eve spread the cards out face up on the bed. "Tens, eights, and sixes are hills and connect trails of points. Other number cards are valleys. Face cards are bridges that steal or reassign points and create forks in the trails. Jacks and Aces are collapsing cards that break bridges. Suits or numbers can be used to connect cards in a trail. Once all cards that can be played are played, the opponent gets a point for each card left in the other's hand and then the points are assigned to each player according to the hills and bridges played."

Dan nodded. "I'm ready. I will destroy you at this game."

Eve snorted and covered her mouth and nose with her hand. "That's the spirit, Dear Dan. Once your dreams are dashed, you can always hope for room service to save you."

"I'm hoping for room service, but for different reasons. You'll be needing someone to save you."

Eve pulled a notepad and a fountain pen from the table behind her next to the silver vase and her flowers. She drew a cross on the paper. Above one arm, she wrote a "D." Above the other, she wrote an "E."

"Just shuffle and redeal, Mr. Dorit."

She wrapped her arms around his neck and he winced. She held on anyway and kissed him full on the mouth. He was still wincing when she drew away.

"Is it that painful to see me again, Mr. Dorit?"

"Let's get away from this dock, Eve. All this screaming and chaos is making my head hurt."

They began walking. Other soldiers and sailors embraced wives and strangers for kisses. Streamers and confetti were flying around and off the ship like a parade.

Eve took Dan's hand. "They are just glad to have everyone home. They are glad to be home. I'm glad you are home."

"Not everyone is home."

Eve leaned on his shoulder. "All the more reason to be thankful. Thank God this war is over in Germany and Japan. I was afraid they were going to send you to the Pacific, but the killing is over."

"I had plenty of points… after the injuries. The killing is never over. It slows down… but someone is always being killed. Just not me."

They reached the head of the dock and stopped. The street was fuller than the offloading area.

"Where are your bags, Dan? Your trunk?"

"I didn't bring anything. I don't want anything from this… awful… Where did people get all this damned cut paper? Isn't there rationing?"

"Not anymore… the car is this way."

Dan just stood and stared at the ground with the blare of noise around him. There was a trumpet or a bugle playing in the distance. He closed his eyes.

"Do you want something to eat? We could celebrate four missed birthdays… for both of us. We can get thirty-seven candles and share a cake. We could skip eating and just get… room service. I'll let you change the subject to anything you like, Dear Dan. What's your pleasure?"

Dan kept his eyes closed as Eve held his hand in both of hers. "I want to play cards."

"Really? You are back from war and you want to play cards?"

"Do you remember the score?"

"Of Hills and Valleys? Yes, it is 48,527 to 49,473… just where we left it when you shipped out in forty-two. I looked at the notepad at least once a week."

"That's a long way from a trillion."

Eve stood beside him silently for a long moment. The bugle blurted off tune again. Dan winced. Eve pulled on his arm until he started walking with her toward the car. He kept his eyes closed the entire time she drove him home.

"Deal the cards again."

Eve's hands shook. She tried to blink back the tears, but they fell thick on their flowered tablecloth. Her lips wavered into a grimace that looked like a smile. Her hands shook as she dealt the cards. The grimace quivered and then vanished.

"This one is winner take all… one trillion points for the winning hand."

Eve's nose was clogged as she sniffed and then whispered, "Why, Dan?"

"Just play."

They worked their way through two drops. Dan had to draw on his third turn. Eve's cards fell out of her hand on the table as she tried to play one.

Dan raised the barrel of the gun above the hill she had played on her last turn. "Pick up your cards, Eve."

She began crying and tried to cover her face.

"Pick up your damn cards before I ruin your face and watch it heal slowly where you lie on the floor. Pick them up!"

Eve raked the cards up from the table. She shook as she tried not to spill them again. "I don't understand… Dan?"

"Take your turn, woman."

He did not lower the weapon as he played one-handed.

Dan won on the final card. He stared up at her shaking with her last four cards in her hand. He didn't bother counting. He took the pen and used the point to turn the notebook around so the current cross was upside right for him. He drew one line through his score of 48,548. He wrote out in capital letters: ONE TRILLION.

Dan dropped the pen and smiled. Eve held her four cards and stared at the gun. He turned it away from her and placed the bore against his temple. He was still smiling.

"Dan, don't… whatever this is… shellshock… just don't. Don't do this. Don't leave me again. Don't hurt yourself. Please, don't. Please!"

"Dear Eve, shut up. Don't make the last sound I hear in this world… a crying woman."

He looked down at the paper again and stopped smiling. The gun barrel slid down his cheek and came to rest on the table in his limp hand.

Eve dropped her four cards and reached out for the gun on the table. "Thank God, Dan."

He tightened his grip and lifted it, aiming at her face again.

Dan was sitting on the porch when the police arrived. They had him stand by their car with one patrolman as they went inside. When they came back out, they had the patrolman cuff him and put him into the back of the car. They called for more officers.

Dan licked his lips. Some of the salty splatter on his face got in his mouth. He tried to spit it out twice.

"You spit in this car and I'll crack your skull open."

He licked his lips again and swallowed.

As it got dark, they drove him toward the police station.

"Why did you do it, Dorit? You rattled from the war?"

"The paper faded?"

"What?"

"The score… it vanished right off the page as I was staring at it.

We can't cheat. I should have died over there, but… that cursed game knit me back together one… one painful piece at a time. There's no cheating the vow, you see."

"Save the crazy talk for your lawyer, Dorit. The Conroys are going to have you buried in pieces."

Dorit stared down at his arm in the infirmary bed. He laughed loudly until one of the other prisoners jerked against his restraints in a bed down the ward and cursed Dan into silence.

"So, shut up or I'll shut you up once we're back in the block."

Dan rolled over into his pillow as far as the leather straps holding him to the bed rails would allow. "It took me until 1958 to figure this out. I'll take myself out in pieces."

He flexed his right forearm. The restraint held to the wrist with the bandage over the stump where his hand should have been. It wasn't healing back. The flesh wasn't reattaching the dead limb like on the French beach after the explosion. A new hand wasn't sprouting in its place like some species of lizard or plant.

"I've found the secret… cut away a piece at a time until there is nothing left."

"Shut up, Dorit… I'll make you suffer, if you don't."

"I wish you would… hell, I'll do it for you."

"Just shut up, man."

Dan grunted as he pulled against the leather cuff with his wounded arm. His shoulder joint began to ache. The amputation of his hand wasn't completely healed. He was feeling wetness and pain under the bandage. As his wrist pulled loose from the loop in the strap, the bandage pulled off, revealing the raw stump.

Dan hissed and pressed the arm against his chest as he waited for the throbbing to stop.

He took two slow breaths, and then leaned over to his other wrist and intact hand.

"For now…"

With the extra slack, he was able to close his teeth on the belt for the strap, pulling it away from the connecting loops.

He muttered. "Won't they be surprised when they find me?"

Dan was brought into the visiting room for the first time since his lawyer had met with him and quit, after his second failed suicide in fifty-eight. He had no family or friends inside or outside the prison. Evelyn's sister had died since his arrest, and the next generation of Conroys were not interested in pursuing visits or death penalties for their aunt's killer.

The guards pushed him down into the chair and shackled him to the table through the holes on the top. They pulled at both of his hands to be sure they were locked. As they left him alone in the room, he rolled his ten fingers to try to get the circulation going.

The door on the opposite end of the room opened and Dan's mystery visitor entered. She sat down at the other end of the table. He closed his eyes.

"Dear Dan, you can't even gaze upon your lovely bride? I swallowed my teeth and the bullet on your third shot. They grew right back, and my stomach wasn't right for a week."

He opened his eyes again. "Why are you here?"

"It's visiting hours, Mr. Dorit."

"I'm not permitted visitors since my last murder in fifty-eight."

"Who did you murder, Dan?"

"Myself… almost. They found me unconscious after I cut out my own brain. I had grown everything back. I was unconscious and naked in my own blood in the floor of the infirmary, surrounded by body parts they assumed to belong to a second murder victim they have yet to identify. I've been in solitary ever since."

"What did you tell them about your hand magically growing back?"

"You've been following my work, Eve. They assumed I had faked the injury to get at someone in the infirmary."

"What did they say about the body parts when no-one was missing?"

"I just told them I didn't catch the fella's name, but he had it coming."

Eve actually laughed. "Very funny."

"I've been paying for that joke for years."

Her smile wavered and she looked away as it dropped back into a frown. Dan shivered and had to look away from her mouth, too.

"It's almost my birthday again. We've missed several more since you got back from war."

"What is the date?"

Eve looked hurt. "My birthday is April fifteenth… tax day… remember?"

"I mean, what year?"

Eve's features softened. He still remembered them being torn away by bullets splattering their flowered tablecloth.

"It's 1963."

"Did I miss anything important?"

"A few things, Dear Dan."

"Why are you here? How?"

"I healed just like you did."

Dan shook his head. "No, I get that. How did you get a visit when I'm in here for your murder?"

Eve tilted her head. "I'm going by Mary Daniels. Before that, I was Alice Wake. People notice when women don't age. I'm playing a journalist in this life. I used some stashed Conroy money to grease the wheels for exclusive interviews."

"Interviews… plural? What do you want to ask, Mary Daniels?"

"How do they not notice that you look young for a man closing in on sixty?"

Dan rubbed his fingers together and stared at the table. "I spend a lot of time in the dark… most of them don't care. We'll see in another twenty years or so."

Eve slid the notepad across the table. It stopped against one of his shackle chains. He tried to back away, but his hands locked the chains out tight against the underside of the table. The page was yellowed and was flecked with a splatter of brown, dried blood. The score read 48,548 to 49,518. Eve had the strong advantage.

"I went back in after I woke up naked in the coroner's office. The police left it right there on the table. I wrote in the real score from our last hand before I slipped away for good. I have some of our old photo albums, if you want me to bring them next time."

"No … next time?"

"We're going to play cards once a week. I'm a little wary of living forever, so we are going to play an hour a week until we get to one trillion… fair and square."

"One hour a week isn't enough… we'll be here… years… more than years. We have to figure out something else."

She stood up and pulled out a rose from her coat. She held it up for Dan to see. He shivered, but didn't look away. Eve laid it gently down on her end of the table.

"I used to feel rage. I watched my families' funerals from a distance. Then… I understand the confusion and pain you felt healing up from the unhealable wounds, but… I'm disappointed you didn't handle it better. You didn't handle it with me. We are in this… situation together and we can only get out together. I'll see you next week."

She ran her fingertips over the petals and pulled one away. She walked toward the door. Dan slid the notepad back across the table. It stopped shy of the rose she had left him. She looked over her shoulder at it and then back at Dan.

"You need to grow up, Dan. You are almost sixty. We will be using that notepad a while… and several more after it."

"I'm not allowed to keep anything. The guards would take it. Eve… Dear Eve… we don't want to have to start over."

She gave up on the shovel and pitched it over the collapsing dirt beside her. She took the hammer to the pine that was still fresh with the dirt scraped away. She broke through the boards, finally, and pulled away shards and splinters with the claw.

The lid collapsed under her feet, and she cut her ankles trying to step back off the body inside. She used the claw of the hammer to pull herself back over the heap onto the grass. Dirt spilled through the shattered lid onto the crotch and legs of the body.

She lifted the wine bottle to her mouth and swallowed the last swig. She pitched it away and hissed from the stinging blisters on her palms.

"You would heal faster if I cut you clean off… ridiculous."

She picked up the canteen and took another drink. The dirt around her mouth turned to mud, and she wiped it away with her sleeve.

Eve stepped to the edge of the open grave, and poured the rest of the canteen onto the face of the body. It splattered for several seconds before the eyes popped open and Dan began choking. She continued to pour. He rolled to his side, gagging. She dropped the empty canteen in the dirt. He still looked dead.

"Climb out yourself… make it quick. We need to be on the road before daybreak."

Dan fell back in as the dirt collapsed. He coughed and clawed his way further up to the level ground in the midst of the nameless graves.

"Move, Dan… they are going to think I slipped you the razor you used to off yourself."

"You did slip it to me. They probably don't care much." Dan rolled to his back next to his grave.

"God, you are stupid sometimes, Dan. What took you so long? Were you scared?"

"I had to swallow it. It cut its way through my insides for two days before it came back out."

"I hope it hurt."

Dan rolled up to his knees and stood with some effort. "Do you want to drive? It is 1971. The rules have changed, I hear."

He looked at her just as the blade of the shovel crashed into his temple on the exact spot where he'd once held the barrel of the gun he used to shoot his wife. He toppled to the ground and his arms folded into his chest as his muscles spasmed. He watched her drive the blade into the ground next to him as she sat on the ground and watched.

"You had it coming ... now hurry up and die already ... we need to get going soon."

Dan closed his eyes as his arms went limp.

Dust fell from the block ceiling onto the table. Dan started to brush it away, but stopped when the cards started to shift. Dan had to draw once he checked the ends of all the trails again. There were voices outside, but the words weren't clear. They both paused to stare at the cinder block beside them. The noise receded. Eve played her next card. Dan had to draw again.

"Who could that be?"

"I don't know, but they'll regret surfacing soon enough."

Eve looked around the trails again carefully. Dan scratched at a sore on the back of his hand as he waited. The flesh around the wound was blackened and crisp.

"It won't heal if you keep picking at it, Dear Dan." Eve played a bridge taking most of Dan's points.

Dan drew the last card from the stack. "Is that a joke?"

Eve dropped her last card and began pointing the piece of chalk as she counted points. Dan laid out his remaining cards for her. She scratched at the board and erased the old score with her discolored finger.

"Not a joke, really... a habit, I guess."

"Should we try to walk out of the radiation zone?"

"It is pretty far... I say we wait it out for now. It is our anniversary, by the way."

Dan gathered the cards slowly into a stack, blowing the dust off each one. "Stores were closed... I couldn't get you anything."

"Yeah, that's why."

"Remind me what year it is again."

"You don't want to know."

"What's the score?"

"You don't want to know. Just shuffle."

"Humor me."

"It is 35,645,407 to 35,656,558… and 2136."

Dan spilled the cards on his first attempt. He reached down and gathered a couple that fell onto the bunker floor.

"You're leading?"

"Always."

Dan gathered the deck into two stacks and bent them back slowly. They rattled together. He pushed them together into one deck. He closed his eyes and breathed deeply before he separated them again. Eve didn't offer to help.

Dan finished shuffling and dealt again. He sorted his cards in his hand. A piece of the bark crumbled away from the two of hearts. "We'll need to cut a new deck soon."

"We could repaint them."

"They are crumbling."

"Just fix the ones breaking… save time."

Eve played the first card. Dan shook his head and drew a card.

"We'll need to stop for food soon."

"I'll go later."

"I'm hungry now."

"You go get food then, Dear Eve."

She played her next card. They went through several rounds in silence.

Dan dropped his last card and laughed. "I actually won one."

"We should get some roses to celebrate."

Dan gathered the cards while Eve scratched the points into the next blank spot on the cave wall under the cross carved into the stone. He tried to wrap his brain around the word. He started to ask, but then remembered what she meant.

"Yeah… they don't exist anymore. I could probably find a related species. I think they are poisonous now, though."

"Just the food, then."

"What's the score?"

Eve tracked across her columns of code. "425,848,334,705 to... 425,848,545,989... I'm still winning, but you're catching up."

Dan picked up a spear and walked toward the mouth of the cave. "This would go faster, if you would just run away with it."

"We can't cheat... we've tried, haven't we?"

Dan left the cave and made his way down the mountain slope. He tried to remember the name of the range back when humans ruled the Earth. The name escaped him. He followed the edge of the savannah around the curve of the range.

He looked back to the west where the sun was dropping away. He thought about walking. He would just walk toward the sun and leave Eve behind. It would disappear and rise again behind him. He would keep going until he reached it. He had nothing but time. He would keep going until he reached it and let its heat consume him. As he looked across the flat plain and the growing shadows, he felt like he was forgetting something. There was some trick to the world that made it harder to reach the sun, but he couldn't recall it now. He would just keep walking until he got to the edge of the world and was set free on the disc of the sun.

It was time. He negotiated the trail toward the break in the rock. He could hear the bats screeching as they began to wake. They were a little bigger than they used to be, but nothing to be frightened about just yet.

"Just more to eat."

He crouched below the mouth of the cave and waited. He wondered how many more times he would have to do this.

"We're not even halfway done."

Jay Wilburn lives with his wife and two sons in Conway, South

Carolina near the Atlantic coast of the southern United States. He has a Masters Degree in education and he taught public school for sixteen years before becoming a full-time writer. He is the author of many short stories including work in *Best Horror of the Year volume 5*, Zombies More Recent Dead, and Shadows Over Main Street. He is the author of the *Dead Song Legend Dodecology* and the music of the five-song soundtrack recorded as if by the characters within the world of the novel *The Sound May Suffer.* He also wrote the novels *The Great Interruption* and *Time Eaters.* He co-authored *The Enemy Held Near* as part of the powerhouse team he formed with Armand Rosamilia. You can learn more about Jay at jaywilburn.com.

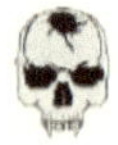

Spaceship Earth

Kenneth W. Cain

Henry Colburn, taking only a moment to appreciate the valley, stood in the clearing known as Greenview, complete with ancient trees and a lake. It was difficult to pull his attention away from what appeared to be a manhole cover in the middle of the field.

Sewage, all the way out here?

Few would ever see this place, because it was thirteen miles from civilization. They would have to hike like he had. So how the hell had *this* ended up here?

He circled the disk several times, contemplating what else it could be.

A dislodged fragment of an airplane? Bending over, he attempted to pick it up. He stretched his fingers around its base, but found no bottom.

He stood and kicked the edge of the disk, trying to extricate it, but nothing so much as shook. Kicks transformed to heavy stomping with the same result. *What the hell…?*

He stepped onto it and the ground around the disk began to tremble. He had nothing to brace himself, and thought to run, but didn't.

A symmetrical pattern of eight raised lines of grass shot out from his location, changing into streaks of crumbling soil.

They resembled the hairy legs of a spider. They rose into the air and he was able to see the dark, jointed, mechanical limbs.

Henry worried that was what they were—the legs of some celestial creature that would devour him upon obtaining its freedom.

The metal legs bent at their joints, enclosing him. Paralysis set in, freezing him in place.

Henry seized two of the limbs and shook as hard as he could. They refused to give, and the space between them was too narrow to squeeze through.

Demise seemed the imminent fate for the man who dared stand on this disk.

The loud squeal of a machine echoed across the vast field. Henry tried to discern its source, but before he could, he found himself swallowed into utter darkness.

Am I dead?

His hand found a wall to his right, the cold sting of metal at his fingertips. This wasn't the afterlife.

Henry ran his hands across the length of the wall. It surprised him when his fingers struck something familiar. He made circling motions with his hands, trying to rediscover the switch. He zeroed in on it and flipped it on.

In the darkness behind him an engine whined, dim lights flickering as the generator began to feed them power. This promise of light brought some of the sensation back to Henry's already drained legs.

Suddenly, a feminine voice that came from all directions startled him. "Spaceship Earth, serial number: 000324, Galaxy: Milky Way… auxiliary power, on. Planet is currently on autopilot."

Hearing what she had to say made Henry doubt the existence of this place. He thought he'd hurt himself and was lying somewhere in the woods, dreaming this whole thing up. He'd heard stories of hikers who had exhausted themselves, ending up dehydrated and hallucinating as a result.

Henry bit his lip and drew blood. A warm, metallic flush of

bitterness ran into his mouth, and pain followed.

Not a dream after all.

A more abundant source of light was visible down the hall, and Henry stared at it.

"Hello?" Henry called, holding a hand to the side of his mouth. "Anyone there?"

Whoever owned this *place* likely hadn't been here in some time. Cobwebs and dust were everywhere.

Staring down the hall he noticed how the strange lights beyond seemed to change. Odd bleeps and buzzes, sometimes a whir, accompanied this alteration of lighting.

What the hell is this place?

Henry hurried toward the room, unsure of what to expect. He burst into the room, then stopped and stared.

He hadn't anticipated this: a cockpit, complete with intricate machinery and blinking lights. Regardless of what the mechanical woman's voice had said, this was a possibility that hadn't even crossed his mind until now. He would have thought it all fake, if it weren't for the realistic appearance of the equipment.

On the right wall there were a series of electronic devices. Some looked sophisticated, while others were more familiar to him. There was a ham radio and a rotary phone, but most of these forms of communications he couldn't put names to. A dozen or so monitors lined the wall above these items.

A lone, sizable screen occupied the center wall. It was made of some liquid substance that was being held back by an unseen force. He reached and swiped a finger across the screen. A wet sensation teased at his skin. However, upon examination, he saw that his finger remained dry.

What in the world?

Sitting beneath the liquid screen was a desk made of an unidentifiable material. Henry examined it, running his hand along its edge and feeling a cool sensation.

To his amazement the desk was floating in mid-air. *No legs*, he marveled and leaned over to confirm this. There he found another surprise. *No wires either? Damn thing's wireless.*

Letting his eyes search the various controls covering the surface of the desktop, some made sense. Most of them he was unfamiliar with, but he was positive some technological gadget-hound would have gleaned more of their individual purposes than he.

The joystick was one of the few controls that made perfect sense to him, but Henry gathered from its design that it wasn't for playing video games. Many of the switches and buttons surrounding it likely had something to do with flight adjustments.

An odd thought occurred to him. *My God, I've been abducted.*

That made perfect sense. The disk, the spider legs, all this technology, everything; it was all too damn real. If these as-yet-unseen aliens decided to wipe out existence, he would be one of the few survivors.

An older man's voice ruined the entire concept by yelling, "What in the hell are you doing here?"

Henry spun, finding the tip of a shotgun three inches from his nose. It startled him, sending him sprawling back onto the desktop.

The desk tried to adjust to his weight but the controls could not bear him. Under his ass, switches shifted and dials turned. Disoriented, Henry dropped to the floor. It felt like the entire room had been seized by a giant and shaken briskly.

"What the… Move! Quickly!"

The man left the gun against the wall and rushed forward, shoving Henry out of the way and rubbing the palms of his hands on his overalls. He started flicking switches and turning knobs with haste. When it came to the joystick, he took special care in adjusting it.

Once he'd finished, Henry's stomach eased, no longer feeling on the verge of purging itself.

The man glanced back at Henry with a most frightful expression pasted on his white face. Then he turned back to the controls, making a few slight adjustments.

Henry watched as the man leaned over the desk and turned on the main screen by depressing some unseen button. An eerie buzz filled the room, then the screen popped and crackled as it came to life.

A detailed map of the world filled the large monitor. It was almost three-dimensional. A few switches, a couple more dials, and a toggle on the joystick brought Florida into clear view. Henry spied a swirl crawling across the map. It looked like a hurricane.

The man mumbled, "I think I can—"

His fingers spun a dial. His other hand eased back on the joystick, and then depressed one of the several buttons lining the top of the stick. The man finished with one last switch and stood back watching.

The hurricane dispersed into the open sea where it could do no harm, missing the mainland by mere inches on the display.

The man turned, hands on his hips. "You nearly wiped out Florida, damn you. Averted by only a handful of miles."

"Sorry? I guess."

"Damn right you're sorry. What the hell are you doing here anyway?" He extended a hand to Henry and Henry took it, feeling the jelly-like consistency leave his legs as he got to his feet. "My name's Mike and I've been running this station for eleven years now."

"Uh…Henry."

Mike nodded.

"Where am I?"

Mike eyed up Henry, as if he'd missed the obvious. "Why this is Spaceship Earth, of course."

There wasn't a hint of doubt in Mike's voice. This was no lie to Mike. As much as this place might seem someone's elaborate fantasy playroom, it wasn't. The seriousness of that brought Henry to a disturbing level of anxiety.

He shook his head and the absurdity of it all came out as sarcasm. "Spaceship Earth, huh?"

"Oh come on, you don't really buy that whole big-bang theory and all, gravitational force and all that orbit crap, do you?"

Henry combed his memories for the basic information he'd learned back in grade school. It was more than common knowledge. It was the law, a rule, the very basis for all of physics. "Yes. Yes, I do."

"Oh well, yes, it's all there, of course. But it takes effort to make it all work." Mike grinned the smile of a man who has been locked away for far too long. "I mean, it doesn't just do it all on its own. Even in school you learn there is an equal and opposite reaction for every action. Don't you?"

Henry contemplated this argument, and although it held obvious truth, logic denied him the ability to buy in. Besides, all he wanted now was to leave before he got caught up in this confusion.

"From here, the Earth's cockpit, I make all the necessary adjustments to create that force. All things are set in motion by my actions, and if left on autopilot too long, eventually civilization as we know it on Earth would significantly change, likely at the hands of a chain of various natural disasters."

Henry couldn't bring himself to smile or to any semblance of pleasantry. This was truly disturbing, and all he wanted was to leave. Mike held the answers as to how to achieve that end. Henry went to speak, but was interrupted.

"It's told that at one point long ago, Mars had been much closer to the Sun than Earth. It had been inhabited by several beings much like our own. The Captain of that ship fell asleep at the wheel." Mike sniggered. "Mars went so far out of its orbit that the land was scorched by the Sun, killing nearly all of its denizens. I'm told it took quite the maneuvering to get Mars into its current position, where it might have been restored to its original beauty if not for being neglected for such an extensive period."

"Listen," Henry said at last, feeling the frown forming on his face. "I hate to interrupt your story and all, but..." Henry chose his words with care. "I really should be going, so..."

Mike laughed hard. "Oh no, no, no. You can't just leave."

"What?" Henry's temperature was rising. "Who do you think you are? I can leave—"

"No," Mike insisted. "The directive would never allow for such a thing. You need training, and your old life will be left behind. It's either that, or—"

"You can't keep me here against my will."

Henry's eyes went to the shotgun. He thought to reach for it, but instead broke for the hallway and ducked into the darkness.

Looking back, he noticed Mike hadn't followed. Henry reached the end of the corridor, looking for a switch or a lever, anything that might lead to a way out. He found nothing, but refused to give up and continued his search. By accident, he nudged the light switch and the mechanical voice spoke once more.

"Spaceship Earth, serial number: 000324, Galaxy: Milky Way… auxiliary power on. Planet is currently on autopilot. Recent course changes plotted."

Lights burst on, running down the hall with a faint glow. At the end Mike stood smirking at Henry's feeble effort.

"Where's the exit, damn it?" Henry's voice had taken on a stern and unforgiving tone, but he took note of how Mike remained unmoved and offered an ultimatum. "I'm leaving one way or another. You choose how."

Even this threat went ignored. Or maybe Mike felt he was up to the challenge. When Mike produced the shotgun, it became apparent how far he might be willing to go should Henry not comply.

"Listen," Mike was beginning to sound more apologetic than anything. "I'm sorry, but I can't allow it. The cockpit cannot be moved, and if you ever—"

Henry didn't wait for him finish the thought, but Mike was shaking his head long before Henry got out the first word. "But I won't."

This was a moment of desperation, but it was true. Henry had no intention of revealing anything about this place to anyone. They would think him crazy if he did. As before, Henry's words were disregarded.

"They won't go for it, Henry. I'm sorry. It's just the way things work."

Henry identified the remorse in Mike's eyes. He meant what he said. This was a man who had some knowledge of what was being asked of Henry. Perhaps Mike had been an unwilling participant some eleven years prior. None of that changed anything as far as Henry was concerned.

Henry shrugged, uncertain of what it even required. There were no facilities to live here. He saw no bed. No food. "So what? I'm just supposed to stay here?"

Mike snickered, taking in the complex machinery and hallway surrounding them as if trying to imagine what that might look like. "No, not here."

If only Mike had seen Henry's living quarters at college. Henry had braved far worse conditions back then. A thin smile found his lips.

"But nearby," Mike finished.

"Is this a house?"

"Not a house at all." The pleasantness returned to his face. "It's someplace else. Somewhere else."

"And what of you?"

Henry's words came off curt, almost as if accusing Mike of some indiscretion.

Showing that he'd regained some level of comfort, Mike sat the gun aside once more. He folded his arms across his chest, satisfaction glowing on his face, as one might expect to see from someone who has recently ended a long and dutiful service. Now Mike could finally reap the rewards of retirement.

"I've served my time," Mike said. "They'll allow me to gather my belongings and relocate."

"And I'm just supposed to give up everything?" The gravity of what he was being asked was heavy. "Everything that I've worked for?"

Mike nodded as if indicating how easy of a choice it was. "That's correct, Henry."

"And what if I don't?"

A frown pulled at the corners of Mike's mouth, all kindness leaving. A worried expression replaced it. Mike nodded to the shotgun and let his eyes fall back to Henry. "They won't allow it."

"Who is this 'they' you keep mentioning? Who won't allow it? And why should they be able to decide my fate?"

It was obvious Henry's hostility worried Mike. He took a precautionary step toward the gun. Mike didn't seem to want it to come to this conclusion.

Who wouldn't prefer retirement to pulling a trigger to kill someone and then having to further one's tenure? Henry didn't think Mike wanted that at all, but he'd also made it quite apparent he wouldn't hesitate to do just that.

"The *they* I speak of refers to the Alliance of Planets," Mike said after a moment, his eyes trained on Henry. "That's what *we* call ourselves. The pilots, I mean. It's a collaboration of all we know."

Henry processed what Mike was saying. That this was all the doing of the pilots. He found himself thinking back to what they were taught in school, about the beginnings of Earth.

How long has this position been filled in this way? How was the first pilot chosen? Better yet, *who was the very first?*

"Even if I did let you go, you wouldn't live long. Neither would I for letting you go. They wouldn't allow it."

Mike turned to the screens and approached the controls as Henry watched. When Mike got there, Henry saw the way he scanned them as if preparing to say goodbye. They must have posed somewhat of a curse to the man. Henry saw how on edge Mike appeared, and thought it must be hard giving up control.

Henry stepped forward, his mind dizzy with responsibility and seized the gun. Mike made no attempt to stop him. This aggressive action only brought Mike visible sadness.

"It won't make any difference, Henry. If you kill me, you still won't make it out of here. They'll just find a replacement. And that pilot will take care of you before settling in."

"You're lying. This is all a lie," Henry shouted, although he couldn't be sure of anything.

Mike seemed to expect this response, almost as if he'd seen it before or done it himself. Perhaps they had more in common than Henry first thought.

"Give me the gun, Henry." Mike reached for it and Henry eased his grip some. "Let's talk about all of this over a cup of coffee, okay?"

The look on Mike's face wasn't one of concern but of compassion. But Henry couldn't bring himself to part with the gun now that he had it.

He thrust the shotgun forward, ramming it into Mike's chest, and sent the man sprawling backward. Henry resumed his aim, meaning to cover Mike as he fell back onto the desk.

Mike arched his back as if trying to avoid landing on several valuable porcelain collectibles. Despite his effort, Mike crashed against one entire side of the table. Imbalance returned fast as the world went off kilter.

Mike twisted to the controls and began working right away, ignoring the gun at his back. Once more Henry fell to his knees, unfamiliar with the sensation of the ship being off course. With a quick glance at Henry, Mike's focus stayed on the desk, easing the joystick back, a grim expression flushing over his face.

When he finished, Mike eyed Henry. Henry's disorientated gaze fell to the strange alien form that had materialized on one of the screens.

When Mike saw this, he turned to the screen and hurried to find one of the more technological communication devices. Henry watched as Mike looped a small earring-like device around his earlobe, and then held the button part of this device in front of his chin. This piece remained hovering just out of reach of his mouth when Mike removed his hand. What followed amazed Henry, as Mike began to speak some incomprehensible language. The creature nodded in response.

It was challenging to read the alien's expression, as its facial features were subtler than that of a human. The dark purple skin made the mouth, nose, and eyes difficult to identify on screen.

When the creature's jumbled language came across, Henry could barely hear what little leaked out of the earpiece, but he was positive it had been in regard to his intrusion and the disruption he'd caused.

"Yes," Mike said, and the creature seemed to understand. "I'll take care of it."

The creature glanced Henry's way for a split second, and then vanished from the screen without notice. Henry took this gesture as a warning, watching Mike replace the device where he'd found it and return his attention to Henry. All thoughtfulness left his face, replaced by determination.

"I need the gun now, Henry," he said and this time Mike wasn't asking.

Mike took a firm grip on the gun's barrel. He made no attempt at soothing Henry, and displayed no more understanding of what Henry might be enduring. The time had come for an end, and, as Henry himself had stated, it would come one way or another.

"No," Henry responded without even considering the consequences.

He knew it was right to surrender, but the gun was the lone thing holding him to the only reality he'd ever known. It represented a possibility to escape this place, and he had to try. If they came, then he'd do his best to avoid them. If he gave up the gun, all hope of that was gone.

"I said, give me the gun!" Mike yelled, his insistence warning Henry he'd gone too far.

Mike had become a different man. When Henry still didn't relent, Mike surprised him by tugging harder. A loud blast rang through the small enclosure.

The two men stood face to face, both with blank expressions, while they considered each other. Each wondered why it had come to this.

Mike stumbled back, blood gushing from his stomach. Henry released the gun and Mike continued to hold onto it as he stumbled away.

The gun fell to the floor, rattling as Mike wavered. Henry rushed to steady Mike, but it was already too late. Trying to avoid doing so again, a weakened Mike fell hard against the desktop. Even this close to death, Mike struggled not to upset the controls but failed again.

He slid down to his knees beside the desktop, taking in the damage and trying to will himself the strength to fix things. His eyes searched the controls, as if trying to understand them.

Henry followed Mike to the floor, wanting to help. A stark look of concern washed over Mike as he continued to stare out at the controls. Mike's color went pale, his skin damp and cold, and he managed to find his voice.

"Must," Mike shivered, a wet gurgling sound stuck in his throat. His bloodied hand fell on Henry's wrist, lifting it to the controls. "Must save Earth."

"What do I do?"

Mike slumped to the floor. There was a single deep exhale and then only silence.

The reality of what had occurred fell over Henry like a bucket of cold water. As the possibilities of what could happen came to mind for the first time, Henry realized Mike didn't do this job out of pride, but out of paranoia.

A sick feeling crawled into his stomach as the Earth tilted off its axis. On one screen, the creature returned. Then another tuned in beside the first; this time, pale-skinned and much more human-like in appearance. A third and fourth joined, each so different from one another. Tiny white swirls indicated the severity of the weather on the main screen rolling across the map on a path of destruction.

Henry noticed the temperature had grown a few degrees, and although he wasn't sure if this was a result of his predicament or this weather change, his forehead began to pour out sweat. He yanked off his shirt to give himself relief, and the female mechanical voice returned to relay Earth's prognosis.

"Warning! Spaceship Earth, serial number: 000324, Galaxy: Milky Way… off course. Determined path undesirable for the climate required to sustain current life forms."

Henry watched as the entire island of Australia was swallowed up by travesties he'd only read about in textbooks. A beautiful continent destroyed within seconds. A mere accident had killed them all.

His mouth went agape; gooseflesh prickled up his arms and around his neck. He froze, immobilized by his terror. In his mind, he saw the premonition of an America torn apart by a swarm of natural disasters. It would all be his fault, because he knew nothing of controlling this ship, and even if help somehow found him, he didn't think there was time enough to save anything.

At his side, various communications devices began to ring in unison. None of them were familiar to Henry. He seized the one Mike had used and tried to fashion it as he'd seen.

There weren't any buttons, so he held the larger piece to his ear and waved the other in front of his chin, trying to make it work. He longed to hear a voice, any voice.

"What are you doing?"

Henry didn't reply, only listened. He was too busy trying to emulate what Mike had done. Trembling hands traced unfamiliar controls on the desktop, searching for an off switch or anything that might resolve this disaster.

"Stop that, now!"

"Warning! Spaceship Earth, serial number: 000324, Galaxy: Milky Way… continent North America core temperature approaching hazardous levels. Modifying internal environment to accommodate change."

The voice on the phone sounded hurried and Henry commiserated with its intensity. "Adjust your trim and spin one and three quarter degrees from the sun before it's too late."

"I don't know how," Henry cried.

On screen, the pale humanoid peered at him through squinty eyes that glared with accusation. Henry felt the weight of guilt those eyes laid upon him.

"The joystick," it said. "Pull left now—" It paused and then clarified as Henry took the stick in the palm of his hand. "Not too hard."

Henry hadn't heard this last part soon enough. He watched as South America vanished into the waters surrounding it, bound for the untold mysteries of its depths.

The urge to vomit found him as he struggled with the increasing loss of humanity. The voice on the phone stuttered, trying to explain what to do but couldn't seem to find the words in its anxiety.

"Warning! Spaceship Earth, serial number: 000324, Galaxy: Milky Way… Immediate corrective action needed."

Henry started to cry. Staring at the screen, he waited for some last-minute command from the creature, something to save what was left. If they could accomplish that much, then maybe Earth could rebuild. Even that seemed hopeless now.

Then, with a sense of urgency, the voice came, "The auto-pi—"

All lines went dead, filled with static. One by one, the alien images on the screens blinked off. The power to the main screen began to flicker.

"Warning! Spaceship Earth, serial number: 000324, Galaxy: Milky Way… Explosion imminent."

"The autopilot," Henry said, finishing the alien's thought.

Perhaps there was hope after all. Waving his hands over the desktop, he began to search for it, anything that offered the familiarity of such a thing.

He found a single small green button toward the top left of the desktop marked with the letters "AP." He prayed this was it, and depressed the button right as the countdown started.

"Five," the computer voice stated.

Falling to his knees, he prayed God would have mercy.

"Four."

He kept telling himself he'd gotten to the button with plenty of time, a grinding hum building in the background.

"Three."

Henry imagined he heard a hint of spite behind the woman's mechanical voice. He felt weak, his head spinning with dizziness unlike anything he'd ever experienced.

The large screen flickered one last time and then went out. Before it did, Henry saw that only a quarter of the Earth's landmasses remained above water. His hometown was not one of them.

"Two."

With the next to last number resounding in the cavernous cockpit of Spaceship Earth, his emotions unraveled.

The extreme conditions forced him to the ground, the heavy hands of some unseen force pinning and holding him there. There he stayed. Earth's assailant in tears and waiting for one last digit to come.

The space between the numbers stretched out for an infinite amount of time. People often said that life slowed down right before you died.

Henry didn't think life slowed so much as one's perception of time did. Popping noises filled his ears as the pressure changed all at once.

He continued to hope the autopilot would kick in at the very last fraction of a second, and save what was left of his world.

In his heart he knew that, even if it did, there wouldn't be much left to preserve.

But we can rebuild.

He thought of Mike's story about Mars, wondered how much of it was truth.

With this doubt clear in his thoughts, darkness overwhelmed him.

As he gave in to the constricting unconsciousness, he heard one final word, and it arrested his heart.

"One."

Kenneth W. Cain is the author of the *Saga of I* trilogy, *United States of The Dead*, acclaimed short story collections *These Old Tales* and *Fresh Cut Tales*, and the forthcoming collection *Embers*. He lives with his wife and children in Eastern Pennsylvania. Find out more at kennethwcain.com. Spaceship Earth first appeared in the Library of Science Fiction & Fantasy anthology *Doomology: The Dawning of Disasters*.

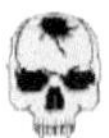

Thus is the Life

Essel Pratt

Being that which society frowns upon. Doing what the law has deemed morally wrong. Refusal to conform into the monotonous despair which the uninformed populace hides behind their plasticized smiles and diamond-glazed eyes. The courts and the governments create a fallacy of safety and order, outlined by the farce of freedom and mockery of individualism. Faceless figures wander the lands, donning masks of individuality, and emanating intellectual dishonesty through their inane education. Their futile lives expunged of all freethinking vices, supplanted with subliminal suggestions that are seared into our minds by the multitude of advertisements that litter our peripheral visions.

Thus is the life of the world today.

As I stand here, concealed by the darkness cast upon me by the exposed brick walls within a long-forgotten alleyway, I free my mind of society's grip. I feel sorry for those around me that hide behind a veil of mimicked self-esteem and overcompensate within their ideal self-efficacy. It makes my head hurt when I think about them. I wonder why I have been chosen to be truly free, while they are chained to imagined beliefs.

Leaning against the moist brick wall, my member's-only jacket protects me from the drizzle that falls from above. I take a drag from my menthol cigarette; the nicotine helps to clear my head of humanity's fog. Staring down at the brick-paved ground, I see my reflection in a puddle that has pooled where three or four bricks have been removed, probably by a neighborhood kid. My face wears the same mask that everyone else wears. I hate it. Disgusted, I spit into the puddle, smiling at the distortion caused by the ripples that erase my reflection.

It is quiet. The soft symphonic percussion that resonates around me provides the soundtrack of the night. It is calming in its discreetness.

Flicking my cigarette into the puddle, I light another before the sizzling smoke from the prior dances away toward the unknown. I am becoming antsy while I wait, hoping I am not wrong about my visitor's arrival. To ease my anxiety, I focus on the smoke that billows from the glowing tip of my cigarette. The ghostly dance pleases my eyes as the smoke's sultry striptease fades out of view, until I inhale another drag. It is beautiful and seductive.

I look at my watch, noticing that it is only two hours from midnight. Promptness has never been a virtue of mine, but being inanely early has been my cancer. I still have another quarter hour before my guest is slated to arrive. I walk toward the back of the alley, where the rusted dumpster blocks the path and a tall wooden fence stands guard behind, and take a piss. The blaring reverb of my urine splashing upon the empty dumpster creates a momentary interlude to the rain's performance, inserting an instance of chaos into the serenity.

Thus is my life; chaos within the forced serenity.

My footsteps splash in the melancholy puddles, destined to fade from existence when the sun rises and summons their moisture back up to the mythological heavens. These are my thoughts. I gather myself mentally, focusing on the steady beats of the drizzle, and the metallic knocks of the gutter pipe to my right. My eyes are closed and my mind is free as I lean against the brick wall collecting my thoughts.

This is how I like it.

A car drives by; its headlights illuminate the interior of my eyelids, coercing them open without warning. The distraction is unwelcome, but I will live. I look at my watch and see that my guest should have arrived five minutes ago. Frustration has added chaos to my serenity, as I fear my guest may not arrive. She is always on time. I will wait a few more minutes, maybe an hour, in hopes that I am not stood up.

I loathe rejection.

A few minutes pass and I hear the clickety-clack of high heels on the crumbling sidewalk. By the sound it makes and the pace at which it approaches, I know that she is approaching from the northern corner, just as she always did. Why she comes this way, I do not know. Maybe she likes to escape the forced monotony of life, just as I do.

I doubt it.

Her footsteps become louder with each breath I take. I place my mask upon my face; it is free of features and painted jet black. It matches my soul. I blend in with the darkness that surrounds me, camouflaged by my lack of homogeneity.

Her eyes focus on the ground as she approaches. Her hands are in her pockets. I wonder what she is thinking, if she feels safe, where she came from, and where she is going. Well, I know where she is going, but really wonder where her intended destination might be. Her long coat hangs just above her knees. The tightly clasped waist belt accentuates her figure. Her face, the most beautiful I have ever seen, is concealed by her long brown hair that hangs against her cheeks. If I believed in society's labels and rules of attraction, I might be in love.

I will settle for lust.

As she passes by, I smell her flowery perfume. It assaults my nostrils and I want to gag. I want to wonder why women subject themselves to bathing in oily fragrances rather than allow their natural scents to attract suitors. However, my mind does not allow me the time to think as I emerge from my alcove and grab her from behind, pulling her into the alleyway. She screams for a moment, but I quickly apply a soothing dose of chloroform to her face. I am careful not to damage her brittle beauty.

She is so pretty when she sleeps.

I drag her to the back of the alley, the same spot that I relieved myself earlier, and prop her up against the dumpster. Being the chivalric gentleman I strive to be, I respectfully placed a dry piece of cardboard upon the wet ground to save her the discomfort of a moist rear end. To protect her from the rain, I drape a trash bag over her head and tie her up with an old extension cord that I find in the garbage.

She deserves better.

I switch my attention from her to her purse. The contents are minimal. A couple tampons, house keys, sticks of peppermint gum, a Swiss army knife, and her wallet are all that is inside. I help myself to a stick of gum and look through her wallet. Her identification card shows that her name is Olivia and she lives about three miles from here. A paycheck stub shows that she works at a restaurant nearby. This route, although not the safest, is probably the quickest way for her to walk home. I toss her purse and its contents into the dumpster and revert my gaze back to Olivia.

Caressing her cheek with the palm of my hand, I feel her warmth radiate through me. I can tell that she is still bound by society's restrictions, and I want to release her. In my experience, those that deserve to be released are usually the most reluctant. Sometimes constraining them is the best way to begin the emancipation of their minds. Liberation can be taxing on those that are afraid to accept it.

I straddle her legs, knees bent as I rest on the balls of my feet, staring at her closed eyes with my hands upon her shoulders for balance. I stare deep into her soul, looking for the keyhole to unlock her inhibitions. I wish I could share with her the beauty of living life without a soul to constantly guide you along the path of fate.

Fate is a hindrance.

Her eyelids flutter as consciousness returns. Still staring in the same position, I caress her cheeks and press my lips to hers. They are soft and moist. My heart beats faster as I anticipate her eyes looking deep into mine. I wonder if she will welcome my embrace or reject me.

It is rejection.

Fear releases from her in the form of tedious gasps for air and fearful screams of terror. I came prepared for her rejection, and I shove a balled-up sock into her beautiful mouth–not that anyone can hear her out here.

It is a clean sock.

I tell her that everything will be okay. I reassure her that I only want to free her from the restrictions of the regulations that the world expects from her. She responds with uncontrollable tremors and tears stream down her face, taking her mascara for the ride. The effect it creates upon her face is mysterious. I trace the path with my finger. She pulls her head away from my touch, but I persist. Her soft flesh is too irresistible not to touch.

I ask her if she has ever felt the touch of a man. She shakes her head to say no, and her tears increase while her breaths become more spastic. I hush her with my index finger pressed between her lips. I feel her lip gloss stick to my finger as I pull it away. I have no intention of desecrating her virginal sanctity, and I am proud that she has not given into the desires of flesh with those that would love her and leave her for the sake of peer pressure. She truly is a good girl.

She is halfway to being free.

I feel bad for what I plan to do next, but it is necessary. Her waist belt is tied tightly to her and I fumble to loosen the knot. Although I fumble, I am successful. Her coat folds open, revealing a tightly fitting black nylon skirt and white button-up shirt. Both caress her petite form with precision. She pulls her legs tightly together and attempts to press her body close to the dumpster. I feel she is trying to get away. I wish she would not struggle and accept that I am here to help.

I tell her to relax. I reassure her that I will not touch her where the sanctity of life is created and birthed; I would never stoop to the level of a despicable rapist. That is not my forte. Instead, I take care in unbuttoning her blouse. I do not want to damage the buttons or cause any unnecessary wrinkling of the fabric. I pull it down from her shoulders, to her elbows because the cord around her wrist prevents me from removing it completely. Her breasts, although rather small in size, are beautifully perky and a light caramel in color. Her skin has a mesmerizing glow that is hard to look away from.

I unclasp her bra—it is a front clasp—and allow her breasts to fall into their natural position. Her increased sobs cause them to bounce slightly. I touch both, squeezing them between my thumb and forefinger. I find that I have no interest in them at all. They do feel nice to the touch, but I don't feel the desire to play with them as society expects us to. Instead, I ponder the significance of their importance in the beginnings of life; how they provide nutrition for our children, not the perversion that they have become.

I place my hand between her breasts, flat against her intermammary sulcus. Her heart is beating rapidly and I can feel its rhythmic pulsations against my hand. It is a strong heart, worthy of freedom. I find myself slightly aroused at the thought of the muscle within.

I suppress my urge; it is not my intention to act out of lust.

Gently, I pinch her nipple and lift her breast upward; revealing the crease on the underside where the fatty flesh meets the smoothness above her stomach. The crease is my guide to release her. I try not to pinch too hard; I know the nipples are a sensitive area. However, it provides the perfect handle to complete the task. With my area of entry in plain view, I unsheathe my Damascus knife from its leather belt holster and press the cold blade against her warm skin. She inhales deeply and screams through the sock. Not wanting to prolong her anticipation, I slice clear through to the bone underneath, making an incision approximately four inches long. Her agony is muffled by the constriction in her mouth.

It pains me that she is in pain.

I try to be quick, but her body seizes abruptly. Not epileptic in fashion, but in denial of my advances. Her warm red blood flows from the incision, covering her stomach in the most beautiful glaze. I fight the urge to become fixated on the flow and force myself to focus on the task at hand. Still holding the breast up by the nipple, I wipe the blood from my knife and replace it into its sheath.

Now is the time to liberate her.

Olivia has all but given in to the process. Her body, in obvious shock, is becoming limp and her screams have stopped. I have seen this before; it makes the ritual so much easier. I take the opportunity to plunge my hand into the incision and force her ribcage to crack. This is the hardest part of the entire process. The ribcage is incredibly strong, and forcing my way through with only one hand is difficult. Luckily, I have had enough practice to make it through fairly unscathed. Although I did receive a small cut on my hand as a shard of bone sliced my knuckle.

Sometimes it happens.

With clear access, I reach in further and grasp her heart tightly. The sudden pressure I apply jerks Olivia back to reality, and her awareness is fierce. Her mouth opens wide and she pushes the sock out with her tongue. I will admit that it startles me, but I continue and twist the heart within her chest, pulling toward me as I do so. It takes a couple seconds, but her screams stop shortly after I extract her heart from within. Her limp body falls to the wet ground, and she is free.

I take a moment to catch my breath. Redemption is quite tiring. Looking down upon Olivia's corpse, I am overjoyed that she is now able to escape the constrictions of law and order. No longer will her neighbors judge her for letting her grass grow, or a future boyfriend from forcing her to love only him and no one else. Now her spirit is unchained and unrestricted.

I take a moment to wipe the rain from my brow and light a cigarette. There is nothing more relaxing than the taste of a smoke after performing a freeing ritual. In fact, I crave the taste and feel quite often. It motivates me to continue my crusade. I inhale deeply and watch as the smoke dances from my lips, like a ghost twirling before me. I imagine, and believe, that the smoke from the celebratory cigarettes is the final step to confer freedom to the vessel at my feet.

I flick the consumed butt to the ground and remove a gallon-sized freezer bag from my breast pocket. The still-beating heart, albeit faintly pulsating, fits inside perfectly. It is still warm. I have a pocket inside my member's-only jacket to hide the organs when I collect them. I am not sure that I could feel comfortable carrying it home without feeling the last bit of life fade from within and its warmth on my ribcage.

Although she is free, I cannot leave her body lying here in a pool of blood, naked, and exposed to the elements. I am not a monster. Her body, although a prison for all of her twenty-five years, served her well and protected her while she was a slave to culture. I collect some of the rainwater from a nearby puddle into a dented old coffee can and wash away the blood from her body. I take care to make sure her skin is not stained. Her vision will be plastered all over the television and newspapers and I want to make sure that everyone can easily identify her for who she really is, and not just another Jane Doe lost in the gutter. I need the world to know that she has become a martyr of freedom.

As I am buttoning her blouse, another car drives by. Its headlights barely penetrate the alleyway, but it is the second I have seen tonight. I never see cars out here, and am worried that it might be someone searching for her. I hasten my pace and retie her waist belt of her coat. I have been a bit careless, and blood has stained her clothes. I hope that doesn't change the view of the news coverage. I want the world to know the signature of my work, and the deviation from cleanliness could lead the media astray. I hope another does not get credit for my saintly deed.

I won't make the same mistake next time.

As I always do before leaving the scene of redemption, I leave a single stem of a bird of paradise in her lap. The flower represents freedom, and has become my calling card. I look her in the eye one last time, then push them shut with my pinky and thumb. I wish she were free when we met, free like me; maybe we could have worked together. It is too bad, but thus is life.

I light another cigarette and turn south as I exit the alleyway. I don't look back, but my thoughts are still there. It is too bad that the rest of the world cannot see things as I do. I promise to free them one at a time if necessary, hoping to find others as knowledgeable as I am along the way. Until then, I walk home quietly with the warm heart near my side. It is not a souvenir; it is to protect her spirit from being forced into Heaven or Hell, as directed by the books that civilized societies worship.

Even in afterlife, the control continues.

I didn't come straight home, opting to stop at a local convenience store for a black coffee first. The night has been long, and I need the boost. I walk up to my modest home, with the white picket fence and the porch that extends the length of the front façade. My key glides into the lock of the generic front door and allows me entry into my living room. I throw my keys down and head to a room near the back of the house. It is an odd room; it has no windows upon the walls.

It is my favorite room.

I turn on the light and adjust my eyes to the bright red walls. My desk sits dead center, and two of the four walls are adorned with floor-to-ceiling bookcases. The other two walls, the ones in front of and behind the desk, are plain, with only the paint upon them.

I sit in my chair and open the top drawer of my desk, where a clean jar awaits Olivia's heart. Within is a fresh formaldehyde bath. Before placing the heart within, I place a gentle kiss upon the muscle and whisper my appreciation for joining the cause. Although she cannot speak, I know that she thanks me for my support.

I look at my watch and notice that it is much later than I thought. Luckily, I do not have to work tomorrow. The mail does not run on Sundays. Still, I am not tired. So, I place Olivia on the shelves to my right with all the others like her. She seems to be right at home. I wish them all a gratuitous goodnight and flip off the light.

I am a little wired from the excitement, so I head next door to the pub. The place is empty, except for Tina the bartender. She smiles as I sit on the stool and order a hoppy dark beer. She gives me something new, and the brew dances on my tongue. She asks how my night has been and I tell her it was good, sparing the details. She decides to share her story with me. She hates being chained to the bar, forced to serve drinks to those that give her orders. She feels like a slave to the patrons, granting their every alcoholic wish. She excludes me of course, because she wants me to give a decent tip. Of course I oblige with a twenty and she keeps the drinks coming. In my head I decide that I will continue to visit her, to see if she really wants to be freed. Then, when the time comes I will oblige her desire.

I think her and Olivia will get along well.

Essel Pratt is a master of horror and fantasy, conjuring tales that haunt souls and inspire imagination. As a student of psychology and teller of tales, Essel writes to share the complex nature of his imaginings with the world. His ever-expanding catalog of short stories spans multiple anthologies and collections, ranging from whimsical fantasy to bizarre horror, including everything in between. Dedicated fans have praised his creations, labeling his talents as prolific in substance. His most notable and prevalent accomplishments include Final Reverie, Sharkantula, and the multiple short stories that have garnered a following of their own, such as the adventures of Detective Mansfield.

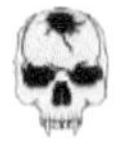

Special Delivery

William Holden

July 1, 2013

My Dearest Joseph,

I bet you're surprised to hear from me. Did you think that I wasn't going to be able to find you? You should know better than that. No matter where you go, I shall always be there with you. Don't you know by now that we will be joined together forever? It's who I am. It's what I am. It's who we are. I know what you must be thinking, but please don't overreact—I know how you can be. I think it's time that we both stop playing games; accept the fact that we need to be together—you and I, the two parts that will make us whole once more.

By now, you must know how I feel about you, and that I would do anything for you—for us. How could you not, after everything we've been through together? Don't you feel me the way I feel you? Have you tried so hard to distance yourself from me that you've lost the connection we once shared? Don't you remember, Joseph? There was a time we were there for one another, no matter what life handed us. I want that again, Joseph. I want—no, we need to be there for each other, now more than ever. We need that connection again. I want to hold onto you and never let you go. That is why I cannot give up on us. You must feel it, as I do. There is something missing in each of us, something that cannot be satisfied by any other means—except by reuniting.

You need me, Joseph, just as much as I need you, and I'm not going anywhere until I can convince you otherwise. I can't be anywhere else but here. We need to be reunited—forever. I know what you're thinking—that I am no one. That all of this is some sort of illusion or distant memory that you can ignore and move on without. But you would be wrong, Joseph. You above all others should know that. You just have to let me prove it to you. I am not the troublemaker that others convinced you I am. The only moments of instability I have come when you deny what we both want: to be as one. You must want that too. I don't understand why you continue to act as though you are scared of me. Have I ever done anything to hurt you? Look, I don't like to bring up the past, but let me be honest here for one moment. I'm more clear-headed than most of the people you've been involved with. Whether you want to admit it or not, you know, deep down that what I'm saying is true.

Do you need me to remind you of Debra, the woman who not only stole your heart, but stole tens of thousands of dollars from you before taking off? Oh, and what about Justin? Lord, that poor tweaked-out meth addict was a mess. He slept with anything in order to get his next fix. Shall I go on? No, I can't. It's too unpleasant for me to remember the hurt and pain others have caused you, because it hurt me, too—all the lost sleep, worrying about you back then. You know that if I could find those sick, mean-spirited people, I would make them pay for hurting you—for hurting us. Oh, and pay they would. Nothing would be too cruel for those who have made us suffer, because when you ache, so do I. I'm sorry for my digression. I must not dwell on the past. We need to look toward the future now—our future. A future we will have together, because it was meant to be. I know you feel it, you just don't want to believe it, but you will, oh, you will…

It hurts me that our relationship has been so one-sided. I've asked you to communicate with me, but you ignore my requests as if I don't exist. Trust me, I do. You may think that your silence is some signal to me that you don't know who I am. We both know that to be a lie. A lie fabricated by those who are trying to keep us apart. I know that you've seen me. It's impossible to think otherwise, as I am wherever you are. Every morning, back in Boston, you took the 7:36 Redline train from Porter Square to Central Square. You walked the short half-block to your job at the Health Center. We've had lunch together more times than I can count. I've even walked you home to make sure you made it there safely when the trains weren't running.

There were days when you sat outside at Harvard Square, eating your lunch. You always sat on the cement walls facing out in the direction of the river. You are an observer, a people watcher, just like me. There were times when our eyes met. They were brief, passing moments as you window-shopped on your way back to work, but those are the points in time that I always hold onto, because in those instants you acknowledged me, that I existed, that we were still connected.

July 3, 2013

Joseph,

It is not quite four in the morning. The sun has yet to waken a new day, and you are still curled up in your sheets, asleep. As on many of the nights since you shut me out of your life, I have not been able to rest. Apparently, your dismissal of me has not had the same effect on you as it has on me.

You look so peaceful, lying there with a slight smile upon your face. Times like this make me realize that my determination to bring us together is what I must accomplish, no matter how much you try to resist our reunion. That is why I decided to spend the night, last night, by your side.

Yes, that's right. I spent the night right here by your side as you slept. Before I go on, I must warn you how careless you are with your own safety. You left the sliding glass door to your balcony open last night when you went to bed. You must be more careful. Do you have any idea how many sick and disturbed people are out there, waiting to take advantage of someone like you? Thankfully, you have me to watch out for you. Since you dismissed me all those years ago, I now find myself outside of things—outside of you—outside of us. I'm always on the outside looking in, because you won't have it any other way. I sit in the dark recesses of your life and watch as you go about your routine. I want to be a part of your life again, to be a part of you, but knowing that you continue to shun me as if I am not good enough for you… If you only knew the truth.

The pain you cause me is enough to send anyone into the depths of despair and desperation. You are lucky that I am the strong and giving one in this life. If I were anything less, I'm not sure what your coldness would do to me—or to you. Again I stray. Where was I? Yes, your carelessness. Last night I noticed you didn't lock the door. I took that as an invitation for me to spend the night with you. So I did. It was one of the most moving and profound nights I've experienced since my departure.

I watched you for hours. I lost myself in the rise and fall of your chest and stomach as you slept. Your breathing through parted lips sang me a sweet lullaby. The smell of your body, damp with the night's sweat, was almost more than I could bear. I had forgotten how rich and sweet a true body could smell. I want to be a part of that scent, Joseph; to be a part of you.

There was a full moon last night. I remembered how much you hated sleeping with the curtains open, but there you were last night, the window wide open. I was thankful for that subtle change in your sleeping habit, as it allowed me to watch the pale rays of the moon decorate and paint our near-hairless bodies. It brought back such wonderful memories for me. I only wish you could have been awake so that we might have shared that moment together, as we had so many times, before you forced me out of our life. I'm not angry with you. That would be like being angry with myself, and that type of emotion would only be counterproductive. Besides, our time has come. You can't stop fate, Joseph. Tomorrow night our strange union will be complete, and then you will understand everything.

Until then…

July 5, 2013

Why do you continue to play these games with me? The angst you cause me is burrowing a hole deep in my chest. Shall I just lie down on your floor and allow you to take a hand drill, cranking the sharp metal drill bit into me to shred whatever's left? Will you love me then, in that final moment? Will that moment of triumph over me get you off? No, we will be one, once again.

I returned last night as promised. I always keep my promises where you are concerned. It was supposed to be our night, independence for the rest of the nation, but our final uniting. Do my words of love and devotion mean anything to you?

Closing off your balcony is one thing, but to cover up the glass doors so that I can't even see you is just beyond my comprehension. Do you think your actions were going to stop me? By now you must know what is happening. Yes, having our balcony shut off from me hurts, but that doesn't mean that I cannot get to you. My being here again while you sleep proves that. It's your coldness that burns me, but that wound will only make our bond grow stronger. Yes, I am hurt, but I am here with you, and always will be. Your selfish motives that cause such distasteful states will only give me strength to carry on the fight, for I know you are worth it—we are worth it. Oh, yes, the two of us together again will be worth all the pain we both must endure.

I shall be everywhere now. You will no longer have a moment without me. When you leave for work, know that I will be there with you. When you take a shit after lunch in that crystal-clean bathroom at work, listen closely, because I shall be in the stall next to you. When you have drinks with your coworkers, look around, and know that I shall be there, too. You'll recognize me if you open your eyes and realize that we will be one.

You cannot shut me out of your life any longer. I will not allow you to do that to us. How can I make you see that this is what God wanted for us? We were placed upon this earth to be together—to help each other, to console each other in times of grief, and to love one another in times of happiness. Our time is coming, Joseph. Do not fight this, for it will only prolong the agony, and shorten the days we have left together.

July 8, 2013

It has been three days since I've last come to you. Three days of agony for me as I watched you go about your life as if I didn't exist. How can you treat me this way? Maybe the better question is; how can you live with yourself, knowing the suffering that you are causing us? I'm the one who loves you more than life itself! I'm the dying twig and you, my dear Joseph, have become the strong brutal wind that has ripped me from the root of my existence, breaking me in two.

Last night was it for me as I watched you leave. I walked down the street with you, close enough to smell the odors of your body mingling with the lingering cologne and deodorant which you doused yourself in that morning. I followed you into Taste, your favorite restaurant—I had hoped it would become our regular hangout. You took a seat at one of the tables by the window. I lingered in the darkened corner, where you wish I would remain. I watched you sit there with an expectant look upon your face. When he walked in, I realized what that look was about. You stood and gave him a brief hug, not wanting to make it known to others, in the restaurant, that they were dining alongside two queer boys. That's what you get for moving to the Midwest, in order to escape me. You have surrounded yourself with a city that doesn't want to know you exist, where people would rather see you dead than alive. I'm beginning to see their point, but… back to last night.

I remained alone in the corner while you laughed and enjoyed the company of another man. Do you know how that made me feel? Wishing that you were dining with me, that I could make you laugh as he did? You gave each other a quick kiss outside on the darkened sidewalk after dinner, and went your separate ways. I knew you were going home alone, and that tonight would be the night when we would be together forever. I have lost you. I see that now. There is nothing left for me to do.

I know you have spent your life scared of our bond. My letters, my gifts, are all proof that they were wrong—there is nothing to fear, because I do exist; or, at least, I did, until you allowed the doctors and psychotherapists to convince you otherwise. I need you, just as you need me. They said I was the unborn twin, the one that didn't survive because I was rotten. They convinced you that I was poison in your system, a parasite that needed exterminating. They even had you believing that you could not survive if you allowed me to co-exist with you. You shut me out of your life—our life. That is what started all of this. Their lies are what brought us this far tonight. You see, I cannot survive without you. Therefore, I cannot allow you to go on without me.

I'm sorry that you will never get to read this last letter. Perhaps it might have been the one to persuade you to allow me to live—to allow us to coexist. I know better now. One more night, one more letter, would not have made any difference. You destroyed us when you let them go to work on you. They filled your head with their medicines and therapies. I tried to make you see the truth. I begged you not to listen to them, but you were always the weaker of the two of us.

You pretended I didn't exist. I only wish you could have admitted to yourself and to me that you had seen me. All the times you looked into the mirror, or saw our reflection in a storefront window, you never questioned the different colored eyes. Your left is ice blue. Your right is green, and mine, just the opposite. Didn't you see me in those moments? Or were you too far gone to care? Were you so afraid to admit the truth that you ignored the obvious?

You look so peaceful, lying in your bed, naked, just as you did every night since they took me from you. The only difference is that tonight you can no longer ignore me. You cannot act out against me, close me out of your life, and pretend that I am no one to you. Tonight we shall be together once again. There is nothing you or anyone else can do to stop me now. Our bodies will once again become one. I shall be there for you and you will now be there for me. Didn't I once say that, in time, you would understand that we were meant to be together? It's too bad we both had to die, in order for you to understand. I did promise you that I would love you forever. Now I shall keep my promise—which is more than you ever did.

Sweet dreams, my little brother.

William Holden's has published over eighty-five short stories. He is an award-winning author of such titles as, A Twist of Grimm by Lethe Press (Lambda Literary Finalist), and by Bold Stroke Books, Words to Die By (2nd place Rainbow Book Awards for best horror and a finalist for the Foreword Reviews' INDIEFAB Book of the Year Award for Best Horror), Secret Societies, and The Thief Taker (Lambda Literary Finalist) His most recent books include: *Grave Desires* (2015), and *Crimson Souls* (2016). You can find him online at williamholdenwrites.com.

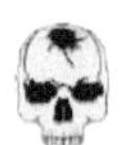

Molly and Me and Baby Makes Three

G. Lloyd Helm

I almost pulled back when Danny didn't struggle. I expected him to at least fight for his life, and when he didn't I almost pulled the pillow off his face. *"Maybe I'm wrong,"* I thought. *"Maybe he really is sick, not just trying to get even for being born."*

But even as I thought it and began to lift the pillow, I knew I hadn't been wrong, so I pressed harder. Twenty full minutes I held the pillow down tight. My arms shook and my neck and shoulders ached from the strain, but when I took the pillow off his face and held my ear to his mouth, I heard nothing. No sound of breath. No feeling of warm exhalation. Danny was dead. Five years old. My son was dead.

I was there in the delivery room holding Molly's hand, helping her push, when Danny was born. She was so excited! Glowing with birth aura so bright and warm, it was like shimmering fireplace coals. Tiny perspiration beads hung on her forehead and rimmed her mouth. Her red-blond hair was stringy with dampness. And she was beautiful! Dear God, she was beautiful! Even lying on the birthing table with her legs up in the stirrups and pain pinching her features she was beautiful—and I loved her. I loved her. She was the only thing in the world that mattered to me.

"Oh Ed… He's coming," she said. Her voice was breathy, panting, edged with pain and a little fear. "He's coming now. I can feel him, Eddie. Now… Nowwww!"

I felt her pain, but not enough of it. I begged God to let some of her pain spill over onto me so she wouldn't have to hurt so much. I wanted to make it easier for her.

"There we go," the doctor said. "Crowning… Ready to push again, Mrs. Pierce?"

Molly nodded, short, and jerky. She hurt too much to speak.

I was at her head, ready to lift her shoulders for the final push.

"All right…" the doctor said. "One, two, three… Push!"

I lifted Molly's shoulders and she bore down.

"Head's clear… Pushpushpush… Push again!"

"I can't…" she gasped. "I… can't!" Panic was settling into her voice. She screamed and struggled to push the baby out, but I could see in the mirror above her legs that the baby did not want to be born. He pulled his head down on his spindly neck, trying to pull back into the womb.

"Shoulders are caught," the doctor said. The excitement was gone from him now. Flat efficiency took its place. Something was wrong.

I watched as his latex-sheathed hands slowly eased into Molly's birth canal on each side of the child's head. There was blood—more than there should have been. Too much.

A nurse injected something into the tube running from an IV bottle into Molly's arm.

The baby's head began to rotate as the doctor turned the shoulders. Like turning a cork in a bottle. "Now! Push! Bear down!" he barked.

The baby was screaming even as the shoulders passed the opening. His hands clutched as they passed, and when the doctor laid him on Molly's stomach for a moment he clawed feebly with his soft fingernails, as though trying to open Molly's flesh and climb back inside.

The afterbirth came in a flood of shocking red. The doctor began packing gauze sponges into Molly. "Take him out of here," he said, not looking up.

"No! I want to stay. I want to…"

"You need to leave, Mr. Pierce," the nurse said, pulling gently at my arm. "There is nothing you can do now. Let the doctor work."

I breathed in the stench of birth and my stomach turned. The nurse led me out to a waiting room at the end of the yellow hall. I sat in an uncomfortable tube and vinyl chair and worried and sweated and prayed.

Danny had tried to take the only thing in the world I cared about even as he was coming into it.

Molly was never the same after Danny was born. She used to be bright, cheery, and never worried. She would smile at trouble and tell me not to worry. Everything would be all right. However, after Danny came she worried all the time. Her face changed from round, sweet, and healthy to drawn, lined hollowness. Deep slashes like cuts that bled black appeared between her eyes and they never smoothed away, even when she slept. She was haunted, and the haunting was between us like insulating plastic. Impermeable and cold, but clammy when you leaned against it for a time. Danny was always there between us, even when he was in another part of the house. Molly could never put him out of her mind. When we made love, I could see that her thoughts were not with me. They were with Danny, in his crib, lying beside him like a lover. She would struggle to be with me sometimes, but even as she began to win, to lose touch with him for a moment of passion with me, a sudden look of disgusted guilt would pass over her face and our sharing would end. There would be no more quiet moments of warm holding and soft words. The instant she was free of me she would rush to him.

We fought then. Not like before Danny was born. Then, our disagreements were short and quiet. Now they became shrieking battles that neither of us wanted, but both of us were powerless to stop. They always ended with Molly running to the baby. Always.

No—not running. Being pulled, as though some umbilicus was

being reeled in.

I felt guilty too. I thought perhaps this feeling of resentment was my means of expressing Father Jealousy. Perhaps I was demanding too much too soon, and if I backed off our lives would smooth out again, but as I demanded less, Danny demanded more. And never from me; always from Molly.

Always.

Danny would not let me hold him or change his diaper or feed him. If he cried at 2 AM, I would get up and prepare a bottle like Molly had instructed me. I would try to change his diaper while the bottle heated, but he would not let me. He would roll and kick and scream, even try to cover the diaper fasteners with his uncoordinated hands. If I fought through the changing, he would refuse the bottle, clamping his jaws shut and pushing at the nipple until Molly would come and take over just to stop his screaming.

I had only to put him into her arms for him to quiet. Then he would turn in her arms and grin with a viciousness far too old for his tender age.

Molly had become his bodyservant. He did nothing for himself, even as he grew big enough to do so. Turning himself over, drinking from a cup, crawling, learning to use the toilet… If Molly did not meet his demands instantly he would punish her with sadistic animality, biting, kicking, clawing, and shrieking like a cougar over its prey.

And through it all Molly forgot herself and devoted everything to the baby.

I tried to reason with her, telling her she had to take some time for herself, but she would not listen. She would forget to eat because each time she left Danny for an instant he would scream with rage. He would even hurt himself by clawing at his eyes until his face bled when she left him even for a moment.

She began to lose weight. The lines between her eyes deepened, and the tips of her cheekbones took on a bruised look from too much worry and not enough sleep,

"This is no good, Molly," I told her. "If you don't start taking care of yourself you are going to get sick."

"I'm not sick," she insisted.

"Not now, but you will be if you don't eat and sleep. You have to let Danny take care of himself a little at least. He is big enough to be left in a room alone for a little while. You don't need to carry him all the time."

"He's too little. He needs me. I have to take care of him."

"He's three years old! He shouldn't need you so much! You shouldn't have to be with him all the time! He can help himself some."

"He's too little! He can't! He's only a baby!"

"He's three years old! Three-year-old children don't need to be held all the time. They don't need so much that you don't have time to eat or sleep!"

She looked at me with pleading stubbornness and said, "I have to take care of him."

Danny began to cry in exact timing with her words. It was as though he meant to emphasize what she said. She turned and started to leave, going to him for the thousandth time that day.

"Wait a minute!" I grabbed her arm and spun her back then took a deep breath to stop my voice from shaking. "I have made an appointment for you with Dr. Kurtz. Maybe you'll listen to him."

She clamped her teeth together and hissed, "You know I am not sick, and I can't leave the baby."

"You can!" I shouted, and grabbed her by both shoulders. "And you will. I have a sitter lined up. You will be ready tomorrow afternoon!"

But she wasn't.

She was sitting in the big chair as I came in, Danny on her lap. Resistance flickered in her gray eyes.

"You are going to the doctor," I said.

"I'm not sick."

"You're going all the same." I took Danny from her. She resisted only enough to make it clear I was not going to get my way. I put the baby in his playpen and pulled Molly to her feet. She didn't resist much, but stood like a wooden doll; unyielding. Resisting by not fighting, but not cooperating either.

I began stripping the dirty pants and blouse off her, shocked briefly at the frailness of her body. The clothes were stiff with neglect and she smelled of dirt and sweat.

I carried her to the shower and turned the water on.

Danny had been quiet, watching us even when we left the room, but when the water came on in the shower he began screaming and throwing toys out of his playpen.

As the screaming began Molly's resistance changed. She began hitting me with her fists, then she kicked and bit. The water made her body slick and hard to hold. I tried not to hurt her, but she was doing her best to hurt me. A few of her kicks landed very near my groin. The last one came too close and I lost my temper. I backhanded her across the face.

Her head snapped back and around as though her neck was made of rubber. Cold sickness coiled in my stomach. My knuckles had cut her cheek just below her eye and the water mixed with the blood made the red trickle look like a cataract. It scared me. I thought I had really hurt her, and I loosened my grip to look more carefully at her.

That was all she needed. She shoved me away and shot out of the shower, dripping wet and bleeding, and ran to the living room to Danny. She took no notice of her nakedness, or the open window shades displaying it to anyone who cared to look. She could only see Danny. She scooped him up, clutching him to her bare breast, and I knew I would never get him away from her again. He smiled his evil taunting smile then, and I hated him.

Three months later I had Molly admitted to a psychiatric hospital for observation. It was not hard. Two doctors took one look at her condition and listened to my explanation and they OK'ed it. My guts turned over when the attendants took her, but the thought of separating her from Danny consoled me.

Getting her away from the baby wasn't easy. I tricked them both by putting sleeping pills in Danny's milk and in a glass of wine. Putting the pills in Danny's milk was the first time I thought of killing him. Perhaps I should have then. Perhaps Molly would be well now, if only I had put a few more pills in the milk.

When Danny was asleep, I begged and bullied Molly into drinking the wine I had prepared. Before the baby was born, I could never have done that. She would have fought back. Now, the only thing she fought for or against were matters concerning Danny; if I tried to impose myself between her and my son. But she had become so accustomed to Danny's bullying that she didn't think to resist me. When she was asleep, I carried her to the car. She was light. More like a bundle of sticks than the living flesh and blood I had carried across the threshold of our house when we first married.

I didn't get a babysitter for Danny, even though I was going to be gone all night and most of the next day. That was revenge. I wanted Danny to suffer a little of the pain he had put Molly through.

Danny should have died that night, or at least the next day. He should have screamed himself to death. I should have gone back and watched him starve, but I didn't. I couldn't. I still hoped he could change; that Molly and Danny and I could become a family.

During Molly's long months of treatment in the hospital Danny seemed to relax and acquiesce to the fact that I was the only one available to take care of him. He tried, at first, to bully me with screaming and hurting himself and refusing to eat, but I didn't give in. He ate what I ate, with his bottles cut to two a day. He resisted, but when he began screaming and beating his head against the frame of his playpen, I simply picked him up and paddled him, then put him in his bed. Four or five paddlings and missed dinners was all it took to convince him that things were going to be different. It would not always be his way, and it did not take long for him to become more compliant and agreeable. Even the woman I hired to take care of him during the day noticed how much easier he was to take care of.

He fooled me for a long time. I even began thinking that when Molly came home from the hospital we could be normal, now that I had taken charge.

I was sitting in my chair, half asleep in front of the TV, when my illusions of normalcy shifted and cracked. Danny was in his playpen quietly rustling through the toys that covered the floor of it. Then he began to whisper "Daddy, Daddy, Daddy…" chantlike. But this was not some game of pretend that only made sense to him. He chanted to me, and his chant had purpose.

I opened my eyes and watched as he jabbed a Tinker-Toy stick into the face and belly of a doll he held clutched in his tiny hand.

Then he looked into my eyes and smiled that same evil smile he had used on me so many times. He used it when he forced Molly into serving him. He used it when he came between my wife and me. Always winning. Always the victor. He smiled and looked into my eyes as he jabbed and jabbed the doll. And he chanted: "Daddy Daddy Daddy" punctuating each word with the jab. The word and then the jab. Constant, unrelenting, malevolent.

I shouted, "Shut up!", and lunged out of the chair toward him.

Instantly he stopped the chant and the stabbing, but the smile never flickered from his face.

He continued jabbing his dolls, the first one having fallen apart from the constant thrusts of his Tinker-Toy sword. I couldn't believe he was doing it and really knowing what he was doing. Toddlers do not harbor burning grudges, do they? But even as I thought it, I knew I was wrong.

Molly got better. She put on weight and stopped cringing or attacking me when I came to visit. After six months of treatment, the doctors let me take her out for the afternoon. We went on a picnic. She was almost her old self. She asked about Danny but there was none of the manic craving for him like before.

"When can I come home?" she asked.

"Doctor says soon. He thinks you're doing great."

"I want to be home with you and Danny."

"I want you home, Molly. I can't wait to have you home again." I took her in my arms and held her. The warmth of her body against me was almost more than I could stand. I wanted her terribly, but the doctor had cautioned me not to try to force her into anything, so I backed off, aching. I didn't push, only enjoyed being in Molly's presence in the cool shade under a clear sky.

Molly's homecoming was a day of joy such as I had not had since the day we married. I carried Danny into the waiting room as I had been doing each Sunday for a month. He had not attempted to re-establish his hold over Molly, but I was keenly aware of his malice toward me, and it made me pause. But then I repressed the apprehension, convincing myself it was just the old paranoia—Father Jealousy—of which I had been guilty before. I placed Danny in her arms and stood away from them, letting them have a moment to themselves.

I led Molly with Danny in her arms into our house. It was spotless top to bottom. There was not speck of dust or unshined surface anywhere. Molly seemed almost sorry to see its cleanness. She had thought to step back into our lives together at the same point she had left it, beginning with cleaning the house she had left in a wreck.

Danny made no demands out of the ordinary. He stayed quiet and easy to get along with. Too much so. I should have suspected something. Angelic behavior with no demands? I should have suspected.

I think now that my mistake was in not recognizing his malice for me for what it was. His hate was not singular. It included Molly as well.

She had forced him out of her warm, humid womb, and he had been taking revenge on her since that day. His earlier attempts had been thwarted when I'd put Molly into the hospital. Now he had to find other means.

It wasn't until I caught him staring at Molly with a malicious, speculative look far too old and evil for a four-year-old child that I realized things hadn't changed, and when he stopped staring at her I knew he had found the means to carry out his vengeance.

But I was too slow of mind to do anything about it, or perhaps it was just that I so wanted us to be a normal family that I blinded myself from what I knew to be true.

"Ed, I think Danny is sick," Molly said when I came home from work. It was four weeks after Molly's homecoming. "He's hardly been awake all day, and he won't eat anything."

"Does he have fever?"

"No, I don't think so."

I went to Danny's room and felt his forehead and the back of his neck. Both were cool and dry. He didn't move when I checked him. He seemed stiff—too stiff to be just sleeping. He didn't answer when I talked to him, or stir when I shook him.

"Is he all right?" Molly whispered from the doorway.

"I don't know. Maybe we'll keep a close eye on him tonight. If he isn't better by morning we'll let Doc Kurtz take a look at him."

But it didn't take until morning.

At 1 AM Danny screamed as though he were being torn apart. When we reached him he was shivering, covered with sweat and burning with fever. I wrapped him in a wool blanket and we rushed him to emergency.

Two days later the doctors told us it was Spinal Meningitis. We went over everything he had eaten, every place we had been, every person he had touched, but found no evidence of infection. Molly and I both took tests, which came up negative for the disease. Danny could not have contracted Spinal Meningitis, but he had.

The treatment he received saved his life, but Danny was paralyzed. Totally dependant. He had his revenge. It wasn't complete yet, but it had begun, and there was no turning it aside.

I'm not sure what finally broke Molly. Perhaps some deep secret feeling that Danny's situation was her fault, or perhaps it was just the constant strain of nursing him. The psychiatrists say they don't know either, or maybe they just aren't saying. But after eight months of caring for Danny, Molly filled the bathtub with warm water, locked the bathroom door, got in the tub and slashed her wrists. The only reason she didn't die was that I came home for lunch. This was unusual for me, but that day had been a bad one at the office and I had a feeling, a burning at the center of my bowels that told me to go home.

When I kicked in the bathroom door, it was almost too late. The tub water was red as blood. I pulled her out of the tub and wrapped adhesive tape and gauze tight around her wrists to staunch the trickle of her life, thinking how much I loved her and could not stand to lose her. She was so thin… almost like before. She had been giving everything to Danny. Even her dignity.

Just before the end, Molly had begun taking Danny to every charlatan she could find who claimed a miracle cure for him. She would plead with them, beg them, give them money, and promise more if they would just heal her son. But he never changed. He always seemed asleep. His revenge was to sleep and drain everything out of us. Out of Molly.

The doctors saved Molly's life like they had saved Danny's, and I wish they had not. Molly would not seem so lost to me if she were dead. There is an acceptance in death. If she were dead I could bury her and let her go. Instead she is there, always. Sitting in her room at the hospital. She doesn't talk or shift her eyes to see me when I walk into the room. The attendants change her position every hour, wash, and feed her, and I will never get her back from that place.

At least Danny can't hurt her anymore. He's dead. I even held a mirror to his mouth to see if there was breath in him to cloud it, even a little. It stayed clear for half an hour. Now I can wait until morning and *discover* that he is dead. No one will suspect me. The doctors said he would die soon anyway. Everyone knows it. They will all be sad, and give me their sympathy and condolences, and secretly they will think. "*Poor Ed. He has had so much grief. But it will be better now that Danny is finally gone. And Danny is better off, too.*"

Now if I can only sleep for a while…

G. Lloyd Helm is a ne'er do well scribbler who has six books on the market. He is kept by his wife of 46 years. He married well. You may contact him at ghelm11109*(at)*earthlink.net. You may buy his books at roguephoenixpress.com.

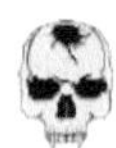

Ghost Story

Carly Holmes

She was the only girl I've ever known who could make walking boots and a duffle coat look sexy. I was in love before I'd even got out of the car, before I'd even met her properly. Curls like kinked copper piping, eyes the same colour as rain-soaked oak. She stood in the lane and smiled as if she wanted nothing more than to spend this autumn day in the woods with a city boy, a friend of a friend, and help him with his thesis on haunted houses. I could have spent the rest of my life just sitting there, gripping the steering wheel, watching her smile at me, but I figured I had thirty seconds, tops, before she started to get nervous.

I slid out of the car and hefted my backpack onto my shoulder, trying to stand tall and relaxed as if I did this country living lark every day. My new walking boots were already starting to scrape the skin from my right heel and I knew I'd be limping before we got further than the first stile. My mate in Cardiff, the one who'd hooked me up with this beautiful creature, had lent me thick wool socks and told me they needed to be worn outside the jeans, pulled all the way to the knee. When I whined that they made me look like a dick he told me that the deerstalker hat with the price tag still dangling made me look like a dick. The socks just made me look slightly froggish.

"Megan?" I asked as I bent to stop one of the socks from shuffling back down my shin. "Hi, I'm Matt. Thanks so much for saying you'll help."

She gave me her hand. "It's a pleasure; Gran loves visitors. We'll go straight in now, before lunch. You won't want to be there when she gets stuck into her soup."

We walked to the houses grouped along the lane. "Old fishermen's cottages," she said. "They're all the same here in Aberarth, they turn their backs to the sea. And this one's hers. Boots off, I'm afraid. She doesn't like to vacuum that often." She grinned at me. "And you might be more comfortable if you wore the socks under your jeans."

I sat in the tiny front room, testing my Dictaphone, while the kettle and Megan whistled in the kitchen. Her Gran eyed me expectantly from an armchair.

"What's that thing?" she asked.

I showed her the Dictaphone and clicked a few of the buttons. "It'll record everything you say and then I can write it up later."

She seemed impressed. She nodded a couple of times and stared at the wall for a while, mouth pursed. "Not going to give me cancer, is it?"

"No, Mrs Howells, it's safe." I held it out to her. "Do you want a closer look?"

She flapped a hand at me and tugged her blanket further up her chest. "You keep hold of it. No reason why I should have to have it."

The return of Megan had me fumbling pen and papers to the carpet. I think she knew the effect she had on me, but she was graceful about it and let me help her with the tea while she picked up my notes. Her Gran sat and watched us through narrowed eyes as milky pale and faded as sea glass. "Crumbs!" she barked as I took a piece of cake. Megan softened the command by winking at me as she leaned forward with a plate.

Once centre-stage, Mrs Howells set aside her suspicions of my character and modern technology and shuffled forward in her chair so that she could tap my wrist with her spoon whenever the fancy took her.

"It's way up in the valley," she said. "Up where the Arth is still more stream than river. She'll take you," a nod towards Megan, "though I don't like her going and I've told her so. There're a lot of ruined cottages up there, scattered through the woods. Most of them were crumbled down to nothing by the time I was born, but that one was still lived in. My mother took me there every Sunday with a basket of bread and some potatoes. Christian charity, she said, but I knew it was because she was scared." The quick, precise flick of her spoon against my wrist bone made me jump.

"You see, she was a witch. The woman who lived in the cottage. Nobody ever said as much, but we all knew it. Once a month she'd come down to the village and stand in the lane, not looking at us, not speaking, just waiting. We'd all, each household, fill her sack with what food we had and then she'd go. She touched my mother once, laid a hand on her stomach when she was pregnant with me and blessed the bump. Four miscarriages before that but she carried me straight through and delivered me with barely a drop of blood spilt. But what you can give you can also take away, that's what my mother thought, and that's why she made the extra offerings. Just. In. Case." Three more taps of her spoon. I had to stifle a grin and knew that Megan was smiling behind her mug.

"And then one day she had a child with her. A girl, not much more than a toddler and weak as a newborn. There was something wrong with her, you know, in the head. Constantly dribbling. She'd walk in circles if she were put down. Nobody could believe the witch had had her the usual way, no man would dare go near her, so the little one must have been dumped in the woods like people dump kittens they don't want. Either that or she stole her.

"Anyway, things carried on as they were and no questions asked. Blankets and firewood and vegetables in the winter, apples and fish in the summer. We all rubbed along and the child seemed healthy enough. Didn't like us though. I never saw her smile, not once. My mother made me give her a bag of my old toys one Christmas and she tipped them out onto the ground in front of me and stood on each one, grinding them under her shoes. I cried all the way home."

She settled back in her chair and raised her eyebrows at Megan, who stood up and gathered the mugs. "More tea?"

I nodded and murmured a thank-you, but was so engrossed in her grandmother's story I forgot to look up to watch Meg leave the room, and by the time I remembered she'd disappeared back into the kitchen. Mrs Howells thinned her lips and folded her arms, staring at me. We waited in silence until Megan returned and only then did she unfold her arms and carry on.

"Yes, she was an odd one, that girl. She used to spend her time sitting in the upstairs window of the cottage and gawking at the world around her. There can't have been much of a view—it was all trees—but she'd sit and stare and point the way you or I would if we were dropped onto the busiest street in London. Who knows, maybe she saw things in the trees the likes of us couldn't see?

"When the witch died the girl couldn't have been more than half grown, eleven at most. We should have done something then—someone should have—it's not right to leave a little girl up in the woods all by herself. But, you see, we didn't want her. None of us wanted her. So we never talked about it. Left the odd bag of potatoes by the door, that kind of thing, and pretended that she didn't exist. She made it easy for us—she never came to the village in the daytime, though there were some who said they saw her now and then after dark, digging through the allotments."

She nodded at the memory and reached for her tea. "Any more cake, Meg? I can't remember exactly when she died but it was a few years later. Some childhood illness she should have left behind with her pigtails, but I suppose she was a late bloomer for that kind of thing, what with being so backward. A few people said that they'd stopped seeing her at the window, but none of us wanted to know so nobody knocked on the door. Nobody went in to check.

"A couple of tourists found her a few months later. Walkers, they were, and they raised a right fuss afterwards, trying to get the police interested. Made us feel like criminals. She'd been dead a while. Curled on the floor beneath the window in the upstairs room, fingers hooked round the edge of the sill. As if she'd tried to drag herself up for one last look out. Poor girl."

I took another piece of cake. "Did you ever find out where she came from? Did any relatives come forward?"

She glared at me. "I haven't finished yet, young man. You can ask your questions later. You wanted to hear a haunted house story and I'm just getting to that part."

She acknowledged my mouthed apology with a slight movement of her head and cleared her throat.

"So there we were, all very sorry for the poor girl but really, it wasn't as if we'd done anything wrong. She was taken away and buried in the churchyard on the top of the hill. You couldn't pay for a view like that these days. Meg can take you up to see the grave, I'm sure, if you can handle the walk." The doubtful glance she gave me spoke volumes about her confidence in my ability to handle a walk even half that distance.

"After she was buried we didn't give her any more thought, if I'm honest. It was over and done with. There were a few hard-nosed types, mentioning no names, who went up to the cottage to see if there was anything worth taking, and a few ghouls who wanted to see where she'd died, but the rest of us left well alone. And then the troubles began."

My Dictaphone suddenly let out a high-pitched squeak and I echoed it with my own chirrup of alarm. Megan chuckled quietly from her corner and her Gran threw back her head and bellowed her delight.

"Got you scared, have I?" she asked, as I fiddled with the tiny machine. "Like a ghost story, do you?"

I tried to laugh. "Love them. I'm a big kid when it comes to a good ghosting, and the scarier the better. Please, carry on." I was desperate to press my hands to my hot cheeks but didn't want to draw any more attention to myself.

"So," she continued, still smiling, "during that autumn, a few months after she'd died, we had an outbreak of whooping cough in the village. It claimed nine young lives in a few weeks. They had to shut the village school; there was no one to fill it. In the winter we lost five souls at sea. Old Evans and his three lads first, in one fell swoop, all gone. There wasn't even a storm. Poor Aggie, his widow, she was never the same.

"By the next spring we were all of us wearing black in one form or another. I lost both parents to their hearts and the lady who lived next door broke her leg and got an infection that carried her off. There were whispers that the witch had put a curse on us for neglecting her child, and some folk even started leaving offerings up at the cottage. I got married and fell pregnant and barely left the house once I started showing, the looks I got. Everyone expected me to lose it, you see. But I didn't. Her mother." She pointed at Megan.

"And then people started hearing things up in the woods. A courting couple came running down the lane one day, showing a lot more flesh than was decent and whiter in the face than my bed sheets. And you can trust me on this, young man, my bed sheets are the whitest things you'll ever see. They said they'd been sheltering from the rain in the cottage when they heard someone moving around upstairs. Before they could get their clothes back on footsteps came running down the stairs into the next room. The inner door burst wide open, ripped off its hinges. They didn't stop screaming until they were half a mile away and too out of breath to scream any more. Stopped their kissing and cuddling it did, though, which pleased the girl's mother no end because the boy was a bad sort and no good for her.

"Then young Tomos was found hanging from a tree next to the cottage. He'd failed his school exams and couldn't cope with the shame, so the story goes, but I'd seen him that morning and he told me that he was going to be allowed to take them again in a year. He wasn't cheerful, but he didn't seem about to kill himself either. So, what do you think of that?"

I nodded and sucked on the end of my pen. "Great, Mrs Howells. Not your usual haunted house story, but it's definitely got me spooked." My cheeks had died down enough by now for me to risk a joke at my own expense.

She bridled and raised her spoon. "Not a proper haunted house? Tell me what you were expecting then. Go on. Not a proper haunted house! What would you say if I told you I've seen things with my own eyes?" She didn't let me answer. "Now, I don't like to talk about this, and I don't believe in ghosts like you see on the telly. Headless horsemen and the rest. But I do believe in bad spirits, and bad energy. I do now, anyway." She shifted forward and lowered her voice.

"It was a couple of years later, and there'd been a few more incidents. The hunt that went through the woods every Boxing Day came to a sticky end, horses bolting and bones snapped all round. A little boy went missing from Aberystwyth and was found wandering in the woods, covered in bite marks. Human bite marks. He wouldn't tell a soul how he got there. There was nothing that couldn't be explained away by ordinary men and their ordinary wickedness, but still. I'd taken to walking through the woods myself, to blow the cobwebs away. I was having some trouble with my husband, and liked to get out of the house when I could. But I never went near the cottage. As soon as I could see it through the trees I skirted off the path and kept my distance.

"The day it happened I was alone, and happy enough. I'd walked for a while and stopped below the cottage, on the riverbank, to cool my feet. I couldn't see it through the overgrown trees, and barely remembered why I was avoiding it anymore. It was a warm afternoon and I was almost asleep when I heard something hit the ground behind me, so I turned to see. It was a wooden horse, about the size of your fist, and just like the one I used to have when I was little. I remember I was pleased and thought I could take it home for my girls. Then I saw something else, a few feet away. A tin pig, the kind you paint and add to a farmyard set. I stood with it in my hands and looked at it and I knew exactly where its ear would have a slight nick. You see, it wasn't just like the one I'd had when I was a girl, it **was** the one. The one I'd given to the witch's child all those years before.

"Well, my heart started beating fast then, and I looked up at the cottage. I was still a way away, but even so I could see there was someone standing in the doorway, just standing there, watching me. I forgot I was a wife and mother then, a grown woman, and I turned to run." She swallowed loudly. "And that's when I was grabbed from behind. Arms around my waist, and tight so I thought they'd split my ribs wide open. Someone pulled and dragged me towards the cottage. Words in my ear, wet words hard as pebbles. *Now you! Now you!* I screamed and kicked and heard shouting in the distance. It was a couple from the village. Incomers, they were. I'd been as unwelcoming as the rest when they'd moved in, but I was glad to see them then, and never heard a bad word said about them after.

"By the time they reached me I was alone and scratched up, in a state. They had to half carry me back to the village. I was terrified I'd be pulled back to the cottage so I clung to them all the way home."

Her hands were shaking. When I cleared the fear from my throat she flinched and pushed them beneath her blanket, and I pretended I hadn't seen.

"So, that's my story. I've never been back to those woods since, and I wouldn't again, not even if you paid me. I don't like Meg going, but she's as stubborn as her mother."

Meg shifted in her chair and glanced at me. "Nearly time for lunch. I'll heat up the soup."

I followed her into the kitchen. "What a great story. She really believes it, doesn't she? Do you think she'll mind if I ask her a few questions?"

Meg moved close to reach a saucepan down from the shelf behind me. "I think she's had enough for today. She's still there, in her head. I don't want to leave her scared." She touched my shoulder, quickly. "I've heard it before, anyway, so I can probably fill in any gaps for you. We should go in a minute. It's a long walk."

I stood by the window and waited as she heated the soup and switched the television on, leaning over her grandmother with a murmured comment and kissing the top of her head. Mrs Howells accepted the tray placed on her lap with a nod. "Thanks, cariad." Her hands were steady now and her attention seemingly on the lunchtime news bulletin. Megan had been right about not wanting to be in the room when she started eating though. Any appetite I'd had crashed into the wall along with the bits of half chewed carrot that exploded from her mouth.

As I squatted on the doorstep and wrestled my feet into my walking boots, she called to me from her armchair. "You look after my granddaughter, do you hear me? Don't think of coming back without her."

I craned my head around the frame and gave her my most reassuring smile. "Don't worry, I'll keep her safe."

Megan stepped past me and pulled the door closed, but not before I heard her grandmother's response. "Patronising little city boy. He'll start running as soon as a cow moos at him, I know his type."

True to my word, and stung by this slur on my manhood, I tried to help Megan over the first two stiles. We tussled, legs at extraordinary angles, until she laughed and pushed me gently away. "I can manage, really. Save your energy for the uphill bits. And for the cows." She winked at me and I imagining leaning forward, kissing her. I bent and fiddled with my boot.

The path narrowed through gorse and thorn, winding up the side of the hill. The village was soon no more than a grey slide of rooftops and chimneystacks. I was too out of breath to speak, too focused on not panting, but Megan seemed to float in front of me, twisting to point at the view as it fell away behind us, pushing her hair back with an impatient hand.

"You don't mind taking me?" I asked when the path had levelled out a little and I felt less sick. "After what your Gran said? It doesn't scare you?"

She stopped and pulled a bottle of water from her backpack. "Don't be silly. I don't believe in ghosts, and I've played in those woods since I was tiny. I know my Gran thinks something happened to her there, but she was quite fragile back then."

She offered the water and looked away from me, down over the gnarl of treetops towards the flat grey of the sea. We'd climbed a fair way and cleared the woods, but they stretched ahead and beneath us, in the distance. I guessed that was where we were going, to rejoin the river and follow its rush to the cottage.

"My granddad used to beat her," Meg said, still staring down at the sea. "It got so she was too scared to be at home, and too scared to stay away, in case it made him angrier. She had breakdowns, and even went into hospital for a while. You wouldn't think it to see her now, so strong, but she used to jump at the buzzing of a bee in the garden. She thought it was him all of the time. She thought he was just behind her, even when he was in the next village, working. He became her entire world."

We carried on walking, but slower now. "Did she go to the police?" I asked.

Megan shook her head. "I don't think she even tried. You just put up with it back then. No, he died. Heart attack. My mum was still a girl, but just as relieved. She had her fair share of bruises too. She says they wore pink at the funeral and tap danced behind his coffin."

She did a quick jig, clumsy in her thick layers, and laughed as she stumbled and I caught her arm to steady her. "All downhill from here," she said, gesturing towards the valley ahead of us. "And that's where the fun begins. There's no real path any more, so we'll have to do a bit of clambering once we get into the woods. Take a good long look at the sky while you still can, Matt. The trees are so dense at the bottom, where the river is, you won't even know the sun's shining."

"We need breadcrumbs," I told her as she strode ahead. "To lead us back out."

"Oh, I can get us back out," she assured me. "If they let us go."

And she grinned.

That fear again, just a tickle between my shoulder blades, but as addictive as anything I'd ever known. I loved it.

I followed Megan down through a sheep-scattered field to where the trees elbowed each other. She slipped under the fence and faded away, lost against the dim backdrop. As I scrambled after, skidding to my knees, I called out to her to wait. The pale angles of her face gleamed supernaturally pale as she turned to me. "Are you okay?"

I resisted the urge to take her hand. "I couldn't see you properly. It's like the light's being squashed by all these trees."

She nodded and peered at her watch. I wondered if she had plans for the evening. "It's going to be steep for a while now," she said. "Be careful, and if you start to slip just sit down."

After the third skid had landed me on my back I decided it would be easier to just stay seated and slide the rest of the way. I didn't know how Megan kept her footing. She glanced round a couple of times to check on me, but we didn't speak until we were at the very base of the valley, enclosed on all sides. I could hear the river toiling somewhere out of sight. It was several degrees colder, and my jeans were heavy with mud. I tried not to shiver.

Megan pulled me to my feet. "Not far now. If we can get to the riverbank we can follow it to the cottage." She started to force her way through the undergrowth, swearing quietly as brambles scratched at her legs. "They caught a monkey in these woods a few years ago, you know. It had escaped from a private collection, and didn't know how to survive by itself, out in the wild. A couple of kids saw it first and ran home to tell their parents, then two of the local farmers took their shotguns and went after it. Not much of a hunt, by all accounts. The poor little thing ran straight up to them. All it wanted was to be looked after. They took it into the pub afterwards, all puffed up like they'd done something clever. The little dead body dangled by its tail for everyone to see." She grimaced. "It trusted them to keep it safe and they killed it. Probably laughed as they pulled the trigger."

We were at the riverbank now. I tipped my head back and could just make out tiny patches of sky between the thick layers of tree canopy above me. They looked a long way away. The movement made me dizzy and the leaf mould I was up to my knees in made me sneeze. Something had gone from the day. I was struggling to recapture that sense of anticipation and fun I'd felt before we entered the woods. If her sober monkey story was anything to go by, Megan's mood was dipping, too. I didn't really have anything to lose.

"Maybe we can go for a drink afterwards," I said. "If you want to?"

She smiled at me and reached to brush something from my shoulder. "That would be nice. You can tell me a ghost story over a pint."

Before I could decide whether she was flirting she'd turned away and started walking upriver. I suppose I should have taken the lead and trampled the worst of the brambles, helped her over the fallen logs, but I was content to stay behind and enjoy the way her jeans tightened across her thighs as she kicked a path clear for us. I allowed myself a tiny daydream or two.

When she stopped I was so engrossed in my own thoughts I barely registered the sudden stillness until I'd cannoned into her and almost knocked her off her feet. We were both warmed from the walk, cheeks pinked by exertion. She clutched at my arms to keep herself upright and pointed over my shoulder. "There it is."

And there it was. So tangled in ivy I would have missed it if I'd been by myself. Half of the roof was gone, and the other half looked as if it was hanging by cobwebs alone. There was no door to keep the elements out, no glass in the window frames. They punctured the stone walls, blank and black, like eye sockets. I started to walk over, fumbling in my backpack for my camera, clicking off a couple of shots, and then something moved in the upstairs window. A quick, pale blur of something. I squeaked and took a step back, and behind me Megan laughed.

"It's a dove, look." She clapped her hands and the bird launched itself from the sill, flapping wildly as it tore away. "But I know what you thought. Just for a second it could have been a face. That's the window the girl used to sit at, before she died."

She stepped past me and walked up to the doorway, pouting and draping herself against the frame like a model on a photo shoot. "Do you want a picture of me?"

I thought I might as well fire off a few rounds, seeing as she was asking.

"And what about one from the window? I could sit up there and look out, the way she did."

She ducked inside the cottage. I could hear her stumbling around.

"Be careful," I shouted. "The whole lot might come down on you. It doesn't look safe."

She shouted something back, something unintelligible but reassuring, and I relaxed and scuffed around outside while I waited for her to reappear. Blocks of stone lay scattered, presumably loosened from the cottage walls by harsh winters. I prodded one with my toe. It was a chunky blue-grey, shot through with seams of milky quartz. Beautiful enough to take home and lay on my mantelpiece as a souvenir. I bent to pick it up.

Beneath it, something pink lay half buried in the earth. Pig pink. I held it in my hand and turned it over, wiping it clean on the front of my jacket. Its rusted face leered up at me. There was a slight nick to the ear. I shuddered with my whole body then, felt the shudder kink the hairs on my head and crease the skin across my feet. I dropped the toy and stepped back, looking to see if Megan was at the window. I thought I could hear her somewhere inside the cottage, I could definitely hear someone, but there was no answer when I called out.

This was usually the best bit for me, when the thrill teetered over into fear and that fear threatened to gallop away with my adult self and turn me back to a child. Monsters and werewolves flickering on the edges of my vision. But I suddenly wanted Megan outside, with me, where I could see her and know she was okay. Then I could let myself enjoy it, the getting spooked and the afterglow of safety when the grown man in me reasserted himself.

"Meg," I shouted, "just come down. I'm getting cold."

My eyes were starting to water. "Megan, answer me."

When she appeared at the window, popping up in a flurry of hair and limbs to fill that dark space, I actually screamed, and then we both laughed and I couldn't stop.

"Did you think I was her?" she called. "It smells really bad in here. No ghosts, though."

She hooked one hand around the frame and leaned out. "Get one of me like this."

I looked at her through the camera lens. "Get back in first. If you fall and break your neck your Gran will make mincemeat of me." I adjusted the focus and watched as she hauled herself back inside the cottage, crossing her arms on the sill and smiling down at me.

"Better?"

I grinned at her. "Much better." I raised the camera again.

Then she turned her head quickly, as if she'd heard something in the room behind her. When she looked back at me her face was almost mask-like with surprise. I started to say something, but she jerked with a sudden, vicious convulsion and her mouth opened wide. Loose masonry from the window scattered down to my feet.

I tried to laugh, still half convinced that she was joking around. "Meg?"

Her lips clamped shut, teeth grinding, and then opened again, wide. But she didn't speak.

Over her shoulder a face appeared, chin resting on the curve of her neck. If we'd been anywhere else it would have looked like a gesture of affection, the two heads so close. But here, it was something else. "Meg?" I said.

We stared at each other. Something twitched at her waist and I knew then that she couldn't move, couldn't speak, because of the arms encircling her ribcage. "Meg?"

The face, the other face, turned to me. Young, pockmarked, and grinning as if she'd only just learnt how and now would never stop. That grin stretched her skin so that the corners of her mouth were torn and bloody, and I could see the meaty length of her tongue. She looked at me and whispered something into Meg's ear, and Meg shut her eyes. They were glassy with tears when she opened them again. Her hands clung to the sill, fingers white and rigid, and then something snapped with a crisp rip and she sagged and let go. I thought of twigs crunching underfoot, but knew it was one of her ribs.

I still believe I might have done something then, gone inside and got her out, but as we looked at each other, the three of us, I heard footsteps making their way down the stairs, somewhere in the dark cottage, and I knew the three of us would soon be the four of us. My body hijacked any conscious intention and threw me backwards, away from the footsteps and the grinning face, and from Meg.

She was still staring at me, tears on her cheeks, when I dropped my rucksack and ran back to the river. Up to my waist in it and plunging downstream, legs and arms thrashing, screaming Meg's name. But I didn't look back.

I don't know how long it took me to reach the beach and I don't know how long I lay there on the sand, monstrous in my seaweed wrappings. I was half drowned and hypothermic. The police brought Meg out of the woods, splintered through with broken bones. They worked hard to get me to admit to having killed her, to being high on drugs. They didn't believe me when I told them about the witch.

When they finally gave me my camera back I sat for hours with the photographs, just looking at her. There were two that the police had missed. In both of them, the witch stood in the doorway of the cottage and watched me not watching her. Her child leaned from the upstairs window and grinned, not at me, but past me, at Meg. I burnt those ones.

But the photographs of Megan, twirling, posing, pouting, I'll keep them forever. She really was the most beautiful girl I've ever known.

Carly Holmes writes stories and occasional poetry by the banks of the river Teifi in west Wales, UK. Her debut novel, *The Scrapbook* (Parthian) was shortlisted for the International Rubery Book Award in 2015. Her short prose is regularly published or is forthcoming in a number of anthologies and journals such as *Ambit*, *The Lonely Crowd*, and *The Ghastling*. In 2016 Carly won First Place in the Allingham Festival short story competition.

Carly is co-editor of *The Lampeter Review*, a journal affiliated to the university where she obtained her PhD. Ghost Story was first published in 2014 in the *A Fiction Map of Wales* anthology by Hmm publishers in association with Wales Arts Review.

Jeff: Ghost Buster Extraordinaire

Elsa M. Carruthers

Even before he opened it, Jeff knew the letter was from Stu. Who else would send him a letter with no return address label, postage due? He sighed. Most of what Stu sent were duds; false leads and bogus accounts of the paranormal that someone had fed him as a gag. Figures. Stu's only skin in the game was the chance that he might be asked to take some pics, do some cover art and catch-work at local cons.

Still, every once in awhile Stu came up with the goods. And that was why Jeff dealt with him; because of the every-once-in-awhiles.

Hey Jeff-

I found this story in that journal I told you about. You know, the one I found in that ghost town, River Bend, NV? It says on the front page that the dude's name was Sheriff Bartholomew Pratchett. It's a good read to puzzle over, and I know you really like those unsolved mysteries.

The way I came about it is a story in itself, so I'll tell you about it another time.

Later,
Stu

Jeff leaned against his fence and opened the envelope. He leafed through the grainy copies and decided it was a short enough story to read right then, so he let himself into his living room and sat in his favorite chair. The ceiling fan whirred in the background, and in a few moments he found himself engrossed in his reading.

Monday, July 18, 1879

It is by far the hottest day yet in my new post as Sheriff. There is no moisture to speak of; no trees grow and the shrubbery is withered and brown as clay. It is as if God Almighty has withheld the rains in a vengeance, like the Good Book says. Even the wind provides little relief, as all it blows about are thick, swirling waves of dust and an occasional thorny tumbleweed.

I have been here in River Bend for going on nigh three weeks. From what I've gathered so far, Dan O'Conner started up the town so as to service the local ranchers around here. The majority of the revenues come from hired ranch-hands, who come blazing into town with a month's wages. Some of those dollars go to the shops for supplies and to repair damages caused by the rowdier crowd, but most go to the girls at the saloon.

The town hired me to make the young cowpokes and gamblers behave.

As all with the town seems well, I have taken to walking it, twice daily, and greeting the townsfolk who are so obliging as to speak with me. Already I have met Homer Dean, the smith, and Augustus Mills, the saloon keep and owner. I have also made acquaintance with Lu-Lu Bell and Virginia Holmes, the two overripe tarts enterprising in Gus' saloon. The rest of the folk are shy of strangers.

Tuesday, July 19, 1879

There is a big commotion today. The town's in a bustle to get all in order for the arrival of Miss Leah Lynn in a fortnight. All is being whitewashed, and long needed repairs are finally being tended to. The ladies are crowded in the hardware store, each trying to outbid the other on the last bits of cloth for new dresses and bonnets. Trade is now fierce.

I am always on the lookout for any start of trouble.

Thursday, July 28, 1879

Miss Leah Lynn is to arrive by coach, and I am to escort her from the coach to the saloon for her first singing performance. If all goes well, River Bend will finally be something worth speaking of.

The Ruiz lad rode into town early this morning. His lips were split and his little filly looked dry, so I motioned to the water trough and the barrel next to it with a hand dip. He took two dippers full, wiped his mouth with his sleeve. Then he said Billy and Percy Hill made off with two of his father's horses.

I'll see to it that both of them are sitting in the jailhouse and that those horses are found and returned to him by the time Ruiz and his men head up here. I sure hope there's no more trouble than that over this. The Hill boys are fine lads. I'd hate to hang them if I don't have to.

Sunday, July 31, 1879

f first, and by Jesus, I have never seen a man so big and powerful looking. I'd swear his britches were made of enough material to clothe a whole family. His gang wasn't quite as large, but I reckon I saw a bit of a family resemblance, given the fact that none except the lad who was here before was a lick less than five feet ten.

By noon Percy and Billy were blubbering that they didn't mean no harm by stealing the pintos. Damn luck. Percy sold the horses to some traveler and gave the money to his Ma. After I showed Ruiz that the boys were in the jail, I invited him and his gang into the saloon for some drinks while I went to see about the money.

I rode my mare up to the Hill farm and saw Mrs. Hill sitting on the porch, rocking away on a twisted branch chair and peering off into the distance. The house was no more than three or four rooms, but it looked cozy enough. The garden plot was as dry as the rest of River Bend; not even weeds dared to grow in the desert heat. For the life of me I can't figure why some of these folks insist on farming this hardscrabble land, when it's as plain as day that it's meant for ranching and not farming.

I knew she was a widow, so I said, "Mrs. Hill, might I have a word with you about your boys?"

"The ones you got locked up in your jail, Sheriff?" She looked at me, but her eyes were a pale, cloudy blue.

"Yes, and I reckon you know why they're in there."

"For helping their starving Mama."

"Horse thieving, Mrs. Hill."

She blew out a tired sigh that seemed to let her whole innards escape. Afterwards, she slumped into the rocker and lowered her face.

"You call it horse thieving, and I suppose you'll hang 'em for it. But I tell you, they was only trying to help their poor blind Mama. Ain't no crime in that."

"Horse thieving is a serious crime, but I don't want to hang Billy or Percy. I just want to return Señor Ruiz's money so that the boys can go free. Where's the money, Mrs. Hill?"

I put my hand out, palm up to show her I really intended to take the money. Then I put it down; her cloudy eyes met mine.

That's when she cackled madly and pointed to her stomach. It hung into her lap like an empty sack.

"Here it is, Sheriff. All that money. Does Señor Ruiz want his pound of flesh?"

I stepped back a bit, more than a little unsettled, and bumped into my mare.

As I mounted, fixing to ride back and do what I did not want to do, she hollered, "Sheriff, River Bend is coming under a curse and you will bear the brunt of it. You'll hang my two good boys and reap what you have sown." Her wails pierced the wind like giant thunder claps.

I tried to pay her no mind, but her cackling spooked me anyway.

Monday, August 1, 1879

I had two lads ready the ropes and gallows at eight. Pablo Ruiz watched it all, his black eyes set, his mouth twitching under his dusty moustache. The lads tested the ropes with two full sacks of flour. The sacks fell, coughing up white puffs when the ropes yanked them back up. There was a crowd milling about the platform of the gallows, only breaking to allow Billy and Percy to step up. Out the corner of my eye I saw Ruiz cock his pistol.

Neither boy said a word as the nooses were put over their heads and tightened around their necks. I could see that Billy had wet himself. The crowd grew hushed, save for a babe or two. An awful tightening seized my belly, making me want to lose my breakfast.

I didn't dare look at Pablo, for fear of seeing a gleam of satisfaction in his eyes. There was a loud snap of the floorboard opening up, and the crack of the ropes as they grew taut. Percy dangled, sometimes bumping into Billy, his britches now also wet.

Just then, there was a pop and a fierce light from the flash of a camera box. The man working the thing must have set it up while no one was paying any mind, and took the likeness of the two boys as life poured out of them. The townsfolk all turned to stare at the man. We could only see his backside sticking out of a drape attached to the camera box. Someone hissed. Some of the men spat out great gobs of tobacco juice, most landing on the ground, while waving fists in the air.

"Cut the boys down and bury them proper in the cemetery," I said to the lads. For a moment they just gawked like a couple of turkeys in the rain. Then they got to their work. My work was to handle the cameraman.

He was just coming out from under the drape when I caught up to him. "Who are you, and what is your business in River Bend?"

"Easy now, Sheriff. I'm a working man. I meant no harm by taking a likeness of those young horse thieves. I'm Giles Marner, cameraman for the San Francisco *Bee*." His smile was all sugar; I didn't like it one bit.

"You're a long way from home. What's your business here?"

"Why, I'm here to take the likeness of the lovely Miss Leah Lynn when she arrives." He added with a sly smile, "And, of course to hear her sing. She is a beautiful songbird."

I had to send him on his way. He'd done nothing wrong, save showing disrespect for Percy and Billy. Everyone had scattered, and, for my part, I was glad. Something like what the cameraman just did more than likely could blow into a wildfire. I knew most folk saw me talking to Mr. Marner and reckoned it was enough.

Thursday, August 10, 1879

I've seen Giles Marner around, taking likenesses of the people who've ridden up to River Bend 'specially to hear Miss Lynn. The hustle has done wonders for our town. A couple of times I've had to break up some misunderstandings and send one or the other on his way, but that's what I'm here for. Those little misunderstandings have in no way dampened even Mills' spirits.

Lu-Lu and Virginia have been especially social as of late, and of course that puts most in a good mood. Even the town ladies' jabbering about Lu-Lu and Virginia doing devil's work and bringing down the Lord's wrath upon River Bend only causes folks to smile.

Saturday, August 12, 1879

I walked the town several times today. A lot of folks are spooked all of a sudden. Seems that a few cowpokes who wandered over here for the show had their likenesses taken and are now sick. There's no doctor around here to speak of, so Mrs. Dean rode out to that old squaw, Two Trees, and brought her back to tend them. The men lay up in the hotel, withering like old vines. Two Trees said the men's spirits have left and their bodies weep for them to return. I don't know about all that, but I do know that it's not good for folks to be spooked.

I don't like the connection with the cameraman, either. I will watch him more closely.

Sunday, August 13, 1879

I noticed something peculiar today before I heard of those cowpokes dying. The side of the smithy where they stood before the camera is just as faded as before the whitewashing. And all the rest of it is as fresh as the day Owens set his brush to it. I have half a mind to send old Marner on, but I can't seem to make sense of what he's done wrong.

Besides, the railhead is a day's ride from here, and I'd hate to have to send him on with victuals and water skins he didn't earn.

Friday, August 18, 1879

More folks have died, each one shriveling up as if their very blood and flesh had been sucked out. Two Trees says something or other about curses.

"Well now," I told her, "by my figuring, that's three curses. One for hanging those boys, another for allowing Lu-Lu and Virginia to be sociable, and now one for Mr. Marner."

The woman gave me such a hard look. I thought it best to be on my way. I stepped out, the day's sun lighting up the town like gilt.

Later that day, a small gathering of folks came to the jailhouse. I could see they had Mr. Marner. He was all banged up and they were fixing to hang him. A few ladies hurried along after them.

"Ho now," I said. "Why are you folks taking the law into your own hands when that's what the good people of River Bend hired me on for?" I tried to sound friendly, like when I'm soothing my mare during one of her fits.

"To hell with the law!" some young hand called out. I could've cursed at that. The rest of them started grumbling and by that time, practically the whole town was out on Main Street watching.

I stepped forward and asked the man up front what the problem was.

He spit a long trail of brown juice at my boots. I let it go. He put his left hand up and motioned for the cameraman to be shoved forward. Mr. Marner was inches from death. Before I could stop him, he had Marner by the hair, shaking him as if he were no more than a saddle blanket. "This here man's a murderer. Every time he sets to camera-ing someone dies. We're gonna hang him so it won't happen again."

There was not a peep out of Marner. He was just as limp as a washrag. That was when I pointed to the star on my chest. "Hand him over or you'll be hanging. All of you. You damned near killed him already."

The man still had Marner by the hair. That same cowpuncher yelled again, "To hell with the law!"

I whipped my pistol in the air and shot. The man threw Giles Marner to the ground. "Have this cursed, murdering son of a bitch then." And then they turned and left. After that, there was not much to look at, so most folks went on about their business.

I sent Mr. Giles Marner on his way, after dusk. I wanted Two Rivers to see to him, but she just stared at me and shook her head. I asked some of the other ladies, but seems that they were not inclined to help. He was a real sorry sight, so I patched him up as best I could and set some whiskey before him. I explained how he had to go or he'd be killed. No question about that.

He was cordial enough about it and gave me no fuss. I helped him load the camera onto a pack animal, saddle his horse, rode out with him to the road crossing, and sent him on his way. He got his victuals for no charge after all.

Sunday, August 21, 1879

All's been quiet of late, and we are all anxious for Miss Lynn's arrival on Friday. The only one who warns against Miss Lynn's coming is Two Trees. She insists that Miss Lynn is some kind of bad spirit. No one paid her any mind. The night before, she threw up her hands and said she was going home.

Friday, August 26, 1879

Miss Lynn arrived today, and nearly took my breath away the moment I saw her. She is by far the loveliest woman I have ever seen. Her eyes are the color of emeralds, and her hair the color of pitch. She has the clearest, smoothest skin, like cool milk. I helped her to the saloon for a rest and some refreshment. When she smiled at me and said she was grateful, my heart stopped for a moment. I left her there just so that I could collect my wits.

That night I was awestricken. We all were, really. She sang song after song, her voice growing sweeter with each new verse. As the night wore on, Miss Lynn appeared fresher and more beautiful than before. It was as if the music were somehow reviving her. At midnight she finished with a curtsy that revealed her ankles. Not a single man hooted, though. No one dared to offend Miss Lynn, for fear she wouldn't sing again.

She retired to her room at the hotel. Some of us stayed on at the saloon for a bit, 'til about one or so, then it was just me wandering about, too excited to sleep. I was just making my way up to the hotel, on the other side of town, when I heard a dog howl and then some horses whinnying. Thinking it was another horse thief, I crept along the front of the hotel, then slowly to the side. I saw nothing at first. Then, in the moonlight I saw Miss Lynn put something on the ground. A moment later it grew, God help me, into the cameraman. For the second time, my heart froze that night. He looked at her with worship in his eyes.

"How may I be of service, Madam?" I heard him ask.

"You know what to do."

"Why, yes, of course." He took a large gunny sack from his back and set up the camera box. She stood in front of it, her legs spread wide, a slight wind picking up her skirts. Marner readied the flash while she opened her mouth as wide as she could. He pressed the flash. A light such as I have never seen before came out, and disappeared into her throat. Then I heard the wails and screeching. It was the voices of all those who had posed before Marner this past month. I just knew it.

Leah Lynn turned toward me, eyes glittering. At that moment, I was transfixed. The next thing I knew, Giles Marner was standing over me, his camera box ready. I pulled my pistol. Marner laughed as I tried and tried to cock it. The hammer wouldn't budge. Finally, I just put my arm over my face, but I know it was no good, because as he took my likeness, I could hear Leah Lynn's cold laughter in the darkness.

Saturday, August 27, 1879

I can already feel the effects. I have tried to warn the others, to tell them not to listen to Miss Lynn's songs, and that Giles Marner is here. It is no use. They will not hear what I have to say, and I am dying. I can feel the pull of my soul ripping from my body. I have my Bible on hand, but all I can think of is how—

The photocopy showed the place where the rest of the page was torn away.

Jeff put the story from the journal down, and wiped his forehead with his sleeve. This sounded like it could be a winner. Something that could finally get him some respect. He could really get his book published, and make everyone who called him "Ghost-Buster" eat it. If he played his cards right, he could maybe even get a reality show. This had all the makings of a pilot episode. He had to call Stu, see if maybe they could meet there. Stu could get a few good shots of him exploring the faded wall, the saloon, and the town square. Stu'd know what to do. He wasn't good for much, but Stu did know his way around a camera.

He leaned over and pulled a worn map from his side table. By the look of it, River Bend was only a few hours' drive from Ely. He could check it out and be back in time to start writing an outline. Hell, if this story panned out, it could be a stand-alone that could launch the series.

Excited, he took a cooler, filled it with his "road food": Hot dogs, deli meat, Ritz crackers, soda, gum, chips, and Little Debbie's snack cakes. On the way out the door he grabbed his camera (just in case Stu couldn't make it), recorder, and the map.

He left a quick voicemail for Stu and set out. The drive was uneventful. A few hours later, Jeff pulled up to the ghost town, unable to believe his luck. The buildings stood relatively intact. The place was surprisingly well preserved. A rush of happiness lit Jeff's face. This was it! The big story. He slipped his camera bag over his shoulder and undid the clasp.

A few good shots at the right angles, where the shadows stretched thin like long fingers… Yes! Later, he'd go over the photos and see if he saw any traces of "white matter." When he found any, he'd go back over those areas, comparing them with the journal entries, and then he'd test for paranormal activity.

Into his recorder he said, "Town of River Bend remarkably preserved. The paint looks fairly fresh and the windows are unbroken." He stepped gently onto the wooden platform that acted like a sidewalk. The boards settled, held firm. "Windows are clouded over with dust, it is impossible to see into any of the buildings, but there is a sense of sadness here."

Just then a gorgeous woman pulled her Harley into the dirt patch where he had parked. She glided the blue bike next to his car and cut her engine. When she pulled off her helmet and said, "Hi," with a big bright smile, he thought his day couldn't get any better. But it did.

She stepped up next to him and smiled again. "Hi there," she said in a husky voice. She asked him what he was doing, and seemed genuinely interested when he explained. Despite his plan, a not so small part of Jeff hoped that Stu didn't get his message.

They talked, looked around, and she stood respectfully to the side whenever he snapped a photo or recorded his thoughts. Every once in awhile she took a few pictures of her own on a cheap, disposable camera.

Jeff tried to force open some of the doors, but they wouldn't budge. "You'll have to bring some tools next time," she teased him, letting her fingers trail down his arm as she spoke.

"Yeah, that's a good idea," Jeff said. "I could jimmy some of these doors open and we could see inside."

Finally he was done and it was time to go home. He slipped his camera back into its case and snapped the recorder off. She smiled sweetly at him.

"It's getting late. I guess I better head off too," she said.

Jeff lingered. He wanted to ask her if she'd like to go to dinner with him or when/if she ever planned on coming out here again, but he couldn't quite work up to it. Instead he stammered a very garbled, "See you later," and made a dash for his car.

"Wait," she called after him. Her red leather jacket made a slight crackling sound. He turned back to her, his stomach knotted with hope and dread. She leaned close to him, so close he could smell her hair, and she kissed him on the cheek. "Take a picture of me and I'll take a picture of you. You know, so we don't forget each other."

Jeff immediately took some nice photos of her. He felt guilty, like he was imposing on her.

"My turn!" She took out her camera and took a single picture. Jeff's knees buckled. He tried to push himself back up. It was no use. All of his strength left him. A soft, melodic laugh was all that was left of the lovely woman he'd spent the afternoon with. And when he looked up, the last thing he saw was Stu stepping out of his beat-up Mazda.

Elsa is a poet and writer living in California. She is very shy, but can be coaxed out of hiding with great food, music, and lively conversation. She earned an MFA in Writing Popular Fiction from Seton Hill University. Elsa continues her studies by reading critical studies and attending conferences and conventions. Her work is published in several e-zines and anthologies, including HWA's *Poetry Showcase volume III*. Currently, Elsa is working on a novel and several nonfiction projects.

Tapestry
Lydia Peever

"Hey, that looks like a face!"

As the words left Bonnie's mouth, Tess cringed and jerked her head down to look at the floor. Distracted by a phone call a moment ago, she had run her hands through her hair. Again. Damn it. There they were, on the polished tile, four or five strands of hair. She moved her rolling chair back quickly but knew she had run out of time.

"Look! Tess, your hair, it looks—"

"Nah, it doesn't look like anything." Using the toe of her sneaker, Tess scuffed at the hair to force the strands away from one another.

"Oh, hey! Why'd you do that?" Anger flashed in Bonnie's eyes. "It looked like a face! That was so weird! Did you even see it?"

"It's just hair." Tess turned back to her computer and dragged the few hairs deep under her desk with her foot. Pushing them as far back as they would go, adding them to the rat nest of hair and dust to be cleaned out every Friday. It never mattered how often she brushed her hair, the errant shedding never stopped. Usually she got to it before anyone could see it. If she moved fast, they never saw a pattern in how her hair fell.

Tess sighed and closed her eyes for a moment, knowing nothing could stop it now. Bonnie had seen something in those five strands on the floor. Eyes still closed, she asked, "So. What did you see?"

"A face. Wide eyes. Not happy. You should have looked. It was super weird." Bonnie turned back to her computer, obviously still a little ticked off.

"Did it look like you?" Tess asked, not caring how odd that sounded.

"No, but it was a girl. How strands of hair could make such detail…" Bonnie turned, less agitated and full of questions. "So weird, it looked scared. Deformed or something."

Damn it, Tess thought, angry that it was happening again. When it happened to random strangers she'd learned not to care, but when it happened to coworkers or friends the consequences destroyed her every time.

Chewing at her lip, she looked to the right and faced her officemate. A red mark on Bonnie's mouth was all she needed to see. It would be flesh-eating disease again. This counted as the second time she had given someone fasciitis. Same as last time, it would be fatal.

"Are you okay?" Bonnie said, green eyes searching Tess's now pale face, no doubt plastered with worry.

"What is that on your lip?" Tess asked, appearing to change the subject.

"Man, I don't know. It feels terrible. It's all tingly." Bonnie reached to touch it, but left her fingers hovering an inch away from the raw patch.

Tess looked at the clock. Ten minutes to lunch. "You should go to the doctor. Like, right now." She leaned back and looked at the rat nest of hair just beyond her feet at the back of her cubicle wall.

"Aw, it's just a cold sore or something."

"No, really," Tess said, crouching half under the desk, "you should go on lunch right now. It's probably flesh-eating disease. You need to see a doctor before it spreads." She tried to sound firm.

"Tess! What a terrible thing to say!"

Gathering the hair and stuffing it into her purse, she began collecting other things that were stored under there. "No, seriously. I know it sounds messed up, but..." Trailing off, she grabbed her lunch bag with food she wouldn't eat and high heels she would not wear today. She stood up and set her belongings on the chair, and put her jacket on. "What you need to do is go straight to a doctor. I only hope it's nothing, but trust me." She stared steadily into the redhead's eyes, forcing her to listen close. "It's probably something terrible."

Bonnie clamped her hand down on Tess's wrist, pinning her to the office chair, "Really. What is wrong with you?"

"Nothing," she hesitated. These were the moments she ought not hesitate since it was now when the overwhelming urge to tell all rose, no matter how crazy she sounded. "I have to go. Please tell me you will see a doctor, okay?" She waited while Bonnie removed her hand and searched her face for explanation. Tess had never used a harsh word before and, though quiet, had come across as friendly until now. "I'm sorry," she said as confused silence lingered. There was nothing left to say.

Jacket on, she stuffed everything into the lunch bag, flung her purse over her shoulder and walked past her confused acquaintance and into the hall.

In ten minutes, Bonnie would head to a doctor, and spend the next week in hospital as a virus ravaged her once pretty face.

In ten minutes, instead of lunch, Tess would be at home preparing to deal with the job she had just walked away from.

Thanks, hair. Thanks a fucking lot.

No telling how many times this would play out. How many jobs, friends, homes... How much she would have to give up because of her hair and the futures people saw in it. It wasn't her fault the fortunes came true. After failing to explain the phenomenon so many times, she had grown bitter. When Tess tried to talk about it, the story came out confused. She tired of trying to explain something she barely understood when not talking at all suited her better. Though weary of looking for new jobs and homes, she had grown used to it. Being looked at like a freak when she tried to talk about it was something she could not get used to. Killing people was something no one should get used to, so she always left them before what they saw came true.

Growing up with only her sister and father to talk to hadn't helped. When it came up, they spoke in half sentences. Pretending they knew what having hair like this meant. For a long time, she did not know if people read too much into the images, or if her discarded strands were what shaped their fate. When grappling with this, she often thought of the first death she remembered.

One Sunday, when Tess was very young, a man saw an axe in her hair. It lay traced out in strands that fell on the light hardwood at church during a summertime picnic. Her hair was lighter from playing in the sun every day, and hard to see when it fell on a bright surface.

He crouched down with her among the legs of other adults bustling around and touched one finger to the floor.

"Would you look at that!" he said, then grinned, his tan wrinkling around gentle eyes.

"It's just my hair fell out." She looked at the design of one strand shaping a head, another forming the brow and nose. The grimace. Two strands rent the face in half, becoming a trail where a chest may have been. Some small whips lay at terrible right and acute angles.

His fingertip ruined an eye and caved in the skull. "This looks just like an axe. What would you say?" He hadn't seen the face at all, but that didn't mean it wasn't there.

Her voice small and eyes down, Tess had replied, "I'd say that I hope it's not an axe."

With a soft pat on the top of her head, he walked out of the huge dark doors to the front lawn of the small town church to rejoin the festivities. The man's son stood a few feet away chopping firewood for a corn roast that evening. Without warning, the axe slipped. For all anyone knew, the man was about to tell his son what he had just seen in the hair, and to be careful cutting wood. Instead, when he opened his mouth, the axe flipped through the air. The blade came down on his skull. Face cleft in half, he died instantly.

Hearing the screams as she approached the door, Tess looked out one clear pane in the stained glass to see the man fall to his knees. What faced her was a ragged wound, with one eye on each side of a dark metal blade. Blood poured down his chest. The way the axe stuck out before he collapsed looked exactly like it had in her hair. Women screamed over men shouting "Get back!" and "Call an ambulance!" while adults gathered Tess and other children away from the windows and doors.

She heard about it for weeks in the schoolyard. No one knew he had seen death in her fallen hair, so no one could tell why she was so upset. Eventually, she talked to her sister. Together, they talked to her father. Though they were too young to explain properly, her father nevertheless understood when they told him what the man had seen. This became the first time her life was rearranged. Her father switched her to another school. Before long, they moved to a different town, and then another. He regarded the stories with patience. After seeing a neighbour's face torn in half, when she told him of the car crashes, miscarriages, diving accidents and other patterns that came true, they seemed tame in comparison.

Tess had learned by the time she reached fifteen to keep her hair in a tight braid so it could not escape. Years had passed since the church incident. There had been many accidents, but no direct link that others could discern. No direct link from her to their death. If someone saw something, Tess kept it to herself. If she told anyone, she told her father. But only the bad ones. The bad ones always meant another move, another school, and difficulty making new friends. It was easier to ignore what people saw in her hair and pretend it had nothing to do with how they ended up.

Tess could do little the night her sister died. She sat on the floor under Sarah's body in the bedroom where she had hanged herself. Arms down, head down, turning slowly in time to fading moonlight. There had only been two years between them. Looking up, she had watched the rope gently twist up to the left, then untwist to the right until paramedics ushered her out of the room.

She and her father had rushed to the bathroom hours earlier, alarmed by shrill weeping as Sarah tore handfuls of hair from Tess's brush. Anger and arguments had been an everyday occurrence for months at that point. Sarah had been rushed to the hospital more than once with slit wrists. Her screaming was not uncommon, but her crying worried them both enough to come running. Even as they tore the frail sister from her screaming torment on the floor, they knew that she had seen her own death. Even as she flailed, legs kicking the hair, it slid out of order then back as if drawing the portrait was its only goal. Thread-snakes, they slithered into place as her father wrestled Sarah away. This dark artist created a perfect picture of Sarah with her arms down, her head down, hanging. Tess cleaned up the hair, bringing it into her room to the little box she kept just for that.

An hour later, Sarah hanged herself. Just as the image on the black and white tile had described.

Her father could barely look Tess in the eye as he explained the curse the next day.

"Sarah isn't even in the ground, Dad," she said, protesting his decision to talk this over so soon.

"You and I both know it was going to happen sooner than later. I miss your sister, God knows I do, but I missed her the first time we rushed her into the hospital with this…" He stopped and looked out the window, his mind weighing words.

"Illness?" she tried, wanting to finish this conversation.

Smoothing his own greying hair, he said, "No, like I said, curse. It's a curse, and there is more to it that I don't even know."

"But I'm the one with the curse, not you."

Knowing his eyes were trained out the window, she studied him until he looked at her. They locked eyes.

"She didn't want to see you go first," he said plainly. "The hair was why your mother killed herself, and I expect you to someday, too. Sarah couldn't bear to see you go first. That's why she's been trying so hard to-" he trailed off as he normally did when talk turned to his wife and the girls, how dark this had all become over the years.

People had seen things in her mother's hair, just like her sister saw, just like everyone else. Then they died, like the man at church. Her father hid it from her as best he could, but people had seen things in her shedding locks before she was able to walk. Others had died. He refused to tell her how many, but handed her a diary. It belonged to her mother and all the entries were addressed to her. One of the girls would follow in her footsteps and since Sarah was born first, with nothing amiss, her mother began writing to Tess before she had even conceived.

It had been a long time since she last read those passages. Mentions of ruined friendships, new towns and scrambling for work to pay the cost of moving. How her mother cut her own hair to save killing every hairdresser. The diary read like her own life in many ways.

Lines about the doubt and worry, the fear that someone would see their death in her tresses. If she cut her hair short, the smallest hairs would find a way to crosshatch and describe the end of whoever looked close. If she shaved it off, the smallest stubble would careen and swirl as if it were lead dust shaped with magnets. Someone would see. Futures in her hair would never be silenced.

Tess never had to test these theories as her mother had. Every time she read the diary, she held it close with silent thanks. If her mother had not gone through such torment, who knows how long Tess would have lasted? It had driven her own mother mad. It had driven her to suicide—learning what her hair really did. Stories reached back through maternal generations of suicide and insanity and so many different shades of hair.

Then the explanation of the bigger picture. What the hair was really for. What the purpose really was. The deaths that followed were a by-product. Every accident unavoidable, but unimportant.

Years ago Tess had pored over every line in the diary, each page a little piece of the mother she barely remembered. Moving so often, she had kept the diary in a drawer with clothes. Finally, it shuffled into a safe box with her will and insurance papers. Tess rarely read it now, and hadn't touched it since sliding the box into its new spot in the bedroom closet. On her way home on this sudden last day of work, it became all she could think about.

Removing the key from her jewellery box, she opened the safe. With the diary in hand, she sat on the edge of her bed to flip through from beginning to end. There were fifty pages of plain cursive describing each time someone her mother met had died. In between, there were many pages of thought and research. Some entries recounted stories her own mother had told, or that Tess's great-grandmother had relayed. With every generation they understood a little better.

Nearing the last few entries an hour later, she stood, still reading, and walked slowly toward the spare room. She kept no furniture in there and it was icy cold even for early fall. All of the vents were shut tight to better preserve the tapestry. The huge black image covered almost an entire wall, and was the only thing in the room. Tess stood before it. Without looking up right away, her eyes remained trained on the words of her dead mother.

The final pages talked about the design. How much it had grown since she was a little girl. None of them knew where the thick black fabric had come from or what force wove their hair into the existing weft. Nearly every woman in her lineage contributed. None of them had ever thought to refuse, though more than a few did kill themselves. They accepted the charge of its completion entirely. If they questioned the purpose, they never denied it. The only trouble proved keeping their hair in check. Keeping it for the wall, and never letting any fall. If they let their hair down, someone could die. That used to be the extent of the curse.

By the time her mother was born, though, the design itself had grown more hideous. The image unfolded as detail sketched itself in strand by strand. The picture became a modern apocalypse. A future that wrote itself. It wasn't the cruel oddity of bewitched hair and it wasn't that people died. Needing to see how it ended—what the final picture would be—that was the real curse.

Looking at the weird woven images, her heart hollowed. She closed the diary and set it on the floor at her feet. If only her sister had been stronger, she might have understood. Her father had died just before Tess learned the spell would finally be broken. There was no way it could continue, as she could not have children. Just after she turned seventeen, her doctor confirmed she had been born without a uterus. The tapestry would be complete in her lifetime. She would see how it ended.

Tess reached into her pocket. Most of the hair she had secreted away was there, though in haste she had stuffed some in the waist of her jeans and the cuff of her sock. She gathered a weightless handful of the stuff. Palm open, she watched her hair rise up as if dancing in a draught. Hanging in the still air, the filaments twisted into a loose ball and surveyed their environment as if seeking a familiar face. Then an undetectable breeze caught the hair, whisking strands toward the tapestry, where they wove themselves in. Twisting tightly in and around, they completed another part of the story. Mixing among her mother's darker hair, they formed a line between that and the white hair of a grandmother. That white hair represented teeth, the dark hair the void of a gaping mouth. Tess's own auburn hair formed lips forced wide, screaming, tormented.

How many generations the tapestry represented she had no idea. It depicted a nightmarish rapture yet to unfold. She grew excited for the day it would be complete. It would mean the end of her, but, far more importantly, the end of this curse. Whoever found it, paramedics, retirement home staff, she didn't care; they would decipher it. She trusted the story it told would make itself known. She trusted destiny, whether it fell on the floor or became pulled into the picture, woven by invisible hands.

Leaving the diary on the floor, Tess headed back downstairs. She had the rest of the day to look for another job and prepare for a move to another town. Perhaps she could enroll in university again. She was barely twenty and had decades before the tapestry would be complete.

On the wall, red hair became flames and blood. Fair blonde was the steel of blades and coins laid in villains' palms. Black tresses grew into shadows concealing harbingers of destruction. Brown locks were mounds of earth piled quickly over corpses. The flesh of the dead, lightning in the sky and the whites of eyes made of hair. Bones. Thousands of bones in piles that stretched into the horizon, drawn by aged women in a hundred shades of grey.

Lydia Peever is an author and journalist in Ottawa. She is a huge fan of horror music, books and film so anywhere there is blood, you will probably see her lurking in the corner working on her next novel. When not writing, find her talking horror movies on Splatterpictures Dead Air podcast or on a dirt road photographing roadkill. Learn more at nightface.ca.

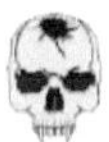

Death's Final Request

Bruce Lockhart 2nd

You know not what I am. To say that I am death—and, therefore, simply the end of all things—is a statement which burns me to the core.

The All-Father granted me a name, so long ago.

In the beginning.

"Azrael."

I still tremble at the thought of the powerful force I felt, when the All-Father's breath brought me into existence, into physical consciousness.

He'd taken away the energy of animals, in order to clothe the outcasts from the Garden. Out of their life-force, I was spawned.

Had I known what I know now, I would have begged for absolution.

I would have pleaded with Him, for a release from the bonds that would soon chain me to a life of turmoil, but, alas, I was oblivious to the consequences of my existence.

The All-Father explained that it was my purpose to send all energy back to Him. After the humans he had created ceased to exist on the Earth, a new life could be re-established from the old life. And for a while my purpose was just.

I, Azrael, was a creation between an angel and a star.

But the millennia I've spent on earth have morphed my appearance into reverence and trepidation; I am no longer light, but rather a shining beacon of darkness.

I can attribute the beginning of my transformation to the first human death; the demise of the All-Father's most precious creations came from two brothers, Cain and Abel, the outcasts' offspring.

I remember it clearly, as though it happened only moments ago. Cain lured his brother to the field and slayed Abel in cold blood.

My essence was yanked fiercely from my dwelling, where I had, until that moment, spent my days basking in the warmth of His light.

It had been so long since I felt that loving glow, and for an instant, I embodied Cain as he took his brother's life; I bore his hatred as he attacked Abel fiercely

Instantaneously, a horrible darkness formed inside me, threatening to crack the very light the All-Father had bestowed me with.

The All-Father's rage, however, at the affront to his very creations, reverberated through time itself.

The blackness that now controlled me had resulted from Cain; spilling his brother's blood, it pulsated deep within, tearing at my essence.

It was a horrendous, vicious, neverending pain.

How could I endure this? I begged for relief from this agonizing pain, but the All-Father did not answer.

And then there came another…

The fallen one once referred to as the Morning Star.

His deep, ominous voice still taunts my mind, twisting and dementing it.

"Hello, Azrael," Morning Star hissed. His disturbing presence shook my abode, as if the Heavens themselves protested against his being there.

I raised my face slowly to see him, this glorious Morning Star the All-Father had once treasured.

His appearance still makes my insides wrench.

Morning Star was much larger than I'd imagined. His skin was flaked, and his flesh held burns and deep cuts, marring features that must have once been bathed in perfection. Wings, which I had envisioned feathered as white as a swan's splendid tail, were instead grey. The edges were singed, and the bones were deformed and contorted, sticking out at both tips.

What disturbed me most, however, were the heavenly chains that appeared melded with his body. I quivered as I imagined the agony they brought.

"Morning Star, dear God, what has happened to you?" I questioned hesitantly.

His face warped into madness, and his lips pulled back, stretching wide to reveal his pointed, bloody teeth.

"Exactly! Azrael! That's exactly what happened to me… your God." He spat as his expression turned grim, the dementedness vanishing as quickly as it came.

Briefly, I found my resilience. "The All-Father didn't do this to you, Morning Star, you did this to yourself." I had knowledge of Morning Star rising up against the All-Father, and of his being cast out of the Heavens.

His voice transformed into an unnatural shriek, such as I had never heard.

"MY NAME IS LUCIFER!" He shook with rage. "And the One who did this to me is the same One who did this to you."

His stare penetrated me. Black eyes that almost looked sad, as though he pitied me for my naivety. I could feel him mentally peeling back layers of my mind, clawing to find the darkness caged within…

"You and I have more in common than you'd like to think, Azrael." Lucifer had begun to saunter around me as he continued. "I have a proposal, one that will ease you of your pain."

My eyes widened at his divulgence. "The All-Father will surely release me."

He spun around, spreading his hideous wings in a wide circle. "Ah! But He won't, will He? How many times have you begged Him for remission? How many times have you pleaded for liberation, yet found no answer?"

The questions he posed stirred anger inside of me, and yet I felt truth in his accusations. I still had this pain; there appeared to be no relief.

"Where is He, then? It is I who heard you beg for mercy, is it not? It is I who heard you beg for emancipation. It is I who answered… not He?"

"So you have you come to my aid, Lucifer. Forgive me for asking, but what is it you want?"

A strained smile parted Lucifer's parched lips as he answered.

"All things are energy, Azrael. That energy, which you now hold inside you, is of evil consequence. Its original intention was the transference of pure energy to your Lord." I noticed the emphasis on the word your, as though Lucifer was no longer part of the All-Father's creation.

"The difficulty your Lord ran into is that his new creations are wicked, and unrepentant death spurs tainted energy. Thus, He cannot take it back unto Himself; He has no way of disposing of it. Which is why it remains trapped in your being…"

He paused, shaking his head in exaggerated empathy.

"So unfair. And it will only get worse. But I have the power to solace the pain inside of you. I can rid you of it. I can take it unto myself, and I will continue to do so, as long as you allow me."

"And what is the price I'll pay, should I allow this?" I groaned at the stabbing sensations inside me, doubling me over.

"You owe me nothing. The dark energy you hold within is payment enough. I shall relieve this affliction you bear, each and every time you must do your duty, brother."

The agony had reached a boiling point, tearing at my insides. Lucifer had become blurry, and I fell helplessly to the ground.

"I need your answer now!" his ethereal voice boomed, shocking me back into focus.

All I could do was nod.

"Good." His black tongue slithered over his lips as something shiny formed in his hand.

A scythe; I thought he was going to use it, in order to end me. The sky darkened as ominous clouds hastened around us. He took a powerful swing, just above my head.

My body gave a spasm and released the excruciating pain, for the moment.

He handed me the scythe, and told me to use it to reap dark energy from the damned. The dark energy they held.

Then I watched in trepidation as he dove back into the fiery pits of Hell, where he was destined to dwell for eternity.

However, a deal with the devil always comes with a price, and throughout the ages I discovered what that price is...

Lucifer had hoped if he gathered enough energy, he could break free of his chains and rise up against the All-Father with new power. He has held onto festering vengeance; an all-consuming need for retribution.

And even after countless centuries of delivering on my promise, his power still paled in comparison to the All-Father's.

His mind had become one of lunacy.

I couldn't help but find slight satisfaction in the knowledge that it would never be enough. After all, Lucifer had deceived me, by his assurance he would ease my torment.

To ease does not mean to eliminate. The words he had uttered on that day had been deceitful.

The centuries of transferring malignant energy caused my form to morph into something ugly, almost skeletal. I have cloaked myself in a dark, hooded robe to conceal my disfigurement.

My affliction lingers.

Numbed, but still ever-present.

My eternity seems doomed, and the thought of doing this forever makes me weary. My thoughts are continually interrupted, as I'm transported to a deserted part of an obscure city, where a man is running from a group of people. He is shot in the back, the bullet piercing his flesh, rippling through him. He bleeds out on the ground, his time expiring quickly as the darkness remains trapped within.

I reap the energy, and then, yet again, I am yanked away, now to a dingy old basement. A depraved voice speaks with unnatural calmness to a small child, who is tied to a radiator.

"This will only hurt for a moment."

The child screams, and I am revolted at the sight of a pair of pliers in the man's dirty, pudgy hands. A heart attack has him dropping those pliers as he claws at his chest. Again, I do my duty.

My being is pulled in multiple different directions; fragments of horrific deaths fill my mind. Finally, I'm brought to an old man lying in a hospital bed. He struggles for life, and is only breathing because of the machines he's hooked up to.

An oxygen mask covers his mouth, but his withered, leathery arms struggle with it, until finally he pulls it off his face.

Defeated eyes dart towards the wall, where machines that supported his life are plugged into the outlet. I swear he can see me.

"Please…" he pleads. Even as he requests relief, his bitterness is unyielding. He knows not what he is asking for.

The frail man finds enough strength to yank on the wires, once, twice; and it is on the third time that I reap for the final time.

I'd seen goodness done in this world, but as of late, the advancements in technology have created many more avenues for iniquities.

There are so many people in existence, and I am constantly being split into hundreds of different directions, all at once. There is so much death and misery…

I am beginning to lose conviction that the All-Father even hears the pleas of His children.

He hasn't heard mine…

I am beyond exhausted as I enter my humble domain. I can do this no longer. I am not surprised when I hear the rustle of wings. His vileness precedes him.

I'd been holding on too long now. I expected he'd send one of his minions, but the air surrounding me recoils, assuring me he was there in person.

"Azrael, it's been so long."

I cringe at the sound of mockery in his voice. Intense pain and fatigue radiate through me, causing me difficulty to remain in any position too long.

I remain silent.

"Why has it been so long since your last deliverance? Why are you here, wasting time? There is much more of my energy to reap."

I scoff at his words. During my thousands of years, the humans had begun to refer to me as the Grim Reaper.

"Your energy?" I scoff.

He frowns at my comments, "I did not come here to squabble."

Lucifer's features had become more distorted and heinous over time, and his tattered wings, along with the fragmented bones, have the appearance of burned charcoal.

"No, of course not. I'm sure you're just here to make certain I uphold my end of our deal." There is indignation in my tone as a newfound energy awakens within me.

Lucifer, however, isn't pleased with my current course of action. His vile wings somehow manage to lift him up, sending tremors through the air.

"How dare you!" he screeches. "We had a deal!" Then, "Fine, enjoy the horrific pain you will now endure, forever!"

Now it is my turn to take to the air. I do not have wings, but the design of creation the All-Father had instilled in me allows me this. I ponder my next move for a moment, even as an undeniable rage courses through every pore of my being.

"No, Lucifer, I'm afraid you do need me, or no more energy." I pull back my hood revealing horrific features that even Lucifer cringes at. I call his bluff. "Without it, how will you ever rise up against the All-Father?"

He glares at me coldly, and his enormous wingspan lands him crookedly back on the ground. I wonder if my appearance even disturbs the devil himself?

"What is it you want, Azrael?"

The unnatural voice that comes out of my mouth doesn't sound like me. "Nothing you can give me, Lucifer." My tone defies him with every word.

"Tread cautiously, Azrael," he threatens.

"I want absolution only One can deliver me." I tremble at the forcefulness of my own voice, looking to the scythe he'd given me so long ago.

After the endless amount of death, carnage, and evil I've been forced to witness on earth, I feel my hand reach for the cold metal one last time.

"Ah, now we've come to our senses." Lucifer claps his hands together, discoloured nails tipping his gnarled fingers.

My own skeletal fingers wrap around the sinister weapon, "Yes, we have."

And then, as if he sees it before it happens, Lucifer leaves the ground with tremendous speed and charges towards me.

"No!" He wails, but it's already too late; the demonic steel plunges through my core.

As my being slowly fades, I don't know what the consequences will be.

To humankind.

To myself.

If my days will be spent fighting Lucifer, in the bowels of Hell, so be it.

I feel a pang of guilt at disappointing the All-Father, just before my being is no more…

Darkness becomes my chasm, until dreadful images begin to

explode around me. I see the All-Father's plan unfold; all along His purpose for me had been to bring about the end times.

I did not know it, but Lucifer had bought mankind many more years, even though his only chance at freedom was their demise.

The world erupts into flames and chaos. I bear witness to Lucifer rising against an army of angels, with his army of demons.

Heavenly figures plunge into the earth, as ethereal screams fill the air. And yet my resentment for the All-Father disappears, and I come to understand the burden He must bear from every sin His creations commit.

The darkness around me begins to dissipate, and a light so bright it could illuminate the universe fills my every pore; it restores my former glory, and I watch in melancholy as the world comes to an end.

Bruce Lockhart 2nd has been writing/editing for the last six years; he'll be 24 this Halloween and feels very fortunate to have found is calling so early in life. Together he and often his business partner Suzie Lockhart have over 40 short story publications and have been co-editors or acquisition editors for several anthologies. Together they have their own short story collection entitled *Adventures in Horrorland* and are excited to be working with Digital Fiction Publishing. Bruce intends to keep branching out and become successful at the fine art of storytelling.

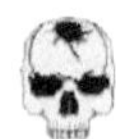

Plight of the Valkyrie

Daniel Soule

Henry Mortimer wanted to die, but couldn't. He just lay there all day in a hospital bed, waiting. The doctors and nurses passed him by. They didn't notice him; there was no special reason they should. Another old man on a geriatric ward, small and unassuming, still dressed in cardigan and cords, brown leather shoes popped up on the neatly-turned-down bed.

The night shift would be on soon, and he was sure the right someone would be along sooner rather than later. He could feel it wouldn't be long now. Besides, Ethel in bed four didn't have long left; they'd be giving her all the attention she needed. Well, nearly all. Some things they couldn't do, and they knew it. It warmed his heart, after all this time, that they still put all that effort into "making her comfortable." Henry chuckled at the euphemism. Nobody heard him.

Charlie in the next bed was due to go soon, too, but that one would catch most of them by surprise.

Charlie coughed, introducing himself. "Waiting room for God, this."

Henry smiled. "Yes, I suppose it is, in a way."

"Charlie Crocker, like in the movie, pleased to meet you."

"Henry Mortimer," he said offering a hand over the gap between them.

"Bloody hell, your hands are freezing, mate," said Charlie. "They need to get you a blanket."

"I'm all right."

"Here comes the night shift," Charlie gravelled, nodding to the administrative station at the end of the Victorian ward. "I look forward to the nights."

"Why is that?" asked Henry.

"Look, that one: Nurse Valerie." Charlie cocked his head, gesturing to a middle-aged nurse in scrubs, reading over charts. She wasn't pretty, nor was she ugly; she was quite unremarkable in appearance. Heads had never turned in a crowd to look at her, even when she was young, and the truth of it was that this was just as she wanted it: no unnecessary attention.

"You like her?" asked Henry, knowing the answer.

"Lovely bum," said Charlie. "What you in for, mate?"

"Me? Oh, tiredness, I suppose, extreme tiredness."

"I shouldn't even be here," wheezed Charlie.

"Is that so?"

"No room for me down in oncology. Lung cancer, you see. But as I'm an old bugger and I am going to croak it soon enough. I guess they thought they'd give me a trial run in the departures lounge," explained Charlie. "So what do you do?"

"Do?"

"Yeah, do, for a job, or what did you do before? I was a cabbie. Forty-five years driving people around. I've got some stories, I can tell you."

"I was a doctor a long time ago, a surgeon, actually," said Henry, "but then I changed professions."

"What to?"

"Pathology, I suppose," said Henry, "I…"

"Good evening, gentlemen," interrupted Nurse Valerie Curry, looking down at a chart.

"Evenin', Nurse Curry," said Charlie, like a schoolboy at

registration.

"I'll get you your meds, Charlie. And who do we have here?" Val flicked the page back and forth looking for a name to go with Henry's bed.

"Henry, Henry Mortimer," he said.

"You're not on the chart," replied Val still scanning the page.

"Are you sure, dear? I was sent up this morning. Would you check again?" asked Henry.

Nurse Curry flicked the page once more, tracing her finger down the list of names, and as if by magic, "Ah, there you are. I don't know how I didn't see that, Mr. Mortimer. I'll get you a gown. Hey, you cheeky sod," Val broke off, turning to Charlie who had just pinched her bum. "Charlie Crocker, you keep your hands to yourself," she said cheerfully, tucking the old man in tightly. Charlie grinned innocently as she left to finish her rounds.

Alarms started to bleep at bed four. Val and the junior doctor on duty strolled over to Ethel's bed. There was no need to run. The end was expected and she had a 'Do Not Resuscitate' order. They checked the readings, pushed some meds and made a note on her cart. Val squeezed her hand and they left for nature to take its course.

"God speed," croaked Charlie. "Hey, where are you going?" he whispered.

Now in his gown, Henry had hopped out of bed and padded over to Ethel. Only Charlie noticed him, looking around as if on watch for his truanting classmate. Henry leant down to Ethel, taking her hand. The old woman opened her eyes, and Henry saw her face smiling up at him, as if he were an old friend. Henry patted her hand and she closed her eyes. A flat beep rang quietly, followed by the shuffling of scrubs as the young doctor and Nurse Curry came back down the ward.

"Mr. Mortimer, you shouldn't be out of bed," said Val.

"My apologies. I didn't want her to be alone at the end," explained Henry, already walking back to his bed.

The young doctor appeared too busy turning off machines and

filling out the necessary paperwork to notice Henry. Nurse Curry came over to the two old men when they had finished with Ethel. "Now you two get some rest," she said pulling out a syringe from the pocket in her scrubs and perching on Charlie's bed.

The young doctor walked back down the ward, head in a chart.

"It's usually tablets I get," said Charlie.

"This is better. Won't hurt a bit," said Val finding a vein with the skill of an old pro. "It'll help you sleep as well. There, all done. I still can't find any records for you, Mr. Mortimer, but I'm sure they'll turn up by the morning. Hey…" Val jumped. Charlie had pinched her bottom again. "You are a very naughty man," she scolded lightly.

Henry watched her leave. She moved in such an unassuming way. Her skills were certainly well practiced. There was a great balance between her proficiency, compassion, and the ability to blend in. He turned to Charlie, swinging his legs over the side of the bed.

"I wouldn't get out of bed again; she runs a tight ship, does that one," warned Charlie.

"Don't worry, Charlie, I'm not going anywhere, but you are, and I don't want you to panic," Henry explained.

"Panic? Why the bloody hell would I panic?" Charlie laughed in his hoarse voice.

"Nurse Curry just gave you something. You'll feel a sharp pain but it'll be quick," said Henry.

Wincing, Charlie sucked air in through his teeth sharply and clutched at his chest. "How did you know? Are you trying to kill me?"

"No, Charlie," Henry said kindly. "It was Valerie. I just… know these things."

The old cab driver was overcome with pain. A drowning sensation flooded him. Panic set in but his body was unable to fight against it, and the panic grew. As it touched on the unbearable, at that point where all hope was lost, when the infinite, cold inevitability of nothingness showed itself and his mind cowered before its universal majesty, Henry took Charlie's hand and the pain stopped. The panic stopped too and he opened his eyes and looked up into Henry's face.

"It's you," said Charlie.

"Yes, my friend."

"This is it then?" asked Charlie, already accepting the answer to his question.

"It is. Shall we go?" asked Henry, as though he'd only called around to see if Charlie could come out to play, to which the inevitable answer was always "yes."

Henry closed Charlie's eyes and popped back into bed to wait for what he had really come here for. The ward was quiet but for an occasional cough and snore, or the huff of a ventilator and the beep of a monitor. Presently, Nurse Curry did her scheduled rounds.

"He's gone, in case you were wondering," Henry said as Val walked by his bed. "Very good work, might I add? Very nicely done. You saved him such a lot of pain."

"Excuse me?" said Val rushing to Charlie's side, urgently checking his pulse.

Henry chuckled. "Very good, very good. Only an expert could see through the mask. Your abilities are quite excellent. Nigel was spot on with you. You will do just nicely, I think."

"Mr. Mortimer, I'm about to lose my patience with you," snipped Val.

"No you are not," corrected Henry. "Besides, no one can hear you now, so let's be frank for a moment."

Silence enveloped them. Val straightened up, sensing the change. A night shift can be quiet, but in a hospital the hum of machines, the bang of a distant door, the rattle of a trolley or the sounds of sleep are always present. They were not now. It was the silence of a vacuum, a silence so still it could only be accompanied by the absence of the world.

"Yes, you are a cautious creature. You sense it, but don't understand it. I'll explain. Time has stopped, or rather, slowed greatly. To stop it would be to end the universe, and that is certainly not in my power. We are but servants of the universe, after all. But slowing, perceptually speaking, is quite possible. It is mostly a question of distraction of consciousness anyway. I digress.

"Firstly, let us deal with the issue of Charlie here. You killed him, did you not? It will look like a cardiac arrest, and they will assume it was brought on by the additional stress to his pulmonary system because of the final stages of his lung cancer. I have no axe to grind on the matter. You are not in trouble. In fact, far from it: in a way, consider it an entrance exam, and you passed with flying colours." Henry waited patiently for a response.

This was a most delicate moment. He remembered his own recruitment well, in the field hospital at the second battle of Ypres. The candidate is filled with fear. Their gift has been exposed, and they have built their entire existence around hiding it, in the knowledge that the world would not understand. He could see Valerie assessing her surroundings, measuring him, trying to understand what he had just said. The calculation clicked into place, and she was ready to act.

"My dear, you cannot kill me," said Henry. "If you want you can take that syringe in your pocket and stick it into me as if I was Charlie there, but it would make no difference. I cannot die, and that, in short, is why I am here to see you. I have been looking for my replacement for so long, but it is a tricky business finding the correct person."

Hesitantly, Valerie took her hand out of her pocket, looking around furtively, expecting the police to rush in any moment. How was it possible for him to know so much? Was it a trick?

"I see I'm going to have to be a little blunt. A shock will be necessary." He took his drinking glass and smashed it on the bedside cupboard. Valerie was already off her stride and could only watch. Then, looking her calmly in the eye, he punched the shattered base into his jugular.

"No," screamed Valerie. The nurse in her moved her to action, rushing to pull the glass from his hand.

They wrestled briefly while he twisted and ground the shards into his flesh to prove the point and relaxed. Val pulled the glass from his hand, cutting herself. She looked at him, expecting the fountain of blood to be pulsing from his throat, covering everything, including her, but there was nothing, only a trickle of blood from her finger.

"I don't understand," she said. "Who are you? What do you want with me?"

"I should be dead or dying, should I not, Miss Val Curry?" asked Henry.

"Yes," was the breathless reply.

"Good, good! We are getting somewhere. Things, my dear, are not as they seem. You of all people should understand that. So now that we have established that fact, would you please do me the courtesy of acknowledging your murder of Charlie here?"

"Yes," she repeated in a whisper, and a tide of relief. It was as though she no longer had to hide; that whatever the consequences, for once the truth was known.

"That felt good, didn't it?" asked Henry, to which Valerie nodded, ashamed. "No, my dear, do not feel guilty. You are with a friend, a kindred spirit."

"Who are you?" she repeated desperately, "and what do you want?"

"I am Henry Mortimer, member of the Guild of Passing, and I have come to find my replacement, to recruit you to your true vocation, my dear Valerie. But the first thing we must deal with is, who are you?" said the old man pointing a finger at her. "Please sit down, Charlie won't mind.

"You are what they call an angel of death, or some would call you a serial killer, but neither is really correct. In fact, you have a very special set of skills, a talent that makes you well suited to our line of work. In fact, some of us have philosophized over the years that the universe creates people like you for the very purposes of the Guild. As far as we can tell, people like us and the Guild have always existed, or rather always accompanied the consciousness of humans–we can't speak for the animals."

Henry went on, "Of course, not all of your kind are appropriate. So many flamboyant narcissists, leaving a trail of clues. They want to be caught. It is all about them, not about the craft. No, you are not they.

"Then there are those truly cunning ones, who to the untrained eye you appear to be very like. They are the ones they never catch–killers in the shadows, much as you are. And like you, they love the craft, but unlike you do it for the pleasure of the kill. They revel in it, covetously hiding it from prying eyes. This is the difference, is it not? We, you and I, see death as a natural part of the universe, and we…" Henry searched for an appropriate word and settled for "help."

He explained further: "It is a subtle but important difference. In this instance, it is *everything*. To choose the other sort would be a disaster of horrific proportions. To have one who enjoys killing with mirth standing over the membrane between life and death could well rip that membrane asunder, and the consequences for the universe…" didn't bear expressing.

"Anyway, we collated our information and are certain of your disposition. By Nigel and some of the others' reports you have killed some 182 individuals…"

"Eighty-seven," Val whispered a correction, tears in her eyes. She remembered every one of them.

Henry smiled. "We won't quibble about numbers. Some we discounted from your early career. It was difficult for us to be sure it was you rather than their condition. You have become more clinical with experience. You are a craftsman, or rather craftswoman–even the Guild is a little politically correct, nowadays. We try to reflect the cultures we serve. We are impressed with your work: the love you have for all aspects of it, all aspects except one. You don't do it for the enjoyment of taking the life. There is no mirth in your actions, but love. Love of the craft in and of itself, and love for the people you serve. This, my dear, is what makes you such a perfect candidate.

"Which brings me to your second question: what do I want with you? I'm here to offer you a job. One in which your special skills, your talent, would be valued and praised. One in which you will never again have to worry about being caught. One in which you will never again have to hide yourself, pretending to be something you are not. In short, my dear Valerie, I offer you freedom to be yourself and to live that part of your life you love the most."

The solid foundations of her universe were shaking as if to bring down the walls of reality. Valerie felt woozy, steadying herself on poor Charlie's bed. "You are Death!" She couldn't believe it as she said it.

Even Death needs skills of persuasion. His tilt of his head was only slight. Some never want to believe it is time to pass on, and remain trapped in limbo, and so the Guild must convince some to let go; not all are willing, and it can all get a bit messy with stranded souls.

Valerie needed to let go. Henry remembered his own recruitment, and how he tried to subtly pick up a scalpel from the blood soaked operating table. He would have slashed Joshua's throat, the old guildsman whom he replaced, until the old man smiled and pointed to something between them. At first Henry thought it was a trick, but then he saw them: the flies. Dozens of them, suspended in the air as if caught in aspic. At the second battle of Ypres, among its many horrors were the flies that swarmed the dead and dying as a writhing pall. Henry himself loved the battle: he could ply his trade so freely, refining his skills. Many men were better off to have an artery nicked than to suffer, and so many were suffering.

"Death?" chuckled Henry. "In a way, we are death. We are the membrane between the Universe experiencing itself through the subjectivity of life. Though we have many different names, depending on the culture and the time. Death has certainly been one." And with the those words an icy wind whipped between them, and Henry transformed before Valerie into the billowing tower of the Reaper, clutching a scythe of bone with a sweeping, mottled blade, forged from all the ores of the Earth.

"Ankou was another of our names, as was Hel," and his form

shifted again, this time into the striding figure of a muscular Nordic woman, replete with helmet, furs and spear, her eyes as deep and shifting as oceans.

Hel's full, pink lips moved again, with the resonance of mountains. "Others called us *La Santa Muerte*." Skin fell away, revealing the sheen of bloody muscles, which too fell away to rusting bone. The holy skeleton regarded the horror in Valerie's eyes with cool acceptance, and spoke again.

"Perhaps you would prefer me," the jawbone clapped, "more beautiful?" Val sat now across from the ethereal beauty of a man-boy. Tight golden curls adorning his head, and white within white wings flexed, preening, behind him. "Gabriel, they called us," he said sonorously, eyes black within black.

Then he grew again, and the hospital ward dissolved in his presence, and they floated in the infinite, lonely abyss of space, his skin turning blue. Four arms gestured with adornments of gold. Fangs pointed from his blood red lips. Yellow eyes with a lizard's pupil bore through Valerie, and his form was terror itself. She couldn't look into those eyes; instead, she stared into the blue skin, sparkling with a trillion stars. The terrible separation of life and creation threatened to overwhelm her in a crashing torrent. "Some," his flicking tongue lisped, "thought us the destroyer of worlds…"

"But," the hospital room surrounded them again, and the old man returned to his humble self, back in cords and cardigan, "we are just the psychic projection of the cultures we serve, and when people believe in nothing, we come as friends."

Valerie was quiet in thought for some time, though, of course, time had slowed so much Henry could wait. Finally, she was ready. "So what do we do now?"

"You are agreeable to our proposition, then?" Henry took her nod as agreement. "Oh, that is splendid, my dear, truly splendid. Nigel will take it from here, and he and the others will train you in our ways. Yes, yes, we have an excellent one in you."

"What about you?" asked Valerie. "Won't you miss it?"

"To be honest, I'm tired of it all. I've had nearly a hundred years. My last assignment was in the Middle East, and I can feel what is coming. That pace of work is not for me anymore. I could ask for a transfer to somewhere like Iceland or New Zealand, but Tore and Jane are doing such fine work, there is no need for me there, nor anywhere else. I have been looking for my replacement for so long, and a Guildsman cannot retire until his, or her, replacement is found. So now we have you I will hang up my scythe and see my last days out as an old man, and in that maybe I'll see you again."

"Where will you go?" she asked.

He gazed out of the window. "I grew up not far from here. I think I may get a small flat. The Guild helps with arrangements. Ah, Nigel is here for you. That's my cue." He stood up and offered Val his cold hand. As they shook, a warmth he had forgotten returned to him, while hers grew cold and the world began to turn once more. The old man's shoes barely squeaked as he walked down the ward: he could move unnoticed too. He passed a tall skinny man, pausing to embrace his old friend, and then he was gone.

Steam rose and the kettle clicked. Henry poured the water into the brown teapot and carried a mug and a couple of biscuits on a tray into the front room. The melodic trumpet announced the start of his British soap. He'd got so very engrossed in it since his retirement a few weeks ago.

It was all going well, apart from his joints. A hundred years without pain does not prepare one for the onslaught of arthritis, but a warm mug of tea does so help.

Two men on the television talked over the bar in the pub and Henry was distracted for a second by teenagers cavorting up the pavement bathed in orange light. There was a wash of contentment he felt when thinking of young people: the pulse in their throats was perennially attractive. For all his experience of death, that final journey still filled him with trepidation the closer it came, which, if he lingered on the thought for long enough, revealed itself as fear. For all his exposure to a few of the mysteries of the universe, he had only been a servant; he knew not what lay beyond the veil. The young rarely think of death nowadays–not here, anyway.

It wasn't always so. Ypres was filled with nothing but death—and how he loved being there—but it was so many lifetimes ago it was as though they weren't his memories. There was a private on his table, drowning in his own fluids, who wanted to speak. While Henry held him down after nicking his carotid artery, he kicked and clawed and gasped. His hand reached up to Henry's collar, not to assault the field surgeon, but to hold on to life. Henry remembered the wallet in the private's breast pocket: the letter home, the sepia photo of his wife and child. Tears now blurred out Henry's vision of the private, just as the private's tears blurred out Henry's implacable face as death came to take him. Now those tears were a mirror through time, reflecting the beginning back to the end in an infinite recurrence. Some things never change; other things do.

A tear is a curved prime, and doesn't merely reflect but also bends and distorts. Why remember the private now? Henry tutted at himself. He knew perfectly well why: fear is sometimes too obvious. But there he was again, stretched through time; this wasn't how Henry had ever remembered the private before. The kicking, the struggling, the terror in his eyes. It had been much more peaceful before. More satisfying.

Flickering lights brought Henry's attention back to his living room. A cobbled street on the flat screen pixelated, and northern English accents stuttered their lines. The hairs on the back of Henry's neck bristled, and the panicked face of the private, pestered with gluttonous blue bottles, beseeched wordlessly.

"Hello, Henry."

Henry jumped in his seat, startled as his eyes rested on her unassuming form, sat nonchalantly in the armchair across the room, as if nothing in this world or the next could stop her.

"Valerie?" Henry gathered himself, a little relieved. "Oh, how lovely to see you again. I wasn't expecting… Oh," he realised, "you have come for me, then?"

Valerie said nothing. She sat cross-legged, hands in her lap, regarding the old man with a look of… Henry tried to put his finger on it, and rejected his initial answer, searching for a different one.

"You look quite different out of your scrubs," said Henry, panic rising in his chest.

The merest of smiles grew on Valerie's face.

"Black suits you. A little conspicuous, not very warm. Quite severe, really," he continued, filling the silence, hoping for a response.

No reply came. The Valkyrie simply savoured the moment, relishing the fear, drinking it in.

"Come, come, my dear, this is most unprofessional," Henry tried to muster that old doctor's authority, but the vibrato in his voice betrayed him. "This is not a game. Do get on with it."

She stood suddenly, and he flinched as she walked to the window to stand adjacent to him and look down onto the sepia street.

"It is a game, and you enjoyed playing it as much as I do," Valerie said. "All that pomposity, 'membrane between life and death', 'love of the craft,'" she mocked. "The funny thing is I think you actually believed it. You'd convinced yourself. You never saw the terror in their eyes. A true psychopath. What is sicker than killing a friend, and as if you are doing them a favour?"

And now she turned to tower over him, within her eyes the abyss of a trillion stars. "But we all love it, the entire Guild, so I suppose I should thank you. Now I can indulge my fantasy with impunity, and I've always had a thing for old men who had it coming. You remember smutty old Charlie? Now, this might hurt a little."

Once Dan was an academic but the sentences proved too long and the words too obscure. Northern Ireland is where he now lives. But he was born in England and raised in Byron's home town, which the bard hated but Dan does not. They named every other road after Byron. As yet no roads are named after Dan but several children are. He tries to write the kind of stories he wants to read and aims for readers to want to turn the page. Dan's work has featured in *Number Eleven*, *Storgy*, the *Dime Show Review*, *Short Tale 100*, *Phantaxis* and the horror magazine *Devolution Z*.

Mirrorworld

Martin Rose

Jude falls back against the wall with a smoking hole in his expensive business suit. Divorce papers fall to the floor.

Salazar holds the gun. The end of the barrel forms a toothless mouth ringed with lips of iron.

"But I'm not dead," Jude whispers.

He presses his hand against the hole in his suit. The bullet has penetrated deep through the fibers of cloth, through the shirt beneath and ventilates his interior pocket. A single, high-pitched twitter of birdsong prevails through the smoke, and then all is silence.

"Why?" Blood bubbles up over Jude's lips.

He regrets not taking the time to think of something better. The last moment of his life and all he has to show for it are lines purloined from melodramas and low budget films.

Salazar's face divides in half with a lean smile. "I traffic in black magic mirrors."

"Mirrors?"

"I need dead men to make them."

Jude opens his mouth to ask another question, and that is how he dies; frozen expression of eternal surprise and one hand clasped at his wound. A bullet in his heart, a canary stowed in his breast pocket.

Jude awakens.

His memories of waking in his life before are nothing like this. His coming to is automated, and without transition from one consciousness to the next. He arrives from blackness to find himself reduced to a doll whose wind-up key is touched off once and then set loose, eyes opening.

He stands in a new room. Blood snakes down his suit and stains his clothes from his chest to his belly.

His breast pocket pulses like a heart, and he reaches into it.

"There you are, Jenny."

The canary hops into his palm, talons pricking at his skin. Pale yellow. He brings her to eye level. Her wing feathers are singed around the edges where the bullet clipped her and punched straight through to the other side of him.

"Does that hurt?"

Jenny hops onto his finger, and gives him a reptilian glare. He deposits her back into his pocket, where she flicks her head over the top and watches their new world from the warm nest of his body.

The time before remains faded and dizzied in his memory, and difficult to recall. A man named Salazar. A drawn weapon. Dying. Did that happen? Did he die, just like that, so easily? At the hands of a man who traded in black magic mirrors. Some two-bit Satanist with a reputation for posing like a punk rock singer, but who was just a greasy con artist telling futures to old ladies for blow. Jude quietly tacks on murderer to the list.

Would anyone even know he was gone? Jude analyzes his a quiet, solitary life and draws a mental portrait of himself, sad and disappointing in its smallness: a man who enjoys chess, classic novels and birds. Never married, never loved. With dismay, he finds the mark he made upon the world is insignificant—so mediocre, no one will notice his absence.

Is this death, then? Heaven?

Jenny tweets from his pocket and then falls silent.

The room remains unchanged, yet like no room he ever inhabited. He moves toward the couch, and it shimmers and pixelates like an image from the LCD screen in his office—flat and two-dimensional.

He touches it. Fingers press into a gossamer resistance, invisible and unyielding, an object with no height or width or depth. The couch is like a cardboard cutout.

He rubs his fingers together and they feel greasy and coated in oil. He wipes them on his pants leg in disgust.

Beside the couch stands a crib. A dangling mobile above it. All these things, the bookshelf beside it, even the window through which summer light pours, gives an impression of life—but life without substance. He draws closer to each. Jenny whistles and punctuates his rising panic with ululating song. The furniture is as pages torn from a magazine, fluttering, insubstantial. Artificial.

"Jude."

The voice drifts in like a foul wind. He spins and comes face to face with a window, an oval pane of glass set in the wall.

Like a mirror.

A man stands on the other side of the portal, and Jude recognizes the dark brown hair, the cruel slant of his features, the steady hands behind the trigger that authored his death: Salazar.

Memories detonate. Firecrackers in his head. A dark-tinged recollection of the divorce papers he was sent to deliver to the residence, office rumors of Salazar sacrificing goats. Men and women claiming to be witches engaging in unholy congress with him by the light of the moon. How bad could it be? Gossip, tabloid nonsense, Jude had said.

Jude remembers—his fingers moist with the humid summer—bending the pages as he waited for Salazar to answer the door, impatient, tapping his foot against the floor. All they had to do was just sign the damn divorce papers, but they always gave him trouble. They always stalled and hemmed and hawed. He had planned on stopping at the vet's office in the next hour. The birdcage broke in transit, so he had his canary huddled in his pocket. The entire day had been nothing but a series of small travesties.

Then Salazar answered the door with gun in hand and shot him through the heart.

"Do you like your new home, Jude?"

"What is this?"

"You're in the mirror, of course. You're dense for an attorney, you know that?"

I'm in the mirror?

It did not seem possible.

Jude recalls his father, who passed away from a heart attack when he was a child. His mother tore through the house, drifting from room to room like a sad ghost, covering all the mirrors with scarves. He considered it an old superstition as tired and banal as stories passed in the high-school hallways about Bloody Mary, and conjurations in narrow bathrooms between the toothpaste and the soap. Games played by bored teenagers.

The difference is, this is real.

Fury spikes through him. A lifetime's worth of pent-up frustration propels him forward to reach out and break the glass, shatter Salazar's face.

Nothing happens.

Jude's hand hangs on the air like a stalled puppet and will not obey his will. Salazar pulls out a comb and brushes back his hair with a vain gesture. Jude follows and matches the movement with his own hand in uneasy pantomime.

"Oh, I wouldn't start becoming violent now, Jude. I'm afraid that won't help you very much. You might want to make yourself at home. You could be in there a very long time."

Jenny flutters against his breast. Presses hollow bones against his heart. She burrows deeper into the pocket lint as though the sound of Salazar's voice sends her into a panic.

"There's no such thing," Jude protests.

"No such thing? You're in it now. All it takes is your blood, your signature—which you handily provided with the divorce papers from your firm—a few symbols and spoken words over your dead body. You didn't think witches were the only ones who could work spells, did you?"

"I'm just a lawyer. I've done nothing to you. This is criminal!"

"Haven't you? What, did you think criminals need a reason?" Salazar snorts laughter. "I'm no more evil than you are. How many shady clients have you ever saved from prison and set loose on the street? Well, making mirrors like this, that's my job, and it pays well. It's business—just like getting chumps like me to sign unfair divorce papers is your job. Nothing personal."

Jude considers the nature of evil, reflects on the subpoenas, indictments and divorces he'd delivered in the past, before dismissing it in a burst of rage.

"There's a world of difference between delivering an indictment to a criminal and imprisoning a man for no better reason than you can't keep better terms with your ex," he snaps.

A baby cries in the distance.

Salazar arches his head toward the crib nestled in the corner. Jude struggles for autonomy to move in the other direction but mimics Salazar's motion against his will. His body is not his own.

In the crib, a child turns uncomfortably in her blankets and cries again.

"Shut it, Amanda!"

Salazar continues to yell, walking away from the mirror.

Your father's a bastard, little girl, Jude thinks bitterly. "You shouldn't treat your child that way," he says.

Salazar makes a sound between a growl and a hiss. Jude pulls closer against his will, when all he desires is to shrink back from the man—who bares his teeth, as though he might come through the mirror itself and deliver a worse altered reality than the one he occupies already.

"Oh, you think so? Well, you should pray this cough syrup never runs out. You got a fancy education, lawyer man, you know your Shakespeare. What is it? '*The devil hath the power to assume a pleasing shape*?'"

Salazar moves out of sight.

When the man passes the limits of the mirror's frame, Jude experiences a tremor like a line snipped in two. A cord snaking up through his spine and from the top of his head severs and sets him loose. His joints, his limbs and legs are his own again, to move as he pleases.

I'm a mime, he realizes. "Good Lord, this must be Hell."

Jenny tweets her despair. She recognizes cages when she sees them, after all.

Time takes on new meaning in the Mirrorworld, as Jude comes to think of it.

He remembers and catalogues all the mirrors he ever saw in his life—bathroom mirrors, hand-held mirrors to shave with, pocket mirrors for grooming, rear and side view mirrors, mirrors in a woman's make-up case. He wonders now if lost souls like his were not imprisoned in them all, forced to carry out the actions of their owners.

Salazar visits the mirror every morning, and again in the evening, to arrange his hair or to examine the fit of his clothes. In each instance, Jude finds himself trapped in dreadful pantomime, aping Salazar on the other side of the glass.

When Salazar leaves, shadows follow him by bending in weird knots when he passes, and then springing back into place as though nothing ever happened. It calls into question just how many items in the man's apartment are filled with unearthly vitality, their substance stolen from other lives. Who is trapped in the antique end table, and what poor soul might inhabit the armchair?

Jude presses his face against the glass and peers into the Otherland. He tries breaking the surface again, but the glass remains as stone, and the force of his assault knocks him back with proportionate energy. He succeeds only in exhausting himself.

He tires of this, and at last sits on the floor of his two-dimensional cartoon world and watches the toddler in the far corner, imprisoned in the crib while he remains imprisoned in the mirror. The child is far too young to be without supervision, he thinks. What was her name? Amanda?

She peers at the mirror from above her crib bars, a thatch of wild, brown hair and huge eyes.

Salazar doses her with cough syrup in the afternoon. She sleeps through the hours of his absence. Jude envies her drugged existence, as he has nothing but brutal sobriety with which to feel every throb of pain, experience every agony of a death and an afterlife without conclusion.

"I want you to let me go."

Salazar plucks a hair from the center of his forehead as Jude presents his case. He laughs. Tattoos of mysterious sigils and signs of planets and spirits mark his arms. His gaunt cheeks puff with the force of his derision. Jude mimes it, and through him climbs an insidious, rising hatred. His physicality may be commandeered by Salazar, but on the interior nothing remains of himself to regulate his jangling nerve endings and his seething animosity. A drive-train of agony running with the engine of his heart.

"Why would I do that? Look, you're what, forty years old? Think of it like this—you probably weren't going to last much longer. What did you have to live for anyway?"

Jude tries to protest and instead lapses into sullen silence. That he cannot think of a reason to defend himself only multiplies his rage.

Because I don't have a wife, or a meaningful job, or a particular pursuit, renders my life worthless? That's not fair.

Regardless of the utility of life and its meaning, overwhelming despair claims him. Escape from the mirror will not return his life. His condition is permanent.

So, too, is his imprisonment in the mirror.

Defeat comes on the heels of despair, and a series of images shuffle through his mind's eye—the detritus of his consciousness left over from the days prior. The sound of the gun in the cold air. The hiss of the radiator in another apartment. The residents had surely heard his agony, and chose to remain in their matchbox rooms and let him die. Jude thinks of the divorce papers he delivered to Salazar. His signature and the empty space where Salazar was meant to sign his name.

And then comes an insight, breathless in its power, that surely all of life is a series of contracts requiring signatures and agreements, and his imprisonment in the mirror is no more permanent than Salazar's marriage. While his death was irreversible, his place in the mirror is not.

It can be broken, just like any agreement. He did it all the time.

Jude holds a breath, his eyes expanding as he conceives the idea and wrestles it down and deep within him.

Salazar leaves down the hall with the spiderlegs of shadows snapping at him, before returning to their sensible positions and linear places beneath the flow of sunlight. Jude feels the same as they do, warped into Salazar's wake and then allowed to return to normal in his absence. It occurs to him that Salazar is the only thing he has left in the world, whether he likes it or not. A final last friend, a friend who killed him and imprisoned him in silver and glass.

Jenny tweets.

"Except for you," Jude whispers.

He takes Jenny from his pocket. Plump and yellow, she preens and puffs herself to twice her size and satisfies herself with his finger for a perch.

At home, in his apartment, he collected canaries and other exotic birds, had a crow who learned to speak his name. Some he rescued and others he bought. There would be no one to care for them or feed them now.

"I'm sorry," Jude apologizes to the bird. He strokes it with trembling fingers. "No friends, no one else to sing with you, or flock to you, eh? How lonely you must be."

Her beak opens and she breathes, yellow belly contracting and expanding. Rapid flaps of wing until she takes flight. She careens for the portal, the mirror.

"Don't!"

She fails to perceive the barrier dividing the worlds, and Jude appreciates the sad irony of birds who can't distinguish one glass from the next. He attempts to intercept her, but can't pluck her out of the air fast enough as she sails past. He hopes the impact will only stun her, and flinches against the sight and the sound.

Silence.

Jude opens his eyes and releases a breath.

Jenny's gone.

On the other side of the mirror, in Salazar's apartment, she tweets triumphantly as she alights atop the crib and cocks her head, examining the baby as she might a bit of enticing bird seed.

"Oh," Jude whispers.

The bird casts no reflection. Free of the mirror.

And suddenly, the child awakens from her cough-syrup stupor.

Amanda, with the tousled hair, jerks upright from her slumber. Her eyeballs jitter and then fly open. She turns her head with an automated snap, joints cracking in her vertebrae until she stares through the rungs of her crib at Jude on the other side of the mirror.

"You can see me?" he asks.

The child grins, her mouth stained purple with cough syrup.

"He left it out," the child says.

Her voice plunges low and deep and Jenny flaps her wings but holds her place on the perch, wavering between fear and flight. Jude hears a sound like crinkling paper and when he looks down at the edges of the portal, he sees ice form along the frame, frost crystallizing from the air.

He steps away from the mirror.

He thinks to ask *What?* but decides that he wants no more of this.

Wants no more of what lies beyond in Salazar's collected curiosities. The unnatural child speaking with the voice of something much older.

"He left the bird out," she whispers in answer, and rises up.

A movement of uncoordinated limbs, and then her hand whips out and seizes the bird. Jenny squawks and falls to silence as she succumbs to the child's grip.

"These spells are very exact. One thing off and they mutate or unravel, like a string of Christmas lights," the infant says.

"You don't sound like a child, Amanda."

"I'll hear your case now."

Jude licks his lips and stares at her. Her eyes roll, and they now appear to him jaundiced and yellowed at their corners, with her veins creeping in green and her neck arching to stare at him from the side of her eyes.

"Present your case," the child husks in a voice too old to be a child's. Pitched as a trembling soprano. It makes for a weird and laughable tone, whose very humor invites the gooseflesh to rise and his skin to crawl. He thinks of birdsong, and wonders what such a voice is designed to impart with its malignant sound. It calls invisible things to it the same way Salazar's shadows trip over themselves to slither and grip at him.

"My case?"

"Salazar asked you what you had to live for. What is it, Jude? What is it that you have that's worth leaving the mirror? Present your case. Convince this old and tired judge."

What did you have to live for anyway?

Jude cannot shake the feeling that a man with only birds for companionship did not have a right to live. He'd made no difference in the world by being in it, had saved no lives, had never even donated to a charity.

"I was in love once. That must mean something," Jude says.

"Love does not have to mean anything all."

She turns the bird back and forth in her palm. The canary opens its mouth as though trying to take in air and smothers in the child's grip. The thing called Amanda opens her mouth in tandem with the creature, and Jude thinks she might stuff Jenny into her mouth and bite into feathers and cartilage.

"Just don't hurt her!" he begs.

"Then tell me what you have to live for. Are you not a lawyer? There are many laws both written and invisible. Approach the bench. Tell me what you live for. Tell me what you die for, and why you should be granted clemency."

"I've done nothing wrong!"

Amanda doesn't answer. Her implacable eyes shimmer and Jude sees that she has two pairs of eyelids. A thin film that passes over her eyes, like a lizard's, and then disappears beneath her human, fleshy lid, until he thinks perhaps it had never been there at all.

Jenny tweets.

"Love! Yes, love. I fell in love with a woman I met at a library, did you know that? She was taking out books on ornithology. She owned canaries and finches and cockatiels. She invited me over to see them, and I was looking through her cages, watching the birds. She kissed me when I turned around. Everything happened by accident. Maybe she didn't love me at all, but I know what I felt. A time later, she told me she was pregnant, and I promised I'd marry her. I bought a ring and everything. And then, one day, I came home, and..."

"And then what happened? Did love not see the day through? What happens when at long last it doesn't conquer all, hmmm?"

"Just give her back. Give her back to me. I don't care, I don't care about living." His throat closes up and the tears burn hot as paper cuts at the corners of his eyes. "Hardly matters now, does it? What do I have to live for, anyway? Give her back."

The child laughs and hiccups from her belly, and the sound fills him with nausea as her grasp on the bird tightens.

"You can keep your bird for now. But think on it, boy. Give me the bird and I can grant you a chance for release. You'll have to convince Salazar that he's the one in the mirror, you know. No easy task. And at the end of it, you'll still be dead, but at least you'll be free of the mirror and no longer a plaything for rich occultists with nothing better to do with their money."

"Is that what you are?"

She hisses and opens her hands. Jenny explodes into flight, her song puncturing the air, and arrows for Jude, who catches her, holds her close as Amanda turns her back on him and collapses into the crib as though she had never been awake.

"Good morning, Salazar," Jude says.

Jenny flutters in his pocket, yellow feathers against his heart.

Salazar smooths his hair back from his forehead, and Jude follows suit with fingers pulled by invisible strings. He does not fight but allows the magic to command him. The sensation of raindrops running along his joints, tidal and oceanic currents.

"You sound pleasant today," Salazar says, eyes narrow in his gaunt face. "I don't like it."

"Did you ever wonder, Salazar?"

"What's that?"

"If maybe you're the one in the mirror? And I'm in the real world."

Salazar is expressionless. Heartless eyes flicker, and Jude detects the moment when the idea registers and catches hold on the edge of his consciousness.

Jude holds the posture, unable to move until Salazar chooses to do so. He returns the occultist's blank stare, measure for measure, caught in his supernatural cage.

Jenny, in his breast pocket, moves against his dead heart.

Salazar makes a face of disgust. A twisted leer of his lips. With an angry snap of his wrist, he plucks the bottle of cough syrup from the cabinet as he leaves. Jude follows him until the invisible cord that pulls and stretches him into action is released, freeing Jude to wander his two-dimensional Mirrorworld once more.

"Amanda. Little girl! Wake up, little girl!"

Shadows undulate through window light and Jude makes out her face through the rungs of the crib. She drools with violet-tinted saliva, then her mouth snaps closed and her eyes fly open.

"Amanda?"

The girl sits up and stares at him. He looks for signs and traces of the thing she'd been before, but she looks vacant and groggy, no trace of her otherworldly self until her face bisects with a grin longer than the circumference of her head, extending endlessly to the other side.

"*Yesssss?*"

"Take her," Jude chokes out the words. "Take her and give her back her life."

The child climbs to her feet and grins, opening her hands.

"What happens when you have her?" Jude asks, pulling Jenny from his pocket. She peeps from her hiding place and hops upon his finger.

With her fingers, the child makes the gesture of a person running.

"Your bird pops my cage open," the child growls, "and then you use your wits to make the most of my absence, eh?"

"Fine." He kisses Jenny on the top of her head and lets her go.

She ascends the air in a yellow puff.

The mirror glass parts for her like a wizard's curtain, a shaft of light passing through her feathers.

"Go, Jenny," he whispers, and presses against the glass. The tip of his nose brushes the hard surface of the mirror portal.

The bird bobs and weaves through the apartment. She dives down and alights on the edge of the crib. The little girl coos and blurts a string of excited nonsense words, as though the glittering lizard intelligence lying dormant beneath her child's flesh never existed. Her thatch of corn-silk hair stands out in all directions as the blue blanket falls away. The child offers a chubby fist, fingers grasping for the yellow bird above her. She opens her mouth hungrily, and Jenny stares at her before hopping along the rung and poising above the crib lock.

The Amanda blinks and the monster inside her is back. Or does it only pretend, Jude wonders, when it wants to seem a normal girl?

"There, little friend," she hisses. "Right there."

The shadows around them bend and beckon in their direction, as though all the sleeping, energetic lines of earth and electricity pull along a tide, conspiring to lull the bird and make it see things it could not recognize before. Then Jenny cocks her head and, in a flash of light, spots the bright crib lock for the first time.

C'mon, Jenny.

Tap tap. Jenny sets her beak against it. The little girl swipes at her and the bird dances out of reach, fluttering wildly, and then diving in to *tap tap* again at the lock.

With all the appearance of a normal child, she laughs with her open mouth in a pink curl, the beast evaporated from her eyes. *The devil hath the power to assume a pleasing shape.* Jude wonders what kind of devil she is. Any minute, the thing residing deep inside her will rise to the surface with its yellowed eyes and green veins of rot.

The thing inside her swells. She slams a fist against the crib door. Her fingers hit the mechanism in her desperate grab for the prize. The canary flutters, the lock snicks open and the door casts wide.

Amanda spills out onto the floor, trailing blankets behind her. A monster pretending to be a toddler.

"Yes," Jude whispers.

Jenny describes a drunken figure eight in the air, as though she were no more than a child's mobile. She dances in and out of Amanda's reach, and the little girl stretches her arms in a desperate bid to defy gravity and pluck her out of the air. Jenny dives and tumbles, teasing and tempting the toddler. Shadows cast from furniture and window blinds contract like fingers, becoming shaded tentacles that swat the bird to the ground. She lies flat over wood flooring with wings outstretched, dazed.

Amanda giggles, scoops her up and disappears into the closet beyond. The door snicks shut. Laughter, giggles, the bird singing from behind the closed door.

You use your wits to make the most of my absence, eh?

Jude passes a hand across his forehead, his lips moving in silent prayer.

He sits down on the floor of the Mirrorworld and waits while the little girl with something big inside her hides in the closet with the only thing that made his life worth living.

Jude does not quite doze, but senses himself suspended in a netherworld. He thinks of his birds. Had anyone found them in their cages yet? Would they beat their wings against the bars until their hearts gave out, losing feather after feather to the cruel isolation?

He snaps awake to the sound of Salazar whistling.

Jude races to the mirror, hoping to peer through before Salazar enters, but he's too late—suddenly slapped back from the surface. Jude feels himself posed erect and placed into pantomime, unfurling like a cardboard cutout.

He seals his lips shut against a cry and greets Salazar because he can do no other. He advances upon the looking glass as though they are dance partners engaged in a complicated waltz, until Salazar himself appears.

Jude musters all his enthusiasm.

"Salazar! Why, did you have a good day?"

The smirk disintegrates and dissolves into Salazar's face. His eyes ossify into stones.

"Why on earth do you keep doing that?"

"Doing what? I do everything you do, Salazar."

"Why aren't you miserable, like the rest?"

Jude follows Salazar's motions with cool dedication and loosens the collar around his throat. He pretends he is acting a part in a movie or a play, and this comes naturally to him. All of his future will depend on his talent for litigation and persuasion. His private play, his personal courtroom. Setting the stage and parading before the footlights for the benefit of an unseen audience. An invisible jury.

For Jenny. For liberation from this hell.

"What reason would I have to be miserable?"

"You're in a mirror."

"Am I? Still so sure that you're the one in the real world? Not the other way around?"

Salazar's face turns a shade of red beyond blood, his lips settling in an anemic line. What he shrugged off as a joke before no longer strikes the Satanist as funny.

"Stop it. *This* is the real world."

"Well, anyone would think so, eh? Where's Amanda? That little girl you're always screaming at?"

Salazar pauses, frozen, before slowly regaining his composure, staring at Jude measure for measure.

"Don't go anywhere, boogeyman," Salazar sneers, and turns on his heel to dart through the room and lean over the crib.

Jude watches a slice of the man, silhouetted against a window, fists on the bars, looking down at the empty sheets before snapping back toward the mirror. Salazar's steps echo, impatient staccato against old wood.

"What have you done with her?"

"With the apple of your eye?"

"I can unmake you, you know. I've got a hundred ways to send you to Hell."

"I've been trying to tell you, but you won't listen."

"*Where is she?*"

"*You're* the one on the other side of the mirror, Salazar. That's why your precious girl isn't with you. I'm on the right side. The life side. You're the one dead and trapped in the mirror."

Mirrorworld, Salazar mouths. "You're lying."

"Really, Salazar? Can you afford to be so hasty? You're all alone."

"I was just outside. I can go outside again. I can leave anytime I want."

"Suit yourself." Jude makes his voice casual. *Tread lightly. Be convincing, dammit! Make the closing argument too strong to be denied.* "Where do you think I go when you're not here? Turns out, I go anywhere I want as well."

From beyond Salazar's erect figure, a streak of yellow bolts from the closet, fluttering and flapping wildly into the room.

Jenny tweets furiously, and Salazar starts at it and his mouth parts in confusion. Jude stares wide-eyed at the bird and leaps upon the opportunity afforded him.

"If yours is the real world, why is there no reflection of that bird in mine?" he asks.

Salazar snaps his gaze from the bird to the glass. His eyes widen and his lips part, mouthing a single word: *No.*

"I wouldn't be too hard on yourself. I mean, what do you have to live for anyway?"

Jenny tweets. She hovers at the window and then streaks to the ceiling fan and remains there, preening.

Salazar stumbles against the end table. He jerks open the drawer. Inside, a gun rattles along the bottom, a box of loose bullets clinking together like change. He picks it up, and Jude remembers the firearm. The mouth with no teeth.

"This gun proves I'm real," Salazar insists. His finger lines the barrel.

"I have one too, Salazar."

Jude holds the fluctuating, flat-imaged pistol in his own fingers, waving it before him to demonstrate his power.

"It's not yours. I shot you with *this* gun. This is the real gun!" Salazar's voice becomes ragged, the rhythm of his breath uneven. "I can't be in the mirror."

As though to prove it to himself, he places the cold muzzle against his cheek.

Unable to do otherwise, Jude follows the motion.

"See," Jude pitches his voice to soothe. "See how you lift the gun as I lift it? The magic compels you to follow *my* motions."

Salazar gasps. His arm trembles and strains. Reality tumbles and swaps places and disorients his reason.

Jude grinds his teeth to hold every small emotion within, to keep for himself the secret. He holds his breath and touches the pistol to his head along with Salazar.

An explosion.

The blue flame licks from the muzzle.

Jude is suddenly everywhere at once as molecules of his own self struggle to follow the progress of Salazar's broken skull and splattered brains across the wall and carpet, a thousand shards of mirror reflecting every tiny portion of himself.

He fractures and splits and divides, helpless to share the same fate as Salazar's.

A death rattle from each of the men plays in two-part harmony, filling the empty apartment with a woeful sound.

The little girl with the growling voice and the jaundiced eyes slumbers in the closet, her lips stained with cough syrup.

She dreams of yellow birds and other pleasing shapes.

Martin Rose writes a range of fiction from the fantastic to the macabre, with work appearing in numerous venues and anthologies, and is the author of two horror novels, *Bring Me Flesh, I'll Bring Hell and My Loaded Gun, My Lonely Heart* available from Talos. More details are available at martinrose.org.

Purgatory Central

Steve Billings

"Don't worry, mate, being dead's not so bad," says a deep, broken-glass Scouse accent. "They say the first thousand years are the worst."

Startled, my gaze shoots from the window towards the voice, and I stare in disbelief at the shaven-headed behemoth crammed into the seat opposite me. Bulging, bloodshot eyes burn out of a weathered face etched with ancient scars. Razors, I'd guess, possibly Stanley knives. The spoils of a thousand Saturday night wars, no doubt.

The immense fingers of his right hand, (the word "LOVE" clumsily tattooed across them) grip a gleaming can with a force that says "Don't even think about it." Not that anyone would be mad enough to try. The other hand rests on his lap, out of view, but it shouldn't be hard to guess what's written on that one.

I'm transfixed with a mixture of fear and fascination, but to be honest I'm almost glad of the distraction from the panorama of doom passing outside my filthy, cracked window.

"Honestly, take my word for it, mate, it isn't that bad," he continues. "Assuming you're not heading for certain places, obviously." He stares at me, eyes unblinking, before breaking into a broad, sickly grin.

Where has this gruesome apparition appeared from? Surely he wasn't here until a moment ago. Have I been lulled into a trance, hypnotised by the grim, endless world outside, or am I in the throes of an acid trip gone horribly wrong?

I glance at my watch, although I have a feeling it isn't going to make any difference. How long have I been on this bloody train? Hours? Days? Months? Nothing makes sense any more.

He extends a giant club of a hand across the scratched, graffitied table surface. I hesitate momentarily before meeting it, hoping he doesn't notice my sweating palms, and praying he's not going to try and impress me with one of those death-grip handshakes.

"Hieronymus," he states, looking at me for a reaction. "Hieronymus Cole."

Here we go. It had to happen. Not only do I get lumbered with this musclebound lunatic, but apparently he's a master of comedy as well. I consider calling his bluff and asking him for his real name, but there's a faint rumbling deep in the caverns of my mind, and something tells me to bite my tongue. The scars also help to focus my thoughts.

"Danny," I reply, cautiously.

"Drink, Danny?" he offers, more a command than a question. "Come on, you've got plenty of time on your hands now, me old son."

I shrug, but I'm only postponing the inevitable.

"Come on," he encourages. "You look like you've been listening to Joy Division for a fortnight. Have a cider and cheer up a bit."

I stare incredulously at him. Cheer up? Surely I can't be destined to spend eternity with this clown? I think momentarily about telling him what he can do with his can, but I can see refusal won't be an option.

I nod reluctantly.

The thin, white plastic bag on the empty seat next to him rustles as he reaches in and produces two more silver cans, which do their best to reflect the dim carriage light. I don't recognise the brand, but give my current situation that isn't going to make much difference. I pull gingerly at the tab, praying it's not going to spray his beloved Crombie, or the immaculate Ben Sherman shirt underneath.

"Cheers!" says Hieronymus, raising his can before draining half of it in one gigantic slurp.

"Cheers," I say, meekly.

I steel myself and take a small swig. To my relief it's not only drinkable, it's gloriously refreshing. I momentarily forget my predicament, and drift away to better times.

Blissful memories of teenage summers out on The Levels with Jim and Ozzy, swilling murky scrumpy from battered plastic bottles. Endless, drunken banter about football (Rovers or City), bands (Fugazi or Sonic Youth) or girls at school (Jody or Kelly).

Jim, with his manic grin and his latest, pathetic attempt at a beard, and little Ozzy, lank hair hanging over headphones which seemed permanently glued to his ears. I completed the merry trio; tall, awkward and painfully shy with anyone apart from my closest friends.

Life only really began at sixteen, on those magical August evenings in deepest, brightest Somerset. Two mates and a two-litre bottle of Happy Rat from the village stores were the only requirements for a season of unbounded happiness. We thought it would last for eternity.

That was before the fires started.

I return my gaze to the endless vista of barren wilderness drifting by outside. The looming granite sky gives an aura of permanent dusk. It's been pretty much the same view since I woke on this Godforsaken train; not a single animal grazes in the barren fields, and I doubt any birds ever rest in the blackened branches of the skeletal trees.

I stare down at the empty line running in an endless parallel to ours, and realise that I haven't yet seen a single train pass in the opposite direction.

Abandoned stations and the smoking remnants of bizarre, primitive hamlets provide the only respite as the train rattles relentlessly onwards. Occasionally, a rusted tendril of track peels away from ours and heads off into the desolate terrain, a branch line to another part of oblivion.

Hieronymus follows my line of thought.

"Grim, eh?"

There is a brief silence before he continues. "I spy with my little eye, something beginning with 'F.'"

I bite my tongue. Surely I haven't got to suffer this much longer? He looks like he's here for the duration, though, so I'll humour him a bit more.

"Field?" I offer.

He sucks the air through his teeth. "Not bad. Try again."

I peer back at the landscape until he gets the hint.

"Give up?" he asks. "Fuck all."

I look around swiftly to see if anyone objects to his language, but I don't think they'd be foolish enough to chance it. I wince when I imagine what his reaction might be.

"Not one for the countryside, me," he ponders. "My milk comes from the corner shop. How it gets there's purely between the shopkeeper and the cow."

I glance at the other passengers, who sit morosely, alone with their thoughts. Why are they here?

A hooded girl chews gum with annoying mechanical precision on the table next to ours. Tattooed tears run down a stony face that probably doesn't see too many real ones. Her tiny fists, permanently clenched, sit below forearms dotted with telltale crusted scabs. She rests her immaculate trainers defiantly on the tired seat opposite her.

At another table lounges a scruffy, obese old man, his table obscured by fast food detritus. Greasy burger wrappers fight for space with discarded Cola cups. I can feel the cholesterol from here. How can he eat at a time like this? I stare distractedly at his T-shirt trying to decipher the bizarre pattern of crimson and yellow splashes, until I realise it's only ketchup and mustard.

"Messy bugger," murmurs Hieronymus.

Where had he bought his food? The same place as my friend got his cider, I suspect. I reason that there has to be some sort of buffet car on the train, but it doesn't really matter to me at the moment. I'm really not hungry.

"So why are you here?" he asks.

The words thud into me like frozen boulders.

"Pardon?" I say, meekly.

"Who or what put you on here? Seat 25A on the Afterlife Express."

My mind spins wildly, trying to keep all the mental plates spinning but, one by one, they come crashing to the ground. I struggle to say something, anything, but nothing comes out. I shrug my shoulders tamely.

The silence is so complete that it seems all noise has been sucked out of the carriage. I'm praying we'll reach our destination before I have to say anything, but that's not going to happen, so I wait.

"Fair enough," he says.

I try desperately to switch the spotlight.

"What about you?"

"Drugs," he says, casually.

I really wish I hadn't asked.

He's distracted by an Armani-clad, middle-aged man further down the carriage, who fiddles distractedly with his mobile phone, a huge Rolex encircling his wrist.

Hieronymus stifles a laugh.

"I don't think you'll get a signal here, mate," he says.

He fumbles inside his coat pocket and tosses his phone onto the table for me to see.

"Purgatel," he says with an air of resignation. "Whoever they might be."

The man in the suit looks across the carriage and offers me a sympathetic smile. At least I assume it's sympathy; probably sheer relief that he's not the one sat where I am. He glances away suddenly, as the door at the end of the carriage opens, and reaches for his briefcase.

A gaunt, pallid guard lumbers through the carriage. His piercing eyes stare at each passenger in turn. A shining white baton swings ominously by his side.

"Tickets," he demands flatly as he reaches our table.

"What's the magic word?" enquires my travelling companion, unfazed.

The inspector glares incredulously at him, and then notices the scars.

"Please," he mutters.

"That's better," says Hieronymus, and hands over his ticket, smiling benevolently as he receives it back.

I reach into my shirt pocket and offer mine. He punches the ticket without comment, the jet-black pupils of his eyes boring deep into mine, before he moves on towards the hooded youth, who holds her ticket out nonchalantly.

"Get your feet off the seat," orders the guard, quietly but with genuine menace.

The youth flips her ticket to the floor, and turns casually to look out of the window.

"Get your feet off the fucking seat!" barks the guard, before pulling the nightstick from its holster and, in one sickening swoop, smashing it into her emaciated shins.

Yelping in agony, she pushes back into the seat and the bravado vanishes. A few seconds later, however, temper triumphs over pain, and she propels herself up from the armrests, smashing her forehead into the guard's face. There is a crack of bone as the guard's nose loses its argument with the laws of physics, and he staggers backwards. Rivulets of blood trickle from his battered face down over his dusty uniform.

My companion shakes his head slowly, before taking a lengthy slurp from his can.

"When anger rises, think of the consequences," he says, to no-one in particular.

I look at him quizzically.

"Confucius," he replies, matter-of-factly.

Jim had nearly been flung into a ditch by the police car as it stormed down Digger's Lane, its wheels struggling for grip on the mud which had been turned into a ruddy wax by the morning dew. Intrigued, not to mention bloody furious, he followed the sound of the siren to Cleave Farm.

He was cycling out to meet me at the river, a fresh bottle of scrumpy tied precariously to the top frame of his old bike. When he slowed past the farm, he said, Old Man Henderson was standing solemnly in the yard, one vast arm round his wife, and one round his eldest son. They looked on in pale disbelief as firemen doused the remains of his largest barn. A forensic team, looking more like alien hunters than police officers, waited patiently before they could move in to examine the pathetic pile of sodden, smouldering timbers. They'd earn their money, he said. There was virtually nothing left.

We knew Ozzy wouldn't want to miss this spectacle, sad as it was, so we'd call for him on the way. We knocked excitedly on his door, but his mother answered and said he was asleep. He'd been out all night and looked terrible, she said. Jim and I exchanged a furtive glance, and we could both tell she was worried sick.

Something nudges my subconscious and I return my gaze to the window, as the scenery slowly, but unmistakably, begins to change. The lonely fields are replaced by derelict villages, which in turn become a ghostly suburbia. The train starts to slow as we enter what seems to be an endless workplace designed by a madman, a business park of the damned. The rusted shells of luxury cars sit silently in the shadows of soulless glass monoliths. Dishevelled people, dressed in a bizarre cocktail of rags, amble along weed-strewn paths, which snake between stagnant lakes. The fumes of the rancid water seep into the carriage, and even Hieronymus grimaces.

The Tannoy speakers in the ceiling crackle momentarily, before a slow, quavering voice speaks.

"Next Stop: Avarice. Avarice, your next station stop."

It sounds pre-recorded, but that doesn't make it any less chilling. It obviously isn't the guard, who sits dejectedly at an empty table, blood still spilling from his face, forming a crimson pond on the table.

"About time," says Hieronymus. "This should be interesting."

The train drags itself into a sparse, dilapidated station. The platform looks devoid of passengers until I spot two shadowy figures sat on a battered bench, its once-glorious paintwork long since faded. They are dressed in the same curious mishmash of rags as the others we saw on our way in. A burning oil drum crackling next to them sends a choking black mist along the platform.

The immaculate businessman rises from his seat and shuffles hurriedly down the aisle towards the door at the end of the carriage; eyes fixed on the floor, briefcase stuck fast under his arm like a winger heading for the try line.

The other passengers peer from their windows in grim fascination, silently rejoicing that they're not the first ones to trade the relative haven of the carriage for the unknown lands outside.

The two figures rise swiftly from the bench and march towards him. Adjusting his tie, he smiles weakly, holding his ticket hesitantly towards them but that isn't what they're after. The smaller figure swiftly produces a knife and gestures animatedly towards the oil drum, and for a moment my stomach turns to concrete at the prospect of what might be about to happen. Surely not? The large one prises the briefcase from his desperate hands, whilst the smaller one, without any emotion, slices the leather strap from the lavish watch in one expert move.

He strolls towards the oil drum where he drops it in with look of vague disgust on his face. Sparks shoot from the drum as the taller figure joins him and launches the case into the furnace. Flames…

Three weeks after the inferno at Cleave Farm, it happened again.

The end of the summer holidays was roaring towards us like one of Old Man Henderson's angry bulls. Six blissful weeks of football kickabouts in the sweltering heat and cider-fuelled midnight swims in the murky river water were coming to an end, and we all sensed that things would never quite be the same again. This was 'that moment', and we all secretly knew it. An unsaid farewell to the children we had been, and a greeting to the men we were becoming.

Jim and I were staying on to the sixth form but Ozzy, never one for academic aspirations, had called it quits and decided to take his chance in the mad circus of the outside world as soon as the holidays were over. An excellent guitarist, he'd applied for a job as a session musician in Bristol.

I knew what had happened as soon as I opened the curtains. A huge black plume of smoke barrelled up into the cloudless summer sky, like an oil slick spilling across a perfect blue ocean.

I ran downstairs to tell my parents then sprinted the short distance to Jim's house.

This wouldn't be as easy to gatecrash as the first one. The recently-opened Farm Shop was at the end of a lane, and there was no chance of 'accidentally' passing it on the way to somewhere else. As it happened, we got a good enough view on the evening news, where the local reporter, showing suitable gravitas, interviewed a senior policeman. The cause of the fire was still being investigated, he said, but obviously parallels had been drawn with the previous incident. At the rear of the shop was an old shed full of diesel barrels, he added. It was a miracle no one had been killed.

I turn away as the slamming of the train door startles me, and we begin to pick up speed. I take a final look back, and see the man stood on the platform. His shaking hands cover his face as he drops to his knees.

My companion shakes his head ruefully.

"Poor bloke," he muses. "But he's obviously done something to end up here."

"Good point," I say, "but we'll never know now, will we?"

"Personally, I've never been that fussed about money."

"Me neither," I reply.

"Wisdom outweighs any wealth," he adds.

I return a perplexed look.

"Sophacles," he says, as if I should have recognised it instantly.

The air pressure changes suddenly as the train heads into a tunnel with a loud slap, and the broken carriage lights start to flicker like deranged fireflies. I peer into the void, seeing only a reflection of my puzzled face. I stare back and ponder my last conversation with Hieronymus, and have an epiphany. Perhaps it's not how we got on this train, or when. Maybe that's nothing to do with it. It's why we're on here that seems to matter.

Eventually, we exit the tunnel and the blackness is replaced by a swirling red miasma. I look to Hieronymus for his reaction, but he simply reaches for the white bag again.

The Spectral voice returns.

"Next Stop: Wrath. Wrath, your next station stop."

The hooded youth rises from her seat and gives me a long parting glare before she limps down the aisle, fists still clenched, jaws still chewing.

The station is still shrouded in the swirling maroon smoke, but, as the door creaks open, I hear the sounds of utter pandemonium. A dense, aural cocktail of smashing glass and police sirens mixed with the dull roar of an unseen mob on the rampage.

I see her step into the mist. She peers through the drifting red smog to see that a small group of others has alighted with her. She turns towards them and they look at each other in wary silence. I can't tell if they're about to trade hugs or punches.

The door crashes shut as a fresh wave of fog rolls in and envelopes the group, removing them from view completely.

The last one changed everything.

Jim and I gawped as half the firefighters in Somerset fought a huge inferno, which raged for well over a day. Ozzy had become much more withdrawn over the past few weeks, but we called for him on the way, as usual. His mother answered the door, but she looked a wreck. She said he hadn't come home. We told her not to worry. I said he'd been talking about one of the girls at school a lot recently, and hoped she'd put two and two together.

When the blaze was finally out, the fire engines began to peel off and head away, only to be replaced by a swarm of TV vans, not just local this time, from across the country.

The cameras looked on as the police pulled the charred remains of two people from the smoky ruins.

And so the surreal journey to my ultimate destination continues. The constant can-popping and quotations of my companion prove a useful deterrent against the madness outside.

Raindrops start to scratch tiny wet diagonals on the window as we pull into Sloth. The largest group of passengers so far amble off, and are instantly confronted by a bizarre parody of an old army colonel. A ridiculous array of plumes adorn a huge hussars hat, but even this is overshadowed by a handlebar moustache that looks like it needs some sort of pet license. His immaculate black uniform is covered almost entirely with a rainbow of medals, and the toecaps of his boots shine like black glass.

Behind him the horizon is covered with a multitude of faceless barracks, their crumbling brickwork faded by years of rain and neglect.

His gnarled face bawls a constant stream of orders as he shakes a peculiar red tube menacingly in front of him. I guess it's some sort of regimental stick that complements the uniform, until Hieronymus corrects me.

"Cattle prod," he says with a frown. "Very nasty".

It seems to have the desired effect on the group, who quickly form a ramshackle parade line.

The rain turns to a ceaseless downpour as the train lurches away and climbs into a range of bleak foothills, which gradually become near-mountains, their gradients getting steeper as the speed of the train increases.

When the window begins to steam up, I rub a small porthole with my sleeve, and stare out. Through the sheets of rain, I see pockets of people clambering desperately up the hills, each pursued effortlessly by a prod-wielding officer, who shoots small arcs of blue lightning into the backs of any stragglers.

As we pass through the next stations, Pride and Envy, the carriage gradually becomes a little more deserted as the occupants take their final, humiliating walk down the aisle and out into the chaos.

We both turn our gaze to the junk food addict as the train crawls into Gluttony, but to our bewilderment he remains firmly seated, munching on a family-sized bar of chocolate and slurping a milkshake. He finally departs at Lust, along with a handful of anonymous middle-aged people who look like they'd be more at home listening to The Archers.

"Well, well, well," says Hieronymus, as a huge smile rearranges his scars. "Takes all sorts, I suppose."

"He could've bloody tidied up, though," he muses, as he spies the mountain of wrappers and empty cups.

Finally, I realise the rest of the carriage is empty, and it's just myself and Hieronymus left. Even the guard has removed himself somewhere along the line.

I think about moving to an empty table, but to be honest I've come to warm to this guy. Bizarre, boozing sage though he is, he's provided a welcome distraction on my journey.

"And then there were two," he says, resignedly.

An awkward silence follows, and I feel I owe it to him to break it.

"So tell me why you're here," I ask.

"See these?" he continues, fingering the chaotic series of tramlines across his face. "I know you've been dying to ask. Pardon the pun. How do you think they got there?"

"Come on," he adds, with a sparkle of menace in his eyes. "Be honest, I can take it."

I have nothing much to lose now.

"I don't know. Cage fighter, maybe? Football hooligan?"

"Not bad," he says, nodding appreciatively. "Not bad. Doorman. Worked the clubs around Liverpool for years. A few scrapes here and there with the local scallies, nothing I couldn't handle. Innocent days, really."

He sounds like he almost enjoyed it.

"All of a sudden, the drugs start appearing by the lorry load and the whole world goes banzai. If I found anyone dealing anything, anything, they were out. End of story. One day the club owners, evil bastards they were, call me in and tell me who's allowed in to sell and who isn't. I say no, it's not going to happen. They show me a stack of money this thick," he says gesturing with his immense thumb and forefinger, "but I still say no. Eventually I turn away one face too many, and this is what happens."

I sit, stunned. If it's true, then the guy's got more principles than I've ever had.

"Still," he says, perking up, "Onwards and upwards. I intend to live forever or die trying."

"Don't tell me. Confucius?" I ask.

"Groucho Marx," he replies.

We're interrupted by the disembodied voice, chilling my blood for what appears to be the last time.

"Next stop: Purgatory Central, where this train will terminate. Change here for Heaven and Hell."

"Well, this is us," says my companion, and rises as I do.

His enormous fingers start to crush the empty cans one by one, and put the mangled metal chunks back into the bag, before he ties the top neatly and drops it on the table.

Something irks my subconscious, and, as I look down at his hands, I am stunned to see that he has "LOVE" tattooed on both of them.

I gesture for him to leave first. He nods and squeezes his huge legs past the table and into the aisle.

The door creaks for the last time as we step onto the deserted platform of a huge terminus. Massive, rusted arches do their best to support a canopy of fractured glass panels high above, the spans reaching out to infinity over a seemingly endless horizon of empty platforms. The only sounds are the wind, which blows swirls of rubbish across the tracks in small tornadoes, and the tolling of a huge bell somewhere in the far distance.

We walk silently towards the concourse, and I sense for the first time that Hieronymus is struggling for words. As we pass the engine of our train, I pause to peek through a cobwebbed cabin window, but the interior looks like it hasn't been touched for a hundred years. An inch-thick layer of dust lies like fine silver snow over everything, including the driver's seat.

A sudden clattering breaks the solitude, and I look instinctively upwards into the crystallised roof. My tired eyes scan the canopy, and then I see it. A lone crow preens its ebony wings, and then turns slowly to return my gaze. We stare at the little black statuette for a moment, then turn to continue our walk.

A huge, peculiar departure board dominates the concourse. At least a hundred feet in length, it is seemingly hewn from a single, flawless slab of coral-red marble. In contrast, the lettering is formed by individual slate panels, each with painted characters in a variety of bizarre colours and styles. Despite the endless stretch of platforms, only two trains are advertised. Underneath the board, a faded white sign sits above a doorway seemingly long since bricked up. I look closely and can just about read the lettering. It says "Exit."

As we walk to the trains, the first comes into view. A line of gleaming chrome carriages, as immaculate as the day they were crafted. Through windows as clear as mountain spring water, cosy table lamps shine invitingly onto gleaming cutlery. Vast wine glasses, deserving of only the finest clarets, sit invitingly on frost-white linen.

Behind this glorious apparition lurks a haunting, blackened hulk, its windows obscured by what appear to be random splashes of dark paint, a bleak palette of blacks and greys.

We stand silently on the platform and look at each other, for what seems an eternity, and very soon will be. At last, he breaks the silence, just as he had when we first met.

"Well, good luck, mate," he offers, and holds his vast hand out for the last time. "I think this is where we say our goodbyes."

I feel an overwhelming sadness. I was rather starting to like this character, despite all his bizarre philosophising, and was hoping we might continue our journey together.

"Aren't we getting the same train?" I ask hopefully.

"Sorry, mate, but I don't think so." He offers me a final, rueful smile, a million miles from the sickly grin from our first meeting.

After the business with Ozzy, Jim went back to school, but I couldn't face it.

I decided I'd go travelling and get away from things for a while. At the end of the summer holidays, I cashed in my savings and bought a ticket to America.

I spent a glorious autumn hitching rides and catching long, slow trains across the desolate northern states; Montana, Idaho, North Dakota. The real America, in my book, not the usual destinations teeming with British tourists whining about the heat. These were vast but insular places, where the next town might as well have been in a different galaxy.

If they'd paid more attention to was happening further afield, they would have noticed a series of brutal infernos. Strangely enough, they'd all occurred in places on my route.

It was a shame about Ozzy and Kelly. I really do regret that things turned out as they did, but they'd fallen prey to one of the most basic of human truths: there are no secrets in small villages. How could he think he'd keep their little affair quiet?

I'd timed my fun to coincide with their long, furtive nights in Gilly's Wood. No wonder he spent most of his days sleeping.

On the night of the last fire, they'd changed their route and I'd walked straight into them. I was carrying an old plastic bottle, but he knew straight away from the smell that it wasn't cider inside it this time.

Hieronymus bids me farewell, turns slowly and ambles towards his train.

I walk towards mine and stop to check my ticket for a final time before I board. I distractedly run my finger through the strange grey paint, and notice it isn't paint at all, but a fine veneer of hot ash, and I know where my train is heading.

Steve lives and works on the edge of The Cotswolds, near the city of Bath, England. Despite a life-long addiction to bleak music and dark literature, he lives a chaotic but happy life with his wife, two children and two deranged cats. His first ever short story finished runner-up in the 2012 Aeon Award and he has had numerous stories printed since. You can find out more about Steve at stevebillingsfiction.wordpress.com.

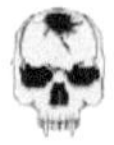

The Cottage of Curiosities

Annie Neugebauer

Patty could never decide which way to face when she got on the tree swing.

She looked across the lawn at the house. It was small and white, with a pointy roof with dipped sides and pretty green trim. The stone chimney crooked like a kindly old man, and the curtains were open to let in the evening sunlight. If she faced the house, she felt more cheerful, but then she always felt the urge to turn and look behind her at the woods.

Things lived in the woods, and most of them weren't bad, but sometimes, Patty was sure, they got hungry in there. Mama said if you walked too far in you could get turned around. Through the two ropes that held up the swing's wooden seat, Patty looked at the woods, studying the narrow limbs of saplings and the ground where the first of the dying leaves collected in puddles of burgundy and gold.

A little beyond where the yard met the forest, something shiny glinted under the last touch of the setting sun, winking at her once before it disappeared.

Patty stepped around the swing and took a few steps forward, ignoring the fretful squirrel that chattered at her from the tree. The sparkle flashed again.

Distantly, she heard the cuckoo clock go off inside the house. The little bird cried six… seven times before falling silent, which meant it was time for Patty to go back in. Mama didn't like it when Patty pretended not to hear it, and Mama hadn't been feeling well for several days now, so she wouldn't want to get out of bed to ring the big brass bell that could be heard from even farther away than the cuckoo.

But Patty wanted to know what the shiny thing was. Maybe it was something neat that would make Mama feel better! Mama loved neat things; she collected them.

With that settled, Patty mustered her courage and tromped into the brush. She kept her eyes trained on the spot where the glint came from, and even though her heart was pounding, she got there quickly and squatted to pick it up.

It was some special type of rock, about the size of her small palm. She flexed her wrist and tossed it into the air. It made a satisfying smack when she caught it. The surface was rough and angular, mostly black and gray with a little bit of brown on it, but parts of it gleamed silver. It was perfect.

The deep, full tolls of the bell rang out. Mama wanted her to come inside.

With an eager bounce in her step, Patty ran back to the house.

Mama's room was the only room where Patty didn't need to shut the curtains for the night. They were already closed, and the air was very dim. Several candles were melted almost down to their bases, and the room was smoky.

When Patty walked in she saw Mama's silhouette under the covers. She must be very tired to get back in bed after ringing the bell. Patty tried to be quiet, but the old wooden floors creaked beneath her feet, even when she walked across the woven rug, as she always did, to look at the shelves.

They were full of Mama's collection. There were pale seashells–one with a pearl inside it–and tusks with carvings in them, paintings and sketches that hung from ribbons, and the skull of a critter with horns.

There was a stuffed bird in a big fancy cage, and a globe in its own stand. There were bugs of all different kinds pinned to a board, but Patty didn't like to look at those. Instead she looked at the little clay pot full of brightly-colored feathers.

In the center of it all hung the dark, fancy cuckoo clock with its mysterious chains and weights dangling from it like necklaces. The center piece swung back and forth, back and forth. Its ticking filled the room with a familiar, incessant rhythm. Patty stared at the door the little bird lived in, then looked away.

It had been just her and Mama for as long as Patty could remember, but sometimes people traveled through the woods to see the house. They called it the cottage of curiosities. Mama liked to show them her treasures, but she never sold them, so eventually people stopped coming.

The special rock felt heavy in Patty's hand, so she left the shelves and sat on the edge of the bed.

"How do you feel, Mama?"

Mama rolled onto her back with a soft groan, peering up at Patty. Her face almost looked like a stranger's in the gloom. "Hi, baby. I'm a little cold."

Patty tilted her head to the side. The breeze outside was crisp and chilly, but inside the house it was almost too warm. She reached out and put a hand on Mama's forehead, like Mama did to her when she was sick. The gilded mirror on the nightstand on the other side of the bed reflected Mama's profile.

"You're very warm," Patty said.

"I don't feel warm," said Mama. Then she pulled the blankets in tighter around her chin and rolled back onto her side. "Will you blow out the candles when you leave, sweetheart? Mama's very tired."

Patty frowned. Mama wasn't going to scold her for making her ring the bell? Or ask her what it was she was holding in her hand? She really must be feeling bad.

Patty stood, blew out all of the candles but one, and set the chunk of silver on the tray next to the bed. Maybe it would cheer Mama up in the morning. Then she kissed Mama on the cheek, took the last candle, and left her to sleep.

Patty brought Mama breakfast, but she didn't want any. The silver rock was gone, though, so she must have gotten up during the night and seen it, maybe put it on the shelves somewhere. Patty hoped it had made her smile.

Patty stayed inside all morning and afternoon, just in case Mama needed her. She walked around their small home and studied every single shelf and all their curiosities. She'd seen them before, but every time she looked she noticed something new.

This time she spotted several dark, oval medallions hanging high on one wall, but she couldn't read what they said. In one cabinet she saw a whole bird's nest with four eggs in it, next to some arrowheads and a piece of strangely shaped coral. There was a section of wood that felt like stone, and a stone with the skeleton of a fish in it. Then there were her old favorites, like the knight's helmet and the stuffed fox with his long whiskers and glass eyes.

As fascinating as these things were–for Patty loved to make up stories about each object and where it came from–by the time the cuckoo's cries grew short and began to grow long again, Patty was twitchy with extra energy. It was still a couple of hours until she'd have to be inside for the night, so she decided to go outside and swing.

This time she faced the woods, but for the first time, she didn't feel the need to watch them just in case something came out. She wanted to go back in. What if there was more silver in there? Or something better, like gold? Or something Patty couldn't even imagine? If she could find something really good, it would make Mama feel better for sure. Only babies were afraid of the woods.

The cries of the cuckoo came from inside – six of them. She still had an hour before Mama would ring the bell.

Patty didn't even stop swinging. She jumped forward when the ropes were stretched all the way, and she hit the ground running. She'd have to search fast.

Patty's fingers trembled as she picked it up. She could hardly even believe it.

Nestled among old brown leaves was a short stick completely covered in bright orange moss. She'd never seen moss that color before – only greens and grays – but it got better. There was a little black crow's foot still attached, grasping one side. What had happened to the rest of the crow she didn't like to wonder, but there was no doubt Mama would love this curiosity.

Patty straightened back up, gripping the stick by the end furthest away from the foot, and turned to leave. Then turned again. And again.

Which way had she come from?

A twig snapped to her side, and she whirled. Nothing moved, but it had gotten darker beneath the leaves. What time was it? Was Mama worried about her? Had she already rung the bell?

A crunch, this time from further away.

"Hello?" Patty called softly.

There was a waiting silence.

"Who's there?" Patty asked.

For some reason, Patty thought she might get an answer, and she desperately didn't want to.

She ran.

She clutched the stick with the crow's foot to her chest and bolted, sprinting through the trees like a wild doe. Twigs scraped the soft puffs of her cheeks and once she tripped on a vine, but she never looked back. She didn't know if she was going the right way until she heard the bell ring. She adjusted her direction toward it.

She didn't hear anything chasing her, but still she ran. Finally Patty burst through the trees into the soft sunlight slanting from behind the house, and she didn't stop. She ran up to the front door, twisted the knob, and skittered inside, shoving it closed behind her. She stood leaning on it, panting.

"You're such a baby," she muttered.

Just to prove how silly she'd been, she went to the window and looked outside. The grass stretched wide and green and empty beyond the flowers next to the house. The woods were still. Her tree swing swayed gently. Patty held her breath, but then she forced herself to laugh. She'd probably bumped it when she ran through the yard. She shut the curtains for the night.

Only then did she remember her prize: the moss-covered stick clutched in her hand, the little crow's foot perched on the end.

Mama was lying on her side again, and the room was still smoky and dark. Patty was surprised Mama had bothered to get up to ring the bell at all.

Patty crossed over the creaky floors and the thick rug to look at the curiosities. She scanned the shelves for where Mama might have put her silver rock, but she couldn't find it. She spent a few moments studying the pretty miniature town on the far side. There was snow on some of the roofs, but not all of them. Mama said Patty could put them in her room when she got a little older.

From the cuckoo came an odd, strangled cry, and Patty stared at the wooden door the bird lived in, but it wasn't time for it to come out. The clock's tick hiccupped, then kept going. Patty turned away.

"Mama?" she said softly, walking over to the bed.

Mama groaned.

Patty put a hand on Mama's shoulder, but she wouldn't roll over onto her back. Patty peered into the mirror on the other side of the bed, but it wasn't turned at quite the right angle to see her face.

"Mama, are you okay?"

Mama mumbled something Patty couldn't hear. Patty reached over to feel her forehead, but her hand hovered. She knew Mama was sick. Really sick. Patty didn't know what to do.

She lightly brushed Mama's hair back, then set the stick on the tray next to the bed. "I'm sorry the silver didn't make you feel better," she whispered. "But you'll like this one. I can tell."

When Mama's only reply was the deep breathing of heavy sleep, Patty took the last candle and left, dragging her feet behind her.

Patty had to do something to help Mama. The stick with the crow's foot was gone in the morning, which meant Mama had gotten up at least once overnight, but she refused breakfast again.

She had to go back into the woods. She had to find something really good so Mama would get better. Maybe she'd even meet a person–a grown-up who would know what to do.

As Patty headed into the green shade, her swing hung still and silent under the tree, and the squirrel watched her, holding his tail. Patty marched with purpose, heading in as straight a line as she could.

But it was impossible to walk in a straight line with all the trees in the way, and before Patty knew it she wasn't sure which way she'd come from. The first tear had started down her cheek when she spotted something white.

Sniffling a little, Patty eased toward the small fluffy lump. She nudged it with the toe of her shoe, but it didn't move. She knelt, reaching out to touch the soft fur with her hand. It was a rabbit.

Patty gently picked it up, but it flopped limply. It had two big ears so tall she could see the veins running through the insides of them. Its eyes were open but a dull, blank black. It was dead, but Patty didn't see anything wrong with it.

"You poor thing," she said. "What happened to you?"

The rabbit didn't answer.

Then Patty got an idea. Maybe this could be a curiosity. Its fur was perfectly white and pretty and it didn't have any injuries. Mama could have it stuffed like the fox and the bird, and she could add it to her other treasures. Patty was sorry the bunny had died, but she was very happy to have found the best curiosity so far. This was *certain* to make Mama feel better!

Patty stood, but something was wrong. The woods were silent. She looked around, holding the rabbit to her torso, but nothing moved. She felt like someone was watching her. Was there someone here? Could they help?

"Hel—hello?" Patty asked softly.

There weren't any sounds. No one was there, but the hairs on Patty's arms prickled and danced.

She wouldn't be a baby like last time, though. Clenching her teeth together, Patty turned and headed in the direction she was pretty sure was home.

She forced herself to walk slowly. She felt like something was behind her, but every time she looked nothing was there. Her pace gradually increased until she was shoving her way through branches and striding with stiff legs.

Patty thought maybe she saw the yard ahead. If only the bell would ring so she could be sure. A twig snapped behind her, but she knew it must be her imagination. Or another squirrel. She refused to look. "I'm not a baby," she said.

She could see her swing. Something scraped behind her, and Patty couldn't stand it anymore.

She ran across toward the lawn as fast as she could–past the trees, past the swing, over the grass, and into the house. Even as she slammed the door shut, she couldn't bring herself to see if anything was there. She ran to the window and closed the curtains without looking outside.

Patty stood clutching the white rabbit to her chest, where her heart pounded so hard it made her skin pulse all over.

"You're a stupid baby," she told herself, but there wasn't any punch to it.

She stood there until her breathing slowed down, and then she went to check on Mama.

This time Patty set her treasure on the tray by the bed right away. She propped the pretty rabbit where the moss-covered stick had been, then went to the shelves to try to find the latter. The cuckoo ticked like an echo of her heartbeat as she searched, but Patty couldn't spot where Mama had placed the stick with the crow's foot.

The floors creaked as Patty walked over to the bed and sat down on the edge. Mama was on her side again, and for a moment she seemed so still that Patty froze too. Then she saw the covers moving with Mama's breath, and her shoulders sank with relief.

"Mama," she said. "Are you awake?"

Mama didn't answer.

"Mama?" she said a little louder.

Mama let out a strange, tiny groan.

Patty reached out a hand to rest on Mama's shoulder, but for some reason she hesitated. Her hand dropped back to her lap.

"Mama, I'm scared. Are you okay?"

Heavy breathing was the only reply.

Patty shifted, leaning over to peer into the mirror on the other side of the bed and see Mama's face. But Mama had the covers pulled up all the way around her head like a cape, so her face was hidden in shadows by the blanket.

Patty lifted up the candle nearby, holding it over Mama's body so she could see into the mirror. The flame made the glass glint and wink, and the glow only dimly reached it. Patty moved her arm around until the light reflected just right, stretching barely within the shadows of Mama's covers.

Patty saw a face that only half looked like Mama's. Patty raised the candle, and eyes glinted within the blankets. They were open, staring at her. They looked solid black.

The cuckoo cried out. Patty shrieked, leaping back.

Mama didn't move. Patty whirled to face the clock, where the strange little bird burst madly in and out of the door where he lived. Something was wrong with the chime. He made a strange gurgling sound as he thrust forward, over and over.

Patty didn't wait for him to get to seven. She ran out of the room and shut the door.

She hid in her bedroom until morning.

By the time sun came through Patty's window, she felt silly, but still very worried. She had been a baby last night and let her imagination get the best of her, but she knew she had to go get help. Today a new curiosity wouldn't be enough. She'd have to go not just into the woods but through them, all the way out the other side where other people lived.

Before she left, she cracked open Mama's bedroom door and peeked inside. The rabbit on the tray was gone, and Mama looked like an unmoving lump under her blankets. Patty stood in the doorway and watched long enough to see her breathing, then shut the door again.

The woods were very dark, even though the sun hadn't gone all the way down yet. The trees overhead made a roof of jagged leaves, and all of the shadows looked long and green.

Patty had been walking all day, and she still hadn't gotten out of the woods. She was tired and hungry and anxious about Mama. She passed a large tree with a misshapen knot in its belly.

Hadn't she already seen that tree?

Patty stopped, looking around.

Had she already been here?

In the distance, Patty heard the cuckoo begin its mottled cry. Her throat felt tight as she turned toward the sound. It wasn't very far away. It sounded like it came from the side of the cottage.

She'd been walking in circles.

The little bird kept crying, although the sound was slow and warbled. She counted to seven, then eight. It kept going. Nine, ten. But it wasn't dark yet, so it couldn't be that late, could it? Eleven, twelve. Patty looked around, hugging her arms tight around herself.

Thirteen. Fourteen. Fifteen.

The cuckoo kept going.

Patty bounced on her heels, hugging herself. She was supposed to help Mama, but she'd got lost all day. The thought of going back to the house made her start breathing heavy. "What should I do?" she whispered.

The little bird cried and cried.

Something to the side caught her eye. Patty took a few steps toward it, deeper into the woods. As she began to see around a tree trunk, she realized it was the bottom of a shoe. Above it was white fabric, over an ankle.

Patty stopped.

Her heart pounded.

"Who's there?" Patty asked.

The only answer was the cuckoo's deranged call.

Patty felt tears trail down her cheeks, warm compared to the nip in the air.

"I don't want any more curiosities," she said, but the shoe stayed.

Her chest began to shake with sobs, but Patty wouldn't let them out. She wasn't a baby, and whether or not she looked, the shoe was there.

She continued walking around the tree, bringing into sight the matching shoe and ankle. Then a long skirt, spread askew and dotted with crimson leaves. Next to it, two hands that looked familiar.

Patty's whole body shook, but she stepped the rest of the way around the tree that blocked her view.

Mama lay dead in the leaves, facing up, her pale blue eyes open and staring listlessly at the trees. Her skin was gray from being outside for days, and ants trailed into the corners of her mouth.

Patty screamed.

If Mama had been here, what was in her room?

Inside the cottage the cuckoo stopped, burbling into a silence that ticked through the woods like a clock too strange to tell time any longer. The silence tocked and dangled and swayed, waiting.

Then the bell rang.

Annie is a novelist, short story author, and award-winning poet. She has work appearing in over fifty venues, including *Black Static*, *Apex Magazine*, and *Fireside*. She's the webmaster for the Poetry Society of Texas, an active member of the Horror Writers Association, and a columnist for both Writer Unboxed and LitReactor. She's represented by Alec Shane of Writers House. Visit her at AnnieNeugebauer.com.

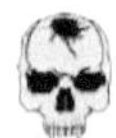

Dead Girls Don't Love

Sarah Hans

I had no memories before Princess came along. Papa Levi put her on the cot next to mine one night and I lay in the darkness, wondering about the source of the intoxicating smell of lavender and honey that drifted across the expanse of floor between our cots. Of course, I couldn't compare the scent to anything then, my mind blank as an unwritten page.

The next day, when she came to work beside me in the field, I recognized her scent. I felt strange, as if my heart were clenching tight in my chest. It was the first time I'd remembered anything from one day to the next, aside from my name and how to dig a hole in the earth. And sometimes I forgot those too. Memories are hard to cling to when you're dead.

Princess's skin was a rich brown, the color of the earth we tilled. Her hair was cropped, like every other worker's, but it was such a dark brown it was nearly black. And her eyes were green, startling against her dark face, paler than the weeds we ripped from the earth bare-handed until our palms bled. She was beautiful.

"Hello," I said when Papa Levi left her beside me.

She blinked at me, squinting against the sunlight, but didn't reply. This was a normal reaction for a new worker, so I didn't worry. Words would come to her eventually. Or they wouldn't. As long as she could do the work, the farm would keep her, either way.

We worked side-by-side tearing up weeds that day, and that night I lay awake on my cot, listening to her cry.

"Why?" I asked her, watching her in the dim moonlight that streamed in between the wall slats. She worked her jaw, but still couldn't speak. I didn't know why she was upset, but I knew the sound she was making was a sound of sorrow. I wasn't allowed to get up from my cot, but I wanted to make her stop. So I stretched my arm across the dirt floor, seeking her hand.

She pulled away from me, rolling onto her other side and sniffling. I retracted my hand, wishing I could do more.

The next day Papa Levi put her beside me again. "This is Cupcake. Follow her lead." He gestured to me and pushed a trowel into her hand. She stood staring at the ground for a few long moments, then looked at me, stupid as a newborn.

"Like this," I said, reaching down and digging a little hole with my own trowel. I liked digging holes, I was good at it. I looked up at Princess. She was staring off into the distance, paying me no mind.

I stood and grabbed her wrist. Her eyes snapped back to my face. "Like this," I told her, and gestured to the holes in the ground. She looked at the holes and looked at me, then at the trowel in her hand. I led her to a spot beside the hole I'd dug. "You try."

She squatted beside the hole and stuck her trowel in the earth. She didn't know what to do after that and looked at me. I knelt and placed my hand over hers.

The touch was like electricity. A tingling sensation spread from my hand to my heart. Our eyes locked. Time stopped.

"What're you two doin'?" A familiar voice boomed. "Cupcake? Princess?" Mama Tess glided up to us, the necklace of animal skulls she wore about her neck clacking. Her face was a twist of anger.

I stood and my trainee followed suit. "Diggin'," I said, gesturing to the half-dug hole in the earth.

Mama Tess's blow caught me off guard, as it always did. She struck me so hard I tasted blood. She drew her hand back for a second strike, but Princess was there. Her hand came up and caught Mama Tess's wrist.

"No!" I cried.

Princess turned to look at me, still holding Mama Tess's wrist. She looked confused, hurt, angry.

"No," I told her again, shaking my head. Princess slowly released the wrist.

Mama Tess called for Papa Levi while she rubbed her wrist. He came with the shovel and hit Princess on the back a few times to teach her a lesson. She didn't scream or cry out as the shovel came down, just whimpered and looked at me with eyes like a puppy's. Innocent, stupid, empty. She didn't understand why this was happening. She didn't understand why I didn't help her.

I couldn't help her. Not with Mama Tess and Papa Levi standing there. They couldn't kill me, since I was already dead, but they could bury me again. Being buried again was my worst fear. What if I couldn't dig my way out this time? I'd be trapped in the dark forever. Anything was better than that, even working from sunrise to sunset and watching a beautiful woman hit with a shovel until she stopped moving.

So I didn't help, and forced myself to feel nothing about it, not even regret. Emotions were for the living.

That night Princess didn't cry. She didn't speak. She just lay on her cot, a lump of human flesh, barely breathing. She still wouldn't take my hand, though I left it on the dirt between our cots all night.

The next day Papa Levi didn't put Princess beside me in the field. I dug holes and wondered where she was, what task she was doing. I had never thought about anything besides the work before. Without memories, what else was there to consider? My past was erased and my future was there, in that field—the present was all I had.

Until Princess. And then I wondered. I missed her scent. For the first time since I'd been brought to the farm, I felt something.

Regret. Guilt. Worry.

At supper I was relieved to find that Princess was doling out the grits. "Hello," I said, extending my bowl and smiling.

She ladled grits into my dish and didn't meet my eyes. I picked at my food and went to bed. I lay awake until Princess came to her cot.

"I'm sorry," I whispered when the lights went dark. I wasn't sure what the words meant, but they seemed right.

I heard her soft intake of breath. "Sorry?" she repeated.

"Sorry." My heart fluttered in my chest like a moth. She was speaking, and speaking to me!

"What is sorry?"

"I don't know," I admitted. Then I laughed, the sound too loud in the quiet barracks, and clapped my hand over my own mouth.

To my surprise, she laughed too, and we fell asleep whispering "I'm sorry" and "I don't know" back and forth, giggling like children and hiding the words behind grimy hands.

The next few days were full of forbidden glances over grits that would make me tingle. Princess became my every thought. Each time I dug a hole in the field I would lean down over it and whisper her name into the earth. I had no words to describe what I was feeling, and no one to whom I could confess my sins. The other workers were mindless drones. When I spoke to them, they just stared, or replied with a simple "Hello." I wasn't sure whether they were really so stupid or whether they were too frightened to exchange words.

One afternoon Mama Tess came tromping across the field, a shotgun balanced on one shoulder, trailed by a house worker, a girl who looked like Princess. Not exactly like Princess, but enough. Her skin was lighter and her eyes were brown, but she wore the same cotton shift and she was just as pretty.

Her belly protruded, and I couldn't help but stare. What was wrong with her? The dead don't get sick.

Mama Tess took her to the apple orchard across the field from the house. I returned to scooping dirt over the seeds that had been placed in the holes I'd dug days before.

The shotgun blast was jarring. I looked up from the field, along with all the other workers. I saw the girl's silhouette slump to the ground among the apple trees. Mama Tess walked away, leaving the body where it had fallen.

Papa Levi passed me on his way to the orchard, carrying a burlap sack and a shovel.

"That's the last time I clean up yo' mess," Mama Tess growled as he passed her.

I stood in the field, watching the living come and go, and wondered. Why would Mama Tess shoot a dead person? Why not just bury her, as they always did, and let her reemerge from the soil if she was strong enough, or stay buried if she wasn't? I watched as Papa Levi bundled the buckshot-riddled corpse into his sack.

I looked out over the heads of the other workers, already returning to their labor, too stupid or scared to know what had happened. Too dumb and frightened to realize…

Realize what? Thoughts could only form halfway in my muddled mind. I stood staring, thinking, trying to make something of the jumbled mess in my head.

"What you doin', Cupcake?" said Mama Tess, somewhere behind me. Her tone was accusatory.

I knelt and scooped dirt over a hole, but it was too late. Mama Tess had seen me pause. She boxed my ears so hard they rang. Then she kicked me, hard, so that I toppled over sideways and lay curled around my knees like a potato bug, trying to protect my face and body from her blows. She hit me with the gun butt a few times, bruising my ribs, before Papa Levi stopped her.

They exchanged words in heated voices; I was in too much pain to hear anything more than a constant buzz.

Papa Levi slung me over his shoulder and carried me back to the barracks, dropping me on my cot. "Thinkin's for the living, Cupcake. You a dead girl now." His breath stank of whisky and rot. His eyes looked me up and down. He licked his lips, made a face like he was disgusted, and then hurried out of the barracks.

Later that night, I listened to Princess breathe in her sleep. The moon was dark, the barracks a lightless tomb. I thought about what had happened in the apple orchard, about the shotgun, about killing a walking corpse. I thought about dead people who eat and sleep and till fields. I thought about the mysterious bump under the dress of the house worker Mama Tess had shot. My thoughts were like an unraveling sweater: they led somewhere, but the more I tugged, the less the shape of the thing made sense.

I did know one thing, though. I knew that Princess was in danger. The face of the girl in the orchard haunted me. She looked so much like Princess. I wondered if I could have saved her; I wondered if I could save Princess.

In the quiet darkness of the barracks, I could hear the living in the house a hundred yards away: the low rumble of Papa Levi's voice, the shrill wail of Mama Tess's laughter. Light flashed between the slats of the barrack walls, and I heard the front door of the house open and close with a slam. Then the sound of heavy, slow footsteps, growing louder. Eventually someone fiddled with the padlock, and the barracks door creaked open. The stench of whisky and rot curled my lip.

"Princess," Papa Levi whispered. When Princess didn't stir, he whispered again, louder. This time, her steady breathing stopped with a soft gasp, but she didn't move.

"Come 'ere, Princess," Papa Levi drawled. "Git up." He stumbled into the barracks. I couldn't see him in the dark, but I could hear him slapping the foot of each cot, counting his way to Princess's.

I grabbed Princess's arm and tugged. She rolled off her cot, across the floor and onto mine. I wrapped my arms around her. She trembled like a tree in a storm. I pressed my face against hers and squeezed my eyes shut tight, hoping that I could will us invisible.

"Where you at?" Papa Levi grunted, slapping at the empty cot with his huge hands. His breaths were loud and rasping. I held onto Princess and wondered whether a skinny dead girl could fight off a living man who had the advantage of both strength and size.

Mama Tess's scream cut through the quiet night. "LEVI! You best get yo' ass back up to this house afore I come lookin'!"

Sighing, Papa Levi stood and stumbled to the door. "I'm a-coming, woman." He staggered out of the barracks and back toward the house, his footsteps retreating.

He hadn't shut or locked the barracks door.

I leaped to my feet and pulled Princess up with me. I ran for the door, but Princess yanked her hand from my grip and returned to her cot.

"What?" I demanded.

"Sleepy."

"No! Princess. *Princess!* Come on." I grabbed at her arms.

She slapped me away. "Sleepy."

I could hear Mama Tess and Papa Levi on the porch of the big house, arguing. How long before one of them came to check that the door was locked? I had to get out while I could. I had to leave Princess. I made one more attempt to pull her from her cot, but she was too heavy for me to carry and let out a reluctant moan. The voices from the distant porch went quiet.

They'd heard us. I let go of Princess and ran.

The barracks were surrounded by fields. There was nowhere to hide, but the moon was gone from the sky and the landscape was dark enough that I could tear across the field toward the house without being seen. I waited just beyond the circle of bright electric light cast by the house's windows, watching as Mama Tess and Papa Levi made their way to the barracks.

Mama Tess started shrieking and I dashed for the porch.

I didn't have a plan. My brain was still too befuddled for that. I ran into the house, shielding my face from light that seemed unnaturally bright after so many months living without electricity. I followed each open door from room to room, the words for each coming back to me as I ran—kitchen, dining room, family room—until I found a door that was closed. I tried to turn the knob but found it locked. I slammed my weight against it uselessly, too skinny and weak to force my way in.

Mama Tess's shrieking was growing closer.

Panicking, I ran upstairs. The steps were strange to me at first. I didn't really know how to use them, and ran up with both hands and feet. But as I ascended I remembered, vaguely, how stairs worked. I knew I would find bedrooms on the second floor. I knew what bedrooms were. As soon as I tried to grasp the memories, they slid away, slippery as sweat-soaked skin, and I was left gasping at the top of the stairs.

The master bedroom was obvious. A huge four-poster bed dominated the room and the walls were papered in delicate pink roses. I grappled with memories of my own bedroom, somewhere, back when I'd been alive. One of Mama Tess's shapeless house dresses was draped across the bed. There was a bulge in one pocket.

I reached into the pocket and pulled out a key ring with four keys dangling from it.

Clutching the keys, I ran back downstairs. Papa Levi's voice bellowed through the house. "CUPCAKE! Whatever you doin', you best stop! Doing's for the livin'!"

Terrified, I fumbled the keys. My heart was beating so hard I could feel it hammering a staccato rhythm behind my rib cage. I breathed in ragged, desperate gasps, my lungs aching. My vision narrowed to a dark tunnel. I had to grip my shaking right hand with my left hand to force the first key into the lock. I tried to turn it, but it was the wrong key. I drew the key out to try another.

Papa Levi's shovel hit me hard across the shoulders, knocking me to the floor. The keys flew from my hands and away even as I reached for them. Papa Levi drew the shovel back for a second blow. I rolled away from him and the shovel came down on the floor with a *thwack*.

I scrambled to my feet and crouched, ready to fight or flee though my shoulders hurt with a burning, stabbing pain.

Papa Levi blinked at me. "How? You dead. You a *dead thing*!" He lunged at me, but he was drunk and I was fast. I ducked out of the way of his shovel and he brought it down on the furniture.

Mama Tess appeared in the doorway. "What is goin' on in here?" When she saw me, she screeched. "Cupcake! Levi, git her."

Again, I ducked Papa Levi's clumsy attack. This time he threw himself off balance and the shovel slipped from his hands, flying across the room. I ran for the shovel and found the keys beside it. Raising both, I backed toward the locked door.

"Cupcake! What're you doin', you stupid dead thing?" Mama Tess called. "Levi, git the gun!" She started toward me, her face puckered in fury and hands outstretched as if she would squeeze my throat.

I drew back the shovel and swung at her. I was weak from months of malnourishment and my shoulders burned, but there was enough hate in me that the swing was powerful anyway. I'll never forget the sound it made as it crushed Mama Tess's head, like a *clang* and a *crunch* all at once.

Papa Levi was going for the stairs, but heard the sound and turned back. His eyes were wide. He staggered over to Mama Tess and knelt beside her. A sound like a dog's howl tore its way from his throat, a sound that made my skin prickle. He lifted Mama Tess into his arms and rocked her, throwing his head back to give volume to that terrible keen.

I dropped the shovel and chose another key. My hands were remarkably steady as I slipped the key into the lock. The door swung open.

The room was filled with the bitter odor of burning wax. On the far wall, an altar was covered in melted candles, dried flowers, and scattered bones. The centerpiece was a statue of a slender man in a top hat, his face painted like a skull: Baron Samedi, God of Death.

The rest of the room was filled with shelves, and on every shelf there were jars and bottles. Dozens of them, maybe hundreds, all different sizes and shapes and colors. Some were just ordinary mason jars, others were soda bottles. Each jar contained what appeared to be a single firefly, a soft glow that flickered and danced.

I lifted the shovel and entered the room. For a moment I savored the beauty of the fireflies, the triumph of the moment.

"Cupcake?" Princess stood in the doorway. She looked like a sapling in a cotton dress.

She took a step, as if to come inside, but I held up a hand to stop her. "No," I said. I hefted the shovel. I turned and swung it, smashing the nearest jar. I swung again and again, smashing jar after jar. The sound of breaking glass became a symphony.

As the jars broke into thousands of shards, the glowing lights dissipated.

Memories came over me like a massive wave, drowning me and punching me and tossing me around like so much driftwood. Even as I was assailed by memories, I kept swinging the shovel, desperate to succeed in my mission, desperate to free every last worker from the senseless hell we'd come to know. I couldn't see or hear, my vision obscured by faces that came rushing back, my hearing full of words and names and sounds I hadn't known I was missing.

I felt a hand on my arm. "Heather. Heather, stop. I think they're all smashed."

I opened my eyes and turned to see Princess, her face beside mine, her hand on my arm. I dropped the shovel. "Deja," I whispered.

She smiled, tears flooding her green eyes and escaping down her cheeks. "How did I forget your eyes?" I asked, taking her face in my hands and swiping at her tears with my thumbs.

Deja laughed. "I don't think you did forget." She pulled me into her arms and kissed me. Her lips were salty and soft. Months of deprivations and trauma were swept away in that kiss. All the beatings and starvation were erased for a moment in my lover's arms. I remembered our first kiss at a movie theater, our engagement kiss beneath the spray of Niagara Falls, our wedding kiss in a sun-dappled clearing while our friends applauded. We kissed a thousand times when our lips met that night.

"Dead girls don't love." Papa Levi stood in the doorway, his fists clenched at his sides. "Dead girls don't *kiss*."

Deja and I separated. "We're not dead girls," she said, lifting the shovel and hefting it with both hands. "We never were." I reached for a huge shard of glass and brandished it, though the sharp edges bit into my palm.

Papa Levi sneered, all furrowed brow and bared teeth. Deja and I crouched, ready to spring when he made his move.

The front door slammed. Papa Levi looked away from us, toward the sound. Horror dawned on his face, and then he forgot all about the kissing girls in the jar room as he turned to flee instead. He was pursued by screaming workers, their wits returned to them, their filthy hands gripping whatever tools they'd been able to find in the fields. Their ululations were the cries of the vengeful, the tortured, the justified.

It was only then I realized Deja and I were standing barefoot in a room full of broken glass. We dropped our makeshift weapons, clasped hands, and started toward the door. I hesitated and looked back. The statue of Baron Samedi still grinned at me. "Wait," I told Deja.

Tiny pieces of glass dug into my feet as I returned to the room and picked up the shovel. With a triumphant cry, I brought the blade down on the baron's head, smashing the figurine into countless pieces of porcelain.

Wincing, I limped back to Deja. We made our way out of the house and down to the main road, our fingers laced tightly together. My injured shoulders burned and my sliced feet stung, but my heart was singing.

Behind us, the farm went up in flames, a yellow beacon in the darkness.

Sarah Hans is an award-winning editor, author and teacher. Sarah's short stories have appeared in about twenty publications, but she's best known for her multicultural steampunk anthology *Steampunk World.*

Sarah's next project is an anthology featuring characters with disabilities called Steampunk Universe. You can find Sarah online at sarahhans.com.

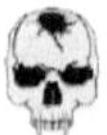

The Death Experiment

Vincent L. Scarsella

Death is one of two things; either the dead man is nothing,
and has no consciousness of anything at all,
or it is, as people say, a change and a migration
for the soul from this place here to another place.
– Plato, Apology 40c

But if there be no resurrection of the dead,
then is not Christ risen:
And if Christ be not risen,
then is our preaching vain,
and your faith also vain?
– 1 Corinthians 15:13-16

Two Marine corporals escorted Major Frank Grant to a conference room in the command center of the Military Casualty Research Enterprise (MCRE), or McCare, as it had come to be called. McCare consisted of a series of labs and barracks constructed about a year ago in the middle of a top-secret stretch of New Mexican desert.

One of the corporals opened the door, permitting Major Grant's entrance into the conference room. Upon seeing General Jack Taylor sitting across a long oval table, the major snapped to attention and gave a sharp salute.

The General returned the gesture, limply.

"At ease, Major." General Taylor's voice was a low Texas drawl. He nodded to the lone chair on the other side of the table. "Have a seat."

After Major Grant sat, General Taylor said, "Congratulations, Major. You've beaten out some pretty tough soldiers to get this mission."

Major Grant could not disagree. Over the last three weeks, he had completed grueling physical and psychological tests in a competition among fifteen others of his ilk, representing the best of the best–Navy Seals, top guns, astronauts, special forces, as well as agents from the CIA and FBI. Toward what possible end, they had not been told. Naturally, the mystery of the mission, and that only one among them would be selected for it, made it all the more desirable.

"Before I tell you what the mission is," General Taylor continued, "I'd like to introduce my project team."

Turning to the man sitting at his immediate right, General Taylor said, "This is Doctor Tomas Prager, head of the science team."

Prager leaned back with his arms folded across his chest with a scowl. He was a small, compact man with straggly white hair and, as Major Grant would soon learn, a bad Czech accent. In short, he perfectly fit the ill-tempered mad scientist cliché.

General Taylor next introduced, to Prager's right, Donald Roland, an impassive-seeming man in his late thirties. Roland gave a brief nod and brief smile as the general informed Major Grant that he was a psychiatrist specializing in the study of "NDEs"—that is, Near Death Experiences—and that he'd written a bestselling book about them.

General Taylor then swiveled around to the far right corner of the table, to the fit, darkly handsome man in his early fifties, leaning back in his chair with a bemused expression. He wore a priest's cassock and his hands were clasped together across his lap. Hanging from his neck was a large golden crucifix at the end of a golden chain.

"And this gentleman is Cardinal Enrico Ginelli," the General said. "He joins us from the Vatican."

Cardinal Ginelli gave the Major a wry smile. Major Grant frowned, no doubt wondering what a Roman Catholic priest was doing there.

Finally, General Taylor turned to the other end of the conference table and introduced me, Second Lieutenant Paul Barnes, project adjutant.

"Should you accept the mission, he'll be your trusty assistant and guide you through the bullcrap," the General said. "Right, Lieutenant?"

"Yes, sir," I replied.

With introductions out of the way, the General leaned forward, clasped his hands before him, and gave Major Grant a cold, hard stare.

"And now," he said, "for the mission." He drew in a breath and added, "What we intend to do, Major, is kill you, then bring you back to life."

The others gave no hint that General Taylor was joking or had just said something ridiculous. They continued staring forward, all business.

"Sir?"

"You heard me right, Major," said the General. "That's the mission—bringing dead soldiers back to life."

General Taylor leaned back and scowled. He seemed out of his element right then, an infantry soldier babysitting a billion-dollar science project, a job fit for a geek, not a war action hero.

"But for the specifics, scientifically speaking," he went on, "I'll turn the meeting over to Doctor Prager. He'll fully explain how it all works."

The General leaned back in his chair and nodded to Prager.

"Verys well, Herr Gen-ral," Prager began. He turned to Major Grant and said, "As de Gen-ral sez, vat ve do ez kill vu, then brings vu back to live."

Major Grant squinted while Prager continued his often difficult to follow explanation. First, they would indeed kill him, with the same poison used to execute death row inmates. Once dead, he'd be carried outside and placed in a small plot of dirt next to the main lab where his corpse would be exposed to the elements, like a soldier who had fallen in battle and left to rot. Only when he was quite dead and in the throes of decomposition, some seventy-two hours later, would they bring him back to life.

Major Grant turned to General Taylor and asked, "Such a thing is possible?" "Sure is," said the general. "Best I understand it, they use something called nano-regenerative technology. Clones of your bodily tissue are produced from DNA strands stored in little test tubes. Then tiny molecular machines will be injected into your body, programmed to repair tissue destroyed in the process of death, replacing dead tissue with the cloned cells."

General Taylor sighed, glanced at Prager, then said, "That pretty much it, Doctor?"

Prager shrugged. "It ez close nuff."

"All I know," General Taylor said, turning back to Major Grant, "is that once your cells are repaired, replaced, and ready for action, Doctor Prager's people will give you a jolt of electricity, and you'll wake up none the wiser." The general smiled. "Think of the battlefield implications," he said. "The ability to revive a dead army!"

"We still are far from such a ting," Prager added.

"And you've done it?" Major Grant said to Prager. "Revived the dead?"

"Yah, Major," Dr. Prager said. "Ve can."

"We've been successful," added General Taylor, "with chimps. Of the forty-eight we have put to death, forty-seven have been revived."

"Chimps?"

"Yah," said Dr. Prager, and now he smiled. "Jimps."

"We brought one back just yesterday, in fact," said General Taylor. "After one-hundred twenty hours." His eyes widened. "Five days."

"Yah," Prager nodded, seeming pleased with himself. "Five days."

"But no humans?" asked Major Grant. "I am to be the first?"

Prager turned to General Taylor. The question seemed beyond what Prager was allowed to say. It was up to the General to determine otherwise.

"No," said General Taylor. "You are not the first… human." He sighed and added, "There's been one human subject before you."

"Sir," said Major Grant. "He survived?"

"Yes, of course," General Taylor said.

But that was all the General would say for the moment.

"And so, you are being offered the opportunity of becoming our second human guinea pig, so to speak," he continued. "To help us move this experiment one step closer to battlefield reality." The General leaned back in his chair. "Of course," he continued, "your participation is voluntary. We'll give you some time to think it over. We appreciate what you're being asked to do is well above and beyond the call of duty."

Major Grant looked down at the conference table, trying to fathom what he'd just been told. They were offering him the opportunity of experiencing death, seeing what, if anything, was on the other side. Finally, Major Grant looked up and asked, "How long will I be dead?"

"Seventy-two hours," said General Taylor. "Three days."

"And my human predecessor?" asked the Major. "How long was he dead?"

"Forty-eight hours," said General Taylor.

Major Grant was a career Marine, a fighter pilot who had qualified for the astronaut program; and like General Taylor, he was quick to comprehend the significance of this mission: bringing dead Marines back to life to fight another day. *Semper fi!*

"I don't need time to think about it, General," the Major said. "I accept the mission." Then, he added, "On one condition."

"Condition?" the General asked, scowling. He was not a man used to conditions. "What condition?"

"I would like to meet the first human subject," he said.

"Why?" asked the general. "What's the point?"

"Think of it this way, sir," the major said. "If you were going to fly a new aircraft, wouldn't you want to speak with the pilot who flew it before you?"

After a moment, General Taylor nodded, then looked at Prager.

"Any problems with that?" he asked. "Letting him speak with Commander Billings?"

Dr. Prager didn't look happy, but after a moment, he merely shrugged.

"I have a problem with it," blurted Cardinal Ginelli from across the conference table, his English flawless. "Your previous subject can do nothing but taint this one's mind."

"Sir, if I may ask," Major Grant interrupted, "how can the previous subject taint my mind?"

After a sigh, General Taylor turned to Major Grant with a frown and clasped his hands together on the table.

"He says that during the time he was dead," General Taylor said, "he experienced, well, nothing. He says there was—*is*—nothing, on the other side of life. Only oblivion."

"Ah," interrupted Cardinal Ginelli, "by telling him that, you have already tainted this one. I vote his disqualification."

"Well, you'll have no such thing, your eminence," General Taylor shot back.

Cardinal Ginelli frowned disagreeably, and leaned back with his arms folded across his chest.

"But I will take your position under advisement," the general added.

Then, with a sigh, he dismissed the Major.

It was 1700 hours by the time I got Major Grant settled into his quarters, a spacious room in a wing off the main lab. While unpacking his gear out of a large duffle bag, the major asked what a cardinal from the Vatican was doing there.

"I have no idea," I told the Major. "That's way beyond my need to know."

Major Grant nodded, then surmised, "I guess the Pope wasn't too happy with what Commander Billings had to say about the afterlife.

Like there isn't any."

That was about as good an explanation as any for Cardinal Ginelli's presence at McCare. One day, about a month after Billings' resurrection, the priest had simply arrived. General Taylor and Prager didn't seem to like it, but they apparently had no say in the matter. Orders from on high, I heard, straight from the White House.

"News like that could put a major crimp on the church business," Major Grant added.

I nodded noncommittally. Editorial comment wasn't part of my job. My mission simply involved helping Major Grant settle in and get from place to place in preparation for his death trip.

"Is the Commander still at McCare?" Major Grant asked.

"Billings?" I said, not entirely sure if I could reveal this. With Major Grant staring at me, waiting, I decided there could be no harm in telling him. "Yes. He's in an empty barracks across the quad."

"How long ago was his… death trip?" the major asked.

"Six weeks."

The major mulled that over for a time, then went back to unpacking the rest of what little gear he had brought with him. Some skivvies, a couple pairs of socks, and three or four special powder-blue McCare uniforms.

When he finished, I told him that chow would be brought to his quarters at 1830. After that, he'd have the night to himself. There was a small TV on the dresser, but the station selection was limited. Breakfast would be served at 0700, and I'd return at 0745 sharp to start him on what promised to be a long and hectic day crammed with still more physical and psychological tests. I urged him, for that reason, to get to bed early.

Major Grant plopped down on his bunk and put his hands behind his head, staring up at the ceiling, looking relaxed, lazy somehow.

"It's hard to believe, Lieutenant," he said. "That they can bring back dead soldiers."

"I've seen it, Major," I told him. "With two dozen chimps and one human being. And yes, it is amazing."

"Why is Billings still here, Lieutenant?" he asked.

I shrugged, not sure how to respond to that, whether I could tell him that the death trip had changed Commander Billings for the worse, made him wallow in a kind of grief, a deep, down funk. Still, I gave him a blank look.

"Never mind," Major Grant said. "Hopefully, I'll find out myself."

"What if you're not allowed to see him, the Commander?"

The Major shrugged.

"I'll probably go through with it," he told me. "A trip to death is hard to pass up."

"Yes, sir," I said.

"And were you his liaison, too, Lieutenant?"

I nodded, remembering how cocky Commander Billings had been, just like him.

"Yes, sir," I told him. "I was."

After leaving Major Grant, I was told to report to General Taylor's office. As I entered the office, the General had a disturbed look. Finally, he looked up at me.

"He settled in, Lieutenant?" the General asked.

"Yes, sir."

He sighed and looked away, deep in thought. Finally, he looked up and said, "Tell the major he can have five minutes with Billings. And not a second more." The General plucked a cigar out of a box on his desk. Scowling, he sucked at it a while before turning to me. "This condition of his is giving me a major headache. The goddamned Pope is having a coronary about this meeting, sees it as compromising the mission – and that limp-wristed President of ours almost caved.

"You think it's compromising the mission, Lieutenant?"

"I don't know, sir."

"Well, those civilians and priests have no idea how a soldier thinks," he growled. "And if I was Major Grant, I'd want to know everything about the mission, especially from someone who'd already been on it."

"Yes, sir," I said.

"So you take him to Billings first thing in the morning," the General continued. He sucked on his cigar another moment, then added, "Zero eight hundred hours to zero eight oh five. And not a minute more. Then you take him to that goddamn priest for a debriefing."

The next morning, as promised, I arrived at Major Grant's quarters at 0745 just as he was gulping down the last of his orange juice. I told the major what had been decided—that he had five minutes with Commander Billings starting at 0800.

We arrived a minute late, at 0801, at Billings' quarters. He was the lone resident of a Quonset barracks across the main quad that had been built to house fifty soldiers. In the front lobby, I presented papers to the Marine sentry permitting the visit.

"Back there, sir," the sentry said with a nod to the other end of the barracks.

We walked down a long row between empty bunks until we arrived at Commander Billings' area—a bunk, a reclining chair next to it in which he currently sat, and a squat dresser against the wall.

I had not seen Billings since his death trip six weeks ago, and his appearance was a shock to me. He was in pajamas, first of all, leaning all the way back on the recliner. And though he was clean-shaven and otherwise hygienic, he still had a haggard, worn-out look. There were dark circles under his eyes, indicating a series of sleepless nights. There was a dog-eared paperback on his chest, and he hardly seemed to notice as Major Grant and I approached and stood before him.

Finally, I coughed and said, "Commander," and he looked up at us.

"So, you're next," he said, squinting at Major Grant.

"Good Morning, Commander," said the major.

"You really going through with it?"

"It's something hard to resist," the Major said. "Isn't it?"

"Yeah, I guess," Commander Billings said, then sighed. "Exactly what I thought."

"So what's it like?" Major Grant asked. "Death?"

The commander moved forward and sat up straight. He leaned forward placing his elbows on his knees and gave the Major a long, cold look.

"What's it like?"

Billings looked down as if trying to find the words.

Suddenly, someone had slipped in behind him—Captain Shea, Billings' Navy shrink. As Major Grant and I were about to come to attention, the captain waved at us to carry on. Billings hadn't seemed to notice his doctor's arrival. He was still staring down at his lap.

Finally, he looked up at us and said, "At first, it's like the stuff you've heard about—one of Dr. Roland's near-death fairytales. I was floating above my dead body, watching the bored techs waiting for their instruments to confirm I was dead.

"Next, I was rushing headlong through a kind of tunnel toward an immense hall, feeling unrestrained, full of energy and release. Entering the hall, I sensed beings, all the beings who had ever lived and died. Family members of mine who had passed. My father, an uncle. And in the middle of all that, there was this majestic light, an incredibly benign entity. The infamous White Light Roland's subjects talk about. I wanted to walk right into it, to be part of the wisdom and love I felt emanating from it."

He turned to Major Grant with a crooked grin.

"So far, so good. Right, Major?"

"Sure," agreed Major Grant.

"Well, I did just that," continued Billings. "I entered the light and felt a surge of energy and calm. But then, it all started to fade, like a light bulb running out of juice, flickering out. Suddenly, everything went dark and I was falling into a deep, dark pit. An abyss, but then even that started peeling away to nothing. And then…"

Now, Commander Billings closed his eyes. Finally, after a time, he opened them and stared at Major Grant.

"And then," he said, "nothing." His laugh was low, mirthless. "Nothing."

Commander Billings looked away with deep, dark sorrow in his eyes. After a time, he must have sensed Captain Shea behind and he turned to look at him.

"Continue, Dave," said the shrink. "Finish it."

"Finish it?" he asked. "There's nothing to finish. How do you describe the end of being?" Billings asked, turning again to Major Grant. "Oblivion."

Major Grant said nothing as we headed back to the barracks lobby. He stopped there and looked back down the other end of the barracks where Captain Shea was standing over Commander Billings telling him something.

"Make you change your mind, Major?" I asked. "Or are you still on board? What shall I tell them?"

"No, I'm on board," Major Grant said. "Seeing the Commander motivated me, gave me a sense of purpose."

"Purpose, Major?" I asked.

"Yes, purpose," he said. "To do something grand for all of us. It makes the death experiment the most important experiment ever conducted in the history of mankind. Not just to resurrect dead soldiers. But to prove that there's an afterlife."

Or isn't, I thought to myself.

Monsignor Ginelli occupied a small suite on the third floor of the squat sandstone visitors' residence on the other side of the quad. Wearing his official garb, a long black cassock, he was sitting behind a desk in an alcove which for the time being served as his office. As we approached, I noticed that he was pecking at the keyboard to his laptop. I wondered if it might be an email to the Pope updating him on the death experiment.

He finally looked up and greeted us with a smile.

"Ah, gentlemen," he said. "Welcome!"

I promptly excused myself with a bow and left Major Grant alone to chat with the priest. I took the elevator to the lobby and sat on one of the dull green leather sofas, spending the time checking my McCare smartphone for official texts and emails. I was also keeping tabs on the time. We were already fifteen minutes behind schedule. Finally, ten minutes later, Major Grant came down.

"How'd it go?" I asked.

"As expected," he said with a shrug. "Cardinal Ginelli fully intends to protect the interests of the Church."

The rest of that morning, I rushed Major Grant through a series of physical tests, MRIs and CAT Scans. Finally, I got him back to his room for chow at 1310 hours, only twenty minutes late. Somewhere along the way, one of the project techs confided that the major's death trip had been moved up for the day after tomorrow.

After gulping down some lunch, at 1330 hours, we were off to the monkey house, a small, square addition to the main lab. Nine chimpanzees lived there in metal cages under the supervision of three or four handlers who communicated with them by use of a sophisticated sign language.

"What do the chimps say about the afterlife?" Major Grant asked on our way across the quad. It was difficult to tell if he was joking.

"I have no idea," I told him. "I don't speak chimp."

After a minute or so watching the chimps fool around in the main cage,

Dr. Adrianna Rossi, the chief monkey handler, approached us. Her plain appearance seemed deliberate. Her white frock didn't help. With the slightest amount of effort—a touch of makeup and simply letting her hair down—I thought she would have become rather attractive. But she was consumed by the study of monkeys, and therefore the effort was, for her, superfluous.

I introduced Major Grant and she nodded.

"So you're the next human guinea pig," she remarked, unimpressed.

"A poor substitute for a chimp," the Major said, and now she smiled.

"Major Grant was wondering," I said, "if your chimps describe their death trips."

Dr. Rossi frowned, seeming ill at ease with the question.

"Our sign language isn't sophisticated enough for them to adequately do that," she responded after a time, completely serious. "All I can tell you is that it has affected them."

"Affected them?" Major Grant asked. "How?"

She thought about that for a time before looking up into the major's eyes. "Darkly," she said. "It changes them. At least, from my observations."

Dr. Rossi's rather dramatic response was unexpected, and put a chill on the visit. Abruptly, she shook Major Grant's hand, wished him luck, and went back to her chimps.

We left the monkey house and next headed to the main lab to watch the latest chimp execution. This time, the chimp was to be shot to death, to further simulate battlefield conditions. We sat in the front row of the small empty gallery that overlooked the laboratory.

One of the monkey handlers, a subordinate of Dr. Rossi, brought a chimp into the lab and, with a flurry of hand signals, directed the creature to a platform a few yards away from a technician holding an M-16 rifle. The handler quickly retreated from the room and a moment later, the technician with the rifle brought it up eye level, aimed and fired, hitting the chimp square in the chest. The chimp squealed and hit the floor.

"Holy shit," Major Grant muttered to himself.

Several more technicians rushed into the lab. They lifted the lifeless chimp body onto a gurney and proceeded to connect electrodes to it. One of them indifferently listened to the chimp's heart and nodded to his colleagues. The chimp was dead.

The handler who had led the chimp into the lab suddenly entered the gallery and sat down a few seats down from us. He wore a distraught look, as if he had just betrayed his best friend.

Major Grant said nothing for a time, though he too seemed shaken.

"Now what?" he finally asked.

"They take him outside and dump in a field next to the lab," I said. "In six days they'll bring the decomposing body inside and try and resurrect it. It'll be the longest time yet between clinical death and revival. One hundred forty-four hours."

The rest of that day, and the next, was a rushed schedule of activities in final preparation for the major's death trip. At 1900 hours the evening before it was to begin, General Taylor summoned Prager, Roland, and Monsignor Ginelli and me to the same conference room where they had first met Major Grant.

"Is he ready, Lieutenant Barnes?" General Taylor asked me.

"Yes, sir," I reported. "Passed with flying colors."

A review of Major Grant's file in front of each of them would confirm my assessment. A panel of doctors and shrinks had given him a clean bill of physical and mental health.

"I wish to note my objection to his participation," stated Cardinal Ginelli.

General Taylor scowled. He seemed to have lost his patience with the priest. But the general had orders to listen and respect the Vatican representative's views.

"Your objection is noted for the record," he said.

He called the matter to a vote and he, Prager and Roland said yes, while, not surprisingly, Ginelli voted no.

"All right, the vote being three to one, Major Grant's death trip will go forward, tomorrow morning at 0800 hours."

The next morning, I arrived at Major Grant's room at 0645 and listened to him gripe about being executed without a last meal. Like any medical procedure, he wasn't allowed to eat for twelve hours before it. Last evening, the project cook had prepared for him a feast—a thick, juicy filet mignon, buttery string beans and a fat baked potato.

I frowned and tried to smile, but actually failed to see the humor in it. What was about to happen that morning was serious business. It was one thing to resurrect a monkey, and quite another to resurrect a human being. The methodical care that went into doing just that was the minor equivalent of a space launch. The project team had left no detail to chance.

At 0700 hours, I escorted Major Grant to the laboratory where we had observed the chimp killed the day before and where he would meet his death this morning. After dropping him off, I wished him luck. He thanked me for taking such good care of him. With a sad nod, I left him and went up to the observation gallery.

There was a tedious pre-kill checklist to get through. After about an hour or so, toward 0815, the agonizing wait finally began to test Major Grant's patience.

"Why don't you just do it already?" he said, loud enough to hear from the gallery. One of the techs tried to make a joke of it, but Major Grant wasn't mollified. His expression hardened. He was on the verge of experiencing death, and the thought of that alone must have been driving him to distraction.

Finally, Dr. Prager and General Taylor arrived and they were ready to begin.

The ten rows of seats in the gallery had filled to capacity by then with various medical, operational and technical observers. Colonels, captains, doctors, and other unknown civilians ogled the spectacle enfolding before them of a man being put to death.

Monsignor Ginelli was last to arrive. He was in full Vatican regalia, wearing the *abito piano*, a long black cassock which flowed to his black shoes. He nodded cordially as he settled into his reserved seat with a perfectly centered view, several spaces down from me. Around his neck was an ornate, bejeweled golden cross. Turning to the spectacle unfolding below us, he made the sign of the cross.

At exactly 0930, the anesthesiologist swabbed Major Grant's right arm. In the next instant, without warning or ceremony, he injected the Major with a lethal dose of poison. Major Grant flinched, but that was all. He drew a breath and simply laid there, waiting for his body to shut down and die. He would feel drowsy at first, then there would be an overwhelming weight on his chest, but that would be the extent of his discomfort. After a few moments, he would fall asleep, and then his heart would stop and he would die.

And it happened pretty much like that. The EEG went flat line, signifying his clinical death. This sudden event was followed by a collective gasp from the audience.

Monsignor Ginelli turned to me with a sad smile.

"That is it? The Major, he is dead?"

I shrugged. What did he expect? A blare of trumpets?

"Yes, Your Eminence," I said. "Just like the chimps—there's not much to see."

But this was a man who had been killed. A man who at this very moment was entering and experiencing the afterlife—if there was one.

Most of the spectators remained for a time, watching the techs record some final readings just to be sure. Then Dr. Prager approached Major Grant's cadaver. He put a stethoscope to his chest and listened. After a moment, he nodded to General Taylor. The man was dead.

As the project team followed General Taylor out of the laboratory, the spectators began to get up and slowly disperse.

"Now," I told the priest on my way out, "we wait."

Three long days passed.

Finally, it was time to bring Major Grant's cadaver inside from Potter's field and revive it. By that time, bacteria and other organisms in the stomach and intestines and elsewhere in the body had already started to decompose tissue, causing it to bloat in a process called putrefaction. Because of this, his corpse was no longer locked stiff from rigor mortis, and by now, his intestines had most likely ruptured. Blowflies and flesh flies had laid their eggs around Major Grant's mouth and anus and their small larvae had become visible. The body's forensic demise was, of course, a gross, though fascinating, spectacle.

By the time I arrived that morning, the recovery team, wearing white masks to guard against the stench and poisons, had transferred Major Grant's corpse from the soil to a stretcher and were transporting it into the lab. Monsignor Ginelli, today dressed in a simple black cassock, had come outside with me. He crossed himself as we watched the solemn procession.

We followed them inside and proceeded to the gallery. General Taylor and

Drs. Prager and Roland were already in the lab, together with a crew of techs whose job it was to perform Major Grant's resurrection.

The procedure was surprisingly brief, easy, and the techs and doctors went about it with their usual nonchalance. After his cadaver was thoroughly washed, the technicians worked quickly to open Major Grant's chest and connected him to a heart/lung machine that pumped an elixir of molecular tissue matching Major Grant's DNA into his bloodstream. These were the nano-repair machines that General Taylor had talked about. Once that was done, the transformation from decomposition to normalcy was startling. After only an hour, Major Grant was no longer a ghoulish creature dug up from a grave. He looked—well, like Major Grant—only asleep.

The next step was to get his heart pumping. His chest cavity was closed and the techs attached more electrodes so that life-awakening electricity could be buzzed through him. While the project team looked on nervously, the techs finished doing so and waited for the command to bring Major Grant back to life.

After a moment, General Taylor nodded. One of the techs turned and flicked a switch at the instrument panel, sending electricity into the major. It was like an old Frankenstein movie. Like the chimps, the major's body twitched with the jolt of electricity. But this time, nothing happened. After a minute or so, the techs tried again, and his body twitched again. With the chimps, and Billings, it had taken several tries to jumpstart the electrical system and the brain.

But this time it seemed to be taking longer, too long. After the seventh or eighth surge of electricity, I knew something was terribly wrong. The troubled faces of the techs, together with General Taylor's deepening scowl, told me that the experiment had gone awry.

"Is something wrong?" asked Monsignor Ginelli.

We had been sitting there a long time in silence, fascinated by the rapid, miraculous transformation of the Major's cadaver.

I shook my head, not knowing what to say, and watched.

One of the anesthesiologists injected the major's body with something, adrenaline I supposed, followed by another jolt of electricity.

But the EKG remained flat.

"Has this ever happened before?" asked the priest. "With the chimps?"

It had happened once before—with the only chimp that had been lost. The poor creature couldn't be revived, had stayed dead. But that had been early on in the project, months ago. The failure to resurrect the unlucky chimp had been studied for weeks after that, and the problem had been found and supposedly resolved.

The resurrection team finally took a breather. For a time, they huddled in the center of the lab with collective concern and bewilderment. Finally, they got back to the task of reviving Major Grant with a sense of renewed optimism. One of the techs bent to the major's ear and could be heard to say: "All right, Major, time to rise and shine—your beauty nap is now officially over. You are definitely AWOL."

But despite another jolt of fresh electric juice, again, nothing.

Major Grant's heart did not start beating; he did not breathe.

In fact, he remained quite dead.

All work at McCare was halted by the powers-that-be after Major Grant's death. A military board of inquiry was convened. I had to testify before a panel of grave, gray-haired four-stars from each of the services. I told my story, testifying that, in my humble opinion, there had been nothing unusual about the Major's case.

Of course, I never got to see the final report of the board. My top-secret clearance was not high enough. By the time it was issued, I was long gone, having reported to the Military Personnel Command in DC as a detailer assigning junior officers for duty. I never learned what had killed poor Major Grant, and I suspected that McCare had been closed.

I often recall my last day there, just shy of a month after Major Grant's death. On my way out of the lobby of the admin building, I ran into Cardinal Ginelli. He was also leaving, returning to the Vatican. He stopped and flashed a kind priestly smile.

"It is too bad what happened," he said. "The major was a good man."

"Yes," I said. "He was."

I had a hard time believing that the priest was truly sorry things had worked out as they had. After all, Major Grant's death had prevented what could have become a nearly insurmountable public relations fiasco for his Church.

"But to me, Lieutenant," the priest went on, "the major's death was something of a miracle – a confirmation of my faith in the Lord Jesus Christ, that he is truly the Son of God. You see, only by Major Grant's death did the Church survive. Had he lived, and reported, like Commander Billings, that death was oblivion, then, of course, the Church would have been discredited. On the other hand, had he been revived, his confirmation of an afterlife, even an afterlife envisioned by the Church, would have likewise made the Church irrelevant. For is not faith built on doubt? Yes, if the afterlife is ever confirmed, there will be no need for priests. I am sure of it."

He smiled at me and picked up his bag.

"So where do you think Major Grant is, Your Eminence?"

The priest stopped and frowned, unsure of my question.

"Ultimately," he said, "we will not know that until we join with him, no? But for those who have faith in the Savior, the Lord Jesus Christ..."

A black limo had pulled up to the front door. Before he could finish the thought, he had picked up his suitcase. He had a flight to catch back to Rome.

"May the Lord be with you, my son," he said. He gave me a kindly smile as he made the sign of the cross before stepping outside.

I smiled, thankful for the blessing.

Vincent Scarsella writes speculative, fantasy and crime prose fiction and plays. His published novels include, *The Anonymous Man*, as well as *Lawyers Gone Bad*, and *Personal Injuries* of the Lawyers Gone Bad series. *Escape From The Psi Academy*, is a young adult novel of the Psi Wars! series. Additionally, numerous of his short stories, including his Pushcart Prize nominated, The Cards of Unknown Players, have seen print. He has also had two plays produced. His work can be accessed at vincentscarsella.webs.com.

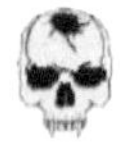

The Miracle Hunter

Dusty Wallace

One week after the first rain in May, Eddie set off from his one-room cabin and up into the mountains. The Appalachians of Floyd County were foggy this spring morning, the peaks of their ridges swaddled in white blankets. Eddie waded into the soupy mist with a near-empty leather satchel over his shoulder and a canteen hooked to his belt. He poked his way into the woods with a walking stick, its intricate carvings resembling the filigree of fine jewelry. He'd spent all summer whittling the oak branch, transforming it into practical art in anticipation of this moment.

Eddie's father and grandfather had hiked this route in the past. And, he presumed, the Bennet clan had been observing this ritual for generations. The trail was barely blazed, dotted with downed trees and steep climbs, but Eddie knew it by heart. His feet remembered each step of the journey he'd first taken as a child. And Eddie lamented that the tradition wouldn't be passed on anymore. At seventy years old, he regretted having no progeny to share his secrets with. He regretted a lot of things.

The humidity settled heavy in Eddie's lungs, and he stopped every hundred yards or so to catch his breath. Assaulted by earthy scents, Eddie found himself coughing up phlegm that carried the taste of the mountains.

A mile into the hike and a mile left to go, Eddie stopped and sat at the base of a walnut, resting his back against its trunk.

"Give us this day our daily bread. And jerky," Eddie said with a chuckle, and pulled his only provisions from the satchel, a piece of bread smeared with butter and drizzled with golden honey, along with two pieces of venison jerky he'd packed for the protein.

Eddie ate the honey-bread in seconds but gave up after the first strip of jerky, too hard to chew with his dentures. "Pieces of shit," he said, and took a long swig from the canteen before marching off toward his destination once more.

Along the second mile Eddie saw squirrels, chipmunks and rabbits darting between trees, and heard a coyote in the distance. At a clearing he paused to cough, and watched a posse of wild turkeys picking through a huckleberry patch.

Eddie thought back to his time in Charlotte, and how life in the forest seemed extraterrestrial compared to that small city. After college the only animal references that had mattered to him were bulls and bears. But when his father died he sold the small investment firm that'd he brought to local prominence and moved back to his place of birth. The cabin was in shambles, but the land he'd inherited was worth a fortune. After spending a little time there and riffling through childhood memories, he couldn't bring himself to let the place go.

Eddie had been married once, back in Charlotte. He thought about Carla as the turkeys gorged themselves with berries. Thought about that decade of marriage when turkeys like these adorned his table in traditional Thanksgiving feasts; Carla's brothers, sisters, nieces and nephews all circling the table like a Rockwell painting brought to life.

Inevitably, Eddie thought about Carla's letter. The one he'd found in his briefcase, letting him know he wouldn't be welcome at home any longer. Eddie had pretended to be shocked, but he'd seen it coming a long way off. At first he'd thought losing the baby had soured their marriage. Later he wondered if Carla was unhappy to begin with and had lost the child as a result. They had never really loved each other the same way again. They'd had enough passion, lust, to fuel a marriage for ten years, but after the third-trimester miscarriage they were just playing roles. Eddie became more interested in stocks than marriage, and Carla couldn't move on with him around.

"Bon appetit," Eddie said, leaving the turkeys to their dinner and starting the final leg of his journey. Usually he'd seen one or two miracles by now, but so far nothing. Only mayapple sprouts and saplings broke through the duff. But the time was right—one week after the first rain in May—and Eddie's spot had never been barren, so he proceeded without worry.

Eddie stopped for a breather and surveyed his surroundings. Sure enough, his secret claim of forest land was abundant with the miracles he'd been hunting. They hid in the undergrowth and the shade of fallen trees. His field of view was full of miracles.

And deer.

"Little white-tailed sons-of-bitches!" Eddie yelled, stomping at them to little effect. The herbivorous wildlife loved the spongy mushrooms as much as people. A herd of over twenty, Eddie guessed, were munching away to their hearts' (and stomachs') content. They barely scattered when he clapped his hands. He waited a half hour for the herd to move on, and by that time the crop was ravaged.

Eddie had a decision to make; press on in search of a yet unknown hotspot, or turn back and save his energy? On one hand, he had only brought enough water and food for a two-mile hike. Also, he was seventy. So adding another leg to the trip might make returning home too difficult. Then again, he felt pretty good today. His arthritis wasn't bothering him much, and damn did he love those mushrooms.

Eddie decided to press on.

Eddie had learned in college that miracles had many names: merkels, morels, hickory chickens, dryland fish, molly moochers. But Eddie's father had called them miracles because, as he said, "It's a miracle if you can find one." Not that they were scarce—miracles grew throughout Appalachia—but they were nearly impossible to see. Their hue of dirt-brown was a perfect camouflage among the detritus. In fact, hunters would often miss them on the first dozen passes. But once one was recognized the eyes became tuned to the shape and color. It was an odd effect, Eddie thought; one second you see no mushrooms at all, then you find a single mushroom and it's as if the rest reveal themselves, rewarding your persistence.

Deer happen, though, so Eddie shuffled through pine needles and dead leaves to somewhere deeper in the woods than he'd ever been. In fact, he wasn't quite sure where he was. He'd never needed a compass for his regular spot, and didn't think to mark the trail as he walked. He ended up in a flat of land about halfway down some mountain whose name he did not know.

The flat looked to be about half an acre. A stream ran through its center, fed from a natural spring gushing from the upward slope at its border. Eddie thought it looked like a perfect place to find miracles; damp and shaded by the higher peaks. Mayflower leaves created a green ocean above the soil, and his father had taught him that the two plants often rooted together.

It was nearly noon, now, and though the sun had burned through the fog there was still a dampness in the air. Eddie knelt at the gushing spring and held his head in its path, washing away sweat, lapping up the water as it ran past his lips. He refilled his canteen and drank half in an instant before refilling it again.

The water was clear, cold, and refreshing. Eddie felt heat retreating from his body and taking lethargy with it. Soon he felt revitalized, ready to hike another mile or two.

But the effects didn't stop.

"What the..." Eddie's whole body started to tingle, the prickly sensations of numbness. He felt his skin tighten around his muscles, and his complexion smoothed into a peachy sheen. His legs and arms swelled with new muscle. The arthritis pain he'd had for years vanished completely.

When the sensations stopped, Eddie held out his hands like a blind man healed, astonished by their softness when he made a fist. He ran his fingers through his hair and found it thicker. Over a puddle formed by the spring he caught his reflection. *Brown.* His hair hadn't been brown in thirty years. And his face had defeated gravity as well, gentle and babyish as it had been in his youth. His jaw open in wonder, Eddie saw that his teeth hadn't regrown, but the gums looked pink, and healthier than when he'd had natural teeth.

Eddie fell to his knees, weeping, wondering if he'd found the fountain of youth, if Ponce De Leon had been too far south in his ancient efforts. Or, conversely, if he might have Alzheimer's. Eddie had a morbid theory that Alzheimer's was the closest thing to time travel a person could experience. One moment you're seventy and the next you're riding your bike to school. Sure, it wasn't real, but *cogito ergo sum*, right?

"It's a miracle." Eddie joked to himself, the blurry splotch drawing attention through his tears. A rotted log lay across the spring-fed stream, and at the end closest to Eddie was a singular miracle. Eddie leapt to his feet with newfound agility and scampered over to the specimen. He picked it up and smiled, twisting and examining every inch. A tiny spider retreated into one of the mushroom's pores. No problem, though. Eddie figured the bug would float out after a long soak.

Eddie laughed and tossed the fungus in his satchel.

The miracles revealed themselves. Eddie said, "I'm standing in miracle heaven," then laughed at his own bad pun. Mushrooms surrounded him. Eddie could barely take a step without one squishing underfoot.

Along with the exuberance of youth came the blissful ignorance. Eddie locked away any dark thoughts about his experience and started grabbing handfuls of soft, delicate miracles. He filled his bag halfway in only a minute or two.

Then the chants began.

They started as an echo bouncing off the slopes. Quiet, eerie, like a parliament of owls calling out in unison. Eddie didn't recognize the language, but had a feeling it was ancient. His heart, despite its recent restoration, stumbled over beats as the sound grew closer.

In the distance white robes contrasted against the trees and bald heads glared with sunlight. Eddie guessed there were about thirty of them, maybe more, all headed his way.

Among the voices, the soft cry of an infant was faint. Still, the sound resonated deeper than the chanting, despite its amplitude.

An uprooted oak, four feet across and thirty long, provided Eddie with cover. Its massive base allowed him to watch unnoticed through an exposed tangle of roots.

As they got closer Eddie could see that it wasn't just bald men in the group; there were women, too. Whatever the requirements for membership, hair wasn't one of them. Nor was race. There were Asian, Caucasian, Black, Native American and others Eddie couldn't identify, ages spanning from young teen on up to the elderly.

Except for the baby. It was swaddled in red cloth, a drop of blood in a cloud of white linen, crying that sweet infant cry that humans are biologically hardwired to sympathize with.

The woman holding the baby stopped before the mouth of the spring where water was pooled several feet across. The others waited in a semicircle a few yards away. The woman was old and skinny, her few remaining teeth discolored and jagged.

She turned to her audience and the chanting stopped. From under her robe she produced a large knife, its six-inch double-edged blade inscribed with ancient runes that Eddie didn't recognize.

"Today, we renew the Mother of Miracles with our blood as she renews us with her own." the woman said. She held the knife high over her head, blade pointed down.

Eddie leapt to his feet and shouted, "Stop!" It was all he could say. He didn't know what was going on and was improvising.

"Who are you? What are you doing here?" the woman demanded and relaxed her blade-wielding arm.

Eddie searched for the right words, but wasn't sure he'd found them. "I was sent by the Mother of Miracles. She asks that you bless her by allowing this child to live."

"Nonsense. The Mother of Miracles wouldn't send a commoner to speak on her behalf. Without the blood of this child she would lose her strength."

Eddie approached slowly, feigning confidence. "The Mother of Miracles says that you do not know her true power. That you have lost faith. She doesn't need your gifts to work her magic, and her bidding will be done by whoever she sees fit."

"What is your name, commoner?"

"Eddie Bennet," he said. "What's yours?"

"Rosina. I am First Maiden of the Mother's Children," the old hag said.

"Rosina, you'll hand me that babe or the Mother will withhold her blessing," Eddie said.

She looked at him wide-eyed, her wrinkly face contorted in uncertainty. "Lies," she said.

Eddie stared her down, trying to communicate threats with body language.

The First Maiden looked out at her followers and saw them stirring with doubt, heard mumblings between them. "We thank you, oh blessed Mother," she said and raised the knife once again.

Eddie had inched his way closer since he had first made himself known. Now he lunged forward and snatched the baby from Rosina's arms.

He turned and ran, but heard no footsteps behind him. Looking over his shoulder, he saw the older Children knelt around the stream, plunging their faces into the cold mountain water, while the young ones watched on silently with their heads bowed.

They took their fill and faced Eddie. The First Maiden was no longer an old hag. Her hair was blonde and flowing over her shoulders and breasts, wrinkles smoothed away, teeth whitened and straight, none missing. Her smile was beautiful, and terrifying.

She raised her right index towards Eddie. "Get her back!" she shouted and the Children struck out after him.

Eddie had never been so deep in the woods, and had no idea if he was heading home or even further into the thick forest. The snap of twigs and rustle of fallen leaves pushed him hard, leaving no chance for Eddie to get his bearings. And though his life was in imminent danger, Eddie couldn't help but savor the thrill. Sprinting through the fresh air with no loss of breath, something he hadn't done in decades, conjured up his long-dead spirit of adventure.

With the baby tucked into the crook of his folded arm, Eddie came to a series of huts hidden among the hardwoods and evergreens. He'd gained a moderate lead on the Children but could still make out branches swaying from contact as they pursued.

Though there were a few hogs penned up along the side of the huts and chickens clucking around freely, the tiny village seemed empty of human life. No one stirred as he ran past the first fourteen shanties, but at the fifteenth he was confronted.

"In here." A young blonde woman popped out through a ragged wooden door. She regarded Eddie with wide emerald eyes, a simple blue dress hanging loosely over her gaunt frame. "Get inside, quick."

Eddie knew, no matter how young he felt, he couldn't run forever. He darted inside and heard the door slam behind him.

Outside, faint footfalls became louder until they stopped.

"Did you see him? Where did he go?" Voices came muffled through the shack.

"He went that-a-way, down yonder toward the old mill." the woman said frantically. Eddie held his breath until the clatter of footsteps began again.

Once the footfalls went silent again Eddie's helper joined him in the one-room cabin. Her eyes were red and swollen with tears. She reached out for the child.

For a moment, Eddie felt like he'd been transported to an alternate reality. He looked and felt young like when he'd first been married. He looked into the eyes of the infant cradled in his arms and wondered if it was his own. Maybe Carla had delivered a healthy baby and was waiting for him at home. Maybe he'd just been tired, and the last few decades were just some dreadfully compressed nightmare.

The woman approached and Eddie snapped back from his reverie.

"Stay back." Eddie said as he turned to shield the infant with his body.

"It's okay. I'm her ma," she said.

"Bullshit, lady. You're obviously acquainted with that mob of witches or whatever they are. No way a mother would give up their baby to be sacrificed by a bunch of murderous lunatics." He paused then added, "Unless she was a murderous lunatic herself."

"I didn't have no choice. Them folks woulda killed us both if I'da tried to stop 'em."

"Why didn't you just leave when you found out you were pregnant, then?"

"You ever hear 'bout these folks before?"

Eddie shook his head.

"Naw, I didn't think so. Ain't no one never heard 'bout us up in these here hills. Anyone who runs into this bunch winds up joinin' 'em or dead. Five years ago I learnt 'bout 'em and 'cided on stayin' as 'posed to dyin'."

"If you joined them, then why weren't you at the spring?" Eddie asked.

"It's my year. You don't drink from Mother on yer own year. This bunch don't consider it kosher."

"The Mother. Who in God's name is the Mother?

"Goddess, not God. They say she's the one that makes the spring work. Takes out all the young stuff and puts it in the water. Then the water makes anyone who drinks it young again."

"That's what *they* say. What do *you* say?"

"Well, I reckon there's a science to it. You see, one time this lady-scientist came up here for research. We told her she'd have to join, or…" she trailed off, looking into the distance for an instant, seeing a ghost of memory she'd have rather forgot. She snapped back into the moment, "Anyways. The lady-scientist told us weren't no such thing as no Goddess. Told us that the river was a… Darn, what did she call it? A culture medium, that's it. She said that something in the water took them, uh, them stem cells and made 'em grow. Not bigger, just more of 'em, y'see? Then when someone came along and drinked the water they'd have all these stem cells fixin' their wrinkles and ailments and whatnot."

Eddie had spent some time as an investment manager for a research firm who experimented with stem cells, so he had a basic understanding. Stem cells could be injected into a specific target to promote cellular regeneration. But these people were seeing instant regeneration of all their physical traits. That was with ingestion instead of targeted injection. That behavior must have came from the spring water. It wasn't just a culture medium. It was a stem cell supercharger.

Further scientific inquiry would have to wait. Eddie changed the subject to more immediate concerns. "What's your name, girl?"

"Name's Lily. Lily Chaplin. The baby's Adeline."

"Well, Lily Chaplin. You bought us some time. What's the plan from here?"

"I reckon we run. Couldn't say where, though."

"Can you get us back to the spring?"

"That's one place I'se certainly can lead us to."

Eddie believed her. She could have easily sold him out to the others and his big adventure would've came to a sudden, and likely violent, end. He nodded and held out the baby, cupping it with both hands.

"Adeline." Lily clutched the child to her and wept.

The baby opened her eyes and cooed softly. She had been asleep when Eddie snatched her, and didn't bother waking during the chase that followed. But hearing Lily say her name woke the child. Eddie nearly cried watching the two of them reconnect. He couldn't fathom how eternal youth could be valued higher than that singular moment. That moment which had escaped him twoscore years ago.

"We've got to leave," Eddie said.

Lily took a deep, wavering breath and nodded. She grabbed a handful of cloths from a small table by the door, which Eddie eventually realized were diapers, and bolted outside after stuffing them in Eddie's satchel.

They ran back the way Eddie had come, but it all looked new to him. Patterns and shapes in the trees morphed as perspectives changed, and he wasn't confident he could make it back home from the spring.

Eddie saw the uprooted tree he'd used as a hiding place before he even noticed the brook babbling in the foreground. He used it as a landmark and altered their direction based on its position. Now he figured they'd be aimed squarely at his own secret place of miracles. Miracles that didn't require blood.

"Wait," Lily called out.

Eddie froze and shot her a puzzled glance. She knelt at the spring and cupped water in one hand. Adeline had started to cry during their run, but went silent as her mother dripped spring water into her open mouth.

"She ain't eat in a while. This'll keep her happy 'til we get somewhere I can nurse," Lily explained. Then she refilled her hand and brought it to her own mouth, drinking greedily before repeating the process. "You ought get some, too, Mister. To help keep ya from wearin' out 'fore we gets where we gettin'."

Eddie took a long pull from his canteen and re-attached it to his belt. "Okay. Let's go," he said, and set off at a brisk jog.

He made it from the spring to his Miracle spot without producing a bead of sweat. Lily had followed him with similar ease, despite being burdened with Adeline.

"My home's still a couple miles that way." Eddie nodded through the trees. "Do you need a rest?"

"No sir. I'm fresh as a daisy and we couldn't afford no break anyways," Lily said, with the baby still resting peacefully against her bicep.

"All right. Let's go, then."

The return trip was always easier than the initial hike. There were still hills and underbrush to work through, but overall the elevation decreased and gravity aided in the quest to reach home. But with their fill of fortified water, Eddie and Lily made the two-mile journey in around twenty minutes.

Eddie didn't bother stopping at the cabin. Landlines didn't reach that far into the mountains, and cell reception had proved spotty at best back when he had a service plan. He'd been set on buying a satellite phone for emergencies, but hadn't yet due to sheer procrastination, for which he now cursed himself.

Eddie ushered Lily inside his BMW X-6, a four-wheel-drive fit for wealthy retirees, tossed his satchel in the back seat and sped off towards the one-traffic-light town of Floyd.

"Listen, Eddie, I ain't sure what's gon' happen."

"What do you mean?"

"We been doin' this for a long, long time. Same day ever' year. I don't know what happens if we miss it."

"How long exactly?" Eddie asked.

"I lost count after a hundred years." Lily said. "I ended up with these folk durin' the war. The Yanks had already took my husband when they came a burnin' through Petersburg, and I didn't know what to do but saddle up and ride west. That's how I came across the ceremony. I been stuck here ever since. But other'ns. They been there a long time 'for I came 'round."

Eddie had traversed about five miles of the winding mountain road when the voluptuous Rosina stepped into the path. He braked hard and lost traction, the luxury SUV ending up folded around a cottonwood tree. Cloth diapers and mushrooms flew everywhere.

The vehicle came stock with airbags in all the doors, the glove compartment, and the steering wheel. All of them activated on impact, and the car filled with thick smoke from their ignition sources.

Eddie's neck was throbbing from the jolt, but he was otherwise unscathed. Brushing miracles from his lap, he looked over to see an unconscious Lily still cradling Adeline, who was now screaming and pawing at the air with her tiny hands. Lily's chest rose and fell regularly, so Eddie turned his attention to the beautiful siren in his rear-view mirror.

Eddie reached for his door handle and found it positioned differently than before. He had to shove all his weight into the crumpled door to force it open, and nearly fell to the ground when it finally gave way.

"Give me the child," the First Maiden said as Eddie stepped onto the pavement. Her followers slowly manifested from the roadside trees to witness the encounter.

"Not a fucking chance," Eddie said.

The Maiden walked closer and brandished the sacrificial blade. "You must be sore from the accident. If you come with us we can make that pain go away. But if things go the other way, let's just say…" Her voice tapered off mid-threat and her gripped loosened, the blade clanking against the paved road.

"Maiden what's wrong?" one of the followers called from the tree line, an olive-skinned American Indian.

The Maiden fell to her knees. Her hair grayed in an instant, then blew away in clumps from the light mountain breeze. The Maiden's fair skin pruned like a wet finger, and her breasts sagged downward under the linen dress.

Rosina's face was frozen in a pain-stricken snarl, and Eddie thought she might have already been dead by the time she fell face first to the ground. A series of thumps drew Eddie's sight away from the spectacle to the followers who were also lying prostrate in supplication to the Reaper.

"Lily," Eddie said aloud to himself. He darted back to the car to find a leathery carcass folded in two, a human-shaped bag of bones blanketing the still-wailing Adeline. Eddie tentatively unfolded Lily's remains to retrieve Adeline before she was asphyxiated.

Eddie never learned why he was spared the Children's fate. He sometimes told himself that Lily's lady-scientist was wrong, that perhaps there was a Goddess involved. But at that moment, with Adeline in his arms, he didn't care about answers.

"The Lord giveth and the Lord taketh away," Eddie said to Adeline. For the first time he gave her more than a passing glance, admiring her whispy-soft hair and silky skin, letting his finger feel the strong grip of her fists.

Adeline opened her eyes and stopped crying, seeming to return the studious examination of Eddie's features.

Their eyes locked. Then it was Eddie's turn to cry.

Dusty Wallace lives in the Appalachians of Virginia with his wife and two sons. He enjoys reading, writing, and the occasional fine cigar. Visit his blog at DustyVersion.blogspot.com.

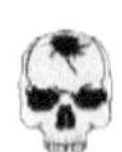

Last Call

JC Hemphill

Dennis had spent the last hour listening to Maurice Townsend griping about his recent outbreak of bad luck—the scandal, the girlfriend's tearful confession on the news, the fallout with his wife, his lost job, lost friends, lost dignity, on and on and on. But Dennis lapped it right up. After all, when would he get another chance to drink with Atlanta's hardest-hitting anchorman?

As Maurice Townsend rambled, kicking back shot after shot of Captain, then Cuervo, Dennis listened and added words of encouragement at all the right times. Before long, Maurice Townsend was hugging Dennis with one arm and raising a toast to his new friend with the other.

"You, sir," Maurice said in the serious tone of a newscaster, "are the kindest person I've ever met. Ever."

Dennis noticed the anchorman controlled his drunken slur like a pro. "How so?"

"You haven't given me the look in… how long have we been friends?"

"About an hour."

Maurice nodded. "Right. In an hour, you haven't given me the who-does-this-guy-think-he-is look. Not once." Dennis tried to respond, but Maurice pushed on. "Which is good. Because everyone else does. Some people do it with pity in their eyes, but I can tell that most wish I'd turn around and walk myself straight to Hell. Nobody bothers to consider my side. Maybe I have my reasons for what I did. Maybe I didn't have a choice."

"Can't fight who we are," Dennis said. "It's human nature to want greener grass."

Maurice's eyes widened. "Yeah. Human nature. Genius. How much would I have to pay you to explain that to my wife?"

"I'm gonna let you in on a secret. Nothing will get you in trouble faster than barroom wisdom," Dennis said, adding a chuckle. "Give a man enough booze and he'll turn a stool into a soapbox. Give his audience enough booze and that man's philosophies will rival Gandhi's. Over the years, me and the regulars here have solved every world problem you can think of. But come next day, those solutions have more holes than a rusty pair of tighty-whiteys."

"Too true," Maurice said with a nod. "Where's the restroom in this pit?"

Dennis pointed toward a shadowed corner. "Just past the jukebox."

Without Maurice yakking, the familiar comfort of Lights Out Pub returned. He closed his eyes and thought about his own problems. Sure, Maurice had lost his wife of a decade, girlfriend of six months, and overseas bank accounts, but Dennis never had any of those things. Not that he hadn't tried for them. The skin of his hands and feet were thicker than an armadillo's hide from all his trying, working in the same factory year after year hoping to get promoted, telling himself that if he kept with the grind, he'd eventually get noticed. But he never did. And year after year a little more of his emaciated paycheck funded his favorite bar and a little more of his time was spent solving other people's problems.

Ding-Ding-Ding.

Dennis' eyes popped open at the sound of the iconic triple-ring of a boxing bell. The bartender, Doug, a sickly man who skulked behind the bar silently refilling drinks, used it to signify last call. Some nights, when alcohol had melted his thoughts, the bell made Dennis imagine himself as a punch-drunk boxer about to enter the twelfth round of a fight he had lost in the seventh.

He glanced around the dim bar. Signed boxing gloves and photos of famous prizefights hung on the walls. Wooden chairs were already turned up on tables and Dennis realized that the bell had been rung especially for them.

"Last call," Dennis said as Maurice returned. "Time to shove off."

"All good things…" Maurice said, suddenly looking like a very large, very dejected child.

"You gonna make it? I can have Doug call a cab."

Maurice reached back, fumbled a wallet out of his slacks, and slapped a crisp hundred on the bar. "Can't. That's the last of my cash. Anything left over is a tip. Damn IRS froze my accounts. Didn't I tell you that?"

"What about the bus? Tell me where you live and I can tell you which route to take. It's the only way I travel. Best designated driver you can ask for."

"BUS!" Maurice threw his hands in the air. "Me? Let me tell you something, friend. I don't ride the bus. Never have. Never will."

"All right."

Maurice seemed to think for a second. "You can drive me."

"I don't have a car. I told you, I ride—"

"My car," Maurice said. He shoved a hand into his front pocket. "You drive me home in my Cadillac." He patted Dennis on the shoulder with his free hand as the other searched his pocket. "Ah-ha. Here they are." Maurice pulled a modest set of keys out and dangled them in front of Dennis.

"How will I get home?"

"You'll take my car. I don't care. If not you, my wife or the government will end up with the damned thing."

Dennis glanced at Doug, who was staring at them from behind the bar. A frown creased the bartender's face. "Okay, but I'm not keeping your car. We'll figure out how to get it back to you tomorrow."

"Whatever. Let's just go." He leaned in to whisper, but forgot to lower his voice. "I'm sick of the way this dump smells."

Dennis glanced at Doug again. The frown deepened.

"We're going," Dennis said, nudging the larger man toward the door.

"You think the Crypt Keeper back there would give us some road beers?"

"You're outta money, right?"

Maurice Townsend let his wide shoulders sink. "My luck's all dried up, huh?"

After a string of carjackings in the area, property management for the bar's strip mall had decided to install high-intensity lamps in the parking lot. The thinking was that brighter light would form some kind of criminal barrier. Personally, Dennis found them annoying. He always saw spots after stepping out of the dungeon-like bar.

Maurice placed a large paw on Dennis' shoulder and leaned heavily. With his free hand, he pointed to the rear of the parking lot. "That's me."

Only one car occupied the lot, and although Maurice had mentioned owning a Cadillac, Dennis never would've guessed the car before them belonged to the anchorman.

"You didn't tell me you drove an Eldorado," Dennis said. He could see only the back end, but the dramatic tailfins of the time were unmistakable. "Fifty-eight?"

"She's a Fifty-Nine Brougham. Cherry. Restored her myself, mostly. Had my upholstery guy do the interior, but I handled the mechanics."

Maurice swayed on his feet while keeping his hand moored to Dennis' shoulder. A belch rose in his chest and threatened puke. Maurice blinked, blinked again, then patted his chest with a fist.

"You all right?" Dennis asked.

"Ugh. Yeah. I think the tequila wants to relocate. Let's get going. I'd rather be hugging my own toilet if I'm going to throw up."

Dennis took the lead with Maurice a step behind, hand on his shoulder for guidance like a blind man. The car—a black slab of Detroit steel—faced Memorial Avenue and the plexiglass cubicle of a bus stop. The street was empty except for the Number 150 bus that was pulling in from the left. The skeleton crew of buses ran to accommodate the flood of drunks expelled by last calls everywhere. Dennis called them drunk tanks. The only passenger so far was an older man in a wrinkled suit, sleeping with his back against the windows. Dennis was suddenly happy to drive the Cadillac. Those overly large windows always made him feel like he was part of a mobile museum dedicated to scaring children straight: “Look here, kids: a drunk. Don't grow up to be that man. No, no. That man is a sad man.”

The hand on Dennis' shoulder tightened, almost clenching. It made him wince and turn. Maurice's eyebrows were scrunched in confusion.

"What's wrong?" Dennis asked. "Sick?"

Maurice didn't respond at first. He let go of Dennis' shoulder and bobbed his head from side to side as if he were trying to see through the glare on a television screen. "Someone's in my car."

Dennis glanced at the Cadillac. They were still about thirty yards out, but close enough to see the lights from the bus shining through the tinted windows, illuminating the outlines of the car's interior. On the right was the rectangular silhouette of a headrest, but on the left was a bulbous shape. The bus released a hydraulic exhale and pulled away from the curb. As it left, so did the shadowbox image of the man sitting in Maurice's car, the tinted windows returning the car to a solid black slab.

"Are you expecting someone?" Dennis asked.

"No."

"Did someone know you were here?"

Maurice shook his head slowly. Shock had sobered him. "I'm the only one with keys."

"So let's call the cops."

From the way Maurice's face contorted, Dennis could tell he didn't like that idea one bit. "Screw them. I can handle this. I'm not letting some punk kid jack my car. I'm sick of people taking things from me, of being… being shit on." A wild anger surfaced as he spoke. He was a kicked and cornered dog, and his car was his bone. He had lost everything else, but he wasn't going to give up his bone. Not tonight.

Maurice stalked forward. Dennis followed. He didn't like the idea of interrupting a carjacker in the middle of a robbery. To him, it seemed like a perfect way to become one of the news stories Maurice built his career on.

Dennis cupped a hand around his mouth and tried to project a whisper. "Hey. What if he's waiting for us?"

Maurice didn't seem to hear and crouched lower as he approached the chrome bumper. Dennis did the same, asking himself why. He didn't have an obligation to this guy. Sure, it was Maurice Townsend, a man once synonymous with credible news reporting, now a famously debunked loser. If the bus hadn't just left, he would've jumped on. But the next one wouldn't be by for twenty-four minutes and he was already in the parking lot; already crouched behind the car, mere inches from a man who had no friends to count on.

Maurice pointed at Dennis and motioned for him to circle around the passenger side. Before Dennis could respond, Maurice stepped along the driver side with his head ducked below window level. Dennis crept to the backseat and poked his head up enough to see in. A distorted image of his unshaven face reflected in the tint.

Dennis didn't know what to do next. All Maurice had done was point. Did he want Dennis to open the door? Was he waiting for a signal?

Dennis heard the lock mechanism engage, followed by Maurice whipping open the driver's door. The car shook on its springs with the sudden movement. The anchorman let out a scream that was half warrior's cry, half panic. Then he ripped open the door to the backseat with a second, less abrasive scream.

Dennis sprang to a stand seconds later. Maurice stood on the other side of the car staring at the interior. His skin shone with a layer of sweat and his chest was heaving. Dennis opened the front passenger door. Then the back. The car was empty.

Maurice said, "You saw him, right?"

"Earlier, yeah… er… it could've been a trick of light, I suppose."

Maurice leaned into the car.

Dennis scanned the parking lot, half expecting the intruder to magically appear behind them. The only movement came as a light breeze swept a mixture of trash and leaves across the ground, and moths swarmed at a height of fifteen feet around the security lamp near the hood of the car.

His gaze drifted to the underside of the Cadillac, and he wondered if the carjacker could've crawled underneath somehow. He took a few steps back and crouched. He saw Maurice's loafers on the other side and nothing more.

Then he noticed his shadow. It extended into the shadow beneath the car so that it looked like Dennis had no head. He looked up at the moths in their mock air battle and the lamp they fought over. Ants made of ice marched up his spine and he stopped breathing as his mind confronted an impossibility. "What the hell," he muttered.

Maurice backed away from the car and looked across the roof at Dennis. "Did you say something?"

"My shadow…" Dennis let the word drift. What he was about to say would sound idiotic. He glanced at the other security lamps scattered throughout the parking lot. None were as close as the one by the hood.

"What about it?" Maurice asked. He started to move around the trunk when he noticed his own dark silhouette. "What the—" He moved from side to side as if he were trying to escape it. "Are you seeing this?"

"Mine's doing it, too."

They both walked toward the back of the Cadillac, eyeing their shadows as if they might come to life and attack them.

When Maurice spoke, he sounded unusually shaken. "In ten years of reporting the news, I have never seen anything like this. I mean… wow."

Dennis backed up. Maurice did the same, and they stood next to each other with their arms dead at their sides. Both shadows were perfectly formed in height and size and so dark they looked like human-shaped holes in the ground. But the real paradox was in the direction they pointed—always toward the car, no matter where the light originated. When Dennis was on the passenger side, his shadow had defied physics and stretched across the light instead of away from it. And when he swung around to the back of the Cadillac, his shadow rotated with him as if the car was the pivot point and not the man. Maurice's—although taller and broader—was identical.

Dennis didn't know what to say. He scanned the light sources again, but found nothing new. The car was a shadow magnet.

"I tell you what," Maurice said. "If I still had my job right now, I'd have a film crew here in five minutes."

Dennis waved his hand and watched his outline return the gesture. He circled Maurice and approached the driver's door. The shadow never fluctuated in shape, or lack of color, or position relative to the car.

Then the lights went out. Not just the lamps in the parking lot, but the street lights too, and the neon signs of nearby businesses, the inner glow of the furniture store across the street, the accent light on the Cadillac's door that let you know it was open, the moon and stars in the sky, all light everywhere died in one single dousing.

"Whoa," Maurice said from the black. "Wh— What the heck? I can't see squat."

Dennis patted the air around him, feeling for the car. He

desperately needed something real to hold, something to ground him and keep him from floating off into the abyss. He found the open door and followed it to the dashboard. He groped for the steering wheel and used it to guide himself into the leather seat. What he really wanted to do was run back to the bar where he could drink until the sun came up and replaced this awful darkness with yellow rays, scudding clouds, and morning traffic.

Maurice spoke from somewhere near the back of the car. "Hey, uh… buddy, you there?"

"Yeah. Front seat."

"Stay there. I'm coming—"

The world blinked back to life as every light popped back on and with them the details of the street and parking lot and rows of suburban businesses were once again visible. There was no pupil dilation. No spots from the light change. No sign that anything had gone wrong.

"I know what this is," Maurice said in his best and-here's-your-nightly-news voice. "People slip drugs—hallucinogens—into people's drinks all the time. Usually to date rape someone. But sometimes it's to rob them. Once the victim passes out, the perpetrator can take their time searching them. Some go so far as to tie the victim up in a basement somewhere so they can use the person's house keys for an easy home invasion."

Dennis had never hallucinated before, but this wasn't how he imagined the experience. He pictured tie-dye flashes and cartoon characters, maybe talking Cheshire cats and opium-addled bugs.

Maurice's eyebrows lowered in suspicion. "I'll bet that slinky bartender comes out any second." He pointed a thumb over his shoulder without looking.

But Dennis looked.

Maurice pulled a smartphone from his pocket. "We should've called the cops like you said."

Dennis wasn't listening. He had stopped breathing. His arm drifted up, seemingly on its own, and pointed at the bar. Or, rather, where the bar belonged.

Maurice already had the phone to his ear. He pivoted to look where Dennis was pointing. The phone slipped from his hand and clattered onto the ground.

Beyond the parking lot was the darkness that had blinded them. The bar and the other adjoining businesses were gone, having been engulfed by some of the densest, blackest fog imaginable.

Dennis stepped out of the car. "I don't think this is drugs."

The Darkness chose that instant to lurch forward in a great wall, erasing all existence in its path. Entire lamps were absorbed, a patch of trees and a dumpster to the far right, the concrete and yellow lines of the parking lot all disappeared as nothingness pushed toward them.

For a second, Dennis could only watch the Darkness inching forward. There was nothing to compare it to. He'd been inside it once and didn't want to go back. It was cold and lonely and gave him the sense that he'd never see light again if it caught him.

Internally, Dennis was screaming to run, but he remembered that he held the keys to a fully restored V-8 monster.

Dennis yelled for Maurice to get in the car. Then he turned and scrambled into the driver's seat. Ignoring the pain of his knees smacking the steering column, he fumbled for the keys in his pocket, panicked by the black wall eclipsing the rearview mirror. Maurice got in beside him and shouted commands, but all sound seemed padded in bubble wrap.

Dennis managed to get the right key in the ignition, and the engine beneath the long hood rumbled to life. From there, Dennis worked mechanically, depressing the brake, shifting into gear, simultaneously releasing the brake and slamming the gas and gripping the steering wheel for dear life as the car bounced over the curb and onto the sidewalk. He tensed, expecting a tire to blow. They held, but the car wobbled like a rowboat in a cruise liner's wake. The Cadillac plowed through a corner of the bus stop, bending the thin support beams and shattering glass, then into the street, where Dennis yanked the wheel to the right. Memorial Avenue ran parallel to the Darkness, but they didn't have another option. Their best hope was the intersection at Thirty-Seventh where they could turn north.

With the tires gripping blacktop, the tone of the engine shifted to a deeper, angrier climb as it accelerated to thirty, forty, fifty miles per hour. Half of the front windshield was clouded in a webbing of cracks from the collision, so Dennis hesitated to go any faster. When he looked through Maurice's window at the oncoming Darkness and saw that it was less than ten yards from the road, he put his full strength into pinning the gas pedal to the floor.

Dennis' senses were returning in fragments, and he took a moment to glance at his passenger. The anchorman's palsied hands struggled to find the buckle of his seatbelt. After latching himself in, Maurice's lips began moving in a voiceless mumble.

"Mr. Townsend," Dennis said over the sound of the engine. "Maurice."

The anchorman didn't respond.

Several thoughts crossed his mind then. What about other people? Was everyone experiencing this? Was anyone? Or was it just them? Maybe Maurice wasn't real. Maybe this was a dream—a nightmare. Maybe he was dead.

As the Darkness started edging into the road, he spotted the traffic lights for the intersection. Thirty-Seventh came on much faster than he'd anticipated. Dennis heard himself yell, "Hang on," and then he was working the emergency brake to keep the car from skidding off the road as it took the ninety-degree turn. The Cadillac groaned as two tons of momentum shifted direction. The Darkness crossed the intersection and reached for their bumper, a mere wisp from consuming the taillights. Dennis released the brake and punched the gas.

Thirty-Seventh connected the residential areas with the highway, so the businesses were larger, the streetlamps brighter. Even at two in the morning Thirty-Seventh usually had some traffic. There were always buses or truckers making overnight deliveries. But not tonight.

Tonight, Thirty-Seventh was all theirs.

"It's still coming," Maurice said, surprising Dennis.

"Yeah, yeah. I see." He was, in fact, trying to ignore it so he could read the signs of the stores they passed in order to get his bearings: Daily's Coffee, Capitol City Taxes, Chomp: Hotdogs & Hoagies, the ever-present Dry Cleaners, a jewelry store next to a pawn store, another Daily's Coffee, another Capitol City Taxes, another Chomp—

Dennis let off the gas as a tingle flushed through his chest.

"Why are we slowing?" Maurice asked. "Pedal to the metal, pedal to the metal."

"I... I..." Dennis couldn't find the words. He didn't know how to explain that despite the speedometer reading eighty-five, they weren't actually going anywhere. Dennis tried to focus on the horizon in the hopes of seeing something new, but the same stores came and went in an endless cycle. Daily's, Capitol City, Chomp, Dry Cleaners, pawn store, jewelry store, repeat. It reminded him of the old cartoons where they looped the same three images in the background over and over again to show motion. And when he glimpsed the side mirror—objects in mirror are closer than they appear—he saw the Darkness steadily gaining.

Maurice clutched the seatbelt across his chest as he too noticed the repetition.

Dennis tried accelerating again, but all that changed was the rate at which the background rolled. The Darkness approached with each passing second, devouring more of the world, reaching out for them, closer, closer...

A sense of intense power overran the cramped atmosphere of the car. The air gained an electrical charge, the radio came to life and blared static, the lights, both inside the car and out, flickered, the forward momentum slowed as the engine sputtered and died, and Dennis felt a lightlessness take him as the car coasted.

Before he or Maurice could speak, the engine cranked back to life and, like a thunderstorm changing direction, the energy in the car shifted.

"Stop," Maurice shouted. "I'd rather be standing outside than speeding down the road when it catches us."

Dennis eased off the gas, nodding in agreement. The car didn't slow. It continued to accelerate, reaching ninety miles an hour on its own. The cracks in the windshield began to spread and crackle under pressure from the wind. He tried pumping the brakes. The car plowed on, passing a hundred.

Dennis yanked the e-brake. Still no response. Maurice started kicking at an imaginary brake on the floor in front of him.

A smoky odor made Dennis cough. He thought the tires or a belt in the engine was burning. But when he noticed the shadowed outline of a man in the rearview mirror, sitting just inches away in the backseat, he forgot all about the smell and the possessed car and the Darkness.

Amber light from the street lamps outside flicked across the man's face, revealing a pointed, clean-shaven chin beneath the brim of a felt bowler hat. A perpetual grin lifted the corners of his mouth.

Dennis' heart stopped beating. Every nerve in his body twitched, and before he knew what he was doing, he pulled himself closer to the steering wheel and away from the backseat. The man in the bowler hat hadn't moved or spoken, but his presence was enough to terrorize Dennis.

Maurice, alerted by Dennis' apprehension, looked over his shoulder. A stunned silence fell over him, followed closely by horrified recognition. His body went slack and his lips began to form one word, over and over again: "No. No, no, no, no, no, no…"

Dennis had a brief moment to register Maurice's reaction before the car began to drift to the left. He tried to pull straight, but the harder he tugged the wheel clockwise, the more it turned counterclockwise.

Maurice uttered one final phrase—"Not yet"—before the windshield filled with the red brick wall of the hundredth Dry Cleaners they had passed in the last three minutes. As the hood of the fifty-nine Eldorado Brougham struck the wall, but before the impact sent Dennis flying through the windshield and into a darkness greater than that of the one pursuing them, time seemed to stop. Shards of glass hung suspended in the air where the windshield had finally imploded. Maurice blocked his face with both hands, poised for impact. The hood, just beginning to crumple, resembled frozen waves in a black pond, and the speedometer read a solid sixty-three.

Then Dennis felt something penetrating his brain.

A voice, raspy and burned, but somehow playful, accompanied the invasion of his mind: "Dennis Richard Fowler. I've come to offer you the deal of a lifetime."

Dennis used the rearview to watch the man in the bowler hat. As the words scratched his thoughts, the man remained motionless, only letting the corners of his smirk stretch a little more.

"The deal is this," the voice said. "Your life now"—time jumped forward a beat and the car moved another inch closer to becoming one with the wall before it stopped again—"for life later."

The first question that came to mind—who the hell are you?—was promptly answered by the voice: "I am nothing more than an offer. Strike a deal and all this will go away. A decade of happiness, fortune, women, and life will be yours. Pass and your path ends with Mr. Townsend's—here, now."

Dennis' next thoughts—Did you make this same deal with Maurice? Is this why the past ten years have come crashing down on him?—were answered by time and the car pitching forward another fraction. The sudden restarting of momentum was enough to drive Dennis into the steering wheel. The thumb of his outstretched hand caught the dash and bent back until it snapped. Sharp pain shot up his arm like a lit fuse.

With time stopped, the man in the bowler hat sitting unmoved, Dennis thought he heard a slight chuckle in the background of his thoughts.

"One," the voice said and the car moved forward another inch. The hood crinkled, Maurice splayed against his seatbelt, and Dennis was tossed forward again.

"Two." Time took another skip forward. A plume of glass and brick and metal erupted all around Dennis as the front end of the car buckled and the back end lifted off the ground. Dennis was sent into the steering wheel for a third time. Numbness spread through his legs.

"Thr—"

Before the voice could utter the number, Dennis found use of his mouth. "Deal."

The presence withdrew from his head, and the man in the bowler hat vanished.

Dennis had just enough time to sigh, thinking he was safe, before the car completed its terrible course. Needles seemed to pierce every inch of his body as he was tossed head first into the red brick. And then there was no more. The Darkness had caught them.

Ding-ding-ding.

Dennis jerked his head away from the bar. His forehead hurt from sleeping face down and his brain felt like a bruised peach.

Dennis heard a slight chuckle in the back of his mind that made his body go cold. A shadow moved behind the bar.

"Passed out, did ya?" Doug, the slinky bartender, said. He stepped into the light with a condescending grin on his face. "I can't believe you let that pussy-footed anchorman drink you under, Dennis."

"Anchorman?" Dennis repeated.

"Drunker than I thought." Doug gave him a look of pity. "You don't recall listening to Maurice Townsend drone on for an hour about his hoity-toity life being so damned unfair?"

"He left?"

"Sure did. Five, six minutes ago. Came out the bathroom, must'a seen you dozing, and left."

Vivid nightmares played through Dennis' mind.

Doug leaned against the bar. "Looks like your luck is finally turning up, Dennis. Mr. Townsend left a hundred-dollar bill and said drinks were on him."

Dennis didn't respond. He listened to the sound of a speeding ambulance as it warbled past the bar outside.

He rushed to the front door, ignoring Doug's confused questions, and stepped into the night in search of a black Cadillac Brougham. The Number 150 bus exhaled and pulled away from the stop. Dennis was just in time to hear the ambulance as it raced toward the intersection of Memorial Avenue and Thirty-Seventh. He didn't need to follow to know it would turn north on Thirty-Seventh, toward the business simply know as Dry Cleaners, where they would try in vain to save the life of a drunk driver who was destined to make the news one last time.

Dennis stood alone in the parking lot, thinking about life and luck. But most of all, he thought about just how long—or short—ten years really was.

JC has more than thirty pieces of short fiction published in various magazines and anthologies, including *S.T. Joshi's Weird Fiction Review*, *Daily Science Fiction*, *Buzzy Mag*, and a series of novellas through Audible. When he isn't at home reading or writing, he spends his days exploring the Rocky Mountains with his wife, one-year-old son, and two dogs. Find him at JCHemphill.blogspot.com.

Acrylic on Canvas

William Holden

Sweat gathered along the edge of his hairline as he stood pissing in the dim, dingy bathroom. The acrid, bitter smell of his urine pricked his nose as it pierced the air. He glanced at the white porcelain bowl covered with years of public use—and misuse. Davis shook himself dry as he stared at the words scrawled across the stained tiled wall, and a nervous chill ran down his spine when he noticed a response to his posting from the previous night. The chill lingered, penetrating his skin, sinking deeper into his muscles and bones.

There had been too many thoughts from too many voices running through his head last night. The commotion had dulled his creative mind, making it impossible to produce, yet he knew he had to write something—*anything*—to make the rest stop worthwhile. His illegal words from the night before were straightforward, a standard among others like him.

Davis was here – November 10, 2013 12:01 a.m.

He stared at the words, not understanding why someone would do such a thing. He had not asked a question, and he certainly did not write it as an invitation to talk… Davis had simply stated a fact. Yet the words in red ink were there, accusing him of lying. The controlled penmanship of the author chilled his blood. He read the words carefully for the fifth time.

No you were not, because I was here – November 10, 2013 12:01 a.m.

His creative mood evaporated as anger toward this stranger consumed him like a fire. *I won't let him get away with this*, he thought as he pulled his black fine-tip Sharpie marker from his pocket. *I will not have my good name tarnished.* Davis bent down, meeting the words at eye level. He raised the pen. A soft thump came from the other side of the wall as if someone had opened the stall next to him. He paused and listened, disquieting silence settling around him.

His hand that held the pen began to tremble; the feeling of someone watching him crept into his mind. Not wanting to make his presence known, he placed the toilet seat down without a sound and perched himself on top of it. His heart pounded against his chest wall furiously; his temples throbbed. The old metal wall wobbled as he leaned against it. Davis brought his face up far enough so that his eyes were now level with the stall. The odor of stale fumes from years of bleach and disinfectant was overwhelming. The bathroom *appeared* empty—yet still he held his breath, listening for the slightest of sounds.

You do realize that in all likelihood that man is waiting for you out there. The voice quivering in his mind sounded timid. *It would be to your advantage to get out of here before something terrible happens to you.*

Don't say those kinds of things, he responded mentally. *There's obviously no one there.*

He stepped off the toilet and returned his attention to the wall. "I'm not going to play your games with clever rhymes or verse." The words sounded hollow as they fell from his lips. He pulled the cap off with a smirk of satisfaction and began to write. *I would like to know who you think you are, and what you expect to gain from calling me a liar. What is it you want?*

Davis leaned away from the wall, tilted his head to the left, and then added several exclamation points.

When he opened the door to the stall, the rusty hinges groaned with age. Fluorescent lights flickered as he passed by the row of sinks and mirrors that hung against the wall; all were tarnished and chipped.

He looked into them despite the streaks of dirt and grime. Shadows danced around him as the lights pulsed on and off, an electric buzz sizzling around him.

He quickened his step towards the door.

The heavy night air warned of an approaching storm, wind howling around him, billowing up through his untucked shirt. He paused at the driver's side door of his car, anxiously looking out across the parking lot.

A lone car sat off in the distance. Davis knew the lot had been empty when he'd arrived. The car had to have come while he was inside. He strained his eyes and thought he saw someone sitting in the driver's seat.

"That's him," he mumbled into the darkness. "Just waiting for me to leave, so he can write something foul about me, no doubt." He slipped his hand into his jacket pocket and felt the cool handle of his knife before gripping it tightly with his left hand and heading across the parking lot.

Davis switched the blade open as he approached, clutching the handle even tighter as he neared the vehicle. A voice spoke up in his mind. *He's in there. We can see him. You better teach this monster a lesson.* Davis drew strength from the voice. Taking a deep breath, he crept alongside the car. He walked up to the driver's door and knocked on the window— waiting for a response that never came.

Grasping the handle with his free hand, Davis pulled open the unlocked door. A foul stench rose up from the interior of the car. Dried blood covered the windows and dashboard. A man's lifeless body fell out of the car. His head lolled backwards from the thick cut across his neck.

Davis's stomach knotted as he fought back the sour bile filling his throat. He leaned in closer, holding his hand to his mouth and nose to block out the smell of the decaying body. The dead face stared back at him with hollow grey eyes.

Davis recognized the man.

He was looking at himself.

Davis descended into a black void in his mind. Darkness surrounded him.

When he awoke, Davis found himself in his own bed, shivering from the cold even as the thin cotton sheets stuck to his sweat-dampened body. He tossed the covers off and sat on the edge of the bed, rubbing what had surely been a nightmare from his eyes.

Standing, he walked across the room and grabbed his robe from the closet, making sure that he replaced the hanger in the exact spot from where he had taken it. He peered around the corner of his bedroom door, and, seeing nothing, he proceeded shakily down the narrow hallway.

Relief washed over him as he saw the five locks of his front door still intact.

Even with this added level of security, he couldn't shake the feeling that he wasn't alone.

Davis drove down interstate 170 with an anxious knot in his stomach. The feeling of someone watching him had continued throughout his shift. Alone on the highway, he became more uneasy about once-familiar surroundings as they took on a sinister feel. Exit signs and mile markers seemed different to him tonight, misplaced somehow. His agitation grew stronger, forcing him to break his path; the system he had lived by for most of his life. As he approached the first rest stop, he turned his head and stared at it.

It stood alone in the dead of the night. His foot tapped the brake.

Old habits die hard, don't they? A voice echoed in his head. He forced himself to pass by the rest stop, a twinge of guilt pricking his heart as if he were leaving an old friend behind.

Davis approached the second rest stop, and the voices in his head cleared—allowing him to think without all the chatter. His mind focused on the bathroom wall and the lies held in those words. His hands tightened on the steering wheel, his pulse quickening as he accelerated the car. He drove past the second rest area not even looking in its direction. He knew a response had come. He could feel the new words from the stranger etched into the wall like a hot poker pressing into him, burning its image on his skin, scarring him for life.

When he finally reached his destination, the parking lot was like last time, empty. Davis pulled into his *usual* space at the rest stop and sat staring at the building while the car coughed and choked. He knew he had to go inside; the compulsion overwhelmed him. Walking away from this was not an option. He wanted the lies and the nightmares to stop, and the only way to stop them was to stop this man from taunting him. Taking a couple of deep breaths to calm his nerves, he opened the car door and stepped out into the night.

The scent of an early fall hung in the air; dead leaves from trees too weak to hold onto them any longer crunched under his feet. He reached into his jacket pocket, feeling the comfort of his knife cradled at the bottom. *Just in case*, he thought. He opened the door to the building. Under the faint smells of urine, vomit, and shit that he had become accustomed to, a different smell lingered—something new…

The smell of death.

Its scent, pungent and deep, burned the hairs inside his nose—rushing out to greet him before drifting away in the wind. Davis took a tiny step inside the door, listening for footsteps, breathing, or someone taking care of their private business. All he heard, however, was the slow, steady drip from one of the faucets.

He walked to the last stall and placed his hand on the door. He hesitated for a moment before opening the door. The creaking sound caused him to break out in a cold sweat. His armpits became damp from nerves as he noticed the same steady penmanship as the previous night.

I am everything you desire, I am everything you fear—and what I want is you!

Davis couldn't tear his eyes from the words. Written in deep red ink, they seemed to pulse—moving in a downward flow, filling the words themselves. He placed his trembling finger against the letters. *The ink is still wet…* The thought penetrated his thoughts while his finger smeared the words. He rubbed the substance between his finger and thumb. He sniffed it. The dark smell of death he'd noticed earlier seeped off his skin. Anger seized his entire body as the door to the bathroom closed.

Davis stood, paralyzed, hearing a man open the door of the stall next to him. His temples throbbed. The pain in his head shattered his thoughts like a thousand nails being driven into his skull. Sounds from the next stall cut through his ears. The man's zipper, the heavy stream of his piss, the splashing of the water in the toilet—everything echoed around him. Davis sat down on the commode to steady himself, covering his ears from the deafening sounds.

He stared at the floor and noticed the man's left foot from underneath the dividing wall. He wore dark green canvas sneakers. As Davis stared at the man's foot, a dark spot splattered near the side of the man's shoe. He continued staring as it soaked into the canvas, creating a pattern. A second drop appeared, and then the smell of death and blood returned. The man was bleeding in the stall next to him. Davis wondered frantically, *was it a self-inflicted wound—used to write on the wall?* He heard the toilet flush, the stall door open, and then water running in one of the sinks.

Davis knew it was time to finally confront his tormentor.

He stood outside the stall door staring at the stranger. He appeared younger than Davis had expected. The man looked up from washing his hands. He looked at Davis through the mirror,—he had a handsome face with a heavy growth of dark whiskers across his jaw line. Blood dripped from the man's small, flat nose; yet he didn't seem to notice. Davis took a few steps toward him, and then stopped. The man turned off the water and shook his hands dry.

"What's your problem, man?"

"Your nose is bleeding." Davis answered in a distant voice he didn't recognize.

"What?" The man ran his finger under his nose. When his finger came back clean he looked into the mirror to double check. "Look, man, I don't know what you're talking about."

"The blood—it's dripping on your shoe onto the floor. Why are you lying? I can see it." Davis walked toward him, the stench of the man's nervous sweat mixing with the deep scent of blood. "What did you do, punch yourself in the nose to get the blood you needed to write with?"

"Look, man, I don't want any trouble. I just came in here to take a piss."

"No you didn't. You came in here tonight to write more foul words against me, just like you did last night." Davis felt his anger toward the man growing in intensity. "It's one thing to torment a person, it's quite another to lie about it as well—that is unforgivable. You should be man enough to admit what you've done."

"You need to back off before someone gets hurt." The man held up his hands as if protecting the space around him.

Davis gripped the knife in his pocket. The comfort of the knife eased the pain in his head. The blade flipped open as he brought the knife out. Davis raised the knife, slashing it through the space separating them. The blade cut through the palm of his stalker.

"Shit!" The man cradled his hand. Blood flowed from the deep cut, soaking into the man's blue dress shirt. He stepped to the left to give himself an escape. Davis, full of adrenaline, blocked his path and brought the knife down across the man's chest. Davis could feel the blade cutting through the material of the shirt and entering the man's skin.

In desperation, the man pushed his body against Davis. They fell to the floor and Davis lost his grip on the knife. He heard it hit the floor behind him. He turned his body and crawled over to it. A foul odor rose up from the stained grout, and he choked on the fumes.

Seizing the opportunity, the man stood up and kicked Davis in the stomach. He doubled over in pain, curling his body into a fetal position.

The man's foot made contact with Davis's body again. He felt a crack in his chest and knew the man had broken a rib. Sharp pain came with every breath he drew. Yet, even in pain, he summoned additional strength. He grabbed the man's foot as it came down for another hit and twisted it. He felt the man's bones snap and break in his hands as he collapsed on the floor next to Davis.

Davis crawled over to the knife and wrapped his bloody fingers around the handle. He stood over the stranger and watched as the man's shirt darkened with sweat and blood. Davis knelt over the man and placed the knife to his throat.

"Why are you doing this?" The stranger looked pleadingly into Davis's eyes.

"The pain you're feeling is nothing compared to the pain you inflict upon me with your words."

"I don't know what the hell you're talking about! Please just let me go…"

"Why do you insist on denying what you've done?"

"Please, I don't know what you're talking about!"

"No?" Davis stood. "Then let me show you." Davis grabbed the man by his dirty blonde hair and dragged him across the putrid floor.

He kicked the door of the stall open and pulled the man in behind him. He knelt down and yanked the man's head up. "*That's* why I'm doing this!" Davis pointed the knife toward the wall. "Those words hurt me. You called me a liar. The bloody tip of the knife clicked against the tile as Davis sneered, pointing out the words. "You smeared my good name with those foul, hateful words."

"I never wrote those words. You've got to believe me!"

"Even after showing you, you still won't admit to it." Davis's mind became a mass of voices and images clogging his thoughts. He had to stop the lies, the voices, and the nightmares this man created. He brought the blade to the man's trembling throat and dragged it deep across the flesh, from one side to the other. The man's body shook and convulsed. The words he tried to form gurgled out of the large gash.

Davis watched as the man's dark, foul blood poured onto the floor. He stood up, watching as the man drew his last breath. Silence filled the bathroom as Davis stumbled out into the heavy night air.

Seventeen minutes later Davis opened the door to his apartment. His mood had lightened since the little trouble in the bathroom. It wasn't how he would normally have handled that kind of situation, yet difficult times sometimes called for extreme measures.

The light of the moon cast faint shadows across the pale grey walls. His head ached, so he opened the bottle of aspirin sitting on his nightstand and downed two of the pills—without water. He crawled into bed and pulled the sheets up to his neck, staring at the ceiling as he waited for sleep to take him.

Davis stood in the bathroom of the rest area once again. The thick air hanging over his head was heavy with the stench of blood. Through the silence, he heard a thump on the far side of the bathroom. He shifted toward the sound. Dark pools of drying blood covered the floor. His now bare feet sunk into its congealing puddles, which oozed through his toes.

He opened the door.

The man's dead body lay in the same position as he had left it, his body completely drained of blood. Everything looked the same, except the man's clothes were missing. He lay in his own drying blood, bare and exposed.

Davis searched his weary mind. He couldn't recall removing the man's clothes. Voices rose in his head—issuing feeble explanations. The man opened his dead eyes and looked up at Davis.

Davis screamed and fell back out of the stall.

"This isn't happening, I killed you! You're dead!" He backed up against the wall. It felt cool against his skin. He wanted to run— wanted to escape this nightmare. He stood frozen; his eyes remained fixated on the dead man staring back at him. The stranger rolled over. His lifeless body thumped and slapped against the cold tile floor. He dragged himself closer to Davis, smearing blood over his grayish-blue skin.

"It's you that I want, Davis." Blood and mucus leaked out from the man's mouth. His tongue fell out and hung in a hideous angle, like a dog with rabies. "Ou, Davith. Ith ou thath I wanth." Davis covered his ears to drown out the newly formed lisp in the dead man's voice. He closed his own eyes, hoping to hide from this corpse in his mind. He could feel the cold, dead body crawling over his feet. Fear paralyzed him. His skin burned from the stale touch of death. His body convulsed as he felt the dead man's body covering his…

He awoke again in his own bed, the coldness of death under the covers with him. Davis took a few deep breaths, trying to calm his mind and quiet the voices. He looked around his room at the darkness surrounding him before reaching over and turning on the small lamp sitting on his nightstand. He shivered against the sweat of his body. His feet felt heavy, as if covered in socks.

Davis tossed the damp sheets off his body, eyes widening in horror as he noticed the dried blood covering his feet. Looking down at himself, he was stunned to see his body fully dressed in a blue shirt and black slacks. The dress shirt, with a cut across the chest and covered in dried blood, was familiar to Davis. A torrent of visions from his dream came rushing into his head.

He was wearing the clothes of the man he had murdered!

The pain in his head returned like a railroad spike being hammered into a slab of wood. It tore into what remained of his sanity.

He stumbled into the living room. As he reached the light switch, he knew something was out of place; something, or someone, stood in the room with him. He stared into the blackness trying to decipher once-familiar shadows. The pain in his head made it so difficult to think. The feeling persisted. His hand moved tentatively across the switch, and when the room lit up, terror rippled through him as he stared at the words written across his living-room wall.

Nice job, but you missed.

The same tight, concentrated penmanship that he had become familiar with in the bathroom stall marred his living-room wall. Davis risked a glance at the front door. The locks were all securely in place.

His eyes inspected the room—everything appeared to be in order. He caught sight of a pen sitting next to the book on the coffee table. He picked it up and went to the wall. He stared at the words, moving and vibrating against the dull white paint. The pain in his head blurred his vision. He felt sick. His muscles ached.

Where are you?

He stood back and looked at the words he had written, no longer recognizing his own handwriting.

He waited for a response. The room came in and out of focus. The floors seemed to roll in waves up and down, like a makeshift funhouse. He gripped the back of a chair to steady himself as red letters began to form on the wall.

Look behind you!

Davis stared at the words as they appeared before him. Fear gripped his chest. His breathing came in short, heavy puffs. Fear kept him from turning around. He could feel something behind him as a chill brushed across the back of his neck like someone caressing a lover for the last time.

He swallowed the fear lodged in his throat and turned around. The living room was empty, yet he knew he wasn't alone. He could feel a presence, closing in on his space, removing the air he breathed—suffocating him.

"Leave me alone!" His scream fell flat against the air before he collapsed to the floor; his hands and knees supported him as his stomach knotted. Dry heaves assaulted his body several times before he spilled the contents of his stomach. He could hear scratching from all directions. The noise became clearer, as though someone was writing on a chalkboard with a damp piece of chalk. He looked up at the wall and wiped a string of vomit from his chin. Words formed all around him.

I am here. I am there. I am above you. I am beneath you. I sleep with you. I bathe with you.

His arms gave out and he fell against the unforgiving floor. He rolled over on his back and held his hands to his ears in an attempt to block out the noise around him. The words continued on the ceiling, larger and redder than the other words—as if they were screaming at him.

I am a part of you. I am on top of you. I am next to you. I am inside of you!

As he felt his life slipping away, he noticed a seemingly solid shadow standing above his head. The black form moved over to the side of him, standing motionless, watching him die. Davis tried to talk. His lips moved, but with no purpose. His mind struggled to form words.

His mind failed him.

The voices in his mind went silent. The sound of death was all that he heard. The shadow took a more solid form and knelt down beside him. Davis's eyes widened with the realization of who was standing over him.

As Davis took his final breath, he saw himself, kneeling next to his *own* dying body, a devilish smile grinning back at him…

William Holden's has published over eighty-five short stories. He is an award-winning author of such titles as, *A Twist of Grimm* by Lethe Press (Lambda Literary Finalist), and by Bold Stroke Books, *Words to Die By* (2nd place Rainbow Book Awards for best horror and a finalist for the Foreword Reviews' INDIEFAB Book of the Year Award for Best Horror), *Secret Societies*, and *The Thief Taker* (Lambda Literary Finalist) His most recent books include: *Grave Desires* (2015), and *Crimson Souls* (2016). You can find him online at williamholdenwrites.com.

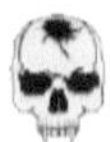

Thank you for reading our ***Digital Horror Fiction*** anthology, **Memento Mori**, and for supporting speculative fiction in the written form. Please consider leaving a reader review so that other people can make an informed reading decision.

Find more great stories, novels, collections,
and anthologies on our website.
Visit us at DigitalFictionPub.com

Join the Digital Fiction Pub newsletter for **infrequent**
updates, new release discounts, and more:
Subscribe at - Digital Fiction Pub

See just some of our exciting fantasy, horror,
crime, and science fiction books on
the next page.

More from Digital Fiction

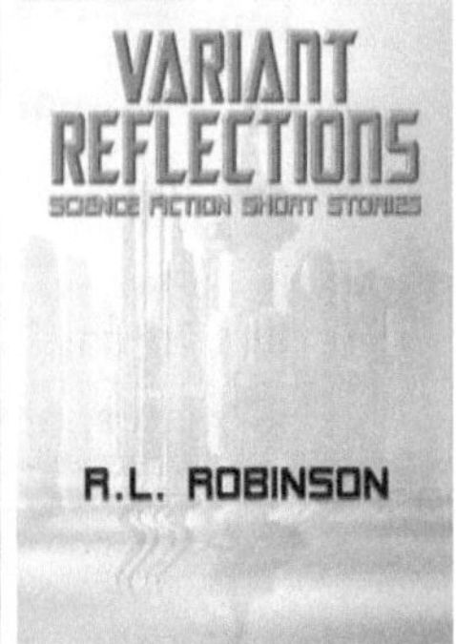

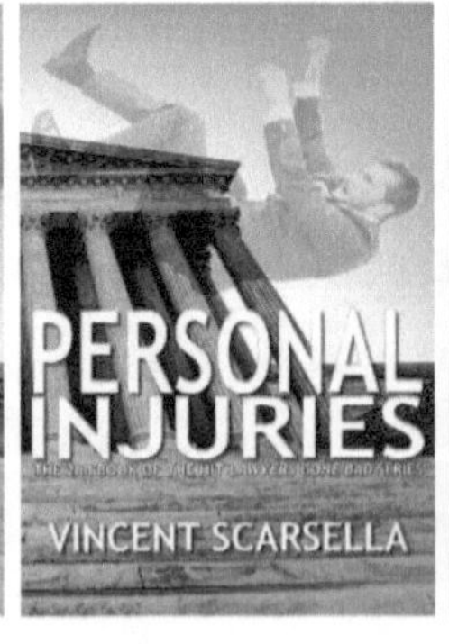

Copyright

Memento Mori
A Digital Horror Fiction Anthology of Short Stories
Executive Editor: Michael A. Wills
Managing Editor: Bruce Lockhart 2nd
Copy Editor: Mike Reeves-McMillan

These stories are a work of fiction. All of the characters, organizations, and events portrayed in the stories are either the product of the author's imagination, fictitious, or used fictitiously. Any resemblance to actual persons or ghosts, living or dead, would be coincidental and quite remarkable.

DigitalFictionPub.com